FIRE AND ICE

FIRE
AND
ICE

Paul Garrison

HarperCollins*Publishers*

HarperCollins*Publishers*
77–85 Fulham Palace Road,
Hammersmith, London W6 8JB

Published by HarperCollins*Publishers* 1998
1 3 5 7 9 8 6 4 2

Copyright © Henry Morrison, Inc. 1998
Map by Dan Osyczka

A catalogue record for this book
is available from the British Library

ISBN 0 00 225651 7
ISBN 0 00 225807 2 (Pbk)

'Fire and Ice' by Robert Frost is reprinted from
The Poetry of Robert Frost by kind permission of
the Estate of Robert Frost, the editor Edward Connery Latham
and the publisher Jonathan Cape

This novel is entirely a work of fiction.
The names, characters and incidents portrayed in it
are the work of the author's imagination.
Any resemblance to actual persons, living or dead,
events or localities is entirely coincidental.

Set in Palatino

Printed and bound in Great Britain by
Caledonian International Book Manufacturing Ltd, Glasgow

For Jackson Cole

Pacific Ocean

Tropic of Cancer

MARIANA ISLANDS

GUAM

MARSHALL ISLANDS

International Date Line

Equator

PAPUA NEW GUINEA

SOLOMON ISLANDS

150°   165°   180°

Fire and Ice

Some say the world will end in fire,
Some say in ice.
From what I've tasted of desire
I hold with those who favor fire.
But if it had to perish twice,
I think I know enough of hate
To say that for destruction ice
Is also great
And would suffice.

Robert

Frost

1

He swung his sextant to the sky.

Night ended abruptly in the equatorial Pacific. In the brief moments when first light revealed the horizon and the heavens still shone, he lowered mirrored pinpoints of Jupiter, Antares, and Capella to kiss the rim of the sea. And, with a careful look around, went below to reckon where he stood among them.

She was asleep on a double berth, hip cocked, long limbs sprawled luxuriously. He plotted the celestial fix on a chart sprinkled with reefs and atolls, and extended the pencil track of their passage from the Marshall Islands.

It was still cool in the cabin, so he crawled onto their berth to cover Sarah's shoulders. She smiled in her sleep, and when she arched invitingly, he kissed her, trailing his beard softly down her spine.

The collision alarm began to scream.

Sarah shot awake, scrambling from the sheets to work the boat. Michael Stone caught her in his arms, felt her

1

frightened heart hammer her breasts. "I got it. I'll yell if I need you."

He ran on deck, his own heart pounding.

The sun had risen, already harsh.

He saw neither land nor another vessel. But they were sailing in a deep valley between two trade wind rollers and lay far below the crests. Before he could see what had set off the alarm, he had to wait for the mountain behind to overtake and lift the boat.

An elderly, sun-bleached thirty-eight-foot Nautor Swan, *Veronica* was small by modern offshore standards. Stone had rerigged her as a cutter, and she was inventively maintained wherever ingenuity could substitute for cash. The only high-tech element of the rig was an unusually tall carbon-fiber mast cannibalized from a racing boat, and, like a Stealth war plane, it made *Veronica* virtually invisible to radar.

Their ten-year-old daughter padded up the companionway in her pajamas. "What's up?" She yawned.

"Something spooked the radar."

"What?"

"We'll see in a minute."

Ronnie swayed sleepily with the motion of the boat and wrapped one arm around his waist. With the other she clung to the threadbare Snoopy backpack in which she stashed her things. Stone bent to kiss her. "Good morning, sweetie. Here, maybe we better put on your life vest."

Ronnie made her standard protest—that the child netting lashed to the lifelines that fenced the deck was insulting enough to a person her age.

"Just till we see what's out there."

He had the blue-water sailor's deep distrust of all equipment. Although he had built the warning system himself, and he was reasonably sure that the radar had simply acquired a target many miles away when *Veronica* had perched atop the previous crest, it would not come as a total surprise to discover the Third Fleet on the far side of the next wave.

He hauled Ronnie's life vest from a cockpit locker,

strapped her in, and debated calling Sarah up on deck. What could go wrong offshore would go wrong.

The sea gathered astern, rising against the sky, muscling under the fiberglass hull. The boat rose like a gull on the wind, soared to the crest, and suddenly the Pacific Ocean spread for miles before Stone's eyes.

He spun a fast circle, searching the horizon. Thin mist astern threatened changes, and a vagueness in the north hinted at the enormous reach of China's winter monsoon, but for now the sea looked benign and so completely empty that he and Ronnie and Sarah seemed to sail alone on the planet.

His gut told him the warning system had sensed a large ship. He turned another circle before the wave raced ahead and *Veronica* sank into its trough. Strange place to find a ship. But the radar couldn't have signalled land. Not yet, although his celestial fix from the moving boat was open to error, especially as time was so critical with the planet Jupiter traveling independently of the stars.

A white tern skimming the water promised they were within twenty-five miles of shore. But his decks and hull did not yet transmit to Michael the feel of waves reflected by land. So the atolls were somewhere between sixteen and twenty-five miles ahead.

"Hey, sleepy face, where are we?"

"We're here," Ronnie yawned.

"Where?"

Ronnie pulled her global positioning satellite receiver from Snoopy's belly. The GPS was a gift from a Japanese solo sailor whose appendix Sarah had removed.

"Pulo Helena, dead ahead. Nice navigating, dinosaur."

"Dinosaur," because Stone still navigated stubbornly by his star shots. He reminded Ronnie that batteries died and most sailboats that smashed into the fringing reefs and submerged mountaintops that grazed the surface of the Pacific Ocean ran aground courtesy of the latest electronics.

Which was not to deny that Ronnie's little marvel had its uses.

"Precisely how far ahead, sweetheart?"

" 'Precisely' fifteen point nine miles." She showed Stone the screen.

He grinned with pleasure. Damned near on the nose. But considering that the little sand and coral atoll group barely broke the ocean surface, it was still out of radar range. Had to be a ship. An enormous ship, standing tall in the water.

"Where are you going?"

"I'm going to check the radar," he said. "Want some orange juice?"

Ronnie thought for a long time and concluded, "I don't know."

"I'll bring you some juice."

To the right of the companionway was a compact galley with a kerosene stove, a sink served by fresh and seawater foot pumps, and a freezer that ran off the main engine. To the left, tucked into a teak bulkhead was the nav station—radar, VHF short-range and SSB long-range radios, and a chart table. The sleeping cabins—Ronnie's forward, his and Sarah's aft—were paneled in teak, but the main cabin was painted an antiseptic white.

Furnished as a compact medical clinic and operating room, its hatches, shelves, and cabinets contained most of the emergency equipment found in a fairly modern ambulance: an intubation unit, a defibrillator, tubing, catheters, and bandages as well as saline and glucose, plasma frozen in the freezer, a primitive anesthesia setup, a tray of operative instruments, plaster of paris for immobilizing broken bones, and a cache of antibiotics, painkillers, vasoconstrictors, anesthetics, Adrenalin, and insulin. Their respirator had served too many years, but compared to it, Stone's radar screen was a genuine antique.

An anemic phosphorous green blip fifteen miles ahead was nearly lost in the sunlight knifing down the open hatch.

The guts of his collision-avoidance system—the scanner spinning inside its radome, the transmitter and receiver circuits, and the wind and solar generators that powered it—were almost as old, bartered long ago in Chinese night markets for no-questions-asked medical services.

He studied the flashing and fading echo with the intimacy of long experience and concluded that a large ship was crossing their course at a right angle, steaming slowly from north to south. Plenty of room—two hours before they crossed its wake—by which time the ship would be long gone. Excellent. Stone relaxed a little, glad to have the ocean to themselves again.

But when he took another look—after he had brewed a thermos of coffee, poured Ronnie's juice, and entered the radar contact and the dropping barometer in the log—the ship had changed course. It had doubled back, prowling slowly among the Helena atolls.

Stone thought its behavior was as odd as its presence.

Pulo Helena—a few wafers of sand and coral between the western Carolines and the New Guinea coast—lay south of the main transpacific Panama-Philippines shipping lanes, and far, far west of the Australia-Tokyo route. It was among the most remote of the stops on the Stones' floating hospital's circuit. They dropped anchor in the lagoon once a year to treat any of the half-dozen nomadic fishing families that happened to be living there at the moment, and now and then a Republic of Palau fishing patrol motored down from distant Koror. But there was nothing there for a ship.

He carried the short-range VHF radio handset, the thermos, and Ronnie's juice up to the cockpit. She sipped a half inch and consulted Snoopy. "Thirteen point eight miles to Pulo Helena—"

Stone picked up a winch handle and headed forward.

"*Now* where are you going? I want hugs."

The Swan was running under twin headsails that spread either side of the bow like a pair of wings. The classic tradewinds rig was self-steering, but it was impossible to see di-

rectly ahead without ducking down to look under the sails
or slewing off course. Stone raised his mainsail, sheeted it
well out over the port side, and secured the boom with a
preventer. Then he furled the starboard headsail. He lost a
little speed, which was fine—give this thing more time to
go away—and now with both sails over the left side of the
boat and the right side clear, they could see ahead.

Ronnie was waiting impatiently in the cockpit. She finished her juice at Stone's request, curled up in his arms after
he had finished adjusting the self-steering vane, and dozed
off with her head on his chest.

The hot morning sun baked perfume from her hair.
Stone breathed it in and wondered if he had ever been so
happy. Once, on another ocean. He tugged Ronnie closer
and searched the sea.

Seventy-five-foot palm trees could be expected to break
the horizon at about twelve miles from the deck of a sailboat. The house of a big ship might stand taller, as might a
hull stacked with cargo containers. He would see something soon.

Veronica's sails, each marked with a huge red cross visible for miles, were stretched out from long, hard use, and
yellowed to a state of dangerous fragility by the sun. But
her splendid hull and towering carbon-fiber mast made up
for their shortcomings, and she was fast.

In less than half an hour she galloped atop a crest and
showed Stone a blurred notch on the horizon. Reaching carefully for his Fujinons, anxious to prolong the moment before
Ronnie tore into her day, he popped the lens caps and focused the binoculars on an immense, angular, sand-colored
ship.

Strange color, almost camouflage; it drifted in and out
of sight like a mirage. A modern freighter's square lines.
Some sort of bulk carrier, he reckoned, hoping its master
knew his business. Their Australian friend Kerry McGlynn,
a salvage tug driver who spun tales of groundings, sinkings,
and fires at sea—swore there were ships in the far Pacific

purchased with American Express cards. What the proud owners saw as a superhighway on the chart was in fact a cobweb of reefs ready to sweep them up.

Ronnie woke up talking.

"Mummy slept right through the collision alarm."

Sarah had been schooled in Britain, and Ronnie echoed her English accent, her inflections, even her gestures. Her intense similarity to her mother was enough to make a man feel his genes were impaired. He was stocky, blue-eyed, and fair under his permanent suntan. Ronnie's skin was a cream-and-sugar blend of his complexion and Sarah's black-coffee black. But her cheekbones were as high as her mother's, her nose as elegant, her carriage as slim and regal.

Occasionally, he did glimpse memories of his own father's level gaze in the child's coal-dark eyes, while she had inherited his blunt craftsman's hands and fingers. And Sarah assured him that Ronnie had his smile. But he watched her grow up with all the delight and awe of a stranger in a sculpture garden.

"Mummy," he reminded her, "stood watch all night so you and I could catch up on our sleep. Now it's her turn."

"But . . ."

"But what?" He knew approximately what was coming next. Last night the two women in his life had a major battle over schoolwork—a book report on a Wole Soyinka tale of postcolonial Nigeria, which Ronnie currently found less interesting than the Hollywood-Coca-Cola-Big-Mac America she called "Daddy's country." This morning they'd be seducing allies.

"Mummy can be a bit of a bore sometimes, don't you think?"

"She's never bored me yet."

Ronnie rolled her eyes.

"And," Stone added, "I've known her a lot longer than you."

"I hope so."

"You *did* catch up on your sleep, didn't you? I mean,

you didn't stay up half the night reading *People* magazines. That wouldn't be why you can't wake up this morning. Noooo, of course not."

At their last landfall, the Kwajalein Missile Range, the U.S. Army nurse, who'd slipped them sealed cartons of sterile needles and a generous batch of insulin, had given Ronnie a stack of old *Peoples*—a dazzling world of buildings, streets, movie stars, and, Sarah had noted, "Grinning Americans turning cartwheels in their gardens."

Ronnie squirmed out of his arms and looked around.

"A ship! Daddy, a ship." She grabbed the binoculars and focused expertly. "Oh, wow. She's big. She's *huge*. Daddy, look at him— Can I go up the mast?"

"To the first spreader—And what do you remember?"

"Both hands for the sailor."

"Leave the binoculars."

She climbed like a monkey, hand over hand up a halyard, toes gripping the mast, which, with the wind on the starboard quarter, inclined only slightly. Thirty feet above a deck studded with steel winches, she scampered onto the spreader and stood, shielding her eyes, straining toward the ship. A prepubescent African goddess. Stone smiled. Godette, the Japanese sailor had called her.

"Both hands!"

"Sorry— Look, Mummy, a ship!"

Sarah had emerged from the cabin with an instinctive glance at the sails, a knowledgeable grimace at the weather astern, and a private smile for Stone.

"Good morning."

The progenitress of the minigoddess aloft was a tall, striking woman, a Nigerian of Ibo and Yuroban parentage, whose fine nose and delicate lips indicted the Arab and Portuguese slave hunters who haunted the African past.

She stood straight, an almost noble figure, heightened this morning by the towel she had wrapped like a turban around her hair, which she had just washed in preparation for landing. A yellow Yap Island *lava-lava* was draped around her torso, baring her shoulders, and a plain gold cross hung on a chain light enough to part if it caught while she was working the boat.

"And what are you smiling at?" she asked.

Stone was deeply in love with her, sometimes wildly. It had occurred to him that this morning he was deep in a wild phase. He stood up and kissed her.

"Single deckhouse aft," Ronnie called down. "I think I see fire stations and piping. It's an oil tanker."

"Kid's got amazing eyes," said Stone.

Sarah glanced at the silhouette. "Rather high in the water for a crude carrier. More likely a liquefied natural gas ship, wouldn't you say?"

Stone could still barely see the thing. He took up his binoculars, focused deliberately, and agreed it was probably an LNG carrier. "Big one. Fifty thousand tons."

"What on earth is an LNG vessel doing here . . . ?" The heavily insulated tank ships were like gigantic thermos bottles speeding gas—compressed and supercooled into liquid—from oil fields to power plants. Fleets of them served Japan. "You don't suppose he's aground?"

"Radar says he's moving."

Both recalled their Australian friend's observation that the second mistake derelict masters often made was backing away from the submerged mountain peak they had just discovered with their bottom, thereby sinking in two miles of water.

Sarah studied it in the binoculars. "Yes, he's all right," she agreed. "Thank God." Frozen in the hold of a fully laden LNG carrier was more thermal energy than a nuclear bomb.

"Ronnie, come down for breakfast, dear."

"But, Mum, it's a *ship*."

"Veronica."

"Yes, Mum."

Stone thought she had given in unusually quickly. The next instant he saw why, as Ronnie whipped off her pajama top.

9

"What is she doing?" asked Sarah. "Oh, good lord, Michael, stop her!"

"Too late."

Ronnie swayed into the sky, wrapped the cloth around the thin wire inner forestay Stone had rigged for the cutter jib, and slid down. Plummeting like a stone, she tightened her grip at the last moment and landed lightly on the foredeck.

"She learned that from you."

"I haven't felt up to that stunt in years."

Ronnie galloped back to the cockpit. "Did you see, Mum?"

"You will give me gray hair before you give me grandchildren."

"Did you see, Dad?"

"I'm impressed," said Stone. "When did you learn that?"

"Pictured it last night in bed. I could see it, so I knew I could do it."

"Please inform me first if you ever picture wings."

"*Daddy*— Do you see the ship, Mum? It's bigger than Pulo Helena. Maybe they'll invite us aboard and serve us lunch and—and show movies and have a swimming pool and video games and TV—I bet they have satellite TV!"

"Perhaps," Sarah said gently, exchanging a look with Stone. "But don't get your hopes up, darling."

"I think they're waiting for us," Ronnie ventured, then embraced her theory with vigor. "Bet you someone's sick and waiting for you to treat them."

Just last spring in the Philippine Sea they had boarded a Danish car carrier to doctor an engineer burned in a pump explosion. The comfortable crew accommodations had looked palatial to Ronnie, the ship a floating storehouse of modern treasures for a child who saw ice cream twice a year. Ever since, she hungered after passing ships like a privateer. Stone was presently at work building a decoder for her for Christmas, so she could watch satellite television.

"Well, if that's the case—and even if it isn't—we'll be landing soon. I want you to go below, eat your breakfast. And then have a nice shower and wash your hair—we'll water at Pulo Helena. See, Dad's trimmed his beard and I'm all spiffed. Call me when you're done and I'll brush it for you."

Ronnie cast a longing look at the ship and dove down the companionway.

The three atolls that formed the Pulo Helena group came into view. The ship lay among them, in the lee of the main island, protected from the rollers, which the islands split. Its house stood higher than their feathery rows of palm trees.

The VHF rumbled to life with the drawl of South Texas. *"Ahoy, sailboat flyin' the red cross. Sailboat flyin' the red cross. You all wouldn't happen to be the hospital boat?"*

"They're waiting for us," said Sarah.

Stone thumbed Transmit. "This is *Veronica*. What can we do for you?"

"Man, are we glad to see you. This is Dallas Belle. We're outta Surabaya bound for Tokyo. The old man's hurt. Took hisself a header. We need a doctor, bad. You want us to come out and meet you?"

Stone looked at Sarah. The Surabaya-to-Tokyo run lay hundreds of miles west of Helena. "Not in these swells. We'll board you in the lee of the atoll. Just sit tight. We'll be there in forty-five minutes."

"You're the boss, Doc."

Sarah took the radio. "When was your captain injured?"

"Yesterday, ma'am."

"Is he conscious?"

"Sometimes."

"Is he vomiting?"

"No, ma'am. Folks on the ham net said you was coming this way. Thank God we lucked out."

Stone released the preventer, disengaged the self-steering, and altered course to swing around the south side of the main atoll. The water was turning confused as the land

11

divided the swells, and he thought he could hear the first faint mutter of the surf that battered the fringing reef.

Sarah touched his arm as they headed toward the sound, and brought up a subject that they'd been debating for days now. "Have you thought about East Timor?"

Stone looked away, scanned the roiled seas, the low round atolls, the reefs, and the sand-colored ship, which had a soft, hazy plume rising from its smokestack. "Darling, I still can't seem to make you understand—it is too dangerous." The Indonesians had invaded East Timor when the Portuguese colonists left and had for years waged a war of terror against the protesting Timorans. Sarah wanted to sail *Veronica* there to treat the wounded.

"Those people are helpless. The world doesn't care. The least we—"

"And what do I do when an Indonesian patrol boat catches us playing doctor in some rebel anchorage? We can't outrun them in a sailboat."

"The boat is plastered with red crosses. How would they know we're not an 'official' mission? Besides, Ronnie won't be there. We're sending her off to school. We've agreed."

"Yeah, we agreed." Hiroshi, the Japanese sailor whose life Sarah had saved, had turned out to be scion of a wealthy industrialist; his grateful father had offered to send Ronnie to the Swiss school his daughters had attended.

They exchanged unhappy smiles. It had to be done, before Ronnie was cut off from her peers forever. And, in fact, she seemed to crave a larger world: when she wasn't mooning over ships, she would lie on deck for hours watching for planes, and at night for satellites on their purposeful courses through the stars.

"I feel an obligation to go to Timor," Sarah said firmly. "We *are* doctors."

Stone looked away at the ocean again. Whether it was middle-aged complacency or male aversion to change, he feared that he was more satisfied with their life than she was. He clung happily to a daily existence he enjoyed for its consistency. When he felt the need for additional excitement, the sea usually obliged with a squall that pumped the adrenaline and burned off excess energy. The endless repairs required by an old boat kept him busy, as did the simple but vital chores of navigation and piloting. But Sarah had grown increasingly restless, almost eager to move on.

He said, "Let's keep Ronnie one more year . . . please."

Sarah stood up. "I promised to help her with her hair."

Stone picked up his glasses and studied Pulo Helena's glassy, green lagoon. Clustered on the white sand beach under tall coconut palms was a tiny village of a half dozen *fales*—open huts with thatched roofs.

"Hey," he called down the companionway. "No one's here. There're no boats on the beach. . . . No, wait. . . ." Steadying the helm with his knee, he fine-focused on the shade under a thatched roof. "Someone's sitting in one of the *fales*."

The next instant *Veronica* needed all his attention as they surfed and pounded through the chaotic intersection, where Pacific rollers with nine thousand miles of fetch smashed past the atoll and raced on toward the Philippines. On the leeward side was a cut in the reef, the pass which ordinarily Stone would have entered to shelter in the lagoon if he hadn't been heading for the ship.

Just past the reef, he seized the glasses again and focused tightly. The little village *was* deserted, but there was one boat, a minuscule sailing canoe beached askew at the edge of the lagoon. A lone figure slumped in the open hut. He tried to rise, but fell back, his head lolling on his chest.

"Coming about!" he warned Sarah and Ronnie, threw the helm hard over, and sheeted in the main. Both sails crashed and crackled across the deck as *Veronica* spun on her keel and shot at the reef. Stone leaned over the side searching for the submerged coral prong that was cited emphatically in the *Sailing Directions*, cleared it by a yard, and surfed into the deep lagoon.

Sarah ran up the companionway. "What happened?"

"Old fisherman, all alone on the beach. I think he's hurt."

"What about the ship captain?"

They looked back at the sand-colored, slab-sided ship, which loomed on the water with the anonymous force of an industrial city.

Sarah shivered. "Horrid looking thing, isn't it? Ugly as sin."

"Reminds me of one of those godforsaken backwater refineries."

"Yes! Like in the Bight of Benin."

"Listen, maybe I should do the captain," offered Michael. "You stay on the atoll here with this guy. What do you think?"

"I'd rather, but Ronnie's so excited. She just said to me, 'It's like we're going shopping at a mall.' "

Ronnie squeezed past her mother. "Are you ready, Mummy?" She was wearing a bright red lava-lava, her Snoopy backpack in hopes of presents, and ribbons in her hair. Her eyes were locked on the ship and when she saw they were inside the lagoon, heading for the rickety dock where the *fales* clustered on the beach, she howled, "Where are you going?"

"Let me check out the ship, first," Michael said.

"No! I want to go with Mummy. She's all dressed and pretty and she wants to go, too. Don't you, Mummy?"

"Well, maybe Daddy's right."

"Nooo. We'll get all hot and sweaty on the atoll."

Stone laughed. "Okay, okay. You take your mother to the ship; I'll do this guy. Grab the helm, hon. I gotta get my bag."

"He'll be dehydrated," Sarah called down the companionway. "You'll want extra glucose and saline."

Stone stuffed the plastic glucose and saline bags into the waterproof backpack that served as his medical bag, and some plasma from the freezer, and plucked the backup VHF handset from its charger. On deck, he said, "You're going

14

to board leeward side. Radio the ship, make sure they've got plenty of hands standing by to fend off."

"Yes, dear."

"Ronnie, run below and get Mummy's pack, then put out all the fenders, both sides. Sarah, don't forget to cut that coral real close on the south side."

"Yes, dear."

"Do I get a kiss?" he asked Sarah.

"Later."

"Careful boarding. Wear your life vest. You too, young lady."

"Yes, dear."

Sarah said, "If they're pleasant, I'll wangle an invitation to dinner."

"Tell 'em the charge for a house call is a raster scan radar."

"Here you go!"

The Swan was closing fast on the dock. Stone stepped over the lifelines, hesitated. The sea was quick. He stepped back into the cockpit, where Sarah had taken the helm. "I'll have that kiss, now."

He took her face in his hands. "I love you."

Her lips were cool, her dark eyes fathomless. "Michael, I want to go home."

"Home? What do you mean? Nigeria?"

"Africa."

"What happened to East Timor?" he asked, belatedly aware that East Timor was old news and that she had been building toward a major pronouncement for weeks.

She returned a defiant stare. "There's plenty to do in Africa."

"We can't go home."

"I am aware that we are fugitives, thank you."

"Strictly speaking, *I* am the fugitive."

"Don't be daft, Michael. Where you go, I go. Always . . . But has it ever occurred to you that being a fugitive gives you the excuse to hide from everything?"

"Dock!" Ronnie called urgently.

Stone swung outside the safety lines with his backpack. "We'll talk."

"No shortage of talk," Sarah shot back. Then she, too, remembered that the sea was quick, and she pulled him to her and kissed him again. "I love you, too. And I always will."

As Sarah steered past, two feet from the edge, he jumped, landed running, and jogged into the glaring white beach. He turned and waved.

Veronica danced across the lagoon, Sarah tall at the helm, Ronnie scurrying around with the fenders, both too busy to wave back. Stone paused a moment to drink in the rare and beautiful sight of his own boat under way, then hurried past the wrecked canoe with its flapping rice-bag sail and tangled sennit ropes.

Up the gently sloping beach, inside the *fale,* the fisherman lay with a dark lava-lava wrapped around his waist, his hands across his belly. His legs were swollen with infected coral cuts. He peered at Stone through milky cataracts.

Those Pacific Islanders who ate their traditional diet and avoided booze, sugared breakfast cereals, and radiation poisoning from the bomb tests, lived long. Stone often found it impossible to guess their age. But this guy had to be in his eighties.

His thighs were tattooed with porpoises—the proud symbol of the Micronesian navigators—and like many of his generation, he had a Japanese rising sun tattooed on his belly. A crucifix gleamed on his leathery chest. A mission convert, which meant he might speak English. Pretty far off his regular track, way down here in the southwest islands, but they went where they pleased.

"Hello, sir. How you doing?"

The old man stared past him at the sea.

Stone smelled the sweet odor of drying copra and he felt the ground reel, his first moment off the moving boat in nearly three weeks. Surf pounded nearby and the trade wind blew hard on his skin, rattling palm leaves.

"Beg pardon?" He leaned closer, smiling, kneeling, trying to put him at ease. He considered himself a barely competent doctor—not a gifted physician like Sarah—better with things than people.

"Too old." The old man opened his hands, revealing a fishing knife plunged into his body.

"Jesus!" Stone gasped. "What happened to you?"

Suicide was one of the plagues of the far Pacific, right up there with drink and diabetes, though they saw it most often among the young. "Is that your boat?" he asked, trying to distract him so he could examine the wound. "What did you do? Sail home and find them all gone?"

"Not my home. I head for Tobi. Stupid old man."

Tobi lay a hundred and fifty miles southwest.

"From where?"

"Puluwat."

"*Puluwat?*" Puluwat was a thousand miles east.

The Carolinian navigators thought nothing of sailing five hundred miles without a compass for a carton of Marlboros or a good party. But the old guy had gotten himself good and lost, then compounded his shame by cracking up on the reef.

"Why you sail alone?"

"Sweet burial," the old man muttered.

The navigator's death at sea.

Gazing into the milky eyes that couldn't have seen any but the brightest stars, Stone guessed that this last voyage had been a test of do or die.

"Excuse me a moment . . . let me just move your hands."

The old man had lost a lot of blood, and as Stone touched him, he fainted with a sigh. Stone quickly ran a saline tube into his arm, and another for glucose. The knife would have to wait for Sarah. Set up an operating room right here in the *fale*. He started to radio the ship to ferry in his Levine tube so he could drain the stomach fluids leaking into the old man's abdomen. But it was too late.

The navigator opened his eyes. A serene smile crossed his lips, when Stone brushed them with water. "Who you?" he asked in a hoarse whisper, even as he craned his neck again to see the sea.

"Just a Sunday sailor, compared to you, sir."

The weathered face rejected the compliment even as the light left his eyes. "Oh, goddammit," said Stone, hoping that Sarah was doing better.

He walked among the fales, looking for a shovel. Nothing. Whoever had been here last had taken everything with them. Get a shovel from the Swan. Or maybe put the old man in his boat and sail him off into the sunset.

A pillar of smoke caught his attention, jetting thick black from the *Dallas Belle's* massive funnel. The trade wind caught it and streamed it west. White water boiled behind the ship and it began to move.

"That was fast."

He walked toward the dock, watching for *Veronica*. But when the *Dallas Belle* had proceeded a thousand feet—its own length—he still couldn't see her.

"Oh, God!" A horrific thought crashed through him. Had the ship somehow run *Veronica* down? Or had its giant propeller dragged her under?

He ran to the old man's canoe. Sarah and Ronnie must have been wearing life vests. They might have been thrown clear, into the water. But as the ship wheeled, presenting a new angle of perspective, Stone slowed to a walk, stopped, stood, and stared in disbelief.

He saw the Swan suspended sixty feet above the water in the sling of a deck crane. The crane swung the sloop inboard, over the gas carrier's main deck. While Michael watched, a party of seamen guided her copper red bottom onto a makeshift cradle and the *Dallas Belle* completed its turn and steamed away.

2

"Mummy. We're moving!"

"*Shhhh!*"

Sarah hunched over her stethoscope, every sense tuned to the old man's heart.

He had not fallen, as they had claimed on the radio. He had been shot in the chest.

Medically, it was the least of his problems. Attempting to remove the bullet, his shipmates had anesthetized the already unconscious victim with morphine. Now he was deep in a narcotic depression, blood pressure plummeting, respiration so faint his lungs barely lifted his ribs.

Sarah shot a half milligram of Narcan into his veins, then listened anxiously for the fibrillation that would tell her that the narcotic antagonist had aggravated some preexisting cardiac disease. He was old. The Narcan could as easily kill him as save him, but she had no choice. She had to get him breathing and increase his blood pressure.

"Mummy."

"Narcan!"

Ronnie slapped a fresh hypo into her glove. Sarah entered a vein, pumped a half milligram, massaged his faltering heart, and listened again.

"Narcan!"

On the third dose, the old man woke up vomiting.

"Quickly."

Ronnie helped her sit him up so he wouldn't choke on his vomit. But just as they had his torso erect he passed out, swallowed, and began to choke. Sarah cleared his airway.

"Captain," she called to the men watching from the sick bay door. "I need the respirator from my boat. And the intubator."

The Texan shouted down the corridor. In moments the mess boy ran in with the gear. The captain's companion, a tall, powerfully built black American, said, "What about the bullet?"

"Would you step outside and close the door, please?"

"Let's get something straight, Doc. Neighborhood I come from every man my age is dead or locked up. Mr. Jack is the only reason I'm not."

"If I can't stabilize your friend he's a dead man. *Get out.*"

From what she could tell without X rays, a small-caliber bullet had entered at an angle, ricocheted off the gladiolus, plowed along the fourth rib toward his shoulder, tearing the subclavius, and lodged deeply in the lesser pectoralis.

Lucky. Until his panicked numb-skull shipmates took it in their collective heads to remove the bullet. A mess boy who had served as a hospital nurse had been drafted to perform the wholly unnecessary operation. Morphine was prescribed to anesthetize the already unconscious victim. Generous in the extreme, they had emptied the ship's dispensary into the old man's veins and set about butchering the remains of his shoulder. The bullet was in deep, and eventually they gave up and left it where they should have in the first place.

That the overdose hadn't killed him outright was either

a miracle or a testament to a constitution of titanium alloy. Judging by his harsh features, Sarah was inclined to believe the latter. His face might have been chiseled from igneous rock: sharp brows, hawk nose, square chin, cropped white hair and nary a jowl or a sag in the skin. And he bore the marks of torture from long ago—his back was crisscrossed with ancient scars, his fingernails and toenails had been ripped out.

Yet whatever luck had kept him alive then and deflected the bullet today had held. The crew had heard on the ham radio cruiser network that the hospital yacht *Veronica* was bound for Pulo Helena. And who should hove over the horizon but Doctor Mike and Doctor Sarah?

"Mummy, we're moving."

The ship was definitely moving, heeling into a turn.

"I know," said Sarah.

"Where's Daddy?"

"I don't know. Help me with this."

"But—"

"First things first—our patient. Don't cry, dear, I need you."

She got him tubed and on the respirator and listened to his heart again. He seemed stable, the Narcan taking at least temporary effect.

"Okay, darling, now we'll find out what the devil is going on here."

She called for the captain. He came, accompanied by the black American.

"How's he doing, Doc?"

"Where is my husband?"

"On the beach," said the black.

"What? You left him on the beach? Where's our boat?"

"We got her cradled up, safe on the main deck."

"You shipped our boat? You can't—"

"Done deal, Doc."

Sarah tried to absorb the impossible. Ronnie looked ready to cry. Sarah put her arm around her automatically.

She was aware that they had in essence been kidnapped, but all she could think about was Michael and the miles the ship's propellers were already churning between them. "You've stranded my husband," she said angrily. "He'll be frantic with worry. You can't just leave him there!"

"You can go back and get him as soon as the old man's on his feet."

"On his feet?" she echoed. "He needs to go in hospital."

The black man shook his head.

"The sooner he's in hospital the better chance he has of surviving."

"He's not going in the hospital."

"We've done all we can," said Sarah. "I've counteracted the morphine overdose. Now he needs a hospital. I can't do any more. Let us go."

"Can't do that. You're the only doctor the old man's got."

"When will you let us go?"

"Soon as Mr. Jack's issuing orders."

"What about my husband?"

"He's not going anywhere. You can sail back and pick him up when Mr. Jack says so." He ran an insinuating eye over her body. "Have yourselves a reunion."

Sarah looked at her patient, pale as snow and barely breathing. His mutilated fingers twitched on the sheet. "You don't understand," she said. "You've *got* to get him into hospital."

"Never happen, Doc."

"What if he dies?"

"He can't die. He's got him a doctor and a cute little nurse."

3

THE TIDE HAD STRANDED THE OLD MAN'S CANOE.

It took brutal minutes and all Stone's strength to wrestle the heavy plank hull into the lagoon. Then he saw the damage: the pillars that connected the outrigger to the pontoon had shattered when the canoe had struck the reef.

He pawed frantically through the empty food baskets and hollow coconut shells that littered the floor of the hull, found the old man's spare rope in coils and lengths of cord neatly skeined. He wrapped the split pillars, and jumped aboard.

The *Dallas Belle* was moving slowly, proceeding cautiously past the northern atoll. Stone sheeted out the sail and lowered the steering paddle, and headed for the narrow channel that cut the leeward reef. The little craft leaped lightly to the wind.

But across the lagoon, the canoe staggered and began to lose speed. Stone—his eyes locked on the ship while he steered standing on the platform over the outrigger beams—

finally looked down and saw that the hull was filling with water.

In the scramble to launch, he had seen the obvious damage but had missed the more destructive consequence of the old man's crash landing. Plank lashings had parted, opening a seam from the bow to the forward outrigger beam—a split nearly six feet long, through which the lagoon poured as the wind pushed the canoe's nose into the smooth water.

Stone ripped off his shirt, stuffed it into the gushing crack. Then he shifted his weight sternward to lift the bow, regained control of the boat, and sailed it through the short passage between the atoll and the barrier reef and into the pass through the reef itself.

Outside, the sea tumbled a dozen rows of mangled surf. The canoe climbed sluggishly onto the first comber, fighting the weight of the water in her hull. The second wave slapped the little boat sideways. A third sluiced it back into the lagoon.

The wind, beam on, banged into its flapping sail and wrenched the outrigger out of the water. As the canoe started to capsize, Stone slashed a stay with his rigging knife. The mast collapsed on the bow with a loud crack, and the canoe wallowed upright, sinking as the sail wafted around it like a shroud.

Stone grabbed the steering oar and paddled for the shallows. Water poured over the gunnels. He jumped overboard and started pulling it toward shore, his lungs heaving, his heart pounding, his mind a blur of shock and despair.

The ship was shrinking in the distance—already smaller than a toy on a boat pond. He'd been crazy to think he could catch it with a canoe. He had panicked, leaping to mindless action, and had nearly drowned himself—Sarah's knight on his charger, catching his neck on a clothesline.

He grabbed his VHF radio, which he should have done immediately, and called on channel 16. "*Dallas Belle. Dallas Belle. Dallas Belle.* Come in *Dallas Belle.*"

There was no response. He called again, "*Dallas Belle.*

Dallas Belle. Dallas Belle. Do you read me, *Dallas Belle?"* and pressed the radio to his ear. Mid-ocean static, a hollow, empty noise, barely distinguishable from the desolate roar of the surf.

He switched to channel 5, which he and Sarah used to communicate when one of them was off the boat. "Sarah. Darling, can you hear me? Sarah! Can you hear me! Sarah!"

He called again and again, until the *Dallas Belle* slipped below the horizon, trailing a smudge of smoke, which the wind scattered.

He was a man of science—a doctor, a navigator, and a self-taught electronics engineer—who believed in God. But neither faith nor science could explain what had happened to his family. That the sand-colored ship had steamed away with his wife and daughter was impossible. A black curtain might more plausibly descend from the sky or thirty acres of farmland suddenly rise from the sea.

What were they doing to his child and his beautiful wife? He tried to rewrite events in his mind. They had put to sea to steady the ship while Sarah performed a difficult operation. Or they were making an emergency dash to a hospital in the Philippines. Events that made even less sense than the event he couldn't believe. But there was no answer he could bear, no fact he could understand.

The phrase, *my beautiful wife,* started racing through his mind. For a second he thought he heard Ronnie scream, *Daddy!* It was a sound so real, so like her frightened shriek the last time she had fallen overboard, that he turned his head to look for her.

His incredulous eyes swept the empty lagoon, the deserted circle of beach that rimmed it. High overhead, the trade wind clattered in the palm leaves. The Pacific Ocean stretched forever in every direction.

He was a hundred and fifty miles northeast of Tobi, which had a radio station. Opposite the direction *Dallas Belle* had disappeared. The Sonsorols, Merir, and Pulo Anna lay far west. But on any of the radio islands, the generator might be broken or out of fuel—with a month to wait for the next state cargo boat.

Angaur, on the other hand, the southernmost of the Palau Islands, had a World War II runway, where he could get a plane to Koror, the capital city. And in Koror was a friend: Marcus Salinis, the president of the tiny Palau Republic. But Angaur was two hundred and fifty miles across the ocean.

Overwhelmed, exhausted from his battle to beach the canoe, he sank to its gunnel and stared. The weather he had noticed earlier was filling the eastern horizon. He looked north, dreaming he would see the *Dallas Belle* steaming back with a perfectly plausible explanation.

A dark spot on the horizon set his heart pounding. It grew, too quickly, and materialized into a flock of black noddies searching for fish. His gaze descended to the lagoon again. A hundred yards down the beach, something large and white was drifting ashore. A dead shark? He watched it, puzzled, as it turned slowly with the current. A frigate bird spiraled toward it and circled tentatively.

A body? Had the navigator sailed in company?

Stone ran. The bird pulled up with an angry shriek. He waded into the shallows, grabbed a cold hand, and pulled it ashore.

It was a man. He was not a Pacific Islander but a pale white European, naked except for boxer shorts and one rubber flip-flop stuck between his toes. He wore a wedding band and a watch. His face had been battered on the reef. But that alone had not killed him, Stone discovered when he turned him over and saw three bullet holes in his back.

"Oh, Sarah."

Stone cast a professional eye on the wounds: small-caliber weapon, the slugs still in him, no single wound instantly fatal. He could have been thrown off the *Dallas Belle* still alive or jumped. Young and powerfully built, he might have drowned before he bled to death.

At that moment Stone seized upon a single truth, the only fact he knew: he had to get off the atoll.

The old navigator's supplies that had floated out of the sinking boat bobbed on the surface of the lagoon.

Stone waded out and quickly gathered baskets and leaf-wrapped bundles of food, coconuts for drinking, sodden rope and twine, bailers, a gourd of palm wine. He dragged two spare spars ashore as well and several huge taro leaves which the old man would have used for shelter from the sun. He bailed the flooded hull and found some yams and breadfruit, a moldy square of canvas, and a long breadfruit twig coated in a sticky substance that stuck to his hands.

Stone sorted what he salvaged into piles and shook his head. The little boat had carried everything a Micronesian navigator needed on the open sea—food and water, shelter from the tropic sun by day and the cold spray at night, and materials for repairs. But unlike Stone, the old Pacific islander had had no need to carry a compass or a sextant or almanacs or a chart. He had held the star paths in his mind, the currents and swell patterns in memory, and had honed his land-finding instincts with a lifetime of close observation of birds, fish, and clouds.

Stone would have surrendered his arm for Ronnie's GPS.

Maybe at night, his own memory of the stars and constellations . . . surely he could hold a course at night . . . and he had learned a trick or two during ten years in these waters. Suddenly his heart flew: he remembered a minicompass he kept in his medical bag to take a bearing if he got caught in the fog in the inflatable dinghy. It was a magnificent break, brilliant luck that energized him for the primary task of making the canoe seaworthy. It would never swim until he found a way to repair the hull.

He looked up at the sun, then checked his watch. Another lucky break. Incredibly, it was only two o'clock.—*My beautiful wife . . . Daddy!*—Taking refuge in the things he knew, he vowed to set sail before dark.

*   *   *

His jury-rigging of the outrigger had pretty much fallen apart, while the split in the hull had been worked wider by the tumbling in the pass. He saw immediately a better way to brace the outrigger, so he put that job aside and concentrated on the split seam. The hull was carvel-built, the long planks meeting flush at their edges. Where a Maine boatyard would have joined the planks with nails, however, the Puluwat canoe makers lashed them together with coir, an elastic coconut fiber. It was the coir—stitched through holes drilled every four or five inches—that had popped.

Stone worked his way along the seam, plucking broken strands out of the holes, and praying that no plank had split. They were all right, until he reached the dent that marked the impact with the reef.

"Son of a bitch."

It had hit right on the seam and *both* planks had split, right along the line of holes, which meant he would have to drill new holes, without a drill. He thought of his orderly tool chests aboard *Veronica*, and felt his heart suddenly pierced with fear.

All the tools he had now were in his medical bag, the backpack he had hung on a peg in the corner post of the fale where the old man had died. He had scalpels and spare blades to cut the coir his Swiss Army knife, surgical scissors and his rigging knife, some disposable cigarette lighters that he carried as gifts, but nothing resembling a drill. If he could find a nail, he could drive it through with a rock and pull it out with his dental pliers. But a nail was not likely on an island where the coconut was the source of every building material.

He ran across the hump of land between the lagoon and the windward reef and searched for driftwood with a nail in it. Nothing but an ancient weathered tree trunk that might have ridden equatorial countercurrents from a Mindanaoan shore, or been pushed four thousand miles from Christmas Island by the tradewinds.

He ran back, eyes everywhere, wondering if he could get away without lashing the planks where they'd split. Two holes. All he needed was two holes, double up on the coir and caulk the split with something. He hadn't considered caulking yet. But without it, water would geyser through the seam with every dip of the sailing canoe's nose and flex of its hull. Maybe palm sap. He jabbed a tree with the Swiss knife, but the sap ran thin. He went back to the fale for his backpack.

The peg where he'd hung it, he noticed at last, wasn't made of wood. It was a brass bolt, tarnished a brown-green color, and he realized with a leaping heart that some long time ago someone had found it in a piece of driftwood and screwed it into the post. Stone gripped it with his dental pliers. Praying it wouldn't disintegrate, he gently screwed it out. With his bag in one hand and the precious bolt in the other, he ran back around the lagoon and knelt beside the canoe, studied the grain of both planks for the safest entry, and began screwing the bolt into the water-softened wood.

He worked from the outside in, taking care not to make the hole too big, and then from the inside out until he joined the holes in the middle and saw light. He repeated the process on the lower plank, screwing in, pulling out, screwing in, pulling out. It took an hour to bore two holes.

Sand kept sticking to his fingers; he finally tumbled to the realization that the sticky substance the old man had carried was breadfruit sap that the islanders used for caulking. They melted it with a piece of smoldering twine; Stone used his lighter. He coated both edges of the open seam and packed it with gauze. Then he stitched twine through the holes and, using his scalpel haft for leverage, twisted it tight.

It was a very small canoe, barely fifteen feet long, designed to sail sheltered lagoon waters inside the fringing reefs, or, at most, a day run between neighboring atolls. That the old man had embarked on a thousand-mile voyage said much for his bravery; that he had almost made it said more about his skills than about his vessel. And yet, when Stone had it launched, rigged and reloaded, he felt his spirits rise on a tide of pride and affection.

It straddled the water like a spider, balanced on a wide stance of hull and outrigger, while the bridge that connected them provided a riding deck high and dry above the water. The canoe might look small beside *Veronica*, minuscule next to the gas carrier, but only by comparison, for it was complete: self-contained, quick, and maneuverable. In the right hands.

He took a practice run back and forth across the lagoon, trying to get the hang of the peculiar Carolinian way of tacking their double-ended canoes. Instead of coming about to change direction, the islanders changed ends, shifting mast and steering paddle to make the bow the stern and the stern the bow, always keeping the outrigger pointing toward the wind.

Standing on the tiny deck that bridged hull and outrigger, Stone stole a glance from the chaotic pass ahead and the reefs on either side, and saw that the seam he had repaired seemed to be holding. No longer leaking so much, less burdened, the canoe rose to each successive wave while the wind, which had not suffered the usual evening drop-off, drove it straight and true onto the open sea.

He noted the time—an hour to sunset—and looked back repeatedly at the atoll, trying to estimate the speed of the counterequatorial current. He kept the swells on his right and the yellow ball of the sun on his left, checking his hand-held compass at frequent intervals.

Streams of black-and-white noddies and terns were flying home to their atoll. From a wave top, he glimpsed them flocking around the dead man on the beach. Then the sun teetered briefly on the rim of the water and dropped off quite suddenly.

*   *   *

The wind grew cool, and cold spray began whipping across the open deck. He felt around in the bilges for a leaf-wrapped lump of breadfruit, which he chewed mechanically, and drank from a hole he gouged with his rigging knife in the soft eye of a coconut while he waited for the first stars to pierce the deepening blue. But cloud had entirely filled the eastern half of the sky, dooming any hope of catching Orion's belt on the rise. Ahead, north, the stars of the Big Dipper began to glow. He traced the pointers to the dim reddish North Star and fixed hungrily on that old friend, only to lose it to the advancing cloud. He looked back, glimpsed the small Southern Cross low in the south. But as he checked it repeatedly over his shoulder, it too began to fade behind the cloud scrim. He fished a penlight out of his backpack to read the compass.

A full sea, shockingly cold, knocked him off the deck into the bilge and slewed the boat out of control. He felt his way in the dark back up to the outrigger deck, found the sheets and the steering paddle, and steadied the canoe by filling its sail with wind again. Quickly, he tied a length of sennit rope around his waist and secured it to the canoe as a life line.

In order to get back on course, he tried to feel whether the swells were still moving from his right, but the wind, stirred by the weather coming from the east, had kicked up contrasting waves. The sky offered no clue either, dark from horizon to horizon.

Were he sailing *Veronica*, he would switch on the binnacle light to confirm his course by its serene red glow. He raised the compass to read it by penlight. The sea reached out like a malevolent child and snatched it from his hand.

He lunged for it, reaching desperately for his last connection to his modern world. But the compass was gone, and his heart sank with it.

He was lost, blinded by cloud, bewildered by the jumbled sea. The wind was backing and veering—crazy shifts that thumped the sail, heeling the canoe, driving it forward, knocking it back. He could still sense the great Pacific swells breathing under the canoe, but the surface was too wild and the night too dark to distinguish their direction.

He stood up, and, gripping a shroud, strained to pierce the gloom. He heard waves collide next to him, but he couldn't see their broken and foaming white crests. *"Jesus,"* he muttered, or thought he did, but his curse transformed into prayer, *"Sarah!"* as he realized he hadn't sailed alone in a decade.

His breath came shallow. He felt his chest constrict, a strangler's hand around his throat, a whisper in his ears that began to roar. When a prickling sensation numbed his lips, he braced for pain, fearing the first symptoms of heart attack. Then he realized with a giddy, choked laugh that it wasn't his body that was under assault, but his mind—tumbling in panic.

A gust headed the sail, knocking the canoe backward, and Stone into the water. He pulled himself aboard by his lifeline. The air was cold. He crouched, shivering, collecting his spirit.

He'd survived worse than this—wedged in pack ice in the Weddell Sea with a South Pole blizzard screaming their way. Now, as then, he heard Sarah's voice, both schoolmarmish and brave. "All right, Michael. Where do we stand?"

Rain struck—a sudden downpour that sizzled icy cold across the sea and shocked him back to the present. He lowered the sail, which the wind was threatening to tear to pieces, secured the heavy boom and gaff. Then he felt in the hull for a coconut shell and started bailing the seawater that was pouring over the gunnels.

Scoop of water. Over the side. Scoop of water. Over the side. Again, and again, and again. Counting each scoop. A moment's rest between each hundred . . .

The canoe skidded on the crests—lurching and sliding. Gusts shrieked against the mast, whistled through the shrouds. When the bigger ones lifted the outrigger from the water, the little boat threatened to turn turtle.

Thunder pealed. Lightning split the dark like a million arc welders, and suddenly the sea and storm were illuminated—the water milk white, the waves jagged, the sky a sickly gray. A powerful blast of wind blew the tops off the waves and sent them scudding along in a dense froth. For a long, impossible moment there was more water than air, air too thick to breathe.

Lightning exploded again—a long, sinuous, liquid bolt toppling slowly, lazily from the sky. By its broad, bright light Stone saw the canoe still half full of water and an enormous wave, double the height of any around, traveling toward him at speed. He threw his arms around the mast and held on for his life. The wave tumbled over the outrigger deck, staggered the boat, pounded his back, and tore at his hands.

The wind grabbed the mast like a handle, levering the boat over as the water punched hard from below. Stone leaned out and muscled the outrigger down with his body. But he knew he had won only a temporary victory. The next lethal wave-and-gust combination could flip the canoe like a leaf.

He felt in the dark for the shrouds and stays, and lowered the mast to reduce windage and stabilize the tiny craft. By the time he tied down the heavy spar he was trembling with exhaustion, while the breaking seas, the rain, and spray had flooded the hull again.

A hundred scoops, rest. A hundred scoops—scraping his hands on the rough wood, salt stinging the cuts—wondering how the frail old man who'd sailed before him had the strength to bail the open boat hour after hour. How could a man in his eighties have fought the sea as hard as he was fighting now?

Suddenly he guessed what the old guy had done. He hadn't fought the sea, he'd embraced it. As he had lowered the mast to avoid the wind, he had sunk the canoe, sub-merging it to protect it from the waves.

Easy to think, a bitch to do, when every instinct said that to float was to survive. Stone reflected briefly, weighed his dwindling options, and accepted that he had no choice. With a sense akin to revulsion, he stopped bailing and emptied the coconut shell back into the canoe.

Quickly, he made sure that his food and gear were tied down. Then he seized a second coconut shell and scooped seawater into the hull with both hands. Breaking seas helped fill it. When a big comber roared out of the dark, it drove the boat under, snapped Stone's lifeline, and swept him away.

Suddenly he was alone in the ocean. In that moment all thoughts of Ronnie and Sarah and the *Dallas Belle* were driven from his mind. The Pacific was miles deep and thick with sharks.

Something brushed his hand. Fear screamed *pull away.* Survival whispered *grab it.*

It tugged hard, like something alive. He battled his senses, got them under control. It was a sennit line trailing from the canoe. He tied it around his waist and pulled himself onto the half-submerged bridge, and fought to keep his chin above the wind-whipped water.

He awakened, shivering with cold, startled that he had slept. The wind had changed. It had moderated. More important, it was blowing rock-steady from one direction. And, judging by the orderly condition of the waves, it had been for some time.

It wasn't quite as dark, either. He could actually see the wave tops breaking. Overhead, an occasional star flickered dully through the thinning clouds.

He felt the first glimmer of hope. December storms in the equatorial western Pacific were short-lived, and the trade wind quickly restored order to the seas. On the heels of hope came reason, the loss of his compass less catastrophic. The night chart of the skies would help him navigate. Already there were tantalizing glimpses of a bright threesome that was surely Orion's belt descending toward the west. Then the Southern Cross anchored her horizon. Soon after, a strong star burning white rose to the left of the wind: brilliant Vega rising in the north, pointing the way to Angaur.

Stone lowered himself into the warm water to lighten the canoe, and began bailing. The sea settled quickly—easing his task—and by three in the morning the hull was riding high. At four he was able to climb aboard. He stepped the mast and raised the sail. Vega had risen too high to shape his course, but the sky had cleared sufficiently for him to see the Big Dipper pointing up the North Star.

Fearing he had already been blown west by the storm, he tacked, laboriously shifting the mast, and sailed east.

He chewed sodden breadfruit and dozed, to wake with the sun in his eyes. It had just nicked the horizon. The sky was clear blue, except in the west, where the remnants of the storm were lit red. He stood up, stiff, chilled to the bone, grateful for the sun's warmth, and studied the sky. Clear east, south, clearing in the west. Clear in the north. A few tall trade wind clouds hung like Christmas ornaments.

He turned a slow, careful circle, praying for a ship, a distant smudge he could hail on the VHF. East and a hair astern he thought he saw something, a wrinkle on the blue seam where the ocean met the sky.

He shinnied up the mast. A wrinkle, a smudge, then a hardness with a feathery top. But not a ship, he conceded reluctantly. Maybe a sail. He gave that up too. It wasn't a sailboat, either. It was land—land he recognized with a sinking heart—the palm-crested Pulo Helena atolls from which he had sailed the night before.

4

"Mummy, what are you looking at?"

"Try to sleep, dear. Mummy's thinking."

"What are you thinking?"

She saw a life raft canister on the afterdeck, far below the porthole where she was watching first light etch the ship against the sea, and her mind leaped to possibilities. It looked like the standard abandon-ship emergency canister, made of white fiberglass, about four feet long and two in diameter, and designed to open automatically when thrown in the water. The raft would inflate to hold four men under a bright orange radar-reflecting canopy. If she and Ronnie could somehow sneak down to the main deck, could they muscle it over the high bulwark and jump after it into the sea?

Sixty feet to the water? From a ship racing at twenty-two knots. They were both fit, both excellent swimmers. But what if they were separated? What if they were knocked unconscious on impact? What if the ship sucked them under?

They could jump from the stern, behind the ship. They could steal life jackets. She would tie them together. But would they injure each other, smashing skulls?

Once safely in the raft, then what?

Drift. Pray their disappearance wasn't noticed immediately. Wait to be picked up by another ship. A speck on the ocean. Better nearer the shipping lanes.

She climbed back into bed and drew Ronnie close.

Escape was too risky. A last ditch. But a hope to cling to. Better, first, to try to radio for help. To that end she had devoted much of the night mapping the ship in her mind.

She had sussed out five possible routes to the radio room: the ship's central elevator; central stairs; private stairs from the captain's cabin; private stairs from the owner's suite, where they were confined; and a narrow balcony aft, which led to a ladder up the outside of the six-story house.

But who was at the top of the stairs, provided she could even climb them without being seen? In the rooms in which she was allowed, there were empty sockets where the satellite telephones had been removed. And the attentive Chinese steward, always ready to bring tea for her and Cokes for Ronnie, was always watching.

"Mummy?"

"Sleep."

Sarah remembered her father as an enormous man, bigger than life, black as coal, as British as Eton and Sandhurst could make an African. Josiah Soditan had been a company sergeant major in the Royal West African Frontier Force before independence, a Nigerian brigadier after. In war, he once told her, women made "jolly good scouts."

He had glanced at his mistress, according her the same honor. She was smoking irritably, anxious for Sarah to thank them for dinner and go home.

"Chaps are natural hunters, don't you see? Focus like field glasses on the kill. Women go on defense: they see everything, threats as well as opportunities."

Puffing his Havana, he had peered at her over his

37

brandy, awaiting some answer. She recalled gazing back like a wary gazelle, wondering what he expected in return for this apparent compliment to her sex.

"Of course," he confided, "this is not a general view in the Service. But I will tell *you* that women are as capable in the killing games as any man."

"Thank you, Father," she had answered with only partial irony, because any compliment from him was rare and thus precious.

"Not *you*, dash it all! You're a physician. Point is, women observe their surroundings more than men. Jolly good scouts . . ."

"Yes, Father," she whispered, half aloud.

Ronnie stirred and slipped out of the crook of her mother's arm and stood up on the bed so she could twirl the propellers on the model World War II airplanes hanging from the ceiling. There were dozens of them, swaying with the movement of the speeding ship. Ronnie knew the names of all. A child of the Pacific, she had snorkeled over the fifty-year-old wreckage of many a battleground.

Dawn was lighting the cabin through the drapes, and Sarah watched Ronnie through slitted eyes. She had been Ronnie's age when the Nigerian civil war had broken out and her father had sent her and her mother to England, where Mother had died of pneumonia, and Sarah had been sent to a convent school.

Ronnie seemed more mature than she had been in some ways, easier in the company of adults. "Ice when the shrapnel's flying," Michael said of her, "like her mother." But she was so young in other ways, much less sophisticated than the American and Japanese tourist children they'd occasionally meet. In the civil war, Sarah had seen her father kill with a sword two men who had attacked her mother. She felt a rage welling up in her that her child should have to endure this captivity, the yacht that was her home plucked out of the water, her father marooned on a deserted atoll, and the sheer terror of not knowing what would be done to them next. She had to control her anger. She feared it as much as she feared the men who held them, for she walked a fine line on the edge of violence.

"I've been thinking," Ronnie said, caressing the belly of a twin-engine bomber. "Daddy's okay."

"Of course he is."

"No, I mean really, Mum. He's got fish to eat and crabs and mussels. Coconuts to drink—except he'll get too much cholesterol."

"We'll put him on a strict diet when we get him back."

"Absolutely . . . He can sleep in a fale. . . . I just hope the mosquitoes aren't too bad."

"Very few mosquitoes at Pulo Helena."

"I bet he's lonely."

"Well, Daddy doesn't really get lonely." Truth. He was maddeningly self-contained, though in recent years he had become increasingly dependent on her as their marriage matured and she became less the sheltered girl and more the woman.

"But he'll miss us."

"Yes, he will."

"And he'll worry, every second."

"But he knows you and I can take care of ourselves."

"I know we can. But I doubt he does— God, I wonder what he's doing. I hope he doesn't hurt himself. You know how clumsy he gets."

"He'll be fine," said Sarah, though in fact she was deeply worried. She knew a Michael Stone their child had never seen.

Ronnie tapped a Japanese Zero to set it swinging, then knelt suddenly beside Sarah. "Mummy, do you suppose he might try to fix—"

Sarah clapped a hand over her daughter's mouth and whispered in her ear, "Careful. What if they're listening?"

"Sons of *bitches.*"

"I will not tolerate that talk."

"Daddy says—"

"Not often."

"Mummy," she whispered, drawing their faces nose to nose. "Are you really not worried?"

"About us . . . ?" She and Michael had always been straight with Ronnie, but she had to censor every fear. "They'll let us go as soon as the old man is better."

Mr. Jack, as they called the old man, lay in the bed next to theirs, attached to the wheezing respirator the ship's crew had brought up from *Veronica*. His respiration was still severely depressed, his blood pressure so low that he was, as Michael would say, two degrees north of death.

"Who do you think shot him, Mummy?"

"I haven't the foggiest."

"But what are they doing? It's so weird. Why won't they go to a hospital?"

"Because they have us."

"We're not a hospital. We're just a clinic."

"Somehow I've got to convince them of that," Sarah agreed grimly. Ronnie's face fell, and Sarah kicked herself for frightening the child. She manufactured a big smile and whispered, "Hey, there. You listen at the door. I'll find out where we are."

They had a big secret—Ronnie's GPS hidden in her Snoopy knapsack. Making a game of using it made things a little less frightening. Creeping around the cabin, touching fingers to lips, they listened at the door with Sarah's stethoscope, then checked that the old man was still asleep, and opened a port.

Ronnie hunched over the stethoscope. Sarah turned on the GPS and held it outside for the moments it needed to touch base with the satellites.

Sarah's heart fell when she read the distance they'd steamed from the Pulo Helena way point. The ship was now making twenty-three knots, over four hundred miles in the eighteen hours since they had left Michael behind.

"They're coming!" Ronnie called.

She jammed the GPS into the knapsack, hung the sack

over the chair where it had been, and shut the port as a soft knock sounded at the door. She exchanged looks with Ronnie and nodded. Ronnie opened the door. It was only Ah Lee, the Chinese servant, with tea and orange juice and breakfast on a tray.

"Good morning, ladies."

"Good morning, Ah Lee."

He laid the table like a room service waiter at the Peninsula Hotel.

Ah Lee was very young, no more than a boy, and hardly any taller than Ronnie, who was fascinated by him. Despite the fact that they had almost no language in common beyond "Good morning," "tea," and "Coca-Cola," she had learned that he was from Shanghai, had no brothers or sisters, and was saving his money to one day open a coffee shop for tourists. He left quickly, after a worried glance at the sleeping Mr. Jack.

"I'm not hungry," Ronnie said.

"Let's pretend there's a storm coming," Sarah told her firmly. "Best eat while we can."

They sat opposite each other at the little breakfast table. The cool aroma of air-conditioned salt air, soap, and furniture polish, the reflected sunlight dancing on the ceiling, and the distant presence of engines many decks below could almost lull her into believing that she and her daughter had booked aboard a luxury cruise ship.

A smile intended to reassure faded at the sharp knock on the door.

"Soon as you got a minute, Doc."

"We're busy," muttered Ronnie. "Come back tomorrow."

"Do *not* provoke them."

Sarah draped her stethoscope around her neck for the authority it gave her, took Ronnie's hand, and entered the incongruously luxurious main salon of the *Dallas Belle*'s owner's suite, which had a spectacular view of the ship's wake.

She saw immediately that the compass in the antique brass binnacle pointed the same NNW 330° it had for the past eighteen hours, then turned her attention to the two men in blue jeans, running shoes, and khaki work shirts, who had assumed the power of life and death over her and Ronnie.

The captain of the *Dallas Belle* was a powerfully built Texan in his thirties. Though he had hailed them on the radio with a deceptively easygoing drawl, he was quick moving, decisive, and thoroughly in charge of the ship, if not of everyone aboard.

That power belonged to the tall black American, Moss. Moss shouldered past the captain, causing Ronnie to edge closer to Sarah.

"When you taking the slug out of him?"

"I'd really rather not."

"I don't give a damn what you'd 'rather' do," he mocked her English accent.

"You've seen too many movies, Mr. Moss. The bullet is the least of Mr. Jack's troubles. What Mr. Jack needs much more is a hospital."

"We got your hospital."

"Try and think of my hospital as an ambulance, Mr. Moss. And a rather minimally equipped one at that. He needs a respirator. Our respirator is old and could pack in at any minute."

"Chief engineer's standing by to fix it."

Sarah ignored the interruption. "Mr. Jack is seventy-seven years old. If he is unable to fill his lungs properly, he will contract pneumonia. He will die—provided, of course, he doesn't die first of the morphine your people poured into him."

"You said you were fixin' that."

"He is not responding to the Narcan as I would like. Though I think he's come around."

"So when he wakes up he'll breathe right. Right?"

"Not only is his respiration depressed by the narcotic,

but once it wears off, even awake, he will have to fight the pain of the bullet wound and your mess boy's surgical skills with every breath."

"Then you got to get the bullet out."

"No. He can't afford any more complications outside of a hospital. Had a man your age been shot I'd be delighted to operate—"

"Without anesthesia," muttered Ronnie.

Sarah squeezed Ronnie's arm so hard she felt her fingers bite the bone.

Moss's mouth formed a wintery smile. "Maybe you want to watch me do your Mom without anesthesia?"

Ronnie looked down at the carpet, and Sarah felt her melt. In the ugly silence, Moss's eyes sought hers. Sarah gazed past, tasting fear for herself as well as Ronnie. Moss seemed to resent the class gulf between them as if she had somehow betrayed their shared African heritage by not suffering poverty.

"I must say, Mr. Moss, among the many things I don't understand about all this is why you, who seem genuinely devoted to Mr. Jack, would risk his life to avoid a hospital. I don't know why you think you have to—and I don't care—but surely you could concoct some story, some plausible explanation how he got shot. It's your and the captain's word to the authorities. Say you were boarded by Indonesian pirates. Or say his gun discharged while he was cleaning it. No one will doubt a ship captain and its owner, particularly as he'll survive. As a physician, I must insist—"

Moss crossed the room in a lightning step, looming, so that Ronnie shrank back.

"Insist," Sarah repeated.

Moss caught her arm.

"Let go of me."

He lifted her and stared into her face.

The captain tried to intervene. "Come on, Moss. Ease up."

Moss ignored him. "I owe that man. He dies . . . you die. Both of you." He flung her aside and pushed out the door.

Ronnie's lips began to tremble. Sarah hugged her hard. "It's all right. Mummy's all right."

The captain tried to smile. "Look here, hon. The sooner your mom patches up Mr. Jack, the sooner you sail back to your daddy. That's the deal, right?"

"Are my daughter and I under your protection, Captain?"

The captain looked uncomfortable.

Sarah was not surprised. "What exactly," she asked, "is Moss's role aboard your ship?"

"Well, Moss looks after Mr. Jack."

"Bodyguard?"

"Among other things."

"Made rather a cock-up of it, didn't he?"

"It's not making him any gentler, Doc. I wouldn't push him if I were you."

"And you have no control over him?"

"He answers to Mr. Jack. Moss is a regular lamb around the old man. So, Doc, if you're reading me right, maybe you realize your best bet is to put Mr. Jack in an upright mode."

"Captain, this is insane. You'll be within helicopter range of Manila in a day and a half. If you don't trust Philippine hospitals, you're only eighteen hundred miles from Hong Kong. Three days to helicopter evacuation. Or in four days you could have Mr. Jack in Tokyo. Though my own recommendation is Manila. The sooner he's in hospital the better."

The captain was staring intently. With a shrewd expression on his sun-freckled face, he glanced at the antique binnacle, then back at her. Sarah realized, too late, that she had foolishly admitted to knowing too much.

"I've been a sailor many years, Captain. It doesn't take a genius to dead reckon our position."

"How'd you know our speed?" he asked coldly.

"This is a gas carrier. They're fast." She nodded at the

broad, flat wake that the ship was grinding out of the ocean.
"I estimate twenty-two knots."

He stared hard. "Close. You got a good eye, Doc."

"Let us go, Captain. You've already taken us more than
a week's fast sailing from my husband. Take Mr. Jack to
Manila."

"Sorry, ma'am."

"Moss is a fool. The bullet means nothing. I've counteracted the morphine overdose. Now he needs a hospital. I
can't do any more. Let us go."

"Can't do that," said the captain. "You're the only doctor the old man's got."

"Then when will you let us go?"

"Soon as he's back on his feet issuing orders."

Suddenly a fire alarm started clanging, and the ship's
horn shook the deck with a series of short blasts that rattled
the glassware in the mirrored bar.

"Jesus H. Christ," said the captain. He bounded up the
stairs, pawing the radio from his hip. The door at the top
closed with a pneumatic sigh.

"What happened?" asked Ronnie.

"Something's wrong with the ship."

The clanging grew louder, the whistle thundered a
seven-note chant. They ran to the stern windows. Nothing
burning on the afterdeck, nothing floating in the wake. The
side ports showed the empty Pacific, the chaos of last night's
storm erased by the trade rollers.

"Veronica." She knelt before her child and took her face
firmly in her hands. "I want you to go in and sit with Mr.
Jack."

"What about you?"

"Do what I ask. Stay with him until I come back."

Ronnie glanced at the stairs, then the door. "But what
if Ah Lee comes?"

"If Ah Lee comes, tell him your mum's in the loo and
wants a fresh pot of tea."

"What if Moss comes?"

"He won't. They've got an emergency."

"I want to come with you."

"You're my lookout. If I'm going to get to a sat phone, you've got to watch my back."

Ronnie looked terrified. Sarah said, "Remember what Daddy says in life-raft drill? . . . Come on," she coaxed, "what does Daddy say?"

A smile emerged on Ronnie's frightened face. "Be British, boys!"

"Be British" was supposedly the captain of the *Titanic*'s last command to his crew, and the way Michael said it was usually good for convulsions, especially when accompanied by a solemn salute.

"But no laughing! Or they'll hear us being British!"

That was good for a grin. Sarah bundled Ronnie into Mr. Jack's cabin. The old man had shifted. His hands were twitching as the Narcan did its work. He could wake at any minute.

"Be careful, Mummy."

"Don't you worry, dear. I'll be *very* careful."

She kissed her, closed the cabin door, and mounted the stairs with a pounding heart. The booming whistle shook the treads. The fire alarms changed. The cacophony—the sheer billowing noise—made it impossible to think. Yet it gave her a strange feeling of being almost invisible.

She was guessing from the various ships that she and Michael had boarded over the years that this companionway would not open directly into the bridge itself but somewhat behind, as light from an entrance would blind the watch at night. At the landing, she opened the heavy door a crack and peered out cautiously and was relieved to find a sort of combination lobby-corridor, which served the captain's and owner's companionways as well as the main stair that rose the height of the house, and the elevator.

To the right was an open door, inside a large computer room, lined with machines and racks of electronics. To the left was the chart room. She entered. Aft, she glimpsed the radio room. Ahead, a curtained entryway. She pulled the curtain an inch from the bulkhead and peered through.

She could see about half the bridge, including the helm—steady in the grip of the autopilot—and, beyond the front windows, an incongruous view of the wind cups spinning on *Veronica's* masthead. The captain was pressed against the glass, staring ahead at a white plume of escaping gas that soared skyward from a valve on the foredeck.

Suddenly he whirled around, firing orders that she could not hear over the noise. His face was drawn taut in an expression that combined command and healthy fear. The whistle blasts stopped abruptly. An officer hurried into view and threw a switch on a control console that shut off the fire alarm. In the freshness of the silence, she heard the captain shout, "Get down on deck and give 'em a hand!"

Sarah ran back into the radio room and hid behind a bulkhead as the mate pushed through the curtain and pounded down the stairs. She located a satellite phone. Her eye lingered on the single-sideband radio's automatic Mayday switch. But a broadcast call for help could be explained away as a mistake, long before any rescue hove over the horizon, and she would surely be blamed.

She crept back through the chart room to the curtain. The ship felt as if it had begun to slow. The captain was shouting into his walkie-talkie.

"Rustle up a mess of blankets, and soak 'em down good— Where in hell are those people going? Stop those gutless sons of bitches. Hold on, I'm coming down there. Any hand off station's going to get his butt whupped."

Sarah ran back to the radio room and hid as the captain raced down the stairs. Before his curses and footsteps had faded, she pulled from her pocket a scrap of paper on which she had written a Palau Islands number, and she punched it into the satellite phone. Holding it to her ear as she waited for the connection, she ran back through the curtain and onto the deserted bridge.

Like the elaborate electronics and computer room, and

the luxurious owner's suite, the bridge itself appeared to belong to a wealthier and more advanced ship than the *Dallas Belle*.

The navigational equipment, the radar repeaters, the engine monitors and controls reminded her of an Australian missile frigate they had lunched aboard with the warship's captain, who was Kerry McGlynn's brother. But this, she realized was even more modern, the latest in technology, for the *Dallas Belle* was an OMBO ship—one man bridge operated.

The giveaway was a glass-walled toilet, elevated with a clear view of the windscreen, and a computer station in front of the helm. OMBO was a cost-cutting experiment that allowed a single officer to stand watch as the fifty-thousand-ton vessel steamed full speed, day and night, fair weather and foul.

At the helm, the computer's thirty-inch monitor displayed course, speed, position, weather, and sea conditions; the *Dallas Belle* itself was represented by an icon of a ship steaming on a pale blue electric sea. If some virus struck down every living soul aboard, the fully automated gas carrier would steam forever on a course dead hands had entered into the computer.

The instant Michael had caught wind of OMBO, he had begun plotting ways to replace *Veronica*'s homemade collision alarm with a modern raster scan radar.

The phone clicked, went silent, and then hummed a dial tone.

Sarah dialed again and stepped to the windscreen, crouching so the men on the main deck sixty feet below wouldn't see her. The captured Swan was lashed to a cradle directly in front of the house. Someone knew their business, she was relieved to see: they had furled the sails and even fitted the sun cover over the boom.

Two hundred yards ahead of the yacht, firefighters were spraying foam on the deck, while two men in gas masks and rubber suits were struggling with the ruptured valve.

The rest of the crew—a half dozen men including their Chinese steward—were watching fearfully from a distance, ignoring the shouts and angry shoves of the bosun.

The sea, as usual, was empty.

Directly below her, she saw the captain and Moss run out of the house, arms laden with blankets. They climbed to a catwalk and raced forward, dropping down to the deck near the plume. Moss shoved a seaman off a fire station and directed the nozzle at the heaped blankets. The captain gathered one up, ran to the plume, and flung it over the broken valve.

To Sarah's amazement, the blanket froze solid instantly, like a sheet of metal. The gas jet blew it high into the air and it sailed away like a metal bird. Of course, she thought. To compress the gas into a liquid, it had to be supercooled, many degrees below zero.

Moss ran up with his arms loaded with dripping blankets. The two men conferred, then darted in through the foam, hurling the wet blankets at the base of the plume. The bosun charged up with a water hose, spraying the blankets as they threw more on.

The supercooled gas froze the blankets and hose water. The plume wavered, curled in on itself like a question mark, and dissipated into thin air. The ruptured valve was soon encased in a solid block of ice.

Moss and the captain high-fived each other and headed back to the house, just as the satellite phone connected to the line Sarah had dialed. One ring. Two. Three. On the fourth ring an answering machine picked up and a recorded voice offered to take a message.

5

A TALL SEA LIFTED THE CANOE. THE SUN HAD BURNED OFF THE morning haze and the air was crystal clear. The triple strands of palm tops brushing the horizon were unmistakably Pulo Helena. Stone cursed the miles lost and the time he had wasted.

How far had the *Dallas Belle* steamed in eighteen hours? Gas carriers were much faster than most freighters. Twenty knots service speed? Twenty-two? He conjured the chart in his memory, drew upon it a distance-made-good circle of three hundred and sixty sea miles. Were the ship still headed north, it had passed the Palau Islands by now— Angaur, his own goal, already a hundred miles in its wake.

Well, Michael. Where do we stand?

Up the same creek we started, sweetheart.

Spilt milk.

He turned his back on the atolls and headed north again.

But when he tossed a coconut shell into the water to judge his speed, the Dutchman's log confirmed that the canoe was a pig upwind. For every mile he gained north he slipped an equal distance to the west. He'd be lucky to make twenty real miles a day.

Built to run before the trade winds, the canoe carried too much sail forward to beat efficiently. The wind kept levering the bow off course. Slacking the sail made things worse: it flapped like laundry. But trimming it to stop the luffing promptly pushed the bow downwind again.

He decided to tear down the rig and rebuild it, using the Swan as a model. He struck the mast, removed the rice-bag sail from the boom, and cut a long triangle out of the cloth with his surgical scissors.

The gaff was the longest spar. With the sail still attached, he stepped it as a new, taller mast, standing it just ahead of the middle of the boat. He stayed it fore and aft and both sides with the old man's sennit rope. Then he fashioned a rope gooseneck to attach the stubby old mast horizontally as a boom. He stitched the triangular strip around the forward stay as a jib, attached lines to control both sails, and sheeted them in. The canoe heeled. He threw his weight on the outrigger, and she darted off on a starboard tack.

He tossed another Dutchman's log. Four knots, he'd swear in any yacht club bar in the South Pacific. Nearly a hundred miles a day. He rigged the sheets to the rudder paddle so the canoe would steer itself and set a course at a sixty-degree angle to the seas.

The tropic sun was nearing its zenith and sending down a brutal light that burned his skin and seared his eyes. He sorted through the items that had survived the swamping, and cobbled together a sun shade. Then he drank from a coconut and ate several chewy mouthfuls of salt fish the old man had stowed in breadfruit leaves.

He ate and drank again before nightfall and stayed on the port tack until after the sun had plunged into the sea, and he was suddenly in the dark. A breaking wave he couldn't see overrode the primitive self-steering and knocked the bow upwind. The wind caught the boat aback, suddenly, and filled the sail from the other side. Stone ducked. The boom whizzed overhead, missing him by inches.

The canoe felt smaller and more vulnerable in the claustrophobic darkness. But as it deepened, the Milky Way grew brighter and brighter, until it illuminated the ocean like moonlight. When he could see the shape of his sail and the gleam of breaking seas, he began to feel hope again. If he could average only three knots north he would make seventy miles a day: Angaur in three days.

Hope, or at least the lessening of despair, opened his mind to bleaker avenues he had not yet explored—the awful leisure to ponder why they had taken Sarah and Ronnie. If they were merely afraid of pursuit, of his radios, it would have been simple to tow *Veronica* behind and scuttle her. But they had taken trouble to hoist her aboard and set her carefully on a cradle. The old sloop had no value—but it was more than a sloop. It was a hospital with an operating room, far superior to a merchant ship's dispensary. Had the dead man shot back? Had he wounded someone who couldn't go to a real hospital?

If Stone was reasoning correctly, if the rambling and convoluted hopes, inferences, and "facts" led to the right conclusion, then Sarah was safe. And so was Ronnie. Safe while she treated her patient. As long as the patient lived.

A frail hope that let him rest. He dozed in five-minute catnaps. Suddenly the cold and the rising wind woke him. But as he rose groggily to drive the canoe harder, an unspeakable explanation suddenly rattled him to the bone.

Had she left him? Had Sarah taken Ronnie and made some deal with the captain to speed them away? He knew he was crazy. But "I want to go home," she had said.

Crazy. Remember the dead man, he told himself.

But he couldn't put from his mind her increasing interest in the changes sweeping Africa, her obsession with Ronnie's studies. There wasn't a nation on the war-torn, disease-ravaged continent that wasn't begging for doctors. You hide from life, she accused. You're a natural fugitive.

Crazy. He got busy with the sail and tried to tether his mind to the night sky. Remember the dead man. Three bullets in the back. That was real. Real, but as inexplicable as the heavens, which were white with stars.

All his guides hung in place: Orion and Betelgeuse, Big Dipper, Southern Cross; Altair, the North Star. He planned to sail north to the latitude of Angaur, then west, downwind, until he found it. North and hang a left. The tricky part was knowing when to hang the left.

Angaur lay seven degrees north of the equator. He was currently somewhere in the vicinity of three degrees north. Each degree was sixty miles. Approximately two hundred miles separated him from Angaur's latitude. But it was impossible to clock those miles, so he needed a fix on the zenith of a star whose high point corresponded with Angaur's latitude. A *fanakenga* star, the Pacific navigators called it, when at its zenith it pointed straight down at their target.

The old guy who'd cracked up the canoe had probably memorized the zeniths of a hundred stars and corresponding islands. Stone knew a few by heart: Altair at nine degrees north promised Kwajalein in the Marshalls, and Yap in the Western Carolines; the high point of Hamal, in Aries the Ram, was close to the latitude of Hong Kong.

And Beetlejuice, as Ronnie called Betelgeuse. Bright red Betelgeuse. He saw it now just north and east of Orion's belt—one of the first he had taught Sarah to identify and by whose light they had "courted" many years ago off the African coast. By some gift of God or Neptune, Betelgeuse's zenith nearly matched the latitude of Angaur.

In theory he could establish Angaur's latitude when he found himself directly under the highest point that Betelgeuse crossed the night sky. But when he tried to practice, the ocean rolled and pitched the canoe; and it seemed impossible to determine the zenith of Betelgeuse as he lay on his back watching the mast arc back and forward like a demented pendulum.

He heard a noise. It was a strange city noise, like a subway platform or a baseball game, so different from the soft sounds of waves and wind that he thought he was imagining it. A crackling sound, like a Japanese yelling in a loudspeaker.

Stone sat up. A brightly lighted ship was coming up behind him less than a quarter mile to his right. A fishing trawler. She was moving fast, deck hands busy under blazing work lights.

He dug his radio out of his bag and shouted, "Mayday. Mayday. Mayday." No reply. He cupped his hands and hailed them. The wind whisked his voice away. He opened his backpack, found his penlights, and waved them at the trawler. When it didn't respond, he shone them on his rice-bag sail.

The ship was catching up. With his hands filled with the lights, Stone sheeted in the sail and altered course to cut it off.

The loudspeaker boomed and crackled. The deck hands bent to their work, blinded by their own lights.

"Help!"

Stone yelled again and again, frantically waving his lights. The trawler passed close enough for him to hear the thunder of its engines. The wind whipped reeking diesel exhaust at him and suddenly backed the sail, flinging it across the canoe. Eyes locked on the fishing trawler, Michael Stone sensed the rush too late to duck.

The wood boom struck him full in the temple.

It knocked him to the floor of the canoe. A loud crunching sound resonated in his skull like breaking glass.

He cried for help. He could only whisper. He tried to drag himself onto the outrigger deck, tried to stand, but he felt himself sliding down a slope of blood-red snow. The last thing he saw was the stern lights of the trawler, half a mile ahead and fading fast.

6

IN STONE'S DREAMS THE TRAWLER LIGHTS MINGLED WITH STARS HE
saw from *Veronica* the nights he and Sarah made love on
the cockpit cushions. As she leaned over him her dark body
blotted out the stars until the sky was black and the sea
empty again. He sat up—not knowing where he was—and
saw the trawler lights converge with a blinking buoy.

He sank back, on *Veronica*, under her, and when he
rose again the buoy was gone, the trawler a distant speck
against the rising sun. Sarah was under him now, gig-
gling, teasing. A whisper of pleasure. Soft laughter. "I'll
be right back. . . ."

His face was burning, his head aching, lolling painfully
with the lurch of the drifting canoe. He heard the sail slat,
flap hard. He tried to shield his face, to move to secure the
sheet. Nausea struck like a fist.

A cool shadow crossed his face. He sensed the sail moving
across the hot white sun. It passed and again he burned. He

knew he should shield his face, find the old man's taro leaf shade, but he couldn't move.

"I'm back. You fell asleep."

"Did not."

"I've ruined you." Laughing. "Is there no cure . . . ?" She descended dark over him and his heart swelled with love until he felt he would explode.

Hull down on the horizon, beating to windward under clouds of white canvas, a giant, many-masted ship sailed a course straight at his canoe. An enormous slab-sided hull painted an unusual light sand color. As it closed rapidly, he recognized the *Dallas Belle*, rerigged as an enormous staysail schooner. She had a bone in her teeth and tore by, laying down a wake that nearly swamped him.

Stone brought the canoe about and sailed after her.

Sarah appeared on the stern, calling down to him, waving, smiling. Ronnie jumped up and down, laughing, beside her. She leaped onto a rope trailing into the water, slid down it, then froze, afraid to let go. "Let go!" Stone yelled. "Let go! I'll pick you up."

Ronnie looked beseechingly up at the ship. "Mummy!"

"Tell her to jump!" Stone yelled. "Tell her to let go. Both of you. Jump. Jump."

Sarah climbed onto the bulwark and began removing her clothes, baring her breasts and her long, slim legs, waving to Stone. She poised to dive. A rush of figures appeared behind her, sailors who grabbed her legs, her body, and bore her down.

Stone's canoe put on a burst of speed and he braced to jump and climb up the trailing rope. But the ship turned even closer to the wind and angled swiftly away.

He awoke in the dark, worrying he was a terrible father. He teased and kidded Ronnie, trolling for laughs when he should give her more; it seemed he should talk to her more, and listen more, or he would end up the remote, dramatic figure his own father had been. He resolved to do better. But still he felt anxious. *Veronica* seemed to be bouncing unusually hard.

His mouth was dry as sand, the pain in his head sharp—pulsing with each beat of his heart. Then, like a garbled radio signal suddenly clear, he recognized his first rational thought since the boom had hit him: he was dangerously dehydrated.

According to his watch, he had been semiconscious for twenty-four hours; baked all day by the tropic sun, seasick and wave tossed, he had passed beyond thirst into a state of muddled lethargy.

Too bleary to make any sense of the sails, he fumbled around in the bilge for the net bag of coconuts, and sliced his hand trying to bore a hole in one.

He sucked greedily at his blood. Eventually he pierced the soft eyes of the coconut, and dribbled sweet milk on his cracked lips.

He drank it dry, counted two more, the last of the coconuts, and drank from one. It wasn't near enough liquid. He debated opening the last. The starry sky meant no rainwater. He'd have to trail the old man's hooks and hope to catch a fish.

Searching for a coconut he might have missed, he found his backpack tethered under the abbreviated foredeck, tore it open, and, with a cotton-mouthed croak of triumph, pulled out one of the saline bags he'd tossed in for the old man. He tied it to the mast, lay down and probed with the needle for a vein. He missed, licked up the blood, and missed, again, despising his weakness and cursing the pain.

A vague memory of the Japanese trawler took shape, interspersed with recollections of crazy dreams of Sarah and Ronnie and the *Dallas Belle*, converted to a schooner. He could only hope that his concussion was a mild one.

He pinched the saline feed, and detached it from the needle, which he left in his arm, and rose on shaky legs to trim the flapping sail and put the canoe back on a northerly course, with the east-rising sun hard on his right hand.

He gnawed a moldy sweet potato and a chunk of hard poi. Then he lay down again to let more liquid into his veins. He pressed his watch to his ear and listened intently. The rapid *ping* raised his spirits like a second heart.

But his head still ached, and a thin red haze hung before his left eye like a dirty window. The crazy dreams kept coming back. Sarah in the arms of the sailors. Ronnie deaf to his pleas. The *Dallas Belle* sailing closer to the wind than he could.

Odd how the mind had chosen a staysail schooner rig with all those free-flying sails and not a boom in sight. . . . He looked up at his own boom, which had nearly killed him. Another unexpected gust, another mistake, and once again the heavy length of breadfruit wood would sweep the deck like a blunt scythe.

He had always prided himself in the simple life he lived aboard the Swan, all his belongings tucked inside a thirty-eight foot hull. But, compared to the old fisherman from whom he'd inherited this canoe, he wallowed in equipment. Sextant. Radios. Three self-steering devices. Diesel generator, wind generator, pumps, engine, winches, blocks, lights, fire hose. He was wondering why he was mentally ranting like a latter-day back-to-the-basics hippie, when a truly radical idea occurred to him. Why not deep-six his boom?

The crazy thing was it worked better without it. When he sheeted in the loose sail, the canoe leaped into motion and sailed a full point closer to the wind. He laughed out loud, razoring pain through his skull. With the wind veering more and more easterly, he could hold a course nearly due north.

A fish struck the line he was trailing. Startled awake, Stone pulled it in slowly, the thin twine slicing his fingers. A small tuna that fought hard, and he was surprised he managed to land it without breaking the line. He killed it with a scalpel thrust in its brain and cut thin strips of flesh, which he inspected closely for parasites before swallowing it raw.

Fixing his position without charts and instruments was like trying to balance a checkbook from scribbles on a cocktail napkin. But Stone had to know exactly where he was before he turned west. The decision was momentous—the heart of any hope of rescuing Sarah and Ronnie—for the instant he turned west he was irrevocably committed.

If he turned too soon—too far south—the trade wind and the rolling seas would whisk the canoe past Angaur deep into the Philippine Sea, where he would face an impossible voyage some five hundred lonely miles to the Mindanao Coast. Turn too late, and he'd be driven between Angaur and the northern Palau Island group or smashed on the fringing reef.

He marshaled crude references, eyeballing the sun by day, the stars at night, estimating direction by the wind and the trades rollers. The canoe's leeward drift west, the counterequatorial current east, and his speed north he guessed from the trail of Dutchman's logs he dropped astern like abandoned children.

The only constant would be the zenith of Betelgeuse, if he could see it. By the fourth night—when the tuna had gone rotten and Stone had tapped the final coconut and finished all but a few ounces of taro—he hoped the bright red star was standing directly overhead. And it probably was—he cursed aloud—several thousand light years above the cloud bank that had rolled in at sunset like the sliding roof of an all-weather stadium.

At midnight, God favored him with a thin smile. A hazy opening appeared in the clouds, and Betelgeuse glared down through it, orange as a pumpkin. Stone lay on the bridge deck and stared aloft. The little orange dot *seemed* to be overhead, but the canoe was pitching in the choppy seas stirred between the counterequatorial current and the trade wind rollers. Before he could be sure, the clouds closed in again.

Devastated, afraid to commit, he stared, cold and tired and hopeless, at the sea. There was light in the water. He looked up, but there was still no starlight to reflect. Then with excitement thickening in his throat he realized it sparkled deeper than reflections. Backwash streaks—long streaks of green light that pointed west like arrows.

"The glory of the seas," the islanders called them. Phosphorescence kicked up by backwash waves. And backwash streaks only occurred between eighty and a hundred miles upwave of an atoll.

Stone cast loose the sheets, set the mainsail over the port side and the jib over the starboard, and turned west. Sailing wing and wing, he began bashing into the counterequatorial current, on the long run downwind to Angaur.

7

SARAH LEANED OUT THE SLEEPING CABIN PORT, TO MAKE SURE NO one was watching from the bridge or the main deck, before holding Ronnie's GPS under the sky. Far below, she could see the life raft canister on the afterdeck. It gleamed white in the morning sun, beckoning. Escape, if she dared. Suicidal, until she knew for sure they were near the shipping lanes.

"They're coming!"

The GPS hadn't been out long enough to lock onto the satellite signals, and its screen was a riot of moving numbers. One and a half days after they had capped the gas leak, she could only guess by the sun that the ship was still making for Shanghai. And only hope they'd enter trafficked waters soon.

"Hurry!"

Sarah shoved the GPS back in Ronnie's Snoopy backpack and was dog-latching the port when the captain of the *Dallas Belle* flung open the door without knocking. His quick eyes noted her at the port, Ronnie backing from the door, and Mr. Jack, still as stone in his bed.

"You're needed down in sick bay, Doc. We got an injured man."

Sarah picked up her bag and reached for Ronnie's hand.

"Leave the kid."

"She comes with me," said Sarah.

"Not in sick bay."

"Ronnie has assisted me since she was eight years old," Sarah said firmly. "She's the best qualified nurse on the ship."

The captain blocked the door. "Take my word for it, Doc. You don't want her down there. Not this time."

Sarah hesitated. Something grave and troubled in the captain's expression made her believe him. "All right. Ronnie, stay with Mr. Jack. I'll be back soon."

"But—"

"It's okay, hon. Your mom'll be fine. She's just gotta help somebody."

"I'm hungry."

"Cook's pullin' muffins outta the oven. He'll rustle you up some breakfast right away. Let's go, Doc."

Mystified, Sarah followed him out of the owner's suite and into the elevator. They descended four decks to the dispensary.

"How's the old man?"

"He should be in hospital," she said automatically. In fact, he appeared to be gaining strength. But her best hope was still to convince them he could not survive on the ship.

"It ain't going to happen, Doc. Better get used to it."

She was frantic for Michael and missed him terribly. The three days felt like weeks. She missed him beside her in bed and longed to hear his voice. To live together on the small boat, they had developed habits over the years that insured each other's privacy. Yet his presence, if only a silhouette in the corner of her eye, was a constant she took for granted. Now she felt as if the air had grown thinner.

But she at least had Ronnie—an active presence and a piece of him—while he was desperately alone. Assuming he had repaired the little lagoon canoe, he was far at sea, perhaps as much as a hundred and fifty miles from Pulo Helena. She tried to close her mind to the danger. Every time Ronnie asked how she thought he was, she whispered that he was a splendid sailor, and if anyone could sail a wooden canoe across two hundred and fifty miles of open Pacific it was Michael Stone. Ronnie would nod, bravely, but she knew as well as Sarah that was an enormous *if*, on an unforgiving ocean.

The dispensary contained the ship's meager medical supplies and a single hospital bed. On it lay Ah Lee, his face battered. His eyes were blackened, his lips bloody. His nose looked broken, and one of his teeth had pierced his cheek. When she leaned over him, the boy flinched.

Sarah laid cool fingers on the back of his hand, and lowered her voice to soothe him. "It's all right, Ah Lee. It's only Doctor Stone. I'm going to help you." Angrily, she motioned the captain into the corridor. "Who did this to him?"

"Took a header down the companionway."

"The devil he did. He's been beaten. Who did this— Moss?"

"The sooner you fix him up, the sooner you get back to the kid, Doc."

She examined the boy's eyes first. When she shone a light into the left, both pupils constricted simultaneously. Good. He probably hadn't suffered a head trauma. "This will hurt just a moment," she whispered, opening a disposable needle and gently injecting local anesthetic around his nose and the pierced cheek. Ah Lee followed her movements with tears in his eyes.

She stitched up his cheek, removed a broken tooth, set and taped his nose, and draped surgical gloves filled with crushed ice around his nose and over his eyes. Then she gave him a tetanus shot and penicillin.

63

"Have someone replace the ice when it melts. I'll look in on him later." She touched Ah Lee's hand good-bye.

The captain was watching from the doorway. "Handled yourself well, Doctor. Lotta class." The captain walked her to the elevator. "I've noticed you Africans know who you are. Problem with our blacks is they don't know and they don't give a damn."

This was not the first of the captain's pronouncements. He had found it difficult at first to believe she was what he called a "real doctor," and seemed to admire her powers as something she had acquired in a jungle.

"Have you discussed your racist insights with Mr. Moss?"

"Moss is different."

"You mean you're afraid of him."

The captain seemed unperturbed. "I'm a seaman, Doc. I steer around heavy weather. And no storm lasts forever."

A potential ally? She wondered. She smiled.

The captain moved a little closer. "You're a good lookin' gal, Doc."

"Thank you, Captain. But as I've told Moss, I am married."

"Well, hell, I'm married too."

Sarah fingered her cross. "I took my vows in church."

The captain pressed the elevator button for the bridge deck.

"Moss wants to see you."

He led Sarah through the curtain. Moss was at the helm, hunched over the big OMBO monitor. "Leave us," he said to the captain.

"No rough stuff," said the captain.

"She'll get what she asks for," said Moss. He rose to his full height and stepped close to Sarah. "Leave us," he repeated, and the captain backed out through the curtain.

Sarah heard his footsteps down the stairs. Moss was standing too near her. She backed up. "What do you want?"

"What do I want?" he echoed, mocking her accent. "You

think you're better than me, *Doctor?* You think 'cause your rich African daddy sent you to college you're better than me. You think this white doctor coat makes *you* white?"

He seized the cloth. Buttons tore loose, exposing her shoulder. He trailed his heavy hand over her shoulder, then under the cloth to her breast. "Black," he said. "Black like me."

Sarah stiffened. His touch made her flesh crawl. But he was far too powerful to resist physically. She tried to contain her panic, looked desperately for something to defuse him. She could sense in him a deep bitterness that had the potential to build to uncontrollable rage. Were she a man he would beat her half to death. But against her it would explode in a brutal sexual attack.

"Your friend needs me," she said. "I'm his only hope."

"I don't see him gettin' any better."

She stared down at his hand kneading her flesh—her fear turning to anger—imagining a scalpel with which she would amputate his fingers. The vision was so bright for a second, she thought she saw blood. Then she realized that her white coat was speckled red.

"You're bleeding."

"Cut my knuckle." He made a fist to show her a deep gash. "Gimme a tetanus shot."

"If I were you I'd pray that Ah Lee isn't HIV positive."

"Say what?" He backed away.

"You've mingled your blood with his," she answered, and felt a deeply satisfying thrill at the raw fear that flickered in his eyes.

"Where the hell would a Chinese kid get . . ." his voice trailed off as the possibilities sank in.

Sarah closed her coat. "Next time you beat up somebody, wear latex gloves."

The black man mastered his fear with a cold resolve that Sarah found as frightening as his touch. "I'll keep it in mind. Next time I have to."

"He's just a boy. Why did you hurt him? Are you demonstrating your authority? I'm already aware of your power over me and my child. I'm doing everything I can to care for Mr. Jack. What more do you want?"

"Ah Lee left his post. . . . We don't allow folks desertin' their watch on this ship." He stared down at her. Sarah looked away, praying he wouldn't touch her again.

"You been married long?" he asked, after a moment.

"Twelve years."

"The guy on the island is Ronnie's father?"

"Of course."

"She's near black as we are."

"A mystery of genetics, Mr. Moss. My husband is Ronnie's father. I'd like to get back to Mr. Jack, now."

"How'd you end up with a white man?"

"He's not a 'white' man, he's *my* man."

"Not at the moment he isn't. And you ain't his."

"At the moment," she retorted evenly, "I am Mr. Jack's doctor."

"And that little girl's mother. I got a word of advice for you, 'Mummy.' Watch your ass if you don't want her face lookin' like Ah Lee's."

Sarah felt her will die. He knew about the satellite phone, her mind shrieked. But before she could control her terror, Moss asked, "You a smuggler, Doc?"

"I beg your pardon?"

"You on the lam?"

"I don't follow you."

Moss walked to the windscreen and stared down at the Swan. "Carbon fiber mast, Doc. Kinda funny on that old boat. Captain tells me that's totally tech. Says customs radar can't spot you. You two runnin' a little dope?" He turned to gauge her reaction.

Sarah failed to cover her smile of giddy relief. "I see. No, we are not drug smugglers."

"What you laughing at?"

"My husband salvaged the mast from a wreck. The owners told us we were welcome to it, but they didn't believe we could actually remove it from their boat and step it on ours. You see, it was just the two of us. Ronnie was only five. And the wreck was on a nasty bit of reef."

"How'd you do it?"

"Frankly, I don't know. He wanted it and we got it. He's quite ingenious."

Moss had studied the guy through the sniper scope and wasn't impressed: a stocky little graybeard with the skinny legs you saw on sailing folk. Not much bigger than Mr. Jack, though he had some shoulders on him.

"He wanted it for smuggling," said Moss. "Chinese art? Body parts? I hear mainland kidneys are hot this year."

"We're not smugglers, Mr. Moss. We sail our clinic to the outer islands. We set broken bones, examine old people, and give children toothbrushes."

"Hey, I'm not judging you. Maybe you run a little contraband to pay for the hospital."

"No. We have benefactors."

"U.S.?"

"Mostly the Japanese. As you might know, they're very involved in the islands."

"Again . . . Funny, I didn't find any weapons aboard."

Sarah bristled. "You have no right to search our home."

"How come no guns?"

"We don't carry guns," Sarah answered.

"I hear boat folks do, these days, what with pirates and all."

"We don't believe in guns."

"Doc!" The captain burst in. "The old man's awake."

Moss stayed behind. He'd only get in the way down there. Better to wait till the doctor got him upright. Then he and the old man could claim some time alone. Funny. He had a grandmother who used to drag him to church in a dirty storefront and make him pray. Last night, scared the old man wouldn't make it, he had given it a whirl. Damned if Mr. Jack didn't wake up.

He turned back to the OMBO monitor, put on the headset. Mr. Jack had once said to him—with that grin that promised they could walk through hell and come out brothers—"You don't know shit about technology, but you know what you like."

That was the truth. The ship's computers were magic. Nothing happened aboard that wasn't on tape. All functions were logged, stored, and available for playback. Every rev of the propellers, every hiccup in the compressors, every change of temperature, every course alteration, every word spoken on every deck in the house, every radio signal in, and every radio signal out.

"You don't *have* to know shit about technology." Mr. Jack had laughed. "You just have to see the opportunity. And you do, Moss." Moss felt his whole body swell with pride at the memory. Mr. Jack had hired a flock of computer nerds who taught him how the machines made magic. But the fact was, he had an instinct how to use them, which was a hell of a lot more important.

He punched up the audio.

A recording he had listened to earlier played again. *". . . hope he doesn't hurt himself. You know how clumsy he gets. . . . He'll be fine. . . . Mummy? Do you suppose he might try to fix—"*

Should have shot the son of a bitch while he had him cross-haired in his scope. Moss played the recording through, but whatever she had whispered after she gagged the little girl was lost. But it was pretty clear that they expected "Daddy" to come after them. Moss had discussed it with the captain, who assured him that even if he did, by some miracle, he'd be way too late.

He hit the speed dial on a satellite phone and activated the scrambler, superencrypting the call so that if the National Security Agency happened to be listening, they'd have to cluster a truckload of Crays to crack it. In his mind's eye, he watched the signal shoot like a bullet thousands of miles into space, ricochet off a satellite, and fall back to earth.

A woman answered like she was standing in the door.

Moss said, "I got a phone number for you. I want to know who owns it."

While he waited, he pulled up the menu on the OMBO monitor, chose Ports from the first set of options, and from the ports listed selected Tokyo. The machine started with an overview showing a broad chart for the Sagami Sea.

Moss hit the Simulator command.

The ship icon appeared on the screen. Moving at sixty times real time, it passed O-shima, the island at the mouth of the gulf, and crossed the Sagami Sea in two minutes. Then it entered the traffic separation lanes and swung into Uraga-suido, the channel to Tokyo Bay. Through the narrows. Past Kimitsu. Yokosuka. Yokohama. Around Tokyo Light, and into the harbor.

Course changes were displayed numerically at each of the many way points as the electronic ship twisted and turned up the narrowing fairway, deeper and deeper into the heart of the city. Depth alarms started blinking as it closed on Takeshiba Passenger Terminal.

"*Banzai!*" said Moss.

The sat phone chirped.

"Yeah?"

The woman had a name and a dossier to match the telephone number the doctor had called. A Palau Islands politician.

Surprised and somewhat relieved, Moss said, "I want to know every call in and out of every phone the sucker owns. Office, house, car, boat, plane, whatever he's got. . . . Number one thing I want to know about is calls to the U.S. Navy, to airlines, or travel agents . . . Say what? . . . Until I tell you."

He stretched his powerful arms and stared out the windscreen at the sailboat's mast.

Why, with one chance to call for help, had she chosen a private number in the Palau Islands? Why leave a message on an answering machine? Why not report the name of the atoll where they'd left her husband?

Why didn't she just call the cops?

She seemed to know her way around the ocean, so she would probably know that if she had sent a standard distress signal, or just tripped the automatic Mayday, they would have canceled it when the calls came in for confirmation.

But their boat was registered in the United States. Why not call the U.S. Navy? Or Interpol? It was a good question and he looked forward to asking her the second the old man didn't need her anymore.

8

A BIRD DIVE-BOMBED STONE THE MORNING OF THE FIFTH DAY, A sure sign of land. By noon, terns and black-and-white noddies were diving and swooping, fishing in flocks. The water took on a peculiar chop between the swells, which themselves began to change shape and grow steeper, and Stone sensed a certain hesitation in the atmosphere, as if air and water were stumbling on an obstacle.

The chop worsened and took on a particularly chaotic quality which, in his exhaustion, he had failed for too long to recognize was caused by a swift current setting to the south. He'd been driven south for hours.

The canoe lurched, and around the sail he was suddenly startled to see Angaur—green and wooded, with a red water tower in the middle. A cluster of buildings at the north end marked an abandoned Coast Guard station.

His chest filled with joy. He was less than two miles off. But his joy was quickly tempered by the realization that he was being swept toward a rock-bound shore.

Soon he heard surf thundering and saw white eruptions as the great swells squeezed through blowholes and shot skyward to fall foaming on the rock. As he neared what looked like the corner of the island, he saw a reef. But it was a small outcropping, not the main reef that sheltered the harbor.

An airplane came skimming low from the north, buzzed out to sea in a lazy circle, and lined up with the island. The Koror flight. Had to be—couldn't be more than one plane every few days for an island with a population of two hundred. But by the time he beat around the island and picked his way through the fringing reef and into the harbor, the plane would be long gone. God knew when the next one went.

The plane touched down less than a mile from him, a minuscule two-engine job floating down a World War II runway built for four-engine bombers, spun around, and buzzed back to the terminal shack. Stone threw the steering paddle hard over and aimed for the little reef, standing high as he could on the outrigger bridge to try to see a passage.

The breakers appeared as a solid snowbank of foam. Then he saw a small, dark break and steered for it. The pass—if it was a pass—looked about six feet wide. The sea was smashing around it in a welter of tumbling water. Michael's boat was swept into the surf, spinning out of control. He fought the steering paddle with both hands, and when he swung his weight into it, it snapped.

A huge comber lifted the canoe like a dart player lining up a shot, and he saw a black gleaming coral bank where he knew the canoe would land. Abandoning the useless paddle, he cut his backpack loose and got one arm through a strap before he had to jump. The canoe shot ahead, crashed onto the reef.

Stone jumped a hair late. The mast cracked, snapped, and plummeted down on him, brushing his shoulder with a blow that knocked him into the water as the sea picked the canoe up again and threw it in splinters.

He was tumbled, somersaulted, driven over jagged coral, found himself suddenly in deep water, swam, and just as suddenly felt sand under his feet. He staggered onto the beach, dazed and bleeding.

A young couple carrying camper's ruck-sacks came running from the road that rimmed the beach, the boy forging ahead, wielding a camera and calling to Stone. Utterly astonished to find himself alive and standing on hard ground, Stone gaped back at them.

"Okay, we take picture, Old One?" the boy asked in tourist-pidgin English, apparently convinced that the sun-blacked Stone was a native and his crash landing a local custom.

The girl was staring, realizing what the boy didn't.

"He's hurt."

Stone broke into a dead run, working his arms into the backpack straps as he pounded along the crushed coral road that mirrored the sun and seemed to jump and leap under his boat shoes. He ran for half a mile, exhaustion vanishing in a burst of hope. The road turned inland. He saw a break in the trees—the clearing of the runway—and heard the plane rev its engines.

"Noooo!"

He saw a tin-roofed shack flying a ragged wind sock, a man in a Budweiser T-shirt sitting in a rusty jeep with PARADISE AIR hand-painted on the hood, and a boxy De Havilland Otter with PARADISE AIR stenciled on its dented aluminum skin. The man in the jeep turned and watched Stone curiously. The propeller pitch rose to a harsh scream and the plane started rolling.

"Stop him!" Stone yelled, his voice thin and shrill.

The man in the jeep cupped his hands and shouted, "Where you going, man?"

"Koror. Stop him."

Stone jumped into the jeep. "Go. Get him!"

The man shrugged, put it in gear, and chased down the runway after the plane.

"Flash your lights."

"Don't have lights."

The plane was drawing away. Its nose began to rise. And then suddenly it slowed, stopped. The jeep caught up. Stone jumped down. The pilot stuck his head out the window. "What?"

"Koror!" said Stone.

"Got any money?"

Stone suddenly saw himself in the pilot's eyes: warm blood streaming down his sunburnt arms, soaking wet, his shirt and shorts in tatters. He held up his backpack. "I got money."

"Passport?" asked the pilot. "They'll hassle you at Koror."

Stone nodded. He had several passports.

"Where you come from?" asked the man in the jeep. "I don't see no boats." Angaurans were famous marijuana growers and notoriously suspicious of strangers.

Stone ignored the question and pointed at the ticket folder on the floor of the jeep. "How much to Koror?"

Having caught up with the plane, the Paradise Air ticket agent now returned to Island Time, slowly extracting a ticket from the folder, laboriously filling it out. Stone fished his wallet from the waterproof knapsack, handed over three American fives, and climbed aboard. The old bomber runway was so long that the pilot took off from where he had stopped.

The plane hopped onto the trade wind like a trained poodle and banked north. Stone looked back at the tiny harbor, a few boats and the sprawling wreckage of a derelict phosphate conveyor disappearing into the jungle. He couldn't see the little reef where he had wrecked the canoe. Below was the blue channel between Angaur and the main Palau archipelago, which looked like a jeweled green dagger set in the filigree of the reef. To his right spread the dark Pacific, to his left the Philippine Sea, dappled in cloud shadows. He looked for a sand-colored ship.

The pilot leveled the plane off at eight hundred feet, turned around and took off his sunglasses, and asked, "You okay, buddy?"

Stone ran a hand through his salt-crusted hair. He opened his pack and wiped the blood off his arm and doused it with peroxide. It stung like hell, but he barely noticed. An old line of Conrad's was running through his head: *The sea gave you a chance to feel your strength.* He felt invincible.

9

"YOUR RADIO WORK?" STONE SHOUTED OVER THE ENGINE ROAR.

"Sure it works," the pilot answered, indignant despite the fact that a third of the dials on his instrument panel were blacked out with electrical tape, and his starboard engine was spraying oil on the windows.

"Would you please radio your dispatcher to call President Salinis and ask him to meet me at the airport?"

The pilot laughed: with a total population of fifteen thousand, the Republic of Palau's president was not a remote figure, but Stone was badly out of date. "He's *Senator* Salinis, again. He got voted out."

When Stone had sailed from Kwajalein, a week-old copy of the Guam *Pacific Daily News* had predicted victory in the election. But politics in Palau were volatile—sometimes violent—to say the least, and Marcus, a hard-driving entrepreneur, had made several trips up and down the slippery slope.

"Who I say wants him?"

Stone gave the name on his primary passport: "Doctor Michael Samuels."

"Hey, you the sailboat doctor?"

"You got it."

"I ain't seen your boat this year."

"She's refitting in the Marshalls."

"How'd you get to Angaur?"

"Can you call him, please?"

Stone closed his eyes, and the next he knew the pilot was shaking him awake. "Koror."

Stone looked around blearily.

"Here." The pilot handed him a comb. Stone ran it mechanically through his salt-caked hair and combed some knots out of his beard, handed it back with thanks, and stepped out into the sun-blasted humidity of a Palau afternoon. A stylish, tall dark Palauan woman sauntered out of the terminal and intercepted him on the apron. "Doctor Mike?"

"Hello?"

"Do you remember me?" She was smiling as if she had a secret. "Joanna Salinis."

Last he had seen her she'd been on a visit home from a Hawaiian boarding school.

"Daddy asked me to collect you. He's up in Bobang. He won't be home till dinner. . . . Are you okay?"

Stone's face had collapsed before her eyes.

He felt suddenly destroyed. Expecting the sturdy bulk of Marcus Salinis, all warm smiles and crafty eyes, instead he found this child-woman, whose tall thoroughbred gait reminded him of Sarah, and who smiled like someone with neither a care in the world nor a brain in her head.

"You look like you need a shower, clothes, and two weeks' sleep. Where's Doctor Sarah?"

"On the boat. Can you take me to a hotel?"

"Daddy said to bring you home."

"I have to make an international call." There was a Comsat station on the island, and international connections in the bigger hotels.

"Use ours. Daddy bought a sat phone."

Joanna drove a brand-new bright red Lexus with a crumpled front fender, already rusting. She drove with the same blithe innocence with which she had shepherded him through the immigration formalities—the self-assured smiles and casual impatience of the republic's elite. Her mother, Stone recalled, was high-caste, daughter of a chief. "Daddy" had overcome lower origins, carved himself an outwardly secure niche in the hierarchy by becoming one of the small crowd that excelled at funneling American aid and Japanese investment into his own pockets. He had built a popular base by fighting for Palauan sovereignty from the U.S. Pacific Trust Territories, and shared the wealth with shrewdly selected supporters.

Stone knew other Palauans, some of equal stature, but none with Salinis's connections to the several worlds of shipping, construction, politics, and Japanese tourism that ruled the Far Pacific.

"Are you hungry? Doctor Mike?"

"Starving."

"Beers and Cokes in back." There was a cooler on the backseat. Stone fished a Coke out of the ice and drained it in one long joyous swallow. "Oh."

"You know you really look *terrible.*"

Stone caught her eye as she stopped for a truck loaded with mangrove logs. "Joanna, I've come to see your dad on business and I'd appreciate—"

"I know. Dad already told me. Keep my mouth shut. I know that, for gosh sakes. I only said you look terrible." She leaned on the horn, blaring until the truck moved, then swung onto a dirt road that climbed a steep hill, and gunned the car over a series of ruts and potholes. "Sorry about the road. Dad says it keeps out strangers."

Stone felt as if his eyes and ears were operating a long

beat behind the moment. "What did you mean, your dad told you?"

"He telephoned me and said you had a problem and I was to pick you up quietly and take you away from the airport. He phoned Immigration to let us through."

"How did he know I had a problem? I didn't talk to him."

Joanna gnawed her lip. "There was a funny message on his answering machine the other day. He right away took the tape out."

"A message? From whom?"

"I don't know, Doctor Michael. He thought it was maybe a joke."

"Where is it?"

"Daddy has it."

"When's he coming home?"

"Soon, soon. Don't worry."

Home, a sprawling modern house of teak and glass and stone floors, was on the side of a steep hill overlooking the Philippine Sea. The humidity had already mildewed the furniture and warped the doors, and the air-conditioning had broken—victim, Joanna explained, of the recurring power outages. But the views were spectacular west to the sea and south to the Rock Islands, which looked like a generous hand had flung emeralds into the lagoon.

"Sat phone?"

"Don't you want a shower first?"

"Where's the phone?"

She led him to a comfortable guest room with a breeze that was better than air-conditioning, and showed him the phone and shower. He waited until she had backed out, then lifted the phone and dialed.

"Kerry McGlynn, please. Doctor Mike calling."

McGlynn was at sea, his secretary replied.

"Can you patch me through to him?"

She could not.

"Doesn't he have a sat phone aboard?" Speed and communication were the key to the salvage game.

"I'm afraid he's rather caught up at the moment. One of our repeat customers has discovered another island new to him. May I help you?"

"I'm a friend. I need Kerry's help."

"Why don't I pass your number on when Kerry radios in? Then he can ring you."

Stone gave her the Salinis's number. "Where's Kerry operating?"

"I'm afraid he'll have to tell you that," the secretary answered icily, as if a friend should damned well know that secrecy was another vital ingredient for success in the salvage business.

"Listen to me. This is personal and very urgent. Is there any place I can meet him?"

"I'm afraid—"

"Please. Please. I have nowhere to turn."

"Hold the line, please."

Stone waited, racking his brain for whom else to call. . . . Lydia Chin in Hong Kong, a shipowner. Or maybe someone from his Navy days. Someone who'd made admiral by now, with the clout to command a search. Someone whom he hadn't seen in twenty-five years? Someone duty-bound to arrest him . . .

"Doctor Mike?"

"Still here."

"I don't know if this helps at all, but it's the best I can do. Before we got this job Kerry had meetings scheduled in Hong Kong. It's possible he will be stopping there in a few days."

"Where's he stay?"

"I can't say."

"Tell him I'll be at the Hong Kong Yacht Club. But if he calls in before, I'll be at this number until tomorrow morning."

He telephoned the yacht club and Lydia Chin. Her office said she was traveling in China, due back tomorrow.

He sat holding the phone, pondering whom else to call. Finally he gave it up and stumbled into the bathroom, where he removed his tattered shirt and shorts. The mirror gave him a shock. He'd lost ten pounds. He could see his ribs, and the bones in his arms showing through a stringy sheath of muscle. His face was dark red, his arms nearly black, his beard hung long from his hollow cheeks, and his eyes, ordinarily dark blue, had the hard silvery sheen of ball bearings.

He stepped into the hot water, cried out as it scalded his sunburn, adjusted to lukewarm, and washed away salt and dried blood with soap and shampoo. When he finally closed the taps, he heard Joanna call, "There's a razor in the medicine cabinet and I'm just reaching in with a robe." A shapely hand and a long arm snaked around the door and hung the cotton robe on the hook.

"There's coffee and Coke and sushi out here when you're ready. Want a beer?"

"Coffee'll be fine."

"Well, *that's* better," Joanna exclaimed. "But you still need a shave."

"Your dad home yet?"

"Soon."

Stone sat at the coffee table she had spread and stared at the food, wondering what else he could do, whom else he should call.

"Joanna, what's my quickest way to Hong Kong?"

"Air Mike to Manila, Air Philippines to Hong Kong." She settled cross-legged on a couch across from him.

"How about to Tokyo?"

"Air Mike to Guam."

"When's the next Manila flight?" His friend—or rather acquaintance—Patrick was in Manila. A semiretired mercenary, Patrick was connected.

"They fly Tuesday, Thursday, and Saturday."

"What day is today?"

"What do you mean?"

"What day of the week, for crissake?" Michael paused. "Sorry. I'm a little confused."

"Today is Monday," she said primly. "Eat something. And you better drink. Want a beer?"

"No. Thank you." He should have been starving, but all he could focus on was his next step. His relief at having made land had already worn off, and his panic about Sarah and Ronnie was escalating. Where would the ship have taken them by now? He ate some cut-up mango and sipped the coffee. Hong Kong offered deeper lines into more worlds than Tokyo, where his friends were more conventional businessmen.

A car slid to a noisy halt on the coral drive. A door slammed, shaking the house, and the next instant Marcus Salinis filled the room. He was a stocky five-six, nearly as broad as he was tall, with a brown face split by a gap-toothed smile. A Micronesian beer belly strained the buttons of his flowered shirt; the tight cloth showed the outline of a gun on his hip.

"Doctor Michael! Joanna take care of you okay?" He grasped Stone's hand in both of his as Stone tried to ask about the message, and squeezed hard. "Joanna, bring a couple of Buds. The man's drinking coffee for crissake and the sun's almost down."

Joanna hurried to the kitchen. Salinis said, "You look beat."

"I need help," Michael said plainly.

"Came to the right place. Listen to this." He released Stone's hand and pulled a pocket tape recorder from his shirt. "I pulled the tape out of my answering machine."

Joanna returned with two cans of Budweiser, which were dripping condensation.

Her father enveloped both cans in one hand. "Hon, I

bought a nice fish. Why don't you light the grill? We'll give Doctor Mike a cookout."

Joanna left sulkily and Salinis turned on the tape. "I don't know if this is a joke or what, Michael. You tell me."

Stone jumped at the sound of Sarah's voice, tight with tension and frustration:

"*Marcus. Marcus. Are you there . . . Bloody hell!—*"

"The machine picked up," Salinis explained. "I was out fishing."

"*Marcus. Marcus, this is Sarah. Please save this message for Michael. . . .*"

Stone felt tears burn his eyes. After all these years, they operated almost as one person. She knew, come hell or high water, he'd somehow get off the atoll, knew when he did he'd head for Palau, and knew that in Palau he would head first for Marcus Salinis.

"*Listen, Michael. We're at nine degrees north, one hundred and thirty-two east, headed northwest at twenty-three knots. We're all right. I've an elderly patient with a gunshot wound. My best guess is we're headed for Taiwan or Shanghai if we don't change course. I'm not sure what they'll do when they don't need me anymore. On the other hand, they'll need me for some time, as they refuse to put the old man in hospital. He apparently owns this so-called* Dallas Belle, *and that is all I can tell you. I frankly don't know who in the world can help us—even if we were free to ask—what navy, what government— They're coming, I'd better ring off. God bless.*"

A hang-up click; Salinis's answering machine whined the dial tone and fell silent. Twenty-three knots, 550 miles a day, 2750 miles in five days—Taiwan yesterday; Shanghai tonight. But if the ship had changed course, it could be anywhere from Guam to Australia to Singapore today, and deep in the Indian Ocean tomorrow.

Salinis was staring at Michael. "Reason I figured it's a joke, she sounds so cool."

"When the shrapnel's flying," said Stone, "she's cool."

"What the hell is going on?"

"We were down in Pulo Helena last week. A big gas carrier radioed for medical help, said the captain hurt himself falling down. Sarah and Ronnie went aboard. I stayed on the atoll where an old fisherman was dying. Next thing I knew they'd hoisted the Swan on deck and steamed off."

"Leaving you alone?"

"Except for some poor guy dead on the beach. Shot."

"That's crazy."

"Just like I said it. I couldn't believe it. . . ."

"How'd you get to Angaur?"

"Fisherman's canoe."

"From *Helena?* You some sailorman, Michael."

His head was reeling, his eyes heavy. "I gotta find the ship."

"Only problem is," said Salinis, walking to the window to make sure they were still alone, "why did Sarah say 'free to ask'?"

"What do you mean?"

"I mean Sarah calls *me* instead of sending a distress signal. And now *you're* holed up in my house instead of at the U.S. Consulate screaming for the Navy."

Stone hesitated.

Marcus probed. "I always figured you were on the lam. Plenty of Americans out here are. But how bad? Sarah got an angry husband looking for you?"

"Bad," said Stone.

"Wha'd you kill somebody?"

"No . . . but I am wanted for murder. Among other things."

"You didn't do it?"

"I didn't kill anybody."

"What were the 'other things'? Drugs?"

"Not drugs."

"So what's left?"

"What if I told you piracy?"

Marcus Salinis looked annoyed, which in a Palauan was a menacing sight. His fleshy face closed up, erased his smile, and gathered heavily around his eyes, which were suddenly small and brittle. "Okay, Doc. None of my business. And fuck you too."

Stone said, "It happened long ago in another ocean."

"Long ago in another ocean? Sounds like the beginning of *Star Wars*. Can you be a little more specific?"

"Forget the details, but I've got a lot of people gunning for me."

"Who? What people?"

"I can't tell you that. I can't tell anybody."

"If you can't tell me, man, maybe it didn't happen."

The politician looked him hard in the face. Stone stared back, and Salinis recoiled from the bleakness in his eyes.

"I lost someone I loved then almost as much as I love Sarah now. . . . That's all I can tell you, my friend."

"And you want my help?"

"I need your help."

Marcus spread his hands. "Sorry, Doc. If I don't know what you're running from, how can I help you?"

"It has nothing to do with this."

"It has everything to do with this if it keeps you from getting normal help."

"I can't tell you."

"Give me a general idea. I don't need the names, but what am I dealing with here?—Come on, Mike, you're in bigger trouble now than you've ever been. You've got to trust somebody or you can kiss your wife and daughter good-bye."

Stone hung his head, silent, wishing he were alone and back at sea, back on the boat, where he never doubted his next move. Here, afraid to say anything that might risk his future with Sarah and Ronnie, he felt paralyzed by indecision.

"Who the hell are you?" Marcus demanded. "Where do you come from? What have you done?"

"Why are you suddenly asking me this?" said Stone.

"Why are you so paranoid? I'm only asking you what

everyone's going to ask soon as you say you can't just go to the cops. What's standing between you and picking up that phone and yelling 'Help!'?"

"No names," said Stone. "No details you can trace. Fair enough?"

"I'll judge what's fair after you spill it."

Again Stone hung his head. "Years ago I sailed into the middle of a political squabble; the murder was a frame-up. I had to steal a ship to get away. Hence the piracy . . . Okay?"

Salinis said, "So who's after you?"

"Two governments and the CIA," Stone answered, wishing immediately that he hadn't.

"How'd you piss off the CIA?"

"It was their ship."

Stone waited anxiously while Marcus digested his story. He knew a dozen men like Marcus around the Pacific, movers and shakers in societies where both moving and shaking were considered peculiar if not suspect. It was a lonely existence for people who'd seen something of the larger world in business travels to Japan and the United States, and one fraught with conflict as they struggled to build miniature versions of superpowers in a region that most outsiders and many locals already thought was paradise.

People like Salinis had always regarded him and Sarah and their work with puzzlement, clearly wondering what they wanted in return in a world where good works were expected of missionaries who burned to convert the natives and Peace Corps types who moved on after a short time. Stone could only hope that piracy in another ocean had no bearing on the power plays and land feuds that kept the blood pumping on Salinis's islands.

The former president gave a deep chuckle. "Yeah, I always figured Sarah had a pissed-off husband looking for you. Any couple that hot had to have run off. . . . Well, seems to me like your situation kind of limits your options. The States sent us a new consulate asshole worse than the last. I'll talk to him if you want. But he'll just pass you along, and you'll be wearing handcuffs before they start looking for that ship, because he's not going to give a damn what happened to your wife. . . . Things are getting kind of heavy around here, in case you hadn't noticed."

"I notice you got a gun under your shirt."

"Another under the car seat. And a pump twelve-gauge in the bedroom. Somebody's following me. Phones are tapped. House, office, even the sat phone. I don't know what the hell they're after. I already lost the election."

"Where's Amelia?" His wife, the chief's daughter.

"Took the kids to her father's till this blows over."

"What's Joanna doing here?"

"I just can't tell with that girl. She's either too dumb to realize what's going on or so damned smart I want her by my side. Probably no big deal. It's been a while since we actually *killed* someone for politics, not counting 'suicides' and botched car bombings. . . . Come here, look at this." He led Stone onto the terrace and indicated a tarnished brass telescope mounted on a tripod. "Take a look."

Stone bent over the eyepiece. A seventy-foot motor yacht leapt into view, anchored in the still water below the hill. It had a satellite dome. Two couples were drinking cocktails in the stern. They looked young and prosperous, the women in bikini tops, gold jewelry, and bright lava-lavas at their waists, the men in loose white shirts and bermuda shorts. A steward came up with a tray of canapés. Clearly vacationers, changed for dinner after a day of diving.

"Been sitting there three days," said Marcus. "Watch the blond guy with the binoculars."

Stone couldn't quite see his face, but the man Marcus indicated had the rugged looks of the summer diver and winter skier. A diamond or gold earring glinted as he casually scanned the sea and the hills between sips from a champagne glass. He swung the binoculars toward the land and raised them to the top of Marcus's hill. For an instant the binoculars locked on the telescope.

The blond man waved.

Stone shrugged. He was so tired, he could barely stand. "Somehow," he said to Marcus, "I've got to track the *Dallas Belle*."

Marcus shook his head. " 'Fraid not. I already asked around. There's a *Dallas Belle* chemical carrier operating in the Gulf of Mexico, where's she's been for years. Looks like Sarah's right about false registry."

"I'm going to Hong Kong," said Stone. "Take my chances with the American consulate, if I have to."

"How are *they* going to track a ship?"

"The Navy used to have a worldwide acoustical tracking system to keep tabs on the Soviets during the Cold War—hydrophone buoys and subs and satellites to record ship noise. Prop wash and engine and driveshaft noise is unique to each vessel, and everything they recorded was stored in a library. Like a fingerprint file. Supposedly, they can call up the files for a ship heard that day in the vicinity of Pulo Helena. Cross-referencing that, the computer will identify who she is. And the files for the days since will tell us where she's gone."

"Assuming the system is still working," said Marcus, "and assuming they don't toss you in the hoosegow for piracy."

"My friend Captain McGlynn's got a brother in the Australian Navy. Stands to reason the navies share data. Maybe he'll help. McGlynn's always had a thing for Sarah."

"Imagine that." Marcus smiled.

"So maybe he'll help, if I can just get ahold of him. Meantime, I've got shipowner friends in Hong Kong, too. Either way, Hong Kong's my best bet. . . . And there's a guy I can see in Manila."

Stone rewound the tape and played it again. He drifted on Sarah's voice, the cool, strong sound and the dispassionate language: These are the facts. This is what I know. All else is empty speculation. . . . He shivered. It was no news to him that his wife was a strong woman, but this was proof of a strength that frightened him, a bloodless quality that he deliberately avoided acknowledging. If she ever decided that he was not for her anymore, she would cast him adrift and never look back.

"Michael, you're falling over dead. Come on, we'll eat some fish and put you to bed."

"McGlynn's calling me from Australia."

"Joanna, give me a hand."

Stone was vaguely aware of Marcus's burly form leaning close.

"Wake me if Captain McGlynn calls."

"Open the bed, Joanna."

"And book me Manila to Hong Kong."

He felt Marcus pick him off the couch like a sack. He smelled Joanna's perfume and then he was gone.

He dreamed the canoe was sinking. He felt weight on his chest and when he raised his head for air, a hand covered his mouth. Lavender soap. Coming awake, he felt Joanna's breasts on his skin and her firm legs entwined with his. Her lips brushed his ear.

"Daddy says don't move," she whispered. "Someone's in the house."

Her body was shaking.

In the glow of the outdoor security light, he saw her dark eyes track movement. A shadow moved across the curtain. The sliding screen door ground softly in its track, opening inch by inch until the shadow slipped through, and into the room.

Steel glinted in the light.

Fully awake now, adrenaline flowing, Stone flipped on top of Joanna, threw the pillow, and grabbed the bedside lamp.

The intruder was covered head to toe in a glistening black wetsuit. When he dodged the pillow, Stone was ready and hit him hard with the lamp. The figure staggered.

From the hall came the steely clatter of a pump shotgun being cocked. Stone threw the lamp, connecting again, and

89

the intruder whirled and ran out the window as Marcus Salinis burst in the door, sweeping the room with a gun barrel yawning like a sewer pipe.

"Get down!"

Stone pinned Joanna under him. Marcus's shotgun roared and gushed flame. The curtains and screen disappeared. Marcus ejected the shell and peered down the hill.

"Missed, goddammit—"

"Get back from the window," Stone yelled.

"Naw, he's still running."

"Daddy, you should have seen it! Doctor Mike faked the guy with a pillow and then *pow!* with the lamp. You were great, Michael."

Marcus looked at his daughter sprawled under the doctor. "Get out from under him. Get some clothes on. Get some beers—And *you*," he turned on Stone, who appeared oblivious of the naked young woman as he rose from the bed to stare in bewilderment at the dark sea. "You want to tell me why a guy coming to kill *me* goes for the guest room?"

10

"Mummy? . . . Mummy! I'm ready for my test."

"What test?" Sarah turned from the window, which framed the same monotone tableau of rain-spattered sea it had since Mr. Jack had ordered the engines stopped.

Adrift, the *Dallas Belle* rolled slightly on the East China Sea groundswell, a regular motion that set the airplane models swaying. Mr. Jack had given no indication why they had stopped. Nor did the small crew seem to be working on repairs. This morning the captain had launched an inflatable Zodiak from the accommodations door at the waterline and motored around the hull. But Sarah attached no special meaning to that, as captains generally enjoyed any opportunity to inspect the trim of their hulls.

Her eye kept locking on the emergency life raft canister on the afterdeck. The deeply laden ship was drifting with the current at two knots, according to her latest GPS reading. But a life raft, which floated on the surface like a feather, would drift with the wind. And the ragged tops of the small waves indicated that the wind was shifting, starting to blow opposite the current. The night could put thirty or forty miles between them and the ship if she could find the opportunity and the nerve.

Her patient was sitting up in bed, a cashmere robe covering his bandaged chest and shoulder, his mutilated fingers clutching his omnipresent coffee mug. Moss stalked about the suite, in and out of the sleeping cabin, menacing as a cheetah, casting dark looks at Ronnie, who sat cross-legged at Mr. Jack's feet. All but lost in a wool sweater from the ship's store, she was holding one of the models, enthralled, as the old man taught her its parts.

"Mr. Jack's going to ask me all the parts of the plane."

"And what happens if you get them right?"

"I win a prize."

"What prize, Mr. Jack?"

His voice was still weak. He had a cutting accent that Sarah associated with Irish-American actors in black-and-white movies about New York City. "First prize: she gets 'em all right, she keeps the plane."

"Really? Mummy, can I?"

Sarah nodded, concerned her daughter was exhibiting the classic signs of Stockholm syndrome, in which the captive fell in love with the captor. Yet she was also aware that the more the child charmed Mr. Jack, the less likely the strange old man would hurt her. Or so she hoped.

"Second prize—if you only get most of them right, I'll tell you a story about the plane. True story. Ready?"

"Ready."

But before Mr. Jack could ask his first question, Moss barged into the sleeping cabin. "About time for some sleep, Mr. Jack."

"Naw, I'm fine."

"Isn't that right, Doc? Shouldn't he sleep?"

"As long as he works hard at deep breaths—deep breaths, Mr. Jack—he can stay up a while longer."

"When I'm done with her, Ronnie's going to know more about World War II than any ten kids her age. Ready, kid?"

Moss folded his arms and glowered from a corner.

"Okay, we'll start easy," said Mr. Jack, holding the plane aloft. "What's this plane called?"

Ronnie sat up primly and answered, "It's a North American B-twenty-five."

"It's got another name."

"A Mitchell."

"And what kind of plane is it?"

"A medium bomber."

"This is the easy stuff, kid. Wait for it. It's going to get a lot harder." He inclined the model toward Ronnie. "What are these little things on the wing?"

"Ice eliminators."

"How fast she go?"

"Three hundred miles an hour."

"How about her engines?"

"Wright Cyclone double-row . . ."

Sarah listened with half an ear as Ronnie gleefully answered every question.

"Who sits here?"

"Bombardier."

"And here?"

"You."

"What did you say?" asked Sarah.

"Mr. Jack was radio operator-gunner, Mummy. He fought the Japs."

"He fought the Japanese— You must have been very young, Mr. Jack."

"We all were."

Ronnie rattled off the statistics he had taught her. Finally he said, "Well, you did pretty good, kid. A little off on the bomb load."

"No, I wasn't."

"You said twelve tons."

"Oh, I meant two. It's twelve tons fully loaded, gross weight. You know what I meant."

"Rules are rules."

"I'll take second prize."

"You're no fun. You give in too fast."

"But the rules."

"You don't want the plane?"

"I *do* want the plane. But I missed a question. Maybe next time."

Mr. Jack looked at Sarah. "She get that from you?"

"And her father."

Ronnie's face fell.

Mr. Jack shot Sarah a wintery scowl. "Give the kid a break, Doc." The scowl evolved into a sly, challenging smirk. "Listen close, Ronnie. The story you won is about the time I took off in that plane from an aircraft carrier."

"No," Ronnie piped up. "It's Army Air Force. Not Navy. Remember, Mr. Jack?"

"Absolutely right, kid. But still, I took off from a Navy ship. Want to know how?"

She hunched closer, clutching the model, her dark eyes wide and steady on the old man's face.

It was, Sarah thought, as if the old man personified for Ronnie the sunken skeletons of the World War II planes and warships they snorkeled over. Or, she mused, as if a gladiator had stepped from the Roman ruins that *she* as a girl had explored in the south of England.

"Okay," said Mr. Jack. "Like I told youse before, I got outta basic right before Pearl and they sent me to radio school. Tops in my class. Got orders to join a squadron out in Washington State. We trained our tails off. Then one night flew to some godforsaken base in the middle of nowhere. My buddy, the bombardier, said it was Wisconsin.

"Should have known right off something was up, because security was real tight. No mail. No telephone. No leave. We practiced short takeoffs. Real short. They had this Navy officer showing our pilots how to do it. Well, all we needed was the goddammed Navy telling us what to do. Pretty soon we was taking off like rockets. So then we loaded up with dummy five-hundred pounders and extra fuel tanks till we was weighted down like freight trains and practiced some more.

"One day we flew west. Put down for fuel in Arizona and did our short takeoff. You shoulda heard the tower: 'You guys nuts?' We kept going all the way to the West Coast.

"Coming in to land we swing over a harbor and there's a flattop, U.S.S. *Hornet,* sitting in the water like a postage stamp, and my buddy the bombardier, who's always doping stuff out first, says, 'That's our ship.' '*Ship*?' " Mr. Jack's eyes got wide and Ronnie laughed. " 'What ship? I thought I joined the Army.' Well, my buddy was right, and before you know it we've got sixteen B-twenty-five bombers sitting on her flight deck like a flock of gooney birds.

"By now, everybody knows something big is up."

"How did you move the planes down to the hangar deck?" Ronnie asked.

"Kid, you got a memory like an elephant." He called to Sarah, who was still staring down at water. "Hey, Mummy?"

Sarah was thinking that there would be less risk of injury jumping from a stationary ship, but a greater risk that someone on deck would hear the splash. Then floodlights and guns and a chase boat launched in seconds—the Zodiak! With an outboard motor near the accommodations door, several decks above the engine room. Could they—

"Yo, Mummy?" Moss snapped. "Mr. Jack's talking to you."

"Yes, Mr. Jack?"

"Your daughter remembered that the Navy planes' wings folded so they could fit into the elevator to the hangar deck. Our wings didn't fold, so we had to lash 'em down topside. The Navy *loved* that. They couldn't launch their own planes with us blocking the runway. So the *Hornet* was a sitting duck for any Japs that spotted us."

Ronnie glanced uncomfortably at Sarah, who said,

"Once again, Mr. Jack. We say 'Japanese' in our family. We have friends in Tokyo who have been very kind to us, very generous. In fact, one gentleman has offered to send Ronnie to school in Switzerland."

"It's a free country," said Mr. Jack. "Call 'em what you want. Having fought the bastards, I call 'em Japs. So anyhow, we go steaming out into the Pacific into some of the worst goddammed weather I've ever seen. Radio silence. Blacked out at night. Eighteen days at sea, sometimes so rough we couldn't see our escort. Weather got worse and the ocean really got mean. I was sick as a dog. You ever get seasick?"

"No."

"Lucky you. How about you, Mummy?"

"Not in years."

"Daddy does sometimes, when we've been ashore too long." Ronnie's face clouded again. And as Mr. Jack resumed his story, describing at length the rigors of the voyage and the myriad technical problems with the airplanes, she began to fidget. Mr. Jack noticed. His face hardened unpleasantly.

"Enough talk, Mr. Jack," Sarah intervened. "You need to rest. Ronnie, it's time for schoolwork."

"No, Mummy. Please."

The old man laughed, then turned pale and gasped from the pain in his chest that the sudden movement caused. "Mum," he said when he had caught his breath, "this is straight-A history. Hey, Moss, tell Mummy what Bob Marley said."

" 'If you know your history,' " Moss muttered sullenly, " 'then you'll know where you're coming from.' "

"Aces, Moss. See, Doc, I got a student, too. Moss, get outta here! You're moping around like a blue-bottom chimp."

Ronnie giggled.

Moss stared her down but did what he was told, heading out the door in venomous silence.

My God, thought Sarah. He's jealous of Ronnie.

And Ronnie, with a ten-year-old's intuition for such dynamics, settled back triumphantly on the bed, clearly the winner. "Then what happened, Mr. Jack?"

"Eighteen days out, most of the escort drops back—so we wouldn't be spotted. We kept going, sitting ducks for the enemy. The ocean got rougher and rougher, bow banging up and down like a roller coaster. The orders come down to top off the tanks and check the engines one last time. . . ."

Sarah's heart was pounding so hard she was afraid Mr. Jack would see it fluttering her white coat. Could she and Ronnie steal the Zodiak? Safer than leaping from the main deck, higher risk of being caught. But the *Dallas Belle* was thinly manned. Only a dozen hands had responded to the gas leak. While the ship was stopped, she could launch it from the accommodations door, just as the captain had. Drift silently out of earshot and, using the GPS to guide them, motor toward the coast.

"All of a sudden, enemy picket ship spotted the carrier. The destroyer and cruiser still with us opened up and blasted them out of the water, but not before the bastards got a signal off. So there we were, about four hundred miles farther from the target than we should have been. The powers that be ordered us to take off immediately, before the whole Jap navy jumped us.

"We cranked up the engines and the colonel took off first, staggering down that little flight deck trying to time it with the rise of the bow. We all stopped breathing. He hit the air, dropped like a rock, and I swear he got his wheels wet before she started climbing. Meanwhile, the Navy boys are rocking our plane, trying to make a little more room for gas, pouring it in from jerry cans. Second guy takes off and almost crashes. Then the third. Then it was our turn."

"Were you scared?"

"You bet I was scared. . . . If I'd been the pilot I wouldn't have been scared, but sitting on two thousand pounds of bombs and enough aviation fuel to burn down a town, I couldn't do a thing but pray—and I didn't really know how. I swore right then and there if I got out of this alive I would never, *ever* put my life in someone else's hands again. If I couldn't run it I wouldn't do it. . . . The skipper revs the engines, the whole plane's shaking. Off the brakes, and down the flight deck so goddammed slow it felt like an ox cart. Heavy. And the end of the ship is coming up really fast. We fell off the end. I was in this turret here; looking back, I saw the ship's bow *above* us. If we hit the water she'd run us over.

"Well, somehow we made it into the air, formed up, wasting fuel waiting for the rest of the planes, and then we headed out, with seven hundred miles of Jap-controlled water ahead of us before we could even reach the target. How long would that take us, Ronnie?"

"Ummmh. Two and a half hours."

"At three hundred knots, yeah. But we were trying to save fuel, so we throttled back to two twenty-five, just hugging the waves."

"Nearly four hours."

"Caught the Japs with their pants down. They were thinking the Navy planes on the carrier they'd spotted couldn't launch farther out than three hundred miles. So while the bastards were hunting the carrier at the three-hundred-mile mark, we were already airborne and coming in low. Took the Jap ground and air defense completely by surprise. Never laid a glove on us.

"We made landfall and flew over these fishing villages and islands, and then the skipper took us up a few thousand feet. There she was, the target. Our group was supposed to hit some dockyards. They were just where the navigator said they'd be. 'Bombs away.'

"The aircraft jumped." He jerked the model into the air, wincing from the sudden movement. "Jumped. I saw the bombs explode like bloody flowers and the dock flying in pieces. And then, dead ahead, this huge tank farm—gasoline and aviation fuel. If we'd saved our bombs and hit that, the whole city would have burned. It was made of paper in those days."

"What city?" asked Sarah.

"Tokyo! What do you think?"

Sarah was confused. By the end of the war, Tokyo had been nearly obliterated by firebombs.

But Ronnie got it right away. "The Doolittle Raid! Remember, Mum. Right after the sneak attack. Thirty seconds over Tokyo? You did *that*, Mr. Jack?"

"Me and my buddies," Mr. Jack answered modestly. "Payback for Pearl Harbor. Taught 'em, if you bomb the U.S., you're going to get bombed back. . . . But, goddamn, if we'd hit those tanks we'd have burned 'em to a crisp."

"Wow. How'd you get back?"

"Getting back turned out to be the hard part. We didn't have enough gas to return to the *Hornet*—she was running for Pearl at flank speed, goddammed glad to be rid of us. So we kept going, heading for China, hoping to land in some part the Japs didn't occupy. Trouble was, they occupied most of it."

"What happened?"

Mr. Jack thrust the model into Ronnie's hands. "Put it back, kid."

Ronnie stood up on the bed and reattached the model to its wire. "So what happened?"

Mr. Jack's expression turned bleak. Ronnie observed him solemnly, then knelt beside him and wrapped her arms gently around his shoulders.

"Enough," said Sarah. "Ronnie, go read in the lounge. I've got to examine Mr. Jack."

Ronnie looked up defiantly. But when she saw the expression on Sarah's face, she scrambled off the bed and out of the room, pausing in the doorway only to insure that Moss wasn't out there.

Sarah checked too, then closed the door. "Five minutes."

Mr. Jack had slumped on his pillows and was staring at his hands, his face dead white. "Jesus, Doc," he rasped. "Kind of overdid it."

"You see why I want you in hospital."

"Why'd you chase Ronnie out?"

"As you said, you overdid it."

"Bull. Listen, Doc. I've done plenty what you'd call bad. And I've plans for plenty more. But diddling little girls was never on the agenda. Your daughter's safe with me."

"You don't hesitate to hold her life as a threat over me."

"I need you, Doc. I'll take any leverage I can get. But I guarantee I won't pull rank. You keep me strong and neither you or your little girl has anything to fear."

"Will this policy be observed by Moss as well?"

"Moss as well."

"What if he strikes out on his own?"

"He won't—unless you give him cause. . . . You planning on giving him cause?"

"You know perfectly well that I'm in no position to give him cause."

"Just as long as you know it. . . ." He glared straight into her face. But she could see that he was tired and weak and in pain, and she wondered, with a sudden stab of hope, whether the Stockholm syndrome might run in reverse if the captive was a doctor and the captor her patient. It had always amazed her when she had practiced in London how even the most incompetent doctors commanded irrational loyalty from a suffering patient.

She sat on the edge of the bed and placed cool fingers against the back of his mutilated hand. Sleep was veiling his eyes. "Tell me," she whispered.

"Tell you what?" he rallied, galvanized by suspicion.

"What you couldn't tell Ronnie. Did your plane make it to China?"

"Chekiang Province. We ditched in a rice paddy."

"You made it."

"Everyone but the bombardier. He drowned."

"Was Chekiang Province occupied territory?"

"Not when we got there. The Nationalists still held it. The village threw us a big party, and then we lit out for Chungking—Chiang Kai-shek's capital."

"You didn't make it to Chungking, did you?" she asked softly.

He lay still and silent for so long that Sarah thought he had fallen asleep. Then he spoke: "Would you like a manicure?"

"I beg your pardon?"

"That's what the *Kempeitai* asked me."

"I'm afraid you've lost me, Mr. Jack."

"*Kempeitai*? That's a Japanese word, Mummy. Japanese for secret police. . . ."

"I see."

"You see." He flung his hand in her face. "You see? You see what the *Kempeitai* meant when they asked if I wanted a manicure? But you don't want me to call them Japs."

"Japan was destroyed at the end of the war, thanks to the bravery of soldiers like you, Mr. Jack. But in defeat, the Japanese people did everything the Allies demanded of them."

"Am I supposed to forgive them because they lost?"

"It would be a Christian act."

"Yeah? Where the hell was Christ when I was screaming for Him?"

Sarah flinched from the hatred boiling in his eyes.

"Out where my husband and I live, the islanders still call the war The Big Fight. It was a very big fight, Mr. Jack, and cruelty abounded. The point, today, is that the Japanese people have been reborn in the past half century as one of the most pacifist peoples on earth."

Mr. Jack sneered. "Because they've had the good old U.S. of A. to do their shooting for them, while they plaster their goddammed Rising Sun all over everything. Are you blind, Doc? We beat 'em fair and square for raping and murdering half of Asia and the second we turned our back they went on the rampage again. Only this time we supplied the muscle to hold off the communists—who'd have stopped them like they did last time. The Japanese're dangerous people, Doc. You don't know them like I do."

"Perhaps I've been more fortunate in my acquaintances, Mr. Jack."

" 'Perhaps I've been more fortunate in my acquaintances,' " he mimicked with another sneer. "Let me see your mitts, Doc— Yeah, you've been 'more fortunate.' Lot more fortunate."

"I don't deny that you've suffered."

"You think it's just me I'm talking about? Christ, Doc. How about the two hundred and fifty thousand Chinese they killed for the raid? People slaughtered. They're monsters."

"Their children and their grandchildren are not monsters."

"Monsters in new faces. They're taking over the world, Doc. And when they're done, they'll take the gloves off . . . and offer manicures to everyone."

"You can't condemn an entire people for the evil acts of a few."

He laughed. "You want to hear the funny thing? I ran into the guy."

"What guy?"

"The *Kempeitai* cop."

"The man who tortured you?"

"Five-six years ago—damnedest thing. I was holed up in Singapore, negotiating gas leases with the Indonesians and I'm feeling some pressure from the outside—like someone's horning in on the deal. I knew right away it had to be Japs, so I invited them to meet in Hong Kong—neutral turf. They sent some mid-level guys—deliberate insult. So I pulled a few strings to torpedo a joint enterprise scam they had going with Beijing. That got their attention. They invited me to lunch in Tokyo—sushi lunch. Ever eat sushi?"

"Of course."

"*Live* sushi? I don't think so, Doc. These guys—real big shots—they eat baby lobsters alive. The little things are still wiggling when they bust them out of their shells. Horrible sight. Cruelty for the hell of it—bragging they got the power to do it. So anyhow, who's at this lunch? The son of a bitch who tore my fingernails out after he got done shoving bamboo splinters under them. Blue suit, red tie, Mr. Corporation Man."

"Are you sure it was the same man?"

"Oh, I was sure. So was he. I was wearing my gloves, but the son of a bitch knew damned well it was me. . . ." Mr. Jack juggled laughter deep in his throat. "His live lobster wasn't going down all that smooth. I let the bastard stew. Didn't say a word the whole time we cut a deal. Till we had an agreement. Then I took my glove off to shake hands."

The old man tugged at the bedclothes, his bright eyes tracking memories. "Funny thing happened to him. A month later he got kidnapped. Down in Djakarta. Some vicious bunch of Muslim fundamentalists got this crazy idea in their heads that he had access to the Japanese stockpile of weapons-grade plutonium."

"The Japanese don't stockpile plutonium."

"Oh yes they do, sweetheart. Enough for an arsenal, in case their peace-loving businessmen run into a market they can't crack with their usual dumping. . . . Anyhow, the kidnappers wanted plutonium—it was all a mix-up. He didn't know the first thing about plutonium—but they'd been misinformed, so they just kept asking him again and again and again until his heart gave out. . . ."

He looked Sarah full in the face and smiled. "Lasted a couple of weeks."

It took every muscle in her body to keep from shuddering visibly. And still trying to court his sympathy, she asked, "Were you satisfied?"

He jerked his hand away with a savage curse and closed his eyes. Then, slowly, he formed a brittle smile. "What do you think?"

11

THE AIR PHILIPPINES' AFTERNOON HONG KONG SHUTTLE CARRIED stylish women speaking upper-class Spanish. Several cast mildly speculative glances at the haggard American who made his way back to economy, which was crowded with sad-eyed housemaids returning to work from visits home. Stone squeezed into his window seat, exhausted but too anxious to sleep, and pressed his face to the plastic to search the South China Sea for a sand-colored ship.

He had struck out in Manila—Patrick had disappeared "in country," according to his girlfriend, who had no clue when the mercenary would be back.

Captain McGlynn still hadn't telephoned when Stone had said good-bye to Marcus at the Koror airport. Nor had Lydia Chin.

"Watch your back," were Marcus's parting words. "I still don't think that guy was after me." But Stone was sure the guest room had provided the easiest entry to the house, and that Marcus, not he, had been the intruder's target. No one knew he was in Koror.

He had emptied their Koror safe-deposit box and bought his tickets with cash. Money would be a problem if he had to spend much more on travel and information.

He hoped there would be messages waiting at the Hong Kong Yacht Club. Somewhere on the maritime grapevine there had to be word of a missing ship, some hint of what had caused the crew to kidnap a doctor.

His best speculation was that the gas carrier had been hijacked for its valuable cargo. Compressed to a liquid by supercooling, the volume of gas in the vessel was enormous and worth millions. And with corruption a way of life on the South China coast long before the People's Republic of China institutionalized it, the hijackers had probably arranged before the theft to sell the gas to a PRC power plant willing to fence it for half price.

Marcus Salinis disagreed. Why, he wanted to know, had none of his contacts, who were scattered throughout Micronesia, heard of any hijacking? And why weren't there any rumors on the ham radio network? "You're talking piracy. Where's the crew? Where's the ship that hasn't reported in and is overdue by now? How come nobody knows she's missing?"

"It's a big ocean."

"Everybody's expected someplace."

Stone suspected a sophisticated paper shuffle. Ships and leases and petroleum cargoes were sold and exchanged routinely. They'd have covered their trail with forgeries documenting false sales, resales, and registrations and backed it all up with phony radio reports. A captain looking down the barrel of an assault weapon would radio exactly what he was told to radio. Just as a doctor with a child would do exactly as she was told.

Clinging to his theory, embellishing it on the Air Mike flight to Manila, he had speculated that the injured "old man"—the captain, in marine parlance—had actually been the hijackers' leader, wounded in the takeover. As they couldn't put into port for medical attention, they had seized

Sarah to doctor him until they sold the gas and abandoned ship.

Here, his thinking turned fuzzy. And frightening.

How would they escape after they got their money? They could not leave the ship moored to the pierhead of the power plant that had paid them. Nor could they sell it. Which meant that they would have to scuttle her—open her sea cocks to sink her out beyond the fifty-fathom line.

But what would they do with Sarah and Ronnie?

The jetliner commenced its descent to Hong Kong. This was his first arrival by air. Twenty-five years ago he had steamed into Hong Kong, a young Navy doctor interning aboard a warship. All his subsequent visits had been with Sarah on *Veronica*.

A dark haze on the horizon firmed up as the blue hills of Guangdong Province rolling northward into the continent. The city's peaks and islands spilled into the sea, dominating an otherwise undistinguished coast. He oriented himself by the hills of High Island and the deep incision of Tai Pang Bay, and on final approach from the southeast saw the jam-packed typhoon shelter at Causeway Bay, its surface carpeted thickly with junks and sampans; the Hong Kong Yacht Club occupied the west end.

Cheklapkok terminal was a madhouse. Neither of the flights nor the quick stop at Manila had prepared him for the crush of people or the noise, to which he was extremely sensitive after weeks at sea. Funneled toward Immigration and Customs, he fingered his passport with a queasy sensation of running naked through enemy territory.

This was Stone's first visit since China had taken over the former British Crown Colony. The communists had promised to allow capitalism to flourish in the quintessentially capitalist city for the next fifty years, but the People's Republic was a dictatorship, and God knew what new computerization the Beijing rulers had added to the British immigration controls, or how thoroughly they would scrutinize his papers.

He caught his reflection in a glass partition. He looked harmless enough. Joanna Salinis had offered him a haircut, and he had trimmed his beard, while a castaway's sunburn wasn't much different from a tourist's sunburn. She had found him fresh clothes, too—khaki pants, a short-sleeved shirt, and an expensive looking oiled-cotton windbreaker that she claimed someone had forgotten in the Paradise Hotel, but which he suspected she had bought. December in Hong Kong, he'd be glad of it.

His worn backpack looked a little off the image of "Physician, retired," which he had entered after *occupation* on the landing entry card. He shrugged out of it and carried it by the handstrap. Hong Kong welcomed all, but it was essentially a business city where a blue suit and a tie commanded respect. Under *purpose of visit*, he had written, "Joining yacht."

He had debated which passport to present. His U.S. document was an excellent forgery, but he hated to use it where a sophisticated system might challenge the false number. It was safer in the remote islands, where he and Sarah were usually greeted as honored guests, and officials were fortunate to possess a working ballpoint pen.

He decided instead to present a somewhat genuine Republic of Palau passport which Marcus had arranged four or five years ago, and which supported the general cover of an American doctor retired to paradise. The Chinese immigration officer scrutinized it and his landing card, on which Stone had given the Hong Kong Yacht Club as his local address, and waved him through.

He removed his U.S. passport from its hidden compartment in the knapsack and stuffed it in his pocket in case Customs searched the bag. But he was passed through without a search, and was carried on a tide of shoppers, housemaids, tourists, and Asian business travelers into a chaotic arrival hall, where greeters from the five-star hotels directed guests to their limousines. A mainland farmer with a cardboard suitcase bumped into Stone, apologizing frantically. A

Beijing bureaucrat shoved between them. Stone disentangled himself from both of them and headed for the doors.

"Would you step this way, sir?"

The voice came from behind him, crisp with authority. He turned to see two uniformed police, a tall blond Brit backed up by a Chinese.

12

THE BRIT WAS TALLER THAN STONE, HIS GRIP FIRM AS HE TOOK HIS elbow to guide him through the crowd, which parted before the uniforms. Surprised to see a Western officer, Stone put on the brakes.

"Who are you?"

"Window dressing," the Brit answered easily. "The Chinese kept some of us on—demoted to sergeant—as the sight of smiling bobbies is supposed to make Western businessmen more comfortable with Hong Kong's new government. Now if you'll just step this way . . ."

"What's the problem?" asked Stone.

"Just a formality, sir. We'll have you on your way in a moment, I'm sure."

"Wait a minute. What formality? I've just been through Immigration."

"So they reported." His grip tightened and the Chinese cop moved in closer.

"Ease up," said Stone. "I'm not going anywhere. I just asked you what the problem is."

He tried to slow their progress, but the Chinese cop took his other arm and now the crowd began to stare at what looked like an arrest. Two cops at the terminal exit saw them coming and held the door open, saluting the tall Brit as they marched Stone out to an unmarked Rover at the curb.

"Wait a minute. What is this?"

Without letting go of his arm, the Chinese cop opened the rear door and the sergeant said, "Let's not make the situation worse, sir. Get in quietly and we'll take this up at headquarters."

Stone stood his ground. "I'm asking you to tell me what the hell is going on."

The sergeant stared hard. "As soon as we get to head-quarters you may ring the American consulate. Unless you oblige me to summon assistance." He nodded toward the cops who had held the door. "In which event, sir, I promise you'll first spend an unpleasant night in a filthy cell. Now— if we understand each other—*get in the car.*"

The last thing Stone could afford was delay. If this was routine, his Palauan passport was good. It had already passed muster at Immigration, and Senator—ex-President— Salinis could confirm it by phone. He had friends at the yacht club. And he could call on Lydia Chin's lawyers.

"All right."

The sergeant climbed in beside him. The silent Chinese cop drove out of the airport, over the Kowloon Bridge and into narrow streets, grinning whenever he whooped the siren. Stone was lost immediately, as they inched past factor-ies and tenements and down twisty lanes overhung with clothing-draped fire escapes and stacked red neon signs. But he had the impression they were heading inland up the Kowloon Peninsula rather than down toward the harbor.

"Corporal Fong," said the sergeant, "ease off on the hooter. It's not like we've caught the Great Train Robbers." He gave Stone an ironic wink, as if to say, Natives will be natives. But instead of reassuring Stone, something he had said earlier at the terminal, which had been nagging at him, now traveled like ice down his spine.

"Do you really think I'll need the American consul?"

"I shouldn't think so," the sergeant replied casually. "Still, good to know they're there. What?"

"It would be," said Stone, "if I were an American citizen."

"I beg your pardon?" The sergeant turned to face him, his eyes glittery.

"Immigration should have told you."

"Told me what?"

"That I'm from Palau."

Corporal Fong glanced in the rearview mirror, then stepped hard on the gas, and as the sergeant reached inside his tunic, Stone tumbled belatedly to the realization that he had not been arrested but kidnapped.

"Who the hell—" he demanded, shock exploding into rage. He'd sailed the canoe two hundred and fifty miles across the open Pacific to find Sarah and nearly died on the Angaur reef. He'd be goddammed if his search would end in a Mong Kok alley.

Stone jammed his shoulders against the seat back, levered both legs with all his strength, and kicked the driver, bracketing the man's ear with his heels. Thrown hard against the window, Corporal Fong's eyes rolled back in his head. The Rover sideswiped a truck and skidded across the street and into a fish stall, scattering shoppers and crushing plastic tubs of live carp.

When it hit the solid brick wall behind the flimsy stall, the car's air bag exploded in Corporal Fong's face, and the sergeant was thrown to the floor. He kicked Stone. Stone punched wildly with one fist and dove into the man's tunic with the other. The sergeant kneed him, knocking the wind from his lungs, but Stone probed deeper, fighting for the gun. A powerful hand closed around his throat. He tucked his chin, found hard metal, and yanked. It was a small .22

caliber automatic—an assassin's weapon. He pushed the barrel into the sergeant's throat. The man let go of him.

"Who sent you?"

"Get fucked."

In the front seat, Fong thrashed around the deflated air bag, which had lacerated his face, and tried to open the door. Stone shifted the gun from the Brit's throat to his eye. "Who sent you?"

"I don't know," the Brit said coolly. "I do know you don't have the balls to shoot."

The door locks clunked; Fong staggered from the car. A crowd had gathered around the wreckage, pointing at the damaged cars and the fish flopping on the sidewalk. The Brit backed away from Stone, feeling for the door. The only way to stop him was to shoot him. But the curious mob had surrounded the car and real cops would be coming any second. Or had he been a doctor too long to take a life no matter how provoked?

"Wait. Tell whoever sent you that all I want is my wife and daughter."

"Come with me. I'll bring you to them."

"Where?"

"Not far," he answered. "Come on."

It was a lie. He wanted to believe, he would give anything to believe. But they wouldn't have pulled the police charade if they had Sarah and Ronnie. The Brit was only a hired killer, which he proved the instant he saw that Stone didn't buy the lie: "Pray the real cops get you first," he said.

He jumped from the car and scattered the crowd, his blond hair a beacon above the small, dark Chinese.

Stone jammed the gun in his backpack and ran the other way. A two-man uniformed patrol rounded the corner, shoving through the crowded lane. Stone turned to run. If the police found the gun in his pack . . . They spotted him. For a second he panicked. Then, suddenly, he felt alert, the adrenalin pumping pure as fire. He ran to the cops, waving, calling, "Can you direct me—can you direct me to the Peninsula Hotel?"

They rushed past him. A thumb jerked toward the street they had come from.

Checking his back repeatedly, he ran until the streets grew wide. He hopped a bus, got off where the Nathan Road was lined with hotels and office towers. Who had hired the Brit? How had he known where to find him?

A busy MTR subway station seemed safe. Stone plunged into it and caught a train under the harbor to Central.

With a moment to think, the truth was chilling. Whoever had taken Sarah and Ronnie on the *Dallas Belle* had the power to strike far beyond the ship.

Marcus had been right. It was he they had come for in Palau. But how had they known he would be there? Had they forced Sarah to tell them where he would go if he got off the atoll? How much had they hurt her to make her talk? She was brave. He tried to close his mind to that. When he couldn't, he prayed that concern for Ronnie's safety would have kept Sarah from being too brave for him.

A different explanation took shape in his mind. A possibility far more palatable, and he clung to it desperately. Could the *Dallas Belle*'s hijackers have traced Sarah's telephone call to Marcus Salinis? Then wiretapped his telephones in case Stone sought help from the same friend Sarah had?

Of course. That was how they had tracked him. Marcus himself had admitted his phones were tapped. But at Koror, Stone had been too tired and confused to challenge the senator's claim that his political enemies were the culprits. They must have traced her call—by sat phone records or signal monitors. The attack at the house and the attempted kidnapping at the airport both followed from there.

The yacht anchored off Marcus's house and the phony cops at Cheklapkok were both complicated, expensive operations, which meant they would try again. He had to learn what he could learn in Hong Kong and get out—before they nailed him.

From the Central MTR station, Stone telephoned Lydia Chin. She was still not back from the Mainland, said her secretary. "Maybe you call back later."

"Tell her I'm at the yacht club."

He took another train to Causeway Bay and walked, heading toward the water and down Gloucester Road, which paralleled a highway that blocked the shore. Just beyond the Excelsior Hotel, he opened an unmarked metal door, scanned the street again for the tall blond Brit, raced down a flight of stairs and through a pedestrian tunnel under the highway. He emerged beside the typhoon shelter. The yacht club was at the tip of the peninsula; anyone getting there had to first cross the parking lot of the Officers' Club of the Hong Kong police.

No messages.

The yacht club bar overlooked the shelter and Victoria Harbor. A thousand dim lights glowed on the yachts and junks and sampans moored gunnel to gunnel, while across the black water, millions blazed on Kowloon's shore.

The bar itself was typical yacht club, shabbier than most but steeped in history: on a wall of burgees from clubs around the world hung a life preserver with the legend, THIS CLUB REOPENED BY HMS *VENGEANCE* SEPTEMBER 8, 1945, commemorating the end of the Japanese occupation of Hong Kong in World War II. He and Sarah cherished the honorary membership they had been given when word got around about their floating clinic.

The cocktail hour was winding down as members headed off to dinner. Among the serious drinkers left was a powerfully built Australian foredeckman known, Stone recalled, as The Beast.

As Stone approached him, The Beast looked up with a glimmer of recognition. "Right! I know that face. Doctor

Mike." He enveloped Stone's hand. "Bob Simmons. Just get in?"

"Flew in, actually. From Manila."

Simmons winked. "Left the boat with the missus and come to Hong Kong for a bit of unauthorized nooky?" He signaled the dour Chinese barman to bring Stone a drink. When the Aussie wasn't sailing, Stone recalled, he worked as a stockbroker. He might know people.

"Cheers." Simmons drained his gin and tonic and motioned for a refill. "You look a little shipwrecked, mate."

"We got beat up off Tobi."

Simmons laughed. "God bless you blokes who own your own yachts. I'll crew any day. Did you lose the stick?"

"Only half," said Stone, milking the lie. "Snapped at the first spreader."

The Beast laughed louder. "Only half. I like that, mate. Only half—say, which half?" He turned red with mirth and pounded the bar. "Which half . . . well, it's an ill wind . . . Now's your chance to upgrade electronics and replace that old wire rigging with rod."

"I don't like gear I can't fix offshore."

The Beast trumpeted the advantages of steel rod stays over wire.

"Did you hear about the hijacking?" Stone asked when he paused to bang his empty glass on the bar.

"Everybody says the Chinese Navy did it."

"What? Big gas carrier? American captain?"

The Beast frowned quizzically as Stone gripped his arm. "No," he said. "I thought you meant the Japanese gin palace they took off Tai Pang. Tossed the boatboys to the sharks and ran for the San-Men Islands."

"I mean a ship. The Filipinos were talking about it in the yard. Nobody knew anything. Apparently she just disappeared."

"Sunk?"

"No distress signal. Word was she'd been taken."

The Beast shrugged. "Chinese gunboats are our biggest

headache. People's Liberation Army navy patrols. They've turned into bloody pirates. . . . Colony went to hell in ninety-seven. Triads running amok—oh, I know what you're thinking," he said, cutting off Stone's next question. "You thought that the communists would drive out the secret societies like they did in forty-nine. No way, mate. Beijing announced the Triads are 'patriotic' organizations, and now the bloody thugs and the People's bloody Liberation Army are working hand in glove. Before turnover, it suited the mainland to make the Brits look like they were losing it—so now that the Brits are out, we've got Triads in the Hong Kong police and Triad-PLA combos kidnapping movie stars, smuggling body parts, stealing Benzes to ship to the mainland. It's the ruddy Wild West— Mate, your's pint's getting old."

"I'm beat," said Stone. "Long day." He felt old and tired and helpless and utterly alone. A porter plodded through the bar, holding up a dirty piece of cardboard with DR. MICHAEL scrawled on it.

Stone ran to the telephone.

Lydia Chin said, "Michael, how good to hear from you. How is Sarah?"

"Not good. I need your help."

"Have you eaten?"

Lydia lived above Central. He asked the porter to call him a taxi and went outside to wait. Sampans darted about in the typhoon shelter. The east wind carried a cool fog and the sound of the televisions from the moored junks. In the distance, he could just make out the blurry top lights of a huge luxury yacht nosing gingerly through the breakwater.

A horn beeped as a cab swung into the driveway. "Taxi, sir?"

Behind him, he heard, "Hold on, mate."

The Beast, swaying on the top step.

Stone said, "I'm going to Central if you want a ride."

The Beast beckoned with one finger, which he then

placed theatrically over his lips as he said sotto voce, "A word, Doctor."

Tight moorings, dirty water, and drunks were three reasons to avoid yacht clubs. "I'm kind of in a rush."

"That's not your taxi, mate."

"I just called him— Oh, is he yours?"

"Unless I'm mistaken," said the Beast, "he'll produce a gun and take your wallet as soon as he gets around the corner."

Stone looked at the car. The driver wore a white shirt and plastic eyeglasses. Jesus Christ, had they found him here?

"I thought they only do that in Manila."

"It's catching on here. So much for the honest workers' state." He lurched to the car, leaned his head in, and said, "Piss off or I'll call the coppers."

The taxi screeched away.

"Are you sure?" Stone said.

"The bloke ran, didn't he?"

Stone looked at the aptly named Beast looming like a belligerent cliff and thought, Let's not panic. The driver could have run in wholly innocent fear of the giant Australian.

"Here's your car now," said the Beast.

"Yeah, maybe you're right," said Stone. "I thought he came pretty fast."

"And, thank you, a lift to Central would be brilliant."

The man's bulk was reassuring on the ride to Central, but after Stone dropped the Beast at the Mandarin Hotel and continued up the peak alone, he braced himself at every dark patch in the road.

Lydia's apartment tower had a garden in front, with a curved cobblestone drive and fountains splashing musically. It was partway up Victoria Peak in a section that, when Stone first visited Hong Kong, had been private homes on terraced grounds.

Security was tight. Two doormen checked his name against a list. An assistant accompanied him through an Italian marble lobby to Lydia's private elevator and pressed the single button.

The car rose thirty floors and opened into a foyer where an elderly Chinese servant greeted Stone and led him to a two-story living room with a view of city lights spreading north toward the darkness of China.

Lydia Chin was Hong Kong Chinese. She had been educated locally and thrust unexpectedly into the family business when her brother proved to be less a businessman than a tennis player; her father, a practical man who had built a shipping fortune out of the Korean War, had preferred to have his daughter in charge rather than a stranger. Her husband worked for one of the old British trading hongs that the PRC had bought, and he lived every other month in Tokyo.

She was a small, precisely-made woman, and spoke with an English Oxbridge accent. "Robert will be so sorry he missed you. Welcome, Michael. Welcome." She greeted him warmly with both hands outstretched, but when he came closer her face fell. "Michael, you look— Are you all right?"

He told her what had happened to Sarah and Ronnie, and when he was done, Lydia said, "That doesn't sound possible."

"It happened," said Stone, grateful that she, at least, didn't start pumping him about his past. "Have you heard anything about a hijacked gas ship?"

"No."

"Nothing? Are you sure? No rumor, no—"

"Nothing, Michael. I've heard of boardings in the Malacca Strait—you know, the usual. They cut loose a container or two. A number of ships around Hong Kong have been raided for their spare change and cigarettes. We had a captain shot in the Pearl River. And the occasional gin palace is stolen to order for mainland customers, but nothing on the scale of what you're suggesting."

"I'm not 'suggesting.' I saw it with my own eyes."

"Yes, of course . . . We had a Honduran car carrier snatched—at anchor, no less—from Hong Kong waters, but that was Chinese Navy. They got the ship back, eventually, minus a few Mercedes, of course." She shook her head. "But I've heard nothing about any gas carrier. Are you quite sure?"

"I saw it with my own eyes. And then, like I told you, she left that message."

"So you said. . . . Well, if the ship was headed for Shanghai, she's there, now."

"Do you have any old friends in Shanghai?"

"Rivals," Lydia answered with a smile. "We're Cantonese."

"I know that. I just wondered. . . ." Most of the great Hong Kong shipowners had come as refugees from Shanghai after the revolution of 1949. Lydia's family was not quite in their class.

"And you're quite sure she didn't radio the authorities?"

"What authorities?"

"U.S. Navy, I would have thought," Lydia replied, watching him intently.

"No."

"Why not?"

He wanted to make up lies—he didn't trust the Navy to believe him, he didn't trust the Navy to initiate a search quickly, he had already asked and they wouldn't help—but Lydia was far too intelligent and savvy and he found himself right back where he had been with Marcus Salinis, afraid that anything he told her now would come back to haunt their future. He said, "You've known us a long time. I have to ask you to believe me when I say that there is something in our past—my past—that won't allow me to ask for official help. Can you accept that?"

"Well," she said doubtfully, "I will ask around, but . . ."

A maid entered and addressed Lydia in Chinese.

Lydia rose. "Excuse me, Michael. I'll be right back. Do nosh on that."

Stone picked at the array of dumplings. He hadn't eaten since breakfast with Marcus and Joanna, but he had no appetite. Not with his mind beginning to flash memories of the close call in Mong Kok. Lydia returned, looking grave. When she spoke, there was challenge in her manner.

"Michael, are you sure you've told me everything?"

"Everything I know."

"Do you know you were followed to my flat?"

"What?"

"My doorman informs me that two Chiu Chau gangsters followed your taxi and are now parked across the street watching the lobby."

13

Whoever they were, the people who controlled the ship and held Sarah and Ronnie were tracking him like an animal. Chiu Chau? Were they Triads? Stone almost wished he were back in the old man's canoe.

He should throw himself on the mercy of the American consul. He wouldn't be any help to Sarah dead. But plead what? "A mysterious ship took my family and boat. And now hired killers and Triads are attacking me." If they didn't arrest him, they'd commit him.

"I ask you again, Michael. As your friend. Have you told me everything?"

Stone went to the windows, but the street was too far below to see. If he told Lydia about the wet-suited attacker at Koror, the phony cops at the airport, the phony cab driver, she would think worse than she was thinking already.

"Of course I have. I'm begging for your help."

"Then why are the Chiu Chau following you?"

"Chiu Chau? Christ, Lydia! How the hell would I know? Listen, everybody's Triad-happy in this town. Guy at the club just told me they've gone partners with the PLA."

"He may well be right."

"Yeah, well, those guys across the street are probably a couple of guys waiting for a date."

Lydia stared.

"Are you sure your doorman isn't fantasizing? I mean, how does he know they're Chiu Chau? Are *you* a Triad?" The secret societies had infiltrated all walks of Chinese life. Stone recalled a photograph of Lydia in *Asia Week* magazine and remembered remarking to Sarah the odd way she had crossed her fingers, wondering if it was a secret Triad sign.

"Don't be naïve, Michael. We own this building. We employ sensible protection."

"You mean your doorman belongs to a different gang?"

"I mean the doorman knows Chiu Chau when he sees them," Lydia answered coldly.

"Lydia, I swear I don't know anything about it."

"What about this 'thing' in your past?"

"It has nothing to do with what's happening now. Absolutely nothing. It was way too long ago."

"Then what are you up to now?"

"Come on, you know what we do. We sail the hospital."

"I also know you're not above repairing the occasional knife wound without informing the police. You do recall when I persuaded the Jockey Club to give you some funding, it was with the understanding you would not have to do that sort of thing in order to pay your bills."

"We do what we have to, but I don't know anything about any Chiu Chau. Listen, I'm wasting your time. I'll see you around."

"Where are you going?"

"I've got to find Sarah and Ronnie."

"Michael. They followed you here. They'll hurt you. Now just sit down a minute and let me think."

Stone sat and tried to think, too.

"Would President Salinis have told anyone you'd come here?"

"No. He's on my side."

"Then how would anyone know?"

"I'm guessing they tapped Salinis's phones and . . ." His voice trailed off. Lydia was looking at him as oddly as he had feared.

"They?" she asked.

"No. This makes no sense," he said. "I'm so confused."

She took his broad, scarred hand in both of hers, which were fine as alabaster, and shook her head sadly. "Oh, Michael, you're such a fish out of water."

"What the hell is that supposed to mean?"

"You do wonderful work out there." A nod east encompassed the vast Pacific. "You doctor people no one else would—"

"I'm not a good doctor," he interrupted, "not like Sarah."

"You sail Sarah where she's needed. *Veronica* is the first to bring help after a typhoon, the first to deliver a child to hospital, the last to run before the next storm strikes. Nothing fazes you at sea. But you're 'Jack ashore,' as the Brits say. Lost on land and lost among landsmen."

Her words troubled Stone. They rang truer than he cared to admit. He was all right if it was physical—"Corporal Fong" would be combing his hair over heel prints for a long time—but he never should have let the Brit trick him into the police car in the first place. And if it weren't for the Beast he'd have blundered into the phony taxi.

Sarah herself said that he was losing the knack of functioning ashore, and Ronnie teased that Daddy was like a sea turtle on the beach. It wasn't an uncommon failing among offshore sailors. But if he was going to get his wife and child back, he would have to become as observant on land as he was at sea. As quick, as clever, and as ballsy.

"I've just got to get my land legs back," he said. "I'll be okay."

Lydia stood up. "I'll have you escorted safely back to the yacht club."

"I can't put innocent people in danger."

"Not to worry," Lydia said with a thin smile. "They can take care of themselves. In the morning I'll get on the phone and see what I can learn about your gas carrier. But I don't hold that much hope. Anything so spectacular I'd have heard about long ago."

Twenty minutes later, the maid came in and spoke to Lydia, who said to Stone, "You'll take the freight elevator to the parking garage."

"Lydia, you don't believe me, do you?"

"I want to believe you. But it's all so farfetched."

"Well, what else could have happened to them?"

"I don't know, Michael. . . . Now listen to me. Under no circumstances are you to breathe a word of this to your 'escort.' "

"I don't understand."

"And whatever you do, don't ask them for help. Do you promise?"

"But I don't understand."

"Jackals," said Lydia, "steal from lions. Failing that, they themselves are quite capable of killing."

"I still don't understand."

"Just promise."

A delivery van was waiting in the garage. A pair of Cantonese in black pants and white T-shirts held open the door to the windowless rear. They indicated a carton of Radio Shack speakers for Stone to sit on. Stone waited for them to close the doors, but they just stood there, until he realized he was being watched through the dark glass of a BMW limousine parked behind the van.

A flashily dressed Cantonese in his early thirties stepped out and sauntered toward him. He peered into the van as if he were considering buying its contents, then hitched up the knees of a tightly fitted tropical suit so white it glowed and climbed in opposite Stone.

"My name Ronald."

A gold watch rimmed in diamonds gleamed on Ronald's wrist. His necktie was silk. He regarded Stone with amusement and, Stone suspected, some disdain for his clothes and beard and stainless steel Rolex.

"Mine is Michael."

His men got in front and drew a curtain across the cargo area. "Just sit back and enjoy the ride."

"What do they see?" Stone asked as the van pulled out and passed the apartment building.

His escort called back and forth through the curtain in Cantonese. There was laughter, and then Ronald said to Stone, "Bruce Lee wannabes."

"Do they recognize them?"

"Low guys. Punks. Why Chiu Chau mad at you?"

"I don't know."

"You owe 'em money?"

"No."

"You sure? They very greedy guys."

"I never met a Chiu Chau in my life. And I sure as hell don't owe 'em money. I just got here."

"Never trust a Chiu Chau. Never. They do anything for money, always work for the highest bidder."

"It must be some mistake."

Ronald shrugged. "Whatever you say, man."

Lydia's warning had had precisely the opposite effect from what she had intended—it had given him an idea. Turn the tables on the bastards and "hire" his own Triad. "Do you work for Lydia Chin?"

"Ms. Chin very fine lady. Chins fine family."

"My wife and I," he said, "have a hospital boat. Lydia Chin contributes to the costs."

"Very fine lady, Ms. Chin."

"I'm a doctor," said Stone. "If I can ever be of some

service—to repay you for this kindness—please ask. I'm staying at the Hong Kong Yacht Club."

"High-price club."

"We have an honorary membership."

"Ms. Chin say you do good."

"We try. What I'm trying to say is, I appreciate this favor and—"

"This Ms. Chin favor."

"I would still like to be of service. Anything I can do."

Ronald looked him up and down. "What kind of doctor?"

"Emergency doctor."

"You mean like accidents?"

"Any kind of accident."

"Like shooting accident?"

"Exactly."

"Knife accident."

"You got it."

"How about girlfriend accident?"

Stone hesitated. "She'd be better in a clinic."

Ronald's face closed up. Stone said hastily, "If for any reason she can't get to a clinic, she'll be safe with me. And my wife."

"How much?"

"No money."

"What you want?"

"Information."

"About what?"

"A missing ship."

"Don't know ships."

"Come on, Ronald, this is Hong Kong—biggest port in the world—and if you work with Lydia Chin, you gotta know ships."

"No say I work with Ms. Chin."

"I'm talking about a big liquefied natural gas carrier that's missing."

"How much worth?"

"The ship's worth plenty. But the cargo's worth a hell of a lot more."

"How much?"

"Millions."

Ronald's shoulders lifted in an elegant shrug. "Ms. Chin very fine lady," he said. "What else you want?"

"Transportation?"

"Take plane."

"Private transportation."

"Where?"

"Shanghai."

"Gas ship in Shanghai?"

"Maybe."

"Big city, Shanghai. What else you want?"

" 'Old friends' in Shanghai?" Stone was asking for introductions.

" 'Old friends?' What else?"

"A visa for Shanghai."

"China Travel Office. Visa, two days."

"I'd like to keep my passports out of the computers."

"You talking big accident, Doc."

Ronald had a word with the yacht club's doorman before he walked Stone to his room. He even checked that it was empty before he said good night.

Stone wedged a chair back under the doorknob, got into bed, and lay awake, wondering how to get to Shanghai. He was scared—scared for Sarah and Ronnie, and scared to-night for himself. Finally he turned on the light, took the Brit's gun out of his backpack, and stashed it under his pillow.

14

WHEN THE TELEPHONE WOKE STONE, HE STILL HAD HIS HAND ON the gun. Sunlight was streaming through the window. His watch said ten. He remembered he was in the yacht club.

"Hello."

"It's Kerry. I'm rushing—meet me at Shit and Feathers at one o'clock."

The salvage captain hung up before Stone could protest: he had no business wandering around the city. At least the Eagle's Nest was in the Hilton Hotel, about as public as you could get. To be on the safe side, he walked over to the Police Officers' Club and shared a cab going to Central.

The Eagle's Nest occupied the top floor. Once-magnificent views of the colossal harbor were somewhat curtailed by newer, taller buildings. But it had retained its popularity as a business lunch place for expat and Chinese alike.

Stone assumed that one of Kerry's major clients must have booked their spectacular window table. The strait between Hong Kong Island and Kowloon, and the vast anchorage beyond, was speckled with anchored ships and edged by liner piers and enormous container ports. He could see west to Lantau Island, north to the mainland, despite the new buildings shouldering close.

Kerry arrived at one on the dot.

The Australian was small for a tugman; short and slim, he couldn't have weighed more than one-fifty. How he had passed his deckhand apprenticeship, muscling heavy lines, could be attributed only, Stone thought, to an aggressiveness that bordered on the ferocious and had served him well in the cutthroat salvage business.

"Where's your beautiful wife?"

"I came alone." Until he saw him cut through the crowded restaurant like an attacking destroyer, Stone had planned to come right out and tell him why he needed him. But if Lydia wouldn't believe his story, why would Kerry?

"What's up?"

He held an unlimited-tonnage, all-oceans ticket and, like most master mariners Stone had met, had the cold eye that accompanied fast decisions and merciless judgment.

"First of all," Stone said, "have you heard anything about a gas carrier being taken?"

"Taken? What do you mean, 'taken?'"

"Hijacked."

"No."

"Nothing?"

"Not a peep."

"You monitor distress calls."

"Every signal in the Western Pacific. Customers calling. What's going on?"

"Okay, let's say they didn't get off a distress."

"Obviously not."

"Have you heard of any ships overdue?"

"No. Except my current customer, of course, who is going to be goddamned more overdue if he doesn't produce some money very soon. But, no. Nothing— Wait." His suntan wrinkled and he passed a scarred hand over his mouth. "Ah. You know the Moluccas?"

"We don't go down there." The Banda Sea touched on Sarah's East Timor.

"No, I wouldn't either—not without a rocket launcher."

"What about it?"

McGlynn squeezed his mouth and gazed across the harbor as if memory would echo somewhere on the blue hills of China. "When are we talking about? Recent?"

"Last week. Tuesday, maybe early Wednesday."

"Yes. All right, mate. Early last week. Somebody tripped twenty-one eighty-two. I have a boat in the yard at Surabaya and she copied and replied. Turned out it was a screwup. Somebody fell and hit the switch."

Stone nodded. Most single-sideband long-range radios had a dedicated emergency switch, like the panic button on a burglar alarm. "They radioed back?"

"Right. 'No problem, thanks for responding, sorry to trouble you. Over and out.'"

"How did you know it was in the Banda Sea?"

"I didn't. But since you asked it occurred to me that a couple of days later another one of my captains came into Surabaya towing a supply barge. He and the laid-up captain were having a pint, and he happened to mention he'd picked up a call about the same time in the Banda Sea. Except he heard his on channel sixteen, VHF."

Stone gripped the tablecloth and leaned closer. Ship to low-lying tug, VHF radio range was no more than forty miles. "What did the ship say when he responded?"

"Nothing. Just the one call, and when he tried to raise her, he got nothing back."

"What did he do?"

"What the hell could he do? The man had a five-thousand-ton barge on a half-mile wire. He put the cook in charge of the radio, told the lookouts to keep a weather eye, and tried to canvass other shipping—there wasn't any."

Stone was hanging on every word, praying for a breakthrough. Kerry misunderstood and got defensive. "No way my captain was going cast the barge loose and start a search pattern on his own. Could have been a screwup. Could have been the last signal before they sunk. Nothing to go on. Just a Mayday. No name, no call sign, no position."

"Like maybe the caller was shot resisting a hijacking and managed to get to the radio room before they finished him off?"

"That's a lot of maybe."

"Maybe," said Stone. But Kerry hadn't been the one who'd found a bullet-riddled body in the Pulo Helena lagoon. "Where would that be, six-seven hundred miles southwest of Pulo Helena?"

"With New Guinea in between. What's going on, Michael?"

Thirty-forty hours steaming for a fast ship. "But no name," Stone asked. "No call signs on either transmission. Wouldn't the single-sideband automatically send a call sign?"

"This one didn't— What's going on? Where's Sarah?"

"You're not going to believe this." Stone told him what had happened at Pulo Helena. The salvage captain listened without interruption until Stone was through.

"Hell of a story. And a hell of a piece of seamanship, Michael. They're going to be mighty surprised to find out you're in Hong Kong."

Would that they were, Stone wanted to say, but Kerry looked incredulous already. "Fact is, the distress calls really tell me nothing, except they strengthen my hijack guess."

"It tells me it's just possible you didn't dream this up."

"Possible?" Stone echoed.

McGlynn returned his coldest captain's stare. "Michael, in my business I see every scam you could imagine. You know how many scuttlings I get called on? They radio me to make them look legitimate. 'Gee, the ship was sinking. The salvage tugs came, but it was too late. Fortunately, they picked up our lifeboat.' Sometimes I feel like a pirate's ferry service."

"Why would I scuttle my boat?"

McGlynn said, "Let me ask you something . . . How good are your papers?"

"What?"

"Is *Veronica* reliably documented?"

"She's registered in Los Angeles."

"Will her papers pass muster?"

"What do you mean?"

"I think you know what I mean. Christ, Mike, everyone knows something's bent about you two."

"I've heard that. Everybody thinks Sarah and I are running from an angry husband."

"I don't," said McGlynn. He had a look on his face of a hanging judge.

"Oh yeah? What do you hear?"

"The only reason I never questioned you was the first time I saw you, you were driving *Veronica* through a pass even the natives wouldn't dare to rescue some little kid. I figured, whatever crimes you did in the past, you were making up for it. But, we were discussing *Veronica's* papers."

"Her papers are in order. She's had a few name changes over the years. She was *Ashante* when we bought her. We changed it to *Sarah*. After Ronnie was born, we changed it again to *Veronica*."

"Bought her?"

"The bill of sale went overboard in Typhoon Mary."

"Along with the canceled check?" McGlynn permitted himself a thin smile.

"We paid cash, actually. That is, Sarah bought her for cash."

"And the seller?"

"A Congo River man."

"Who just happened to own a top-of-the-line Finnish-built sailing yacht. Did you get a good price, for cash?"

A trace of McGlynn's smile lingered, so Stone said, "He

did recommend an immediate name change and a cruise in foreign waters."

"And some name changes for you two as well?"

Stone thought it was fair to answer that question enigmatically. "You know us as who we are."

Kerry's expression hardened. "A stolen yacht isn't why you're running. What'd you do, mate? What do you need me for? Why can't you just go to the U.S. Navy?"

If there was anyone he could trust, it was this friend who cared so much for Sarah. But he had been hiding his past as much from himself as from the world, and the habit died hard. He had to accept he had no choice.

"I'll give it to you in a nutshell, Kerry," he said briskly. "I'm wanted for a double murder, which I didn't commit, and piracy, which I did."

"If you want my help, mate, you better come up with a bigger nutshell."

"Give me a break, Kerry."

"No, you give me a break. You want me to believe you? Convince me."

Stone took a deep breath. "We never told anybody. You'll see why. . . . Sarah's father—the general—was assassinated in a coup attempt. When the coup collapsed, they got the idea of covering themselves by pinning the murder on me."

Kerry's reaction to the revelation was to ask coolly, "What were you doing in Nigeria?"

Stone was still trying to form a careful answer, when suddenly he felt the old pain return as raw and startling as an explosion in his face. He took a moment to compose himself.

"My first wife's name was Katherine. We'd cashed in our shares of an ultrasound medical probe we'd developed, and gone sailing. Sort of a second honeymoon, since we'd been too busy for our first. Bought a big fat Halberg-Rassy centerboard ketch. Your basic first boat when you have more money than sense. Rolled our guts out crossing the Atlantic, and finally anchored up in London. That's where I met Sarah. She was interning at King's Hospital."

"Found yourself a new first mate?" Kerry smirked, but his voice trailed off when he saw Stone's eyes glisten.

"Kerry, there isn't a night on watch I don't grieve for Katherine. Or wonder what the hell I could have done different to save her life."

"Sounds like you still love her."

"I do."

"More than Sarah?"

"No. Of course not. If I had a thousand lives I'd never find again what I found with Sarah."

"Sorry, mate." The salvage man looked away. When he could finally face Stone again, he saw him fighting back the tears.

"Katherine and Sarah hit it off—the three of us became great friends. Sarah was younger than we, just surfacing from the drudgery of medical school, so excited to be alive again. It was fun to be around her. So when her old man ordered her home to Lagos, we promised to sail down to pay her a visit. Landed smack in the middle of what turned out to be a very short-lived coup. A gang of junior officers liquored up by our local CIA agent."

McGlynn stared down at a sea-battered PRC freighter cutting off the Star Ferry. Stone took a long breath and struggled to get the details right.

"Sarah's father was one hundred percent committed to civilian rule, which made him their first target. What they didn't realize was that his units would remain loyal; he'd trained them like British soldiers, taught 'em to stay out of politics. When the coup went sour, the bastards got the bright idea of making the assassination look like a murder— a crime of passion—like I'd caught the general making love to Katherine and killed them both in a jealous rage."

"They murdered your wife too?"

"For verisimilitude. Shot her in her bed. Dumped the general's body on top of her. Stripped them naked. That's how we found them. . . . Sarah's father and my beautiful Katherine . . ." Bitter details, grounded in true loss. "The worst thing was the terror on Katherine's face. She must have woken up, seen them crowding into the room. I can never get out of my mind the fear she felt before she died. I would do anything to change that."

"Did it work?" Kerry asked. "Did they get away with it?"

"Yeah, it worked. If it weren't for Sarah, I'd have been shot 'resisting arrest.' But it worked anyway, and I was running for my life."

"Why didn't you run to the American embassy?"

"It was the CIA guy who told the Nigerians to frame the white American."

Kerry looked skeptical. Finally he said, "How'd that turn into piracy?"

"The cops and the army impounded my sailboat and were tearing Lagos apart looking for me. They had roadblocks and the airport was impossible. Sarah said they would shoot me. I didn't care. With Katherine dead, I wanted to be dead too. But Sarah wouldn't allow that." Stone shook his head. "I can still hear her screaming at me— *demanding* I survive. By then, we'd figured out that the CIA front in Lagos was an outfit that ran offshore oil rig tenders. So I did a run up the middle and split in one of their tugboats."

"Sounds more like grand larceny than piracy."

"Yeah. But the CIA guy came after me. Caught up in a Nigerian patrol boat, about a hundred miles offshore . . ."

"And?"

"I rammed the patrol boat."

"Did it sink?"

"I was driving a six-thousand-horsepower steel tug. Last I saw, their bow was drifting toward Africa, the stern toward Brazil."

"How many did you drown?"

Stone looked at him. "None."

"How do you know?"

"Both halves were raking me with machine guns."

"How'd you get away?"

"Sarah—who was totally in the clear and could have stayed there—risked her life to empty one of her father's safe deposit boxes and hire a smuggler to pick me up. She stayed aboard to nurse me—I'd been hit. The smuggler took us to Moanda, to his Congo River friend, and Sarah bought the Swan. They were still after us, but she insisted on coming with me. Got pretty hairy."

He glanced at Kerry. The Australian was shaking his head. Stone said, trying to convey the nature of Sarah's selfless acts, the truly important thing, "Get this, Kerry. I was a mess. When I wasn't bleeding I was crying. So we're not talking about the heat of passion—that came later."

"Love?" Kerry interrupted.

Stone sighed. "You don't understand. Sarah and I fell in love the first time we even saw each other. At a distance. But it was the sort of thing neither of us would have ever acted on. I did truly love Katherine. You know, if you're happily married you accept that God plays jokes. You meet someone—your instant soul mate—but you honor your love and your commitments.

"Don't get me wrong, by the way, I'm not *that* noble. I wouldn't have stayed for commitment alone, but I really did love Katherine. . . . Still, Sarah and I clicked from the beginning. But nothing ever would have happened. . . . But what I'm telling you is, Sarah didn't stay only for love. She stayed for honor too. The right thing. Katherine was an innocent victim and so was I. Sarah felt responsible, even though she was as innocent as we were."

"Ever ask yourself why you deserve such a woman?"

"Every day." Stone smiled. "But I'm never giving her back. Never."

Kerry's expression turned inward. "Somehow your story would ring truer if Sarah had stayed to avenge her father."

"Truer? You don't believe me?"

"And you, your wife."

"Oh, I wanted to kill them all. Hatched a plan to get the officers who did it. And that son-of-a-bitch spook. Sarah wouldn't hear of it. She's a Christian in the deepest sense."

"Turned the other cheek?"

"You could call it that. . . ." said Stone. "I wasn't as forgiving, but she helped me understand that all the killings in the world wouldn't bring Katherine back. And of course the Nigerians and the CIA were still coming after us with all four feet," he continued, spinning the story into its natural conclusion.

Pursued to Antarctica, then into the Drake Channel and around Cape Horn, they had disappeared among the islands of Micronesia, which were scattered like dust across eight and a half million square miles of ocean. Their trips to "civilization" for supplies and amenities were few, their stops brief and unpredictable. They felt reasonably safe, though they tended to avoid contact with the growing legion of American cruisers. The Japanese and Hong Kong Chinese who helped support the hospital boat had no reason to question their past, and they might have gone on as they had forever, had the *Dallas Belle* not happened upon them, needing a doctor.

"Hell of a story," Kerry said, again.

Stone ignored him.

"Point is, even though all this happened years ago and fifteen thousand miles east, the U.S. Navy isn't going to be any help— Now the way I see it, whoever grabbed Sarah had stolen the ship for the cargo. Somebody got hurt in the hijacking, and they took Sarah to doctor him. Your unexplained Mayday fits right in with the dead guy on the beach."

"Maybe."

"Is the U.S. Navy acoustical tracking system still in operation?"

"SOSUS," Kerry McGlynn answered, "Sound surveillance system."

"If they could call up their files for the Pulo Helena vicinity, they could ID that ship and track it to where it is now."

"Possible," said Kerry.

"I can't go to the U.S. Navy. But I'll bet you could. Or your brother. I'll bet anything the Australian Navy can tap into the U.S. system."

McGlynn was shaking his head.

"Why not?"

"You're asking me to risk compromising his naval career."

"I'm asking you to help me get Sarah back."

"I don't see how you can without coming clean."

"I've got two problems with throwing myself on the mercy of the U.S. consulate. We have a child. If the price of getting my wife back means we'll both go to prison, what happens to Ronnie?"

McGlynn offered no answer.

"But even if I took that chance, there's no promise they'd search. I know this story sounds crazy. My friend Lydia Chin looked at me like I was out of my mind. And now you are. How would you like to persuade a bunch of bu-reaucrats to call in the Navy? Christ, it would take days, weeks. In the meantime, where the hell is she? What are they doing to her?"

McGlynn looked him hard in the eye. "Take a bearing on your story from my position."

"What do you mean?"

"It *does* sound crazy. Crazier than your pirate tale."

"Crazy? Or don't you believe me?"

Kerry sighed. "I'd like to. I wish I did. I've known you and Sarah a long time. On and off."

"If I'm lying, where's Sarah?"

"I can think of two possibilities: One, she packed it in and left you; or, two, you left her."

"Left her? Where's my boat?"

"You tell me, mate."

In that instant, Stone saw the hidden cost of isolation. A true friend could not conceive of such a lie; but he had never made Kerry a true friend, only an acquaintance, like Marcus Salinis, like the others on their Pacific circuit, like Lydia Chin. He had one friend and one friend only, Sarah. The rest occupied the edges of his life. Where, he had to admit, he had placed them deliberately—or allowed them to drift, which amounted to the same thing. With Sarah at his side, it had never bothered him. Without her, he was completely alone.

"Why," he asked, "if I left her, would I come to you with this story that a gas carrier picked up my boat and took them away?"

Kerry sighed again. Cold-eyed captain or not, he seemed uncomfortable with his implications.

"Why?" Stone pressed. "Now *you* sound crazy. If I left her, why would I bother making up a story?"

"Maybe you needed a story."

"What? For what?"

"To explain—"

"Explain what?" Stone demanded, with an awful feeling that he was a beat behind the salvage captain.

"Explain why she and your daughter went missing."

"You're losing me, Kerry."

"Look at me! If she left you, you'd to have some story you could live with. Or at least tell your friends."

"I swear she didn't leave me."

"Michael, I don't know if you left her or she left you or what." Kerry swirled the beer in his glass. When he spoke again, he was gentle. "People do some crazy things at sea. You get out there alone, you think weird stuff. Sometimes, you do weird stuff. I'd bet once a month some seaman just picks up a fire axe and kills his best mate. . . . Last year, bloke on a supertanker wanted to go home, so he wired a cutting torch to a valve on the foredeck, thinking a fire would get him helicoptered to Sydney. It did, in a coffin;

ship was empty, so the tanks were filled with residual gas pockets. Blew the bloody bow off."

"Jesus Christ. You think I did something to Sarah?"

"It happens."

"I just told you what she means to me. I love her.

"I heard you."

"And my daughter?"

"It happens."

"And then I scuttled the Swan?"

"Your words, not mine."

"I love them. But aside from that fact, I'm not capable of hurting someone. Christ, if I were, wouldn't your teeth be on the deck right now?"

Kerry reddened. "Try it, mate."

"Fuck this, you don't believe me." Stone bent to grab his pack. A heavy blow smashed the back of his neck. The force knocked him off his chair and under the table. He thought that Kerry had rabbit-punched him. But somehow the window had broken. Cold wind rushed in. A woman screamed. And Kerry was toppling from his chair, dragging the tablecloth and the dishes on top of him, bright red blood spurting from his shoulder.

A wine bottle exploded musically on the next table and a bucket shattered, spraying Stone with ice. "Get down!" someone yelled. "They're still shooting!"

15

STONE DOVE ONTO KERRY AND JAMMED A WADDED NAPKIN against the wound.

The salvage man was white as the table linen and gasping for air. "What happened?"

"They missed *me*."

All around the restaurant people were screaming and diving at the floor. Others stood frozen, pointing at the holes in the window. A middle-aged American shoved Stone aside, yelling, "Get out of my way. I'm a doctor."

"Run for it, mate," Kerry whispered.

Stone sprinted for the door. The maitress d' was shouting into the telephone for an ambulance. Stone ran to the elevators, saw them suddenly as a trap, and fled down the stairs.

Fifteen flights down he heard the pounding boots and sergeant's shouts of a police squad storming up the stairwell. Stone pushed through a fire door, into a hotel corridor, hurried to the elevators, and waited anxiously for a car, praying that the police hadn't panicked and shut off the system. He heard the cops on the stairs.

The elevator arrived, doors opening on a frightened crowd fleeing the restaurant. Stone squeezed aboard. An Englishwoman stared at him. "I say, weren't you with the man who was shot?" Flustered, Stone shook his head and looked away.

In the lobby, word of the shooting had people huddled by the windows, staring into the street, where police cars and ambulances were stacking up around the entrance and blocking traffic.

Stone went to the telephones and called Lydia Chin. The shipowner was in a meeting. "Get her out of it. This is urgent. . . ."

Lydia came on and before he could speak, said, "No one has any information about a missing gas carrier. No such ship is reported overdue. Anywhere in the world."

"Tell your friend Ronald I want to talk."

"No, Michael. You're playing with fire."

Across the lobby, he saw the woman who had questioned him in the elevator talking to a policeman. "I'm already in the fire, Lydia. Tell him. Or give me some number I can call."

"They will consume you."

"I have nowhere else to turn. They're my last shot."

"No," said Lydia. "I can't be part—"

"Forget it," said Stone, hanging up. "Your friend just found me."

The Triad man was sitting in an armchair, ignoring the chaos and watching Stone with a calculating expression on his lean face. Jackals, Lydia had called them. They wanted the stolen ship. They wanted to steal it from the thieves and sell the cargo. Terrific. He'd ride along and somehow rescue Sarah and Ronnie before the shooting started.

As Stone headed toward him, the Englishwoman pointed him out to the policeman. Ronald noticed and got up quickly and strode to the parking garage elevator. Stone ran after him as a pair of Cantonese who had been sitting near him jumped up, blocking the cop's path. Ronald veered through a fire door, beckoning Stone down stairs that led to the garage.

"What the hell are you doing here?"

"Hey, sailorman. Chiu Chau still looking for you."

"They just shot my friend."

"Missed you."

"What are you doing here?"

"Boys follow. My boss wants to meet you. "

"What about?"

"Explain in car."

A Toyota was already waiting with a driver and a man in front. Both men wore baggy shirts with room for side arms. Stone and Ronald climbed in, and they pulled away without a word.

The car headed toward Causeway Bay.

"How you make Chiu Chau mad?" asked Ronald.

"Told you before, I don't know. What does your boss want?"

"Maybe they mad about ship? Maybe you step in their way— Hey, sailorman. Who buy it?"

"What?"

"The ship with your family. Who buy the gas?"

"Power plant. Generating station."

Ronald pulled a flip phone from his jacket, spoke a few words in Cantonese, and listened intently, his eyes on Stone. "Cops," he said, when he snapped it shut, "looking for sniper. Tall Brit. Yellow hair." He smiled at Stone. "Sounds like guy who stole cop car at airport yesterday. . . . You hear about that?"

Stone looked out the window. Everywhere he went, strangers knew more than he did. At Causeway Bay, the car wove through the tangle of tunnel and expressway ramps and pulled up to a high-rise hotel less than three hundred yards from the yacht club.

Ronald escorted Stone through the lavish lobby into an elevator.

"What does your boss want?"

"Don't piss him off."

"What's his name?"

"You call him Mr. Chang." He led Stone into a suite with glass walls overlooking the typhoon shelter.

Seated on a couch was a heavyset, middle-aged Cantonese whose conservative attire—a Hong Kong businessman's sober blue suit—and quiet jewelry—a gold signet ring and thin wedding band—contrasted sharply with Ronald's gangster costume.

Ronald presented Stone. Light flashed from his wire-rimmed eyeglasses as Mr. Chang nodded, but he neither rose from the couch nor offered to shake Stone's hand. A covered teacup sat on the coffee table. Across the room was a conference table on which was spread a chart, with glass ashtrays holding down the curling edges.

"Want tea, Doc?" asked Ronald.

"No."

Chang spoke, a deep rumble. "You look for ship?"

"I'm looking for my wife and daughter, who are *on* the ship. . . ."

"Where's the ship?"

"I think they're in Shanghai." Stone tried to penetrate Chang's glinting eyeglasses as he answered. "I want to get to Shanghai without anyone knowing. And I want documented backup for my cover story."

"What cover story?"

"I'm going to say that I'm scouting locations for foreign investors to build a Western-style yacht marina."

Chang looked interested. Or at least his stare grew more intense.

After a cautious look at his boss, Ronald grinned. "Neat."

"I want a guide. A translator who knows the waterfront."

"Like I said before, you need a lot, Doc."

"And a boat for the river . . . Also, I'll need some money."

"Last night you say you no want money."

"Walking-around money. Bribe money. I'm prepared to give anything I can in exchange."

Chang was expressionless, but Ronald cracked another smile. "You no fun, Doc. What kind of bargain?"

"You know damn well I don't have time to bargain," Stone shot back. "You know what I need. And you know I'm on the run. I'm a doctor. I'm willing to do whatever you want that I know how to do."

Chang spoke again. "China's got plenty a doctors."

"Then what the hell did you bring me up here for?"

Ronald walked to the windows. "Come here, Doc." Quietly, he murmured, "Guy talk like that to Mr. Chang fly out window."

Twenty-seven stories below, Causeway Bay's typhoon shelter looked orderly, a far cry from the tangle of mooring and anchor lines, hulls gunnel to gunnel, vessels so tightly jammed together that much of the sprawling boat basin could be crossed on foot by stepping deck to deck.

"You see down?"

"Yeah?"

Ronald pointed a manicured finger at the west end. "You see down there?"

"What? The yacht club?"

"Hong Kong Yacht Club."

"Okay. I see it."

"Your club. Honorary."

"So?"

"Okay." He pointed at the opposite end of the shelter, some half a mile east. "End of row. You see yacht."

"With the helicopter pad?" A circle near the stern was marked with an *H*.

"Motor yacht."

"What about it?" Stone had seen it arrive last night

while waiting for the taxi. It was the biggest in the shelter, more than a hundred feet long and bristling with antennas. White domes covered satellite communication dishes.

"Tin Hau."

"The sea goddess." It was a very common boat name in Hong Kong.

"Big yacht. Go anywhere."

Maybe Mr. Chang planned to use the yacht to smuggle human organs down the Pearl River from Guangzhou. Trouble was, the Triad leader had an inflated opinion of Stone's medical prowess.

"Ronald, I told you last night. Emergencies. I don't know the first thing about transplants."

"No problem, Doc. Like Mr. Chang say, we got plenty a doctors."

"Then what do you need me for?"

Instead of answering Stone, Ronald looked to Mr. Chang. Chang shook his head. Ronald could not conceal his disappointment. He started to protest. Chang shook his head again, grunted a word of Cantonese, and stood up. Two bodyguards, dressed as conservatively as he, appeared from another room and escorted him out of the suite.

Ronald waited until he heard the door close. "Mr. Chang likes you."

Stone was surprised. He had thought the byplay between the two men had indicated Chang was against them. "Does he like me enough to help me?" he asked.

"Mr. Chang has very good friend in Shanghai. Businessman. Used to be high PRC official. Ran state cotton factory. Day before he retire from government, he sell factory to 'private enterprise' stock company owned by wife. Next day, he own state factory. Very important man, Mr. Chang's friend. Very rich. He want fine thing in life. Mr. Chang think old friend like that yacht."

Stone stared. "What?"

"No Triad ever steal yacht from typhoon shelter. Tanka boatboys hate us. Like watchdogs. They see me coming, they bark. But they don't bark at *gweilo* honorary member of Hong Kong Yacht Club."

"You're nuts."

"You gonna make me famous gangster, Doc. Rich and famous. Hit the big time. And Mr. Chang be my very good friend."

"I'm not a thief," said Stone, but he was only buying time. Stealing a boat beat stealing body organs; the only thing was, it looked impossible.

"You got no choice, sailorman. I hear they shooting people at the Hilton."

"How am I going to get it out of there, assuming I can even get aboard?"

"I check you out. Everybody say you big deal sailorman. You say that yacht too big?"

"I can handle her. But what about the boatboys? She'll have a couple sleeping aboard."

"You take care of boatboys."

"I will not kill people."

"No killing. Tie 'em up. We let 'em go later."

"I'll bet. . . . What about the cops? Even if I get out of the shelter, what if a harbor patrol boards me?"

"Fog tomorrow night. They can't see you."

"They have radar."

"We have ECM."

"You're joking."

Ronald's face hardened. "Mr. Chang don't joke."

"Electronic countermeasures?"

"He got latest PLA jammers. We jam water cops' radar. All you got to do is get away from the harbor patrol and meet up with the PRC patrol and you home free."

"How far?"

"Thirteen miles."

Ronald took him to the table. The chart was an old Defense Mapping's 93733, a pre-Turnover small-scale rendering of Hong Kong and its immediate waters. Ronald traced a route east from the shelter, south around Hong Kong Island into the Tathong Channel, and east again between Joss House Bay and Tung Lung Island. From Tung Lung, it was a long run straight east through mostly open sea toward a dotted line that represented the former boundary between "Hong Kong (United Kingdom)" on the near side, and "Guangdong Sheng, China" on the far.

"PLA friends wait there," said Ronald. "Cross that line, you home free."

It looked more like sixteen miles. Stone said, "What do you mean, home free? What about the harbor patrol? The water cops are PRC now, too, aren't they?"

"Maybe some Hong Kong water cops belong to Chiu Chau. Maybe some PLA navy patrol friends with Mr. Chang," Ronald answered. Then added with exaggerated patience, "You know L.A., sailorman?"

Stone hesitated.

Ronald laughed at him. "Your boat registered L.A., you remember? L.A., you got Bloods and Crips. Crips steal truck on Bloods turf, Bloods pissed. Same thing Hong Kong and mainland. Any more questions, sailorman?"

"Yeah, Ronald. You're asking me to trust that when I hand that boat over to you at sea, you'll keep your side of the bargain."

"Why not? You old friend of Ms. Chin. Besides, maybe you help us in Shanghai . . . "

"Doing what?" Stone asked warily.

"This your main chance, sailorman."

He was getting in deeper and deeper. The question was, was he getting any closer to Sarah and Ronnie? In answer, he felt a weird little smile tug his mouth: it was one way to get the fish back in the water.

"Hey, where you going?"

Stone was out the door. "Let me take a look at her."

"I'll drive you. Chiu Chau everywhere."

"Wake up, Sweetie," Sarah whispered. The ship was still drifting, rolling gently on the swell.

Ronnie awakened cranky. "What?"

"Shhh. We're going to run for it."

She blinked. "Really? When?"

"Now. Here's your foul-weather jacket— Leave your pack."

"It's got all my stuff in it."

"We can't take our bags. If they catch us, we'll say we're going for a walk. I'm sorry. I'm leaving my stuff too. Here." She gave Ronnie the GPS. "Hide it in your pocket. "I've got a water bottle and the radio."

"They'll see us."

"No, the fog's turned a real souper. See?"

Ronnie peered dubiously out the port. "I'm scared."

"Me, too."

"What about Mr. Jack?" Ronnie whispered, with a fearful look at the old man in his bed.

"I gave him a sleeping tablet. Let's go."

"Where's Moss?"

"On the bridge."

"Are you sure?"

"Come on."

She took her daughter's hand. Ronnie cast a longing look at the now familiar cabin, the swinging airplanes, and her Snoopy backpack. Then Sarah led the way boldly into the empty lounge and out the door and down the main stairs.

"Someone's coming up the stairs."

"We're just taking a walk, remember?" Sarah put her arm over Ronnie's shoulder and smiled at the Chinese deckhand who was trooping up to the crew mess in his boiler suit. He ducked his head. Down they spiraled, below the main deck, down into the hull. It was eerily quiet with the main engine stopped, and even when Sarah opened a door on the accommodations deck the only mechanical noises they heard were a distant murmur from the auxiliary generator that powered the lights and the rhythm of the compressors cooling the cargo. It felt too easy. Or maybe they were just lucky.

"Look!"

The Zodiak, a twelve-foot semirigid inflatable outboard skiff, was propped on its side to save space beside the accommodations hatch. Its little outboard was still attached, tubed to a single six-gallon fuel tank.

Unlike the emergency raft, the inflatable had no canopy, no shelter at all. But they had their foul-weather jackets, though they were rather lightweight for winter this far north. Sarah went to the hatch, turned the heavy dogs that latched it. "Help me."

Ronnie had dropped to one knee and fiddled with her sneaker. "Help me, Mum."

Exasperated, Sarah knelt beside her. "What is the matter with you?"

"Don't look up."

"Why?"

"There's a video camera pointing at the hatch."

"Oh my God, what have I done?"

"It's not your fault, Mummy," Ronnie whispered. "It's way hidden— Pretend you're helping me."

Sarah tried to think. "Then we'll get up and walk away."

"No, we can't. It saw me see it."

"Bloody—"

"Let's dance!"

"What?"

She jumped up before Sarah cold stop her and waved at the camera, which was half-concealed in a steel pillar. "Hi, Mr. Jack. Are you watching? Hi, Moss.

"Come on, Mummy. It's Mr. Jack. Hi, Mr. Jack. Hi, Moss. Come on, Mummy." She dragged Sarah to her feet and hooked her arm around her waist and kicked. "One, two, three, kick. One, two, three, kick. We learned the can-can at the officers club in Kwajalein," she called, as if neither knew he was drugged in his bed. "Sorry, Mr. Jack. Mummy won't do it, she's very British, you know. Bye-bye!" She steered her mother out the door and up the stairs. "One, two, three, kick!"

Three decks up, they ran into Ah Lee carrying a tray with whiskey, glasses, and ice. His battered face fell when he saw them. "No allow. No allow."

"It's okay, Ah Lee. It's just us. Walk."

"No allow."

"Walk."

"Go back."

"Walk."

"I tell Moss."

"Please. No."

Ah Lee hurried up the stairs. Sarah ran to the steel hatch that led to the afterdeck. The fog was so thick she couldn't see the bulwark. The raft canister was a nebulous white glow.

"Hurry."

It was lashed down beside a hinged gate in the bulwark. But the gate was frozen with rust. The only way they could launch the raft was lift it over the bulwark, which rose as high as her forehead. She knelt by the canister, feeling for the ropes that lashed it down.

"Get up, Mum. Someone's coming."

Sarah sprang to her feet and was just backing away from the raft when Moss loomed out of the fog. "What the fuck are you two doing out here?"

Sarah drew herself up to her full height. "Would you kindly moderate your language around my daughter?"

Moss grabbed her arm, grinding it through the thin wind-breaker. "Inside."

Moss shoved Sarah into Mr. Jack's sleeping cabin so hard she crashed into the bed. He pushed Ronnie in after her. The old man awakened, groggy. But when he saw the expression on Moss's face, he snapped alert and austere, as if overcoming the sleeping tablet by an act of sheer will. Or was it fear? He looked afraid.

"Wha'd they do? They get off a signal?"

"Caught 'em prowling around the main deck."

Visibly relieved, Mr. Jack struggled to sit up. He shook

Sarah off when she went to help him. "What the hell were you doing on the main deck?"

"We went for a walk," said Sarah. Her arm burned where Moss had dragged her, but she refused to give him the satisfaction of letting him see her rub it. Ronnie's eyes were big as saucers and she was breathing hard.

"They was checkin' out a life raft."

"Were not," said Ronnie. "We were taking a walk."

Moss said, "It was right after the video picked them up at the accommodations door. Mess boy spotted them heading up, again."

"He scared us," said Ronnie. "And you're scaring me now." Her face crumbled. "Mr. Jack, why—"

"Can it, kid. I seen better acting on a pig." It was the sort of joke line that usually got the old man a laugh from the child. But not when he looked harsher and crueler than Moss.

"Mess boy reported they tried to talk him into helping them launch the inflatable."

"That's a lie! He didn't say that."

"That's what he told me, Mr. Jack."

"That's 'cause you beat him up!" Ronnie shouted.

"Shut up."

"He'd say anything so you wouldn't hurt him again."

"Both of you, shut up."

A steam whistle shrilled across the water.

Sarah whirled to the porthole.

A long, dark hull materialized out of the murk, steaming straight at the *Dallas Belle*. Then another. And a third. Tugboats, sea-battered and filthy, pluming thick smoke into the fog. Sailors in black crowded their towing decks. Red flags flew with the yellow stars of the People's Republic of China.

She was still praying they meant rescue, when the captain hurried into the cabin.

"Tugs alongside, Mr. Jack."

The old man propped himself up higher on his good elbow, eyes burning.

"Cloud cover holding?"

"As promised. But the fog's lifting. We ain't got much time."

"Hook 'em up. Let's blow this joint— Ronnie, go get some ice cream."

"I don't want any."

"Shut up! Moss, take her down to the galley."

Ronnie looked stricken. He had never yelled at her before. But all Sarah could do was nod, helplessly. "Go ahead, dear. I'll talk to Mr. Jack."

Moss jerked a thumb at the door. Ronnie dodged him and ran ahead. Mr. Jack turned a cold eye on Sarah.

"You dumb cunt," he yelled. "Risk your life and your kid's."

"We went for a walk," Sarah said doggedly. "Ah Lee was frightened. He didn't understand. Or, more likely, Moss lied."

"Doc, you're cruisin' for a bruisin'."

"I don't know what you mean. We merely went for a walk."

"Can the lies. You tried to escape."

Sarah started to protest, again, lost heart, and shook her head, bitterly. "We didn't. But wouldn't you?"

"My head feels like mud. You slip me a mickey?"

"A mickey?" Sarah asked, though she knew what he meant.

"A pill. Did you drug me?"

"Yes. I gave you a sleeping tablet. You're too active. You refuse to rest."

"No more pills without telling me."

"If you insist," she agreed.

The old man sighed. "Doc, you're really pissing me off."

"Mr. Jack, I'm only—"

He cut her off with an angry gesture. "I'm going to give you this one chance. You try one more stunt like that—you disobey me in any way, shape, or form—one step out of line, and you'll be punished."

"*Punished?* How dare you! I saved your life, for God's sake. How *dare* you threaten me!"

He leveled a mutilated finger in her face.

"When Moss has you crawling on the deck, begging for mercy, don't say I didn't warn you. . . . And don't look for mercy from me, because I'm going to be right there, making sure he does you like you'll never forget."

"Considering your state of health, Mr. Jack, it would not be in your best interest to have your physician laid up in sick bay."

"I'm not *stupid,* Doc. Moss ran whores when he was sixteen years old. He can make a woman hurt like she wants to die. And still put her on the street that same night. . . . You want a little demo when he comes back?"

She dropped her eyes before he could see her rage or her fear.

"Answer me! You want a demo?"

The carpet blurred through her tears. "No."

The telephone rang. Mr. Jack fumbled it off the night table. "What? . . . I'll meet him in the lounge. Send up plenty of strong coffee. I gotta clear my head for this guy."

He swung his feet off the bed and let her help him stand and put on his robe. "Don't forget. Last chance."

"Where's Ronnie?"

"On her way up."

He shuffled out the door.

Five minutes crawled like days. Ronnie came back, unharmed and still shaken but blessedly distracted by something she had seen.

"Mum, it was the funniest thing. Some Chinese guy came to see Mr. Jack, but he fell overboard."

"Off the ship?"

"No. From the tug, when he tried to board. At the accommodations hatch? He was wearing a suit and the sailors caught him but his pants were soaked right up to his waist. And his shoes were squishing. You should have seen him pouring water out of his briefcase!"

Ronnie started laughing, and then it all caught up with her and she began to cry. Sarah squeezed her and held her tight until she had calmed down. "I think it's nap time, darling." By the time she got her into bed, Ronnie was yawning, and her eyes wore the film of sleep.

"Did anyone say who he was?"

"Who?"

"The Chinese guy."

A big yawn turned into a grin. "His name was Ah Wet!"

"Very funny, young lady." Sarah laughed. "All right, now, close your eyes."

Sarah sat with Ronnie until her breathing leveled into sleep. Then she put on her stethoscope and listened through the door.

She couldn't hear every word—they must have been on the far side of the room. "Ah Wet" was soft-spoken, while Mr. Jack's voice was slurred from the tablet—but the subject was finance, a highly technical discussion of an ongoing scheme to purchase stock options at markets around the world. She understood little, except that the sums were enormous and the long-term project seemed to be nearing completion.

Ronnie slipped behind her. Sarah jumped. She hadn't heard her get out of bed. "Mum, be careful. Moss said he'd beat you up if we tried anything."

Sarah drew her close. She had to comfort her child, but she also had to save her life. "Don't worry, dear. Mr. Jack would never allow that. He likes you too much."

When Michael Stone went to borrow a dinghy, the lunchtime shooting at the Hilton was the talk of the yacht club bar. The word was Kerry McGlynn had a smashed shoulder. Stone called Matilda Hospital, which confirmed that the tugman was in serious condition.

Children watched Stone curiously from a makeshift raft as he launched the dinghy into the typhoon shelter water and negotiated the maze of narrow channels. Old women darted past in motor sampans, ferrying goods and people to the junks and yachts. Several times while dodging sampans he bumped into anchor lines and caught his oars on jutting hulls. The water was filthy, a dead gray color, and stank even in the coolness of December, home to thousands who were born, lived, and died on their boats.

And yet the floating city was a village, rural in character, and he could see that a Triad interloper would instantly be recognized. He drew curious stares as he pulled his oars, then blank faces when they catalogued him: a *gweilo*, a white ghost person from the West, seeking exercise in what normal people considered work. Eccentric, harmless, and vaguely absurd, though perhaps a source of income.

A sampan hailed him, selling fish balls. He bought a basket of the spicy food and drifted while he ate. The instant he had finished, another sampan materialized to sell him hot tea. And when he finished the tea, yet another boat putted alongside, piloted by a smiling, middle-aged woman who swept an inviting hand toward the mattress under the canvas top and called, "Fuck-fuck?"

Stone shook his head silently, trusting neither his survival Cantonese nor Tanka to make a refusal clear or polite, and rowed on, working his way eastward through the moorings, past the junks into the slightly less chaotic area where the sailing yachts clustered.

He was struck by the extraordinary number of superb sea boats—big, modern, high-tech cruisers and racers that could sail circles around his old Swan. Most reflected the spit and polish of the professional live-aboard crew, and everywhere he looked, boatboys in black pajamas were cleaning, fitting, and overhauling. There were easily a hundred boats ready to sail to the Philippines on an hour's notice. He rested on his oars, pretending to admire a big Baltic sloop so he could take his first good look at *Tin Hau* moored at the end of the next row. The Baltic's boatboy came up immediately from the cabin and eyed Stone quizzically.

"Help, sir?"

"Handsome boat," said Stone, dipping his oars and moving on to another vantage. *Tin Hau*, glimpsed through a forest of aluminum and carbon-fiber masts, appeared to be the archetype for the phrase "floating gin palace." The bulkiness of its navy blue hull was cleverly disguised by a smooth, ultramodern superstructure, which, while quite high, was made to look sleek by long strips of black-tinted glass. She looked, Stone thought, like Italians had designed a shopping mall for speed.

As he rowed closer, a flimsy-looking helicopter buzzed in across the harbor and fluttered onto her afterdeck. Two boatboys came running and helped the pilot tie the aircraft down and unload cases of liquor. Stone rowed the length of her, spotted the accommodations door midships in her side, and kept going toward the passage in the rock breakwater that led to the harbor. He paused there while a sampan picked up the helicopter pilot at the accommodations door, and studied her mooring.

No anchor, thank God. Both anchors were secured within the bow, and the yacht was tied to a permanent mooring. He rowed back along her length. Her stern was tied to another permanent buoy; better and better. But when he looked between her and her smaller neighbor, he noticed they'd exchanged lines fore and aft.

He imagined a sequence: when the tide flooded the passage, he would cast off the side lines first, then the stern line. Then start the engines. Race forward and cut the bow line. Run back to the bridge and try to slip away without waking up half the typhoon shelter.

But he still had to get aboard and he still had to deal with the boatboys, who were total innocents. And possibly armed. Guns were restricted in Hong Kong, but who knew on a big private yacht? For that matter, a rigging knife in the hands of a fit twenty year old would be weapon enough, particularly at two against one.

He thought of rowing out again, at night, and climbing up the stern line. But then he'd have to search a yacht he didn't know, to find the crew. He dipped his oars again and started slowly back to the yacht club.

Night was falling, and the hillsides were lighting up. A cool wet wind came in from the east. Despite the exercise at the oars, Stone closed his windbreaker. A floating restaurant sampan came along, with a European tourist couple reclining on cushions in the stern, while an old Chinese woman served them dinner. Another sampan came by with an off-key string trio playing "Moon River."

Rowing slowly, Stone backed water to allow the restaurant sampan to cross ahead of him. It pulled alongside a big motor yacht. The cook rapped on the hull. A boatboy appeared and lowered an accommodations ladder for the woman.

Stone let the dinghy drift. In a few minutes she came back, slipped the boatboy some money, and stepped down to the floating restaurant. "You should have seen it," she told her date. "It had a bidet. Marble. With gold faucets."

Half an hour later he was back in the hotel room with a cup of tea in his hand and Ronald at his side, staring down at the typhoon shelter.

Stone waited, silent, and finally the Triad man asked, "Okay?"

"Tell me about this ECM."

Ronald shrugged. "All I know is I push a button and the water cops' radar goes bye-bye."

"You're going to operate it?"

"No. I got a kid—engineer kid. I tell him when he pushes button. Hey, relax. Comes straight from the People's Liberation Army."

"Where are you going to operate it from?"

"No more questions." He took a pair of VHF radio handsets from a leather case and gave one to Stone. "I guarantee, you radio me to jam the radar, I blind water cops."

"They can hear us on this."

"Hey, you think we amateurs? Scrambled. Nobody hears but you and me. Any more problems?"

Stone studied the chart for a few minutes. Then he went to the window and gazed down at the shelter. "I'll need a woman."

"You got her."

"Not a hooker. Just an ordinary-looking Westerner. Preferably blonde."

Ronald thought for a moment. "No problem."

"She's going to need a gun and know how to handle it."

"No problem."

"We'll need handcuffs for the boatboys."

"Already got 'em."

"Tell her no shooting. She's got to look nice and ordinary, till she takes the gun out. Then she's got to look tough."

"She is."

"Tough enough to convince the boatboys not to fight."

"I get it," said Ronald. "What else?"

Stone went back for another look at the chart, then returned to the window and stared east at the route through the strait between Hong Kong and Kowloon.

"I'll do it tonight."

"Fog tomorrow night."

"There'll be fog tonight."

"The met report says tomorrow."

Down in the shelter, Stone had smelled it on the wind. "Trust me," he said, "fog tonight. The tide turns at ten. Tell your woman to meet me in the yacht club bar at nine-thirty."

"You got it."

"What's her name?"

Ronald shrugged. "What name you want?"

Sarah was the name he wanted. "Katherine."

"You got it."

"Is she American?"

"Yes."

"Tell her she should act like a North Dakota school-teacher on Christmas vacation."

"Like apple pie."

In the yacht club library, Stone read the Shanghai section of the *Sailing Directions* for the east coast of China, and studied the charts. The city was immense. For twenty miles, both banks of the Huangpu River were lined with industrial belts of factories, railheads, coal yards, refineries, tank farms, power plants, and piers. It looked like a perfect place to hide a ship, and a terrible place to look for one.

He telephoned Falconer Nautical in Central to deliver Defense Mapping Agency Shanghai charts 94219 and 94218, and a copy of the *Sailing Directions*. Then he went into the bar and bought a carton of Marlboros. Sarah would kill him, but a pack of American cigarettes could buy a lot of friendship on the Mainland.

When "Katherine" entered the clubhouse bar at nine-thirty, Stone saw instantly that Ronald had delivered as promised. She looked exactly like she could be a school-teacher from North Dakota—a tall, big-boned, pleasant-looking woman in her early thirties. She had her hair in a ponytail, a friendly, open smile, and the slightly bedazzled expression of a recent arrival to the East.

"Katherine!" he called with a wave, and he went to greet her.

She stood half a head taller than he and greeted him in the tentative manner of a new friend. "There you are. What a neat place."

Stone introduced her to the Beast, with whom he had been drinking, and several of Simmons's friends. The bar was busy, with people crowding in from dinner. Stone ordered Katherine the Seven and Seven she requested, and while she was chatting with the others, the Beast asked, quietly, "Old friend?"

"I met her on the Tram."

"You dog. She's too tall for you, mate. She needs a big handsome Aussie, like me."

"She told me she's more interested in stamina than looks," said Stone.

Some people went out onto the terrace, and as they opened the sliding doors, a cool wet breeze entered and stirred the cigarette smoke. The lights in the shelter were turning buttery as fog rolled in from the harbor. By ten, the lights of Kowloon had disappeared and now, whenever the doors were opened, Stone could hear horns and whistles on passing vessels.

Katherine seemed thoroughly caught up in the part she was playing. She touched his glass with hers. "So how you doing?"

"Great. How about a boat ride?"

"Now? Sure. Where to?"

"We'll take a little row. Show you the shelter."

"The dog," the Beast muttered beside him.

Stone asked the bartender for a bottle of champagne and two glasses.

"Nice meeting you, everybody," said Katherine, swinging off the barstool and slipping on her big shoulder bag. "See you later."

"I like your friends," she said, loud enough for some to hear as they headed out. Stone picked up his backpack at the desk and led her down through the boat launching area to the dinghy he had borrowed. On the dock, Katherine took off her shoes. Stone helped her in and had her sit in the back, and he faced her as he rowed.

A hundred yards from the dock, whose lights were fading in the fog, he said, "Might be a good idea to open the champagne."

"In a minute." She fished in her bag. Stone glimpsed a big machine pistol. Handcuffs clinked. She came up with a capsule. In one smooth motion, she broke it under her nose, inhaled sharply, and tossed the husk overboard.

"Hey, wait a minute. I need your head on straight."

"Fuck you."

Stone back-watered one oar and turned the boat around. "Where are you going?"

"I'll drop you at the dock," he said, stroking deep and pulling hard.

"No, wait."

He saw sudden terror on her face. "If you think I'm boarding that yacht with a drug addict waving a gun, you're even crazier than you look."

"Wait. Wait. Just listen."

"You're carrying a goddamned automatic. You'll probably pull the trigger and forget to let go."

"I know how to use it. I'm a cop."

"*Cop?*"

"Ex-cop."

"You're an ex-cop? How'd you end up—"

"You really want to know how I got from Minneapolis to Hong Kong? Let's go. Please. They'll kill me if I don't deliver. Please. I'll do whatever you say. Just let's do it. Now. Please."

Stone turned the boat around and rowed. "Open the champagne."

Shifting heavily to make room for the glasses, she fumbled with the bottle, sent the cork sailing, and poured to the brim. She drained her glass in one swallow and filled it again; then, eyes bright, she leaned closer with his glass and dribbled the wine over his lips while he rowed.

"So what's the scoop?"

"See that sampan with the couple eating? If, during dinner, the woman wants to powder her nose, the sampan driver will take her to a yacht, where, for a tip, the boatboys will let her use the bathroom."

" 'Powder her nose?' Where'd you beam down from, Mars?"

"The scoop is we're going to knock on the side of *Tin Hau*, wave twenty bucks, and ask to use the facilities."

"And they're just going to let me aboard?"

"Like any other tourist who has to pee."

"And if they don't?"

"We'll do something else."

Katherine fell silent as Stone rowed down the twisting channel between the junks. Music and televisions blared. Sampans darted, bearing families on visits, and tourists and prostitutes. She studied one passing and said, bleakly, "That's where they'll put me if I screw up."

"So don't screw up."

"Fuck you. What are you doing this for? Money?"

"Do you really want to hear how I got to Hong Kong from Minneapolis?"

A smile made her mouth pretty, and she fell silent again. As they drew near *Tin Hau,* Stone shipped his oars and reached for his champagne and refilled Katherine's glass.

"Am I allowed?" she asked.

"Pretend you're having fun."

"I thought I'm supposed to look like I have to pee."

The dinghy drifted into the channel where the yacht was moored. Stone made a show of draining his glass. "Hang on, I want to eyeball her, see who's aboard."

Her decks were deserted, her lights out except for the ports in the bow, the crew's quarters. Her anchors were still stowed and her mooring lines had not been exchanged for chain. The stern line drooped, but the bow line was stretched tightly as the flood tide pushed her stem. A generator sputtered from her side, probably the auxiliary, as the main generator wouldn't be needed with the yacht essentially shut down for the night.

"Hey, look out!"

"Just waking them up," Stone told her as he bumped the dinghy into the high hull. Then he rowed to her midships and knocked on the accommodations door. He had money in his hand.

Nothing happened. He knocked again. And while he waited, he looped the dinghy's painter around a miniature Panama chock beside the door.

"I hear someone," she whispered.

The dog latch turned in its recess. Stone said, "You're on," and, to the face that peered out the crack in the door, he said, "Could the lady use your head?"

The boatboy took in the dinghy, the champagne, and Katherine.

"Oh, please," wailed Katherine. "I'm dying. Tell him in Chinese."

"He's not Chinese," said Stone. "He's Tanka."

That Stone knew the distinction drew a smile. The boatboy swung the door inward, lowered a pair of hanging steps, and offered Katherine his hand.

"Right back, honey," she called and disappeared onto the yacht, accompanied by a second boatboy, while the first stayed with Stone.

The Tanka appeared to be in his twenties, well built, and in peak condition. He gazed down from the yacht, expressionless, until he noticed Stone's waterproof backpack stowed under the seat—odd gear for a champagne row. Suddenly his eyes got big and his body stiffened. Stone caught the glint of the gun barrel against the back of his head and heard the sharp click of handcuffs snapping shut. Prodding him from the doorway, Katherine called down, "Welcome aboard."

Stone scrambled up, closed the door, and followed Katherine and her prisoner down a corridor to the head, where she had already chained the other boatboy to the plumbing. He huddled, terrified, his lips parted by a gag. Stone spread his hands wide and said, "Nobody'll be hurt."

Katherine chained his partner and gagged him too.

"Careful he doesn't choke on that."

"It's a ball gag," she said matter-of-factly. "They use them in the brothels."

The Tanka were watching anxiously. Stone said to the man who'd let them aboard, "You speak English."

He nodded.

"Okay. The sooner we're out of here, the sooner I can put you off in the dinghy. Do you understand?"

Both nodded.

"Do I have to switch on fuel and oil pumps in the engine room, or can I just crank her up from the bridge? Katherine, take the gag off this one. . . ."

"From bridge."

"Just switch them on and hit the starters?"

"Yeah."

Stone squatted down beside him and locked eyes. He jerked his thumb at Katherine. "She's a crazy drug addict. If there's trouble she's going to start shooting. I can't control her. So I'm asking you again, can I just crank 'em up from the bridge?"

"All on bridge."

"Good. Now you got single bow and stern line?"

"Yes."

"Any more lines?" Stone asked, to see if he would lie.

"Two lines yacht beside."

"Good. Katherine, stay with them."

"He's lying," she said, "or he's holding something back."

Stone squatted down again. "Anything else I should know about? Just so nobody gets hurt?"

The Tanka exchanged sullen glances.

"What? I'm warning you guys, you don't want us getting caught."

The man they had ungagged said, "Port engine, kaphlooey."

"What do you mean?"

"Changing oil pump."

"Christ on a crutch." Stone rocked back on his heels, cursing Ronald's lousy intelligence. "How fast will she go on the starboard engine only?"

"Twelve knots."

"Is that bad?" asked Katherine.

"It means they can chase us with sailboats."

16

"Okay. Take 'em down to the engine room. You guys fix the oil pump—don't tell me you can't. You're not getting off till that engine's up again."

The boatboys exchanged a look. The one who spoke English said, "No part."

"What do you mean?" But Stone knew. Halfway through the job they'd had to stop to wait for a part. A gasket, it turned out. There'd be no oil pressure without it. "Okay," he told Katherine. "You stay with them."

"What about the engine?"

"If we can get out of here without waking up half the typhoon shelter, maybe we'll be okay."

"Maybe."

"You owe Ronald. My family's counting on me."

On the main deck he kept to the shadows, cast off the two side lines and the heavy stern line. Then he found a fire axe and laid it beside the taut bow line.

Up on the lofty bridge deck he could see over the tops

of the smaller boats. The typhoon shelter looked quiet, with only the occasional moving light of a sampan. He could see over the stone breakwater. The harbor was enveloped in thick fog. But as he hunted for a switch to light the control console, he saw a blinking blue light approaching the breakwater pass.

Stone froze, eyes locked on the pass. It was a patrol boat, emerging from the fog. There were two cops aboard, one steering, one on the radio. Had he tripped a silent alarm?

The boat entered the pass slowly, circled the small basin which was surrounded by moored boats. It was a semirigid inflatable powered by a pair of enormous outboards, capable of thirty knots. A stanchion on the bow held a radome. It went out again into the harbor, sped up, and vanished.

Stone played his penlight over the console and moved a toggle with trembling fingers. The starboard engine gauges gave off a faint red glow. He turned the key. The fuel alarm buzzed discreetly. He ground the starter.

Needles spun and from far below came a muted rumble. He turned on the radar, the depth finder, and the running lights. Then he hurried down to the main deck and ran forward. The bow line was taut as steel cable as the tide pushed the hull. Standing clear, Stone swung the axe at the point where the two-inch line met the mooring bollard. The rope knocked the axe out of his hand and twanged into the dark.

The yacht began to drift back on the next line of boats. He raced to the dark main cabin, up the stairs, into the darkened bridge, guided by the red lit console. A glance aft showed *Tin Hau*'s stern was yards from the bow of a big staysail schooner and closing fast. He engaged the starboard prop. The deck trembled and the tachometer dropped precipitously as the cold engine threatened to stall.

He fed it fuel, gently nursing it. The tach needle trembled. He looked back. The staysail schooner's masts were gyrating wildly. He thought that *Tin Hau*'s stern had crashed into her bow. But as *Tin Hau* moved ahead, he realized it was only her prop wash that was manhandling the schooner.

He throttled back and aimed the bow at the pass, abruptly aware she was a very long boat. For all his I-can-drive-anything-that-floats claim when the Triad asked if he could handle it, the fact was that Tin Hau was practically a ship—three times the length of Veronica and fifteen times her bulk. With only one engine it would take a fine touch on the helm to squeeze through the breakwater without crunching the rocks.

He lined up the bow and looked back to check the stern. Someone was standing on the schooner's foredeck shaking his fist, a boatboy rudely awakened. Another boatboy appeared on the motor cruiser that Tin Hau had lain alongside. He watched as Stone eased the big yacht toward the pass and then he noticed the lines Stone had cast into the water.

Stone couldn't tell what he did next because he was too busy trying to steer the ungainly hull. Rudder hard over, he started to power into the left turn the boat was refusing to make. But just then a cotton billow of fog rushed across his bow from the east. He throttled back instead, hoping that the wind gust would push the bow around for him. For several long seconds the bow hung in stasis. Then it swung toward the pass. He gave the engine some power, and the yacht lumbered between the rocks and into the harbor.

He lined her up on a compass course to the east and looked back. Already the typhoon shelter was a barely visible soft hint of light. And when he looked again—after setting the radar to short range and fiddling the gain knob—the glow astern had vanished. Ahead was fog, black as the inside of a barrel.

The radar was the latest commercial Furuno, a unit he would have killed for on Veronica, with all the bells and whistles and a big full-color monitor that displayed the shoreline, and the vessels in the harbor with the startling clarity of a big-screen movie.

The way ahead was clear. He pushed the throttle forward. The big yacht squatted heavily in her stern and gradually picked up speed. It took her two long miles to peak at fourteen knots—two better than her boatboys had predicted. Stone shoved harder on the throttle, but she had reached her limit. Without her second engine, the hull would not lift onto a plane.

He engaged the autopilot and coaxed it to compensate for the off-center thrust of the single engine. Then he surveyed the radar screen for obstructions ahead and pursuit behind. He set the ARPA plotting aid to track two vessels: a slow-moving, ship-sized target a half mile ahead and a swift echo behind he suspected was the patrol boat heading north toward Kowloon. He nudged the ARPA cursor over each to monitor their direction and speed and instructed the computer to warn him if either changed course.

Suddenly Ronald spoke on the scrambled VHF radio, his voice loud and clear. *"Hey, Doc. Why you no go fast?"*

"I 'no go fast,' you son of a bitch, because you didn't tell me they had an engine down."

"Down?"

"They're changing an oil pump."

"That's okay, man. No sweat. We got you on the radar. You home free."

"Bullshit!" It was still a long thirteen miles to the PRC border. And the worst five were coming up—narrow channels and crowded waters.

A diamond-shaped signal winked on the radar screen. The ARPA was warning him that the police boat, which had been heading toward Kowloon, had changed course. He radioed Ronald: "I think water cops got me on their radar."

"No sweat. I jam 'em."

Stone's radar screen turned a bright shade of red. On the radio, he could hear Ronald laughing. *"He's blind. He's blind."*

"So am I," Stone radioed back. "Turn the damned thing off. I've got a ship dead ahead."

The Triad cut the electronic countermeasure signal.

Stone's radar screen flickered, and suddenly the harbor was back, showing the shores of the Tathong Channel on either side, a ship an eighth of a mile ahead. Four miles astern, the police boat altered course and zeroed in on him like a laser.

He radioed Ronald to jam their radar again, but he didn't answer, and the police boat kept coming.

"Ronald."

No response.

Stone steered for the ship.

Then he locked the helm and stepped out the narrow wing deck to eyeball it. The wet wind tore at him, stinking of bunker fuel. He was staring into the fog when he sensed bulk overhead and saw a freighter towering over him as the yacht tore along her side.

He took the helm again, edged away, then slipped in behind her stern as he and the ship passed in opposite directions.

Katherine spoke and he jumped. He hadn't heard her come up and had no idea how long she'd been standing behind him in the dark.

"How are we doing?"

"Fog's so thick the cops can't see without radar. I just put a big ship between us. They won't be able to track us for a minute."

"Ronald told me he had all these high-tech electronics."

"Ronald's deeper in cyberspace than reality. Another mile and we can swing east again. Get the boys to the accommodations hatch. Have a look, make sure the dinghy's still attached. Take this handset. Give me a yell when you're ready. I'll stop the boat so you can put them over the side."

"Why bother?"

"My problems—and yours—aren't their fault."

Four minutes later, when he was ready to turn between Joss House Bay and Tung Lung Island, he tried again to radio Ronald to jam the radar. No response. "Off!" he yelled, but the picture on the radar screen remained intact.

As the distance grew between them, the ship wouldn't screen him from the police radar.

He throttled back and ran below. Katherine—who he had half feared would murder the two men—had her hands full, trying to unlock their handcuffs and still control them. Miraculously, the dinghy, which he had snubbed close, was still attached, banging alongside as the yacht made a knot or two against the tide.

"Where's the emergency locker?" he asked the boatboy.

Behind a teak panel were life raft canisters, flashlights, wooden plugs, life preservers, space blankets, and food and water. Stone yanked a raft canister from the locker and threw it out the door. The white cylinder popped open when it hit the water and the bright orange raft inflated.

He threw the second raft after it.

Then, while Katherine covered *Tin Hau*'s boatboys with the gun, he opened two of the space blankets and wrapped the shiny foil squares around their shoulders and ordered them into the dinghy. They went quickly, relief visible on their faces.

Stone released the painter with a quick jerk and cast it into the dinghy as the little boat fell behind. Then he latched the door and raced up to the bridge, with Katherine running after him. "Wha'd you throw all that junk for?"

"Same reason I gave the boys blankets."

On the bridge, he jammed the throttle full forward and spun the helm. The yacht dipped its stern and careened toward the east, leaving behind three bright echoes on the radar screen—the two life rafts and the dinghy carrying the Tanka boatboys wrapped in reflective blankets.

"By the time the cops sort out who's who and pick up the boatboys, I'm hoping to hell we'll be on the other side of Tung Lung."

At fourteen knots, it took four minutes to slip between the island and the bright lights of Joss House Bay. Ten minutes later, Stone was steering through a cluster of small islands and beginning to believe he had pulled it off. Almost to the open sea.

"What are all these?" Katherine asked, leaning over his shoulder to point to a group of new echoes that suddenly appeared in the south. The radar hadn't distinguished them at first from the bright target of Waglan Light. Stone hit the Acquisition button again and set the cursor to track them. It took the ARPA two minutes to develop a vector on the new targets. They were traveling at forty knots on an intercepting course.

Stone radioed Ronald to shut down their radar. No response. He tried again and again.

"What's the matter?"

"Ronald's still lost."

"What are you going to do?"

Stone switched on the port engine. It might start in its present condition, but it wouldn't run long. The fuel alarm sounded. He hit the starter. The diesel fired up instantly. He shoved the throttle wide open.

Tin Hau surged as if struck from behind.

Katherine pointed at the oil pressure gauge. The needle was pegged at zero.

"The new owner is going to need a new engine."

"How long can it run without oil?"

"Pray for five minutes."

The knot meter flashed as the broad hull rose on a fast plane, pounding the tops of the swells, shaking the yacht and heaving spray into the fog. Twenty . . . twenty-five . . . thirty-five knots.

But the port engine temperature gauge was climbing relentlessly into the red. An alarm shrilled. The engine stopped as suddenly as it had started. The yacht plowed down into the water, losing speed so abruptly that Stone and the woman were thrown against the control console.

"Fuel cutoff to protect the engine. Son of a bitch!"

Katherine pulled her pistol from her bag and headed for the door.

"What are you doing?"

"I'll hold them off."

"Forget it," said Stone. He had once glimpsed inside the arms locker of a Hong Kong water patrol, which had hailed *Veronica* for a drug check. Remington shotguns and automatic rifles. "Put it away," he told her. "You're outgunned."

"I'm not going to a Chinese prison." She cocked her weapon and pushed through the door.

Stone thumbed the radio again. "Ronald? Ronald?"

The radar display filled with blinking diamond light symbols as the pursuit boats came into the threat zone. Three blinking diamonds astern. And now, suddenly, two ahead on a converging course.

17

"THEY'RE COMING FROM BOTH SIDES," HE YELLED TO KATHERINE. "Come on, we'll swim for it."

The wind tore her voice from the darkness overhead. "Fuck you."

Stone raced below to the accommodations door, pulled a life jacket out of the emergency locker, strapped it on, doused the light, and opened the door on the water rushing three feet below the sill. The longer he waited to jump, the closer the yacht would bring him to the coast, but the more likely the patrol boats would spot him in the water.

A form took sudden hard shape alongside and a spotlight pinned him in the doorway. He gathered his legs to jump.

"Follow me!" Ronald's amplified voice echoed over the water. "Follow me!"

A fast motor cutter flying the lighted flag of the People's Liberation Army pulled alongside. The Triad himself was standing in the light, waving as the wind tore at his white suit and whipped his tie over his shoulder.

Stone ran back up to the helm. The cutter tucked in under his bow and altered course. Stone turned with him, then checked the radar. A half dozen winking diamonds began to drop back.

Katherine bounded through the door. "What happened?"

"That's Ronald ahead of us with his PLA pals. And those"—pointing at the screen—"are PLA gunboats informing some very pissed-off cops that it's finders keepers."

"Now what?"

"Now we'll see if Ronald is an honorable gangster."

In the lee of the San-Men Islands, Ronald radioed Stone to stop the yacht and turn on her floodlights. The cutter's own lights illuminated heavy machine guns on the bow and wheelhouse. Seamen secured the two vessels gunnel to gunnel. Stone watched from the bridge as Ronald was helped between them. He trotted up the companionway, beaming.

"Good job, sailorman!" He walked around the bridge, peering at the instruments, and clapped his hands proudly on the helm. "Good job."

Stone nodded toward Katherine. "Your young lady was a big help."

"Mr. Chang very grateful."

Out of the fog, a thirty-foot wooden fishing junk approached the pool of light cast by the vessels and eased alongside the gunboat. "Okay, sailorman. Here comes your ride."

Stone put on his backpack.

"What about me?" asked Katherine.

"You stay."

"What?"

Ronald swept his hand in a broad gesture of appreciation for the lavish yacht. "Mr. Chang say beautiful boat, beautiful hostess."

"Wait a minute. You're telling me I have to go to the *Mainland*?"

"Package deal. New owner gets deluxe package."

"I don't want to go to the Mainland."

"No one ask you."

Katherine turned to Stone. "This isn't fair. I delivered. Tell him I did my job."

"She did," said Stone. "I couldn't have done it without her."

Ronald returned a cold smile. "Sailorman, I go to big trouble for you. Shanghai. Papers. Hotel. Guide. Everything for your gas ship."

"All I'm saying is give her a break."

"You want to go Shanghai? Or you knight in shiny armor?"

"You wouldn't have your boat without her."

Ronald paused, pretending to consider that argument. He said, "Okay, shiny knight. *You* deliver yacht," and Stone realized a beat too late that he'd been set up. The Triad wanted another service and had counted on the foolish American to back himself into it.

"To Shanghai?"

"Those guys," Ronald explained, nodding at the PLA boats, "maybe they steal yacht from me and Mr. Chang. We trust you more."

"You said you'd put me on a steamer."

"Keep hostess. Turn on autopilot. Eight hundred miles fuck-fuck."

"Not on one engine."

Ronald leaned out the door and streamed a torrent of Cantonese. Four men and a boy scrambled aboard and trooped down to the engine room. "They fix."

"There's a gasket missing."

The Triad laughed. "Mainland mechanics poor people. Fix anything. Make new gasket from helper's skin."

"What about Shanghai Customs?"

"Yangtze fish boat bring new papers offshore."

"You coming too?"

"No way. Patrols catch, cut balls off. Hers too. Deal?"

Stone looked at Katherine, who said, "Beats his last offer."

"Katherine goes home from Shanghai?"

"First class," Ronald promised. "And you use yacht to find gas ship."

"In Shanghai? This thing'll stand out like a Maserati."

Ronald shrugged. "Any boat you want. But no screwup, no mind change. Mr. Chang get pissed, he send choppers cut my hands off. Before he get me, I get you, sailorman. I take big chance on you."

Pumped up by the run from Hong Kong, Stone suddenly saw that he had cast his lot with a juggler who had too many balls in the air.

"You want the gas ship, but you couldn't talk Chang into it. All he wanted was this boat."

Ronald got an angry glint in his eye. "Mr. Chang grateful for ship of gas."

"Bull. He knows he's thin on the ground in Shanghai. Probably afraid you'll start a turf war with the locals."

The gangster gazed back impassively, the glint of anger less extinguished than concealed. Stone shut up. He knew he was right, but it was too late to change allies on the stolen yacht. "You got to leave me a mechanic. If she breaks down in the Taiwan Strait, we're both screwed."

"Okay, okay, I give you mechanic."

Katherine had caught Stone's mood. "Make it two in case we need more skin."

Ronald crossed the distance between them in a single liquid step and slapped Katherine so hard she staggered. She held her face, saw blood on her hand, and whipped the machine pistol out of her bag.

Ronald stared contemptuously into the barrel. "You shoot Triad?"

Stone, regretting already he had stuck his neck out, stepped between them. "Put it away."

"I'm going to kill the fucker."

"You owe me."

"Both owe *me*," said Ronald. "No forget."

Tin Hau's Sea Talk system integrated GPS, radar, depth finder, and ARPA, which made navigation pretty much a matter of feeding in a course and turning on the autopilot. Stone trusted none of it, not in coastal waters heavily fished by wooden trawlers.

He slung a hammock in the bridge house. But soon after he showed Katherine how to use the system, he came to trust her judgment and slept relatively peacefully when it was her turn to stand watch.

They cleared up Ronald's eight-hundred-mile "fuck-fuck" the first night when Katherine said, "I owe you. But don't think I want it."

"Thanks, but I'll pass," said Stone. "I got worse problems."

It had been eight days since the ship had taken Sarah and Ronnie. Ample time to steam twice the distance to Shanghai. They could be in any of fifty ports. Or drowned in fifty fathoms.

18

"Not exactly Shanghai, is it, Doc?" Mr. Jack called mockingly from the bed. His voice was stronger, his New York accent sharper.

Sarah was at the porthole, watching the tugs.

Belching steam and coal smoke, they were working the ship alongside a pier in a cold, driving rain. But instead of the 1920s European skyline of Shanghai's Bund, all she could see was gray marsh and mud flats that stretched to the horizon, dwarfing an electric power station that could have been any coastal generating plant in the world.

The pier extended a half mile into an otherwise empty bay. Across the marsh, the flat sweep of the land was briefly interrupted by four tall chimneys. At their feet crouched the turbine house, a building of mud-colored brick. Pylons marched inland, while a pipeline connected the plant to the domed liquid natural gas storage tanks that huddled like gigantic igloos along the shore.

The old man's mind was labyrinthine, as complex as the

mare's nest of piping that connected the gas manifolds on the pierhead to the storage tanks. But this much Sarah had learned since her patient had regained his faculties: he said nothing without a purpose; every question was a test.

And so she answered, "I've never seen Shanghai."

In fact, thanks to Ronnie's GPS, she knew their position to the degree, minute, and second. If her memory of Shanghai's coordinates was correct, then they were fairly close, perhaps an inlet of the Huangpu River or along a stretch of Hang-chou Bay. Surely the power pylons marching off to the northeast served a city.

The mud flats could be on the Yangtze River a bit north or Ch'ung-Ming Island in its delta or the city of Hang-chou south and west. The *Dallas Belle*'s chart room would hold the answer, she supposed, staring gloomily out the rain-streaked glass.

She felt herself sliding deeper and deeper into depression, drugged by it, unable to think clearly. The long days and nights of captivity had been blending together ever since the tugs had picked up the drifting ship.

Endless days adrift, engines stopped, in fog and rain, until the terrible afternoon she and Ronnie had crept through the bowels of the ship: Moss materializing like a creature from hell, Mr. Jack's vicious threat to order Moss to "punish" her. The word made her feel as powerless as a slave.

His threat had coincided with the sudden dramatic appearance of the trio of tugs flying red flags and billowing smoke like a Turner seascape. And had lingered throughout the long tow at four knots. What landfall beside this marsh in the middle of nowhere would mean to her and Ronnie, she didn't want to guess.

Now she counted time by the degrees Mr. Jack strengthened and poor Ah Lee's bruises yellowed. She hardly remembered the gas leak—the pluming cloud in the sky—and her frantic run for the satellite phone, when she still felt brave.

"Hey, kid!"

Ronnie looked up from the book he had given her. "Yes, Mr. Jack?"

"Run down and tell the cook we want ice cream sundaes."

Ronnie looked at Sarah. She nodded it was all right. As soon as she was out the door, Mr. Jack said, "Say, Doc? Ronnie's told me all about growing up on the sailboat. What about you? Where you from? You a Brit?"

"I'm Nigerian," she answered, wondering at his sudden interest.

"Talk like a Brit."

"My father was a soldier. He sent my mother and me to England during the Civil War. We lived with his former C.O. My mother died and I was sent to convent school."

"Your father was a British soldier?"

"Until Independence. Then he helped form the Nigerian Army."

"What was his name?"

"Soditan. Josiah Soditan."

"Really? I met him."

"You're joking."

"Let me tell you something, sweetheart, if you're in the oil business in Nigeria, you damned well better know the generals."

"My father was not corrupt."

The old man shrugged, winced. "I wouldn't know. Pulled out twenty years ago when I saw the whole kit and kaboodle sliding downhill. What a mess they made of that country. Nigeria could have ruled Africa. Your father mixed up in those coups?"

"No."

Mr. Jack looked at her sharply. "Big man, wasn't he? Bigger than Moss?"

"Much bigger," said Sarah, and, to her surprise, she started to cry.

"Hey, hey, hey. What are you crying for? I told you you'll be okay if you don't step outta line."

"I'm worried sick about my husband."

The rocky planes of Mr. Jack's face softened and he looked, Sarah thought, almost grandfatherly, almost gentle.

"Relax, Doc. He's doing fine."

"You don't know that!"

"He's holed up in the Hong Kong Yacht Club."

She didn't dare believe him. It had to be a trick. And yet . . . She watched with hope flaming inside her as Mr. Jack fumbled for a manila envelope that lay on his night table. Unable to pick it up with his nailless fingers, he slid it off the table onto the bedsheets. She took it gingerly, not knowing what to hope for.

"Open it."

Sarah opened the flap and extracted a fax of a photograph. Her heart jumped. It was shot at long range through a window, but the thrust of his shoulders and the demanding angle of his head could only be Michael Stone.

"This was taken at the Hilton."

Sarah felt suddenly so light she could float. She turned to Mr. Jack with joy that Michael was alive and an almost overwhelming sense of gratitude.

"Thank you." But even as she uttered the words, the cruelty made her sick: she was thanking a monster for inflicting less pain. Ronnie wasn't the only one susceptible to Stockholm syndrome.

"How did you—how did you get this picture? How did you find him in Hong Kong?"

"Come on, Doc, who do you think you're messing with here? We monitor everything incoming and outgoing. You telephoned Marcus Salinis in Koror. Moss had my people tap Salinis's phones and your husband called Hong Kong. When he flew there we were waiting for him."

She was shocked. She had feared they knew about the satellite phone call, but it had never occurred to her that Mr. Jack's power ranged so far beyond the ship—that he was part of something much larger. Or that simply escaping from the ship would not guarantee survival.

"Who's the man he's talking to?" Mr. Jack asked.

Every instinct demanded she deny she knew Kerry; but surely he knew the salvage man's identity already. Mr. Jack was an intriguer. And this was, under the guise of kindness, another test of her trustworthiness. "That's Captain McGlynn," she admitted. "He owns a salvage company."

"Good answer, Doc. What do you think they're talking about?"

"I'm sure you can guess, Mr. Jack."

"Yeah, well . . ."

"When was this snapshot taken?"

"Couple of days ago. How in hell did he get off that atoll?"

Sarah smiled. Her heart was swelling with relief and pride. "Sailed, I would think."

"What do you think he's going to pull next?"

"God knows."

"God isn't here. Care to guess?"

Sarah shook her head.

"I'm just curious," said Mr. Jack. "He's no threat. No way. I just hope for his and your sake he doesn't pull some dumb stunt."

Sarah looked down at her hands. She knew Michael too well to suppose he would sit around the Hong Kong Yacht Club very long.

Mr. Jack chuckled. "Tell you something, sweetheart. If I'd been functional the day we met you, I'd have brought him aboard with you and the kid. What do you think he's up to? You told him you thought we were heading for Shanghai or Taiwan. Where you think he'll go?"

"I honestly don't know."

"Think he'll go to the authorities?"

"I don't know."

"But you don't think so."

Again she looked away, her mind racing as she realized

belatedly that their entire conversation, including his assurances about Michael, had been a prelude to this interrogation.

"You'll find," he said silkily, "another picture in that envelope."

An extreme close-up fell into her lap. It showed the hairs in Michael's beard, the squint lines radiating from his eyes, and the several scars that chronicled the accidents of a life at sea. He looked thin and haggard as he leaned closer to Kerry. She was startled and saddened by how much gray had permeated his beard, a spreading stain she had barely noticed when they were together but which in this photograph spoke of the age of an exhausted, desperate man.

She touched the white crescent scar under his eye. It never tanned, and every time she looked in his face it reminded her of the demon in her heart.

"What's that?" asked Mr. Jack. He nudged her finger. "Is that a birthmark?"

"A scar."

His shrewd eyes raked her face. She wondered if the truth might fool the old man into believing she had warmed to him. It was worth any advantage.

"I hit him with the binoculars."

"You? Miss sugar and kindness? Why?"

"He told me he didn't love me."

"So why are you bugging me to let you go back to him?"

"He was lying."

"Why?"

"To protect me."

"From what?"

"It was many years ago. I was very young. I'd never been in love before."

"Marriage cure you of that?"

Sarah fixed him with a deep and steady gaze. "He is the air I breathe."

Michael had been trying to protect her, insulting their

love in a clumsy attempt to drive her away. To this day she could feel the weight of the binoculars in her hand, and the snarl lifting her lips from her teeth like an animal. She would always be the soldier's daughter, she thought bitterly, forever failing to smother her father's blood with high ideals and her faith in God.

"Moss thinks you two are on the lam. Wha'd you do, rob a bank?"

It was hard to concentrate: she was so happy for this proof that Michael was alive.

"Hey, it doesn't matter to me," the old man said. "I don't give a damn who your husband asks for help. He'll never find the *Dallas Belle*. We don't exist. . . ."

"Is that by plan?"

"Better believe it. It took a lot of planning not to exist. A lot of planning and a lot of money."

"Why?" she asked.

"Why don't you just worry about keeping me alive?"

"Which is precisely why I want you in hospital." As she spoke her hand drifted automatically to her stethoscope. She slipped the other into the side pocket of the steward's jacket she had taken to wearing as her white medical coat. "I am worried about infection. I'm worried about pneumonia."

"I've known plenty of people have caught infections and pneumonia in the hospital, Doc. I'm better off on the ship than in some filthy Chinese hospital."

"It's a two-hour flight from Shanghai to Hong Kong," Sarah retorted.

"Can't do it, Doc. Besides, I don't see Shanghai, do you?"

She ignored the jibe. "I am particularly concerned about the potential for a stroke."

"Stroke?" He looked at her sharply. "What are you talking about?"

"By all reports, and by the strength of your constitution, it's obvious to me that you are an active man."

"There's a room full of Nautilus machines on C deck. I keep in shape. That's why I'm healing fast."

"Yes, quite. But in my experience, sudden layups like yours spawn strokes. Lying immobile, day after day, is dangerous for an older man who is ordinarily active."

"I'm not getting any strokes."

"I can't treat a stroke. Treatment in the first twenty-four hours is crucial to minimize the damage and ensure the recovery. Surely a man your age has seen friends struck down by stroke. You know the results."

"Not in the cards, Doc. . . . You think maybe I should have some therapy. Physical therapy?"

"Perhaps Moss can walk you about . . . perhaps a little work on your machines. How long will we be here?"

"Not long."

"Then what?"

"One step at a time, Doc. . . . " He smiled. "Besides, you wouldn't believe me if I told you."

Sarah retreated to the window. The rain was falling harder. The ship had stopped moving so gradually she hadn't noticed, and it was now tied to the pier. The three tugs were steaming off into the rain, flags snapping in the wind, trailing the acrid stench of burning coal.

God knew what Mr. Jack was up to, but at least she had managed to frighten him with talk of a stroke.

"Hey, Doc," he called across the cabin, "if you're practicing any kind of African voodoo mental telepathy with your husband, tell him he won't be as lucky in Shanghai as he was in Hong Kong."

"What do you mean?" she asked, alarmed that he had already tried to hurt Michael and would try again.

"Shanghai is *my* town."

19

A SHANGHAI PILOT TOOK *TIN HAU'S* HELM SEAWARD OF THE BAR, and Stone felt his sense of time shift backward as he compared the riverbanks to chart 94219. Cold, damp air muffled the sound of engines; horns and whistles moaned. Coal smoke hung heavy on a lifeless wind. Pungent in his nostrils, stinging his eyes, it spread across the mud flats, mingling indistinctly with the sky.

The sight of three ancient steam tugs preceding the yacht up the channel—the immediate source of the smoke—furthered the impression of being far away in another time, as did the wooden barges, lighters, and motor sampans, and legions of seamen doing the work of machines. Dickens's London would have *smelled* the same.

Stone shifted his attention to an enormous Wusong shipyard coming up on the starboard side. Icy rain swept the deck. He backed into the cabin, water dripping from the winter-weight trenchcoat Ronald's Yangtze fishing boat had delivered along with their visas.

After two days' study of the chart, he knew both banks of the river by heart. But the Huangpu snaked through the biggest city in the world, and paper and ink had not prepared him for the sheer size of the harbor, the breadth of the river, or the endless stretches of mud flats.

The Donghai yard began to rise on the riverbank. He was stunned by the immensity of the search he had set himself. In this yard alone, a forest of gantries and derricks crowded around a dozen hulls; some were practically curtained from view by bamboo scaffolding, while over one slip stood a shed roof broad enough to shelter a battleship.

According to the chart and the *Sailing Directions,* there were nine such shipyards in the fifteen miles of navigable water depicted, six dry docks, a refinery, and ninety-eight wharfs alongside tank farms, terminals, and factories. Fifteen creeks, canals, and rivers slipped off into the interior, some possibly deep enough for the *Dallas Belle.* And, as the *Sailing Directions* dated from 1979, when port development had just begun, the numbers might easily have doubled by now.

The next shipyard had its slips covered by a pair of sheds so broad and tall that the gantries stood under their roofs. One berth was empty. The other contained a cruise liner. In the gray morning, he saw the purposeful wink of welding and cutting torches and fiery cascades of sparks as workmen swarmed on the bamboo scaffolding that crosshatched its wedding-cake superstructure.

The cold rain came down harder. Things could be worse, he thought. December was a month notorious for morning fog. Suddenly the rain became a cloudburst, dense as fog. As it swept in, it obscured the riverbanks, imprinting upon Stone's eye a murky, gray impression of thousands of Chinese commuters under black umbrellas and slick raincoats crowding onto the pontoons of a ferry head.

"Look at all those people." Katherine shuddered. "Millions of 'em. Like ants— God, I want to go home."

Stone said nothing. She had been a good shipmate, quick to help with boat chores and always ten minutes early on watch. She had known when to talk and when not to, and despite her myriad problems, she moved with a brave assurance that he found appealing.

But "home" was not an option for a cop who'd been caught riding shotgun for her drug-dealer boyfriend. She'd told him about it the second night as *Tin Hau* pounded through the Taiwan Strait. An assistant DA, hot for her, had warned her in time to flee the indictment.

When at last the squall moved on, he could see fading astern a petroleum tank farm where the *Dallas Belle* might be unloading. He marked it on the chart. Ahead, on either bank of the river were more ferries, the passengers arriving on bicycles. Then another shipyard, half hidden up a broad creek.

Rain swept the river again, and again he couldn't see a hundred yards. He paced the deck, traversing the yacht, frustrated and confused, his binoculars useless, his chart soaked. After an interminable wait, while shipyards and piers slipped by, unseen, the rain lifted briefly. He glimpsed a coal yard, hundreds of sampans crowding its docks, and then, on the east side of the river, the enormous Shanghai Shipyard, where he searched in vain for the sand-colored *Dallas Belle*.

The rain descended like a curtain, and again he was blind. When at last it lifted, the Bund stood a mile ahead, rising above the chaos of the river like a Wizard-of-Oz vision of stately colonial banks and trading houses, stone skyscrapers, and a nineteenth-century clock tower. Stone looked back. Astern were miles of riverbank he hadn't seen.

The slow-moving yacht stopped and the pilot worked her against a wharf. Stone threw lines to longshoremen, who singled her up and secured a gangway. People's Liberation Army soldiers in green uniforms took up position at its foot, and a customs officer in navy blue boarded. He stamped Stone's and Katherine's visas, which allowed them three months in China.

Stone changed into dry clothes, a business suit sent by

Ronald with a note, *You dress like slob, sailorman.* It fit the cover story that he was scouting sites for a luxury marina. Katherine had to help him knot the first tie he had worn in years. She said, "I guess I'm supposed to wait here. Maybe I'll catch you later."

He packed his papers, letters of introduction, and business cards, took his backpack. "Thanks for everything." He would have embraced her with a friendly hug, but all her defenses were up. He offered his hand.

"Good luck with your family."

A passenger ship had docked ahead of them and the pier was crowded with waiting relatives, watched impassively by the bored-looking PLA soldiers. It was, he thought, despite the washout of his river surveillance, almost too easy.

Five soldiers. A couple of plainclothes cops. And a neatly dressed Shanghainese waving from the edge of the throng. Stone worked his way through hugging relatives and cardboard boxes and introduced himself.

"I am William Sit," said the Shanghainese, with a shy smile. "I will be your translator. I am an English teacher. It is certain that your visit will help me a lot in learning modern English."

"Your English sounds great."

"Maybe there is a bit difficulty in understanding the idioms and slangs. You will give me more help and courage."

"You got it," said Stone, hefting his backpack impatiently. "Shall we . . . ?"

Sit looked confused. Confusion turned to embarrassment. "Shall we . . . ?"

"Go," said Stone. "Shall we go?"

"Go! Yes. Yes. My friend has a taxi. He will drive us." His friend, who wore a black suit and a chauffeur's cap, was named Wang. *Mr.* Wang. His taxi was black, shiny, and well kept, and Sit explained as they got in that Mr. Wang drove for a state factory but had taken time off to drive Stone.

"Shall we?" asked Sit. "Shall we go to the hotel?"

"Do you have any messages for me?"

"No."

"How close is the hotel?"

"Only one mile."

"Fine." Ronald's letter had said that "certain people" might contact him at the hotel. "Then we'll drive around the waterfront."

"Mr. Wang will drive you if you prefer, but your friends have arranged a boat."

"Okay, let's just hit the hotel and then—"

Sit looked desperate. "Hit?"

"I want to check in and get my messages, and then he can drive us to the boat."

"Shall we?" responded Sit, with a smile.

William Sit spoke to Mr. Wang—explaining to Stone that he was speaking the Shanghainese dialect Wu—and the taxi drove out of the Waihongqiau dockyard past a long procession of the other ship's passengers carrying their bundles into the city.

"The great changes have taken place in Shanghai," said William Sit as the taxi left the shabby dockyards behind and crossed Suzhou Creek. The rain had lifted again, and from the arching bridge they could see in every direction hundreds of office towers under construction—steel and concrete girders soaring inside cocoons of bamboo scaffolding—and hundreds more completed buildings standing dark. He searched the piers for the *Dallas Belle*, but saw only passenger liners and excursion boats.

"Shanghai is not the same as the old Shanghai, but perhaps soon we will overtake Hong Kong."

Stone had heard that talk around the Pacific for years. Only first they'd have to wire the city for modern communications; improve the port by inventing some way to deepen the mouth of the Huangpu so ships wouldn't have to offload half their cargo at sea; permit a freely convertible currency; establish a legal system to solve business disputes; and eliminate the grim, damp winters.

"The traffic has been being improved," said William Sit. And in the park beside the river, he told Stone, he could watch tai chi at dawn. Stone had already spotted a landing where the boat could pick him up.

The Peace Hotel, a huge old structure, lowered over the park and the river. Faded grandeur—gloomy coffered ceilings, dark woodwork, and shoddy new partitions—was enlivened by a clientele of Hong Kong salesmen on the make.

Check-in went smoothly. An English-speaking assistant manager plucked Stone from the line and registered him personally. Again, it felt too easy, and he worried about the ultimate price.

Somewhere between Hong Kong and Shanghai he had begun a transition from fugitive sailor to the city man he had been for the many years he and Katherine had lived in New York. Taking stock of the hotel lobby, he realized he almost felt comfortable. It seemed that the ground had stopped rolling underfoot, and his senses had refocused on a more human, warier scale than sailing alone with his wife and daughter required.

"One message, sir. Shall I translate?"

William Sit, who had hovered so deferentially, snatched the paper from the assistant manager's hand. "I will translate. . . . You are invited to breakfast at Huxingting Teahouse." He puffed with pride. "Dim sum. Mr. Wang will drive us."

"Who invited me?"

"Mr. Yu. Consultant to Fuxing Islet container terminal. Mr. Yu would know many sites for your marina."

"I don't have time. I have to get to the boat."

"This message says boat not ready."

Stone's jaw tightened. Less invitation than command. "Okay, let's go."

"You no want see room?" asked the manager.

"Later." Stone picked up his backpack and headed for the street. William Sit scampered after him. Stone asked, "Is Mr. Yu a Triad?"

William Sit's mouth dropped. He laughed, covering his lips. "Why ask such a question?"

"Where I come from, waterfront 'consultants' are gangsters."

Sit gave Mr. Wang their destination and climbed in beside Stone, clearly upset.

Stone asked him, "How'd you get the job translating for me?"

"Friend of wife's cousin," Sit answered, his English suddenly clumsy. There was an elegance about him which suggested he came from an educated family that would have suffered terribly during Liberation, Great Leaps, and Mao's Cultural Revolution. Now, in boom times, a teacher hard-pressed by inflation would seize any opportunity for extra income.

Wang drove them up the Bund and stopped in the narrow streets of the Old Town. They walked to the Yu Garden. Just inside the gate, Sit led Stone across a pool on a zig-zagged bridge into a two-story wooden teahouse with dragon-decorated roofs. The tables were crowded with older Chinese and a sprinkling of Western tourists. Middle-aged waitresses carried trays of dim sum around the restaurant.

"Your President Richard Nixon drink tea here," said William Sit.

"Terrific. Is that Mr. Yu?"

At a window table by the pool sat a beefy Shanghainese in a business suit. He had the hard eyes and battered face of a man who won street fights, and was pretty much what Stone had expected: an Asian version of a bad-tempered Irish or Italian mobster on the Brooklyn waterfront. His companion, seated with his flashily draped back to the door, jumped up and crossed the room, hand extended.

"Welcome to Shanghai, sailorman."

"Who's your pal, Ronald?"

193

"My new 'old friend' Mr. Yu. Mr. Yu no speak English. I no speak Wu. William Sit translate."

Stone did not believe for one minute that a "consultant" to as rich a source of bribes and kickbacks as the Fuxing Islet container terminal did not speak the universal tongue of international shipping. "Let me tell you something, Ronald. That guy speaks English as good as you or me. Why don't we talk face-to-face and save a little time?"

Ronald flashed a look at William Sit, and the translator backed out of hearing. The Triad spoke softly. "Sailorman, we on land, now. On land, we no say every little thing we know. Maybe, you, me, we get leg up on Mr. Yu."

"Sorry. Okay."

"Shanghai his town. He think he pull wool on stupid Hongkonger and dumb-ass barbarian. Let him."

"I got it."

They sat with Mr. Yu, who waded impatiently through the introductions, then spoke at length.

William Sit translated: "Mr. Yu welcomes you to Shanghai and wishes you lucky in your quest to locate a yachtsman marina. He is sure that Shanghai offers many such places and that you will be overwhelmed in choosing the best. He has suggestions, which he has conveyed to your boatman, and letters of introduction to show the patrols . . . "

Tea was poured and baskets of translucent dumplings spread on the table.

Yu picked up chopsticks, snared a dumpling, and spoke again.

"Mr. Yu further says that the Fuxing container terminal, while unable to offer river frontage for a yachtsman marina, would be pleased to invest in such an enterprise—"

Mr. Yu stirred, ominously.

William Sit faltered. "Perhaps, I use the wrong word. By invest, I mean Fuxing would make proper introductions for land your company could rent."

"Words confusing," Ronald said affably.

Stone cut in, "Tell Mr. Yu he's too kind, and that the sooner I board the boat he has so kindly arranged, the sooner I can bring him a profitable deal. Tell him I thank him for his letters, his boat, and this delicious breakfast, and now it's time to go to work."

William Sit translated. Yu grunted.

Stone started to rise. "Could you ask Mr. Yu one more thing?"

"Yes?"

"Tell him it is obvious he is an expert with deep knowledge of the port of Shanghai. Could he tell me which of the electric power plants burn natural gas?"

Sit asked. Yu growled in reply.

"There are none."

"None?" What the hell . . . "Are you sure he said none?"

"He said they don't allow such dangerous storage facilities in the port itself."

"None?" Stone echoed, stunned.

Ronald leaned in with an ingratiating smile. "Please could you explain to Mr. Wu that we are very ignorant of Shanghai and could there be such a power plant nearby?"

William Sit's elegant features gathered in a grimace that suggested he would rather not question the consultant too closely, and he asked Ronald, "What does gas have to do with marinas?"

Stone saw that Ronald was caught off guard by the translator's unexpected temerity. He stepped in quickly, shrugging at Yu as he told William, "Ask him. All I know is the bankers want to know."

Yu's answer was, "Electricity plants burn natural gas on the Hang-chou Bay. Thirty miles from here."

"At Jianshan?" The *Sailing Directions* cited a tanker terminal there.

"He say, Yes. Little north of terminal."

Their good-byes were perfunctory, and moments later Stone and Ronald, trailed by Sit at a respectful distance, were zigzagging quickly across the reflecting pool. "Nice go, sailorman. You fast read."

"What happens when new 'old friend' Yu figures out this whole scam is cover to find the gas ship?"

"What scam? Cover super idea."

"You want to build a marina?"

"With foreign money on state land? You bet, sailorman. Beside, I get private place to load boats."

"But the letterhead you printed for me is a fake."

"No, no. Mr. Chang make it real company. East-West Yacht Marina, Ltd. Registered Hong Kong. You vice-president site procurer."

"So you don't want the ship?"

"I no say that. I want ship real bad. Bad as you. But thanks to cover story, I not so thin on Shanghai ground— That remind me, Katherine stay till you find ship. Bodyguard your back. Watch for Brit."

"Here?"

"I'm here. You here. Why not Brit?"

"What do they want from me?"

"Looks like they want your life, sailorman."

"But why? All I want is Sarah and Ronnie."

"Relax. Wang take you to boat."

"I don't get it," said Stone. "What in hell are they up to?" But Ronald had already slid into the crowds converging on the Yu Garden gate and disappeared.

William Sit caught up at the car.

"Ask Mr. Wang for a map of the area around the city," Stone requested. When Wang obliged, Stone studied the large-scale map and pointed to a road that ran along the coast of Hang-chou Bay. "How long?"

"One hour."

"Fast as he can."

Chinese newspapers had come aboard the ship, and when Sarah and Ronnie joined Mr. Jack for his late breakfast, they found the old man ranting about the Japanese. He rattled the paper and spread it over the plates. "Look at that."

In among the long columns of characters was a photograph from the New China News Service of a warship flying the Japanese Rising Sun. "The sons of bitches are rearming. Just launched themselves a new helicopter carrier. So much for your 'most peaceable people on the planet,' Doc." He glared up at Sarah. "What do you suppose they need an attack carrier for?"

"Aren't helicopters used primarily for rescue?"

"Sure thing, Doc. Handy too for attacking the capital cities of their former colonies in southeast Asia."

"That sounds a bit farfetched, Mr. Jack."

"Then what do they need it for?"

"I guess it's inevitable, with the United States Navy cutting back its presence."

"Yellow bastards."

Sarah touched the newspaper. "What," she asked, "do the Chinese say about it?"

Mr. Jack gave her a look. "Yeah, I read Chinese—don't push, Doc. I warned you not to get out of line. That includes curiosity."

Ronnie cringed beside her, frightened by his tone. Sarah apologized, trying to smooth it over. "I'm sorry. I was merely curious how the Chinese feel about it."

Mr. Jack gave her another probing look. Then he said, "Says here the Japs' actions are, quote, 'provocative and threaten to unsettle the balance of power in Asia.'"

He stood, walked painfully to the window, and picked up his walkie-talkie. "Captain, where the hell are those tugs?"

The captain responded immediately. *"Radar just picked them up out on the bay. They're heading this way, Mr. Jack."*

"Tell 'em to step on it. Cloud's breaking up. The sooner we're under cover the better."

"Sir, you've got some more visitors just coming on the pier."

197

"Send 'em up. Tell 'em we're sailing, but they can get off on the pilot boat. And tell those tugs to get the lead out."

Stone's taxi driver knew shortcuts out of the massively congested city. And as the Old Town was relatively near the western suburbs, they were, within twenty minutes of crossing the river, heading briskly through diked farmland which was lively with new construction despite the gray day and the muddy winter fields.

"Rich peasants," explained William Sit. "Now farmers build their huts of brick." Wang gunned the taxi around what looked to Stone like old-fashioned three-wheeled Gravely lawn tractors pulling trailers heaped high with construction materials.

Ahead, on a flat horizon broken by leafless trees standing like feathers on the dikes, he saw high-tension power lines. When they reached where the power lines crossed the road, Stone motioned for Wang to take the gravel road that ran beside the pylons.

"No," said William Sit.

"It'll run straight to the power plant."

Wang and Sit both shook their heads, and the translator pointed at the large Chinese characters on a sign hanging from the nearest pylon.

"Restricted area. It is not allowed."

Wang spoke and Sit said, "Is safer on coast road."

In another twenty minutes they attained the coast road and headed south beside a broad alluvial plain that spread to the indistinct shore of the bay. For the second time that day, Stone had the eerie impression of sailing on dry land. He was reminded of Holland on an enormous, bleak scale. Road traffic was sparse and the bay, though dotted with small craft, was devoid of ships.

"There!" said Stone.

Four immensely tall and remarkably narrow chimneys had materialized as a rain shower thinned to mist. Closer, and he could see the outline of a squat generator building and then to the left, on the water's edge, a tank farm sparkling like aluminum cookware in the thin light. He took out the binoculars he had liberated from Ronald's yacht and traced the piping that served the tanks to a pier that jutted far into the bay. The end of the pier was lost in a rain squall.

Far ahead, the road dipped under a massive pipeline that carried fuel from the tanks to the power plant. When they were two hundred yards from the pipeline, the squall blew aside. The pier was empty.

Stone told Wang to stop. The driver and the translator exchanged glances.

"Stop, dammit!"

He jumped out, focusing the glasses on the water beyond the pier. He felt drawn to the murky, indistinct middle distance and kept fine-tuning the superb glasses, trying to pierce it. His senses seemed unusually alive. He felt the cold damp wind and had a feeling of being watched. William Sit hurried up behind him, whispering, "Soldiers. On the pipe."

There was a catwalk atop the pipeline and, on it, uniformed militia stared in their direction. "Not good," said Sit. "Not good. Thank you for coming. We go now."

Stone lingered. He looked at the chimneys. Burning natural gas, the power plant emitted invisible smoke, invisible only as heat waves dancing on the chimney tops. Why did he smell coal smoke?

He shifted the glasses back to the water. A squarish shape, less a shape than a hint of presence, seemed to hang in the distance. A ship in a squall?

Wang called urgently, and Sit's voice grew shrill as he pleaded, "We must go, sir."

Wang did not wait for agreement. He shot the taxi ahead, and turned it around in the middle of the road, his gaze locked on the soldiers who had started down a stairway from the catwalk.

The squalls merged, a mile offshore, obscuring behind a bank of hard, dark rain whatever it was that Stone had sensed was out there.

"We go!"

"Okay, okay. Tell Mr. Wang, back to Shanghai. To the boat."

Wang gripped the wheel with both hands as they raced down the coast, then inland through the farms, weaving among bicycles and tractors, dodging pedestrians, trucks, pigs. William Sit cowered, hands folded in his lap, as if not daring to look up for fear they would be flagged down by the People's Liberation Army. Stone, who was urging Wang to go faster, doubted either man would work for him tomorrow.

He tried to collect his own spirit. He couldn't afford to panic, couldn't lose focus wondering whether the *Dallas Belle* had come and gone; or if the crew was heading out to scuttle her, having sold her cargo; or if Sarah and Ronnie's lives had ended days ago.

He had to search the port of Shanghai as if he were convinced that the *Dallas Belle* was moored to one of its many piers. Experience offshore had taught him that it was almost impossible to see what you didn't believe existed. A boat, even a ship, remained stubbornly invisible until the observer accepted the possibility it was there; an unexpected landfall appeared with shocking suddenness.

He looked at his watch. It was still early—a gift—just one o'clock. He took out his chart, spread it on the backseat. "Ask Mr. Wang where the boat is."

Sit asked, then turned around and, puzzling over the chart, finally pointed to a coal yard on the near bank of the river, two miles upstream from the Bund. The taxi was already within the suburbs, and he said, "We will arrive in twenty minutes."

Wang made it in fifteen, through the gates of a vast, drab coal yard, steering between gray-black mountains of soft coal to the wharfs. Hundreds of sampans were tied to the offloading docks and, rafted to each other, jutted ten deep into the river. The coal was being unloaded from the sampans by shovel and primitive conveyor belts.

Mr. Wang got out of the car with a brusque gesture to follow, ending any doubts that he worked for the Triad and had recruited his friend William Sit instead of the other way around. The schoolteacher lingered by the taxi.

Stone reached to take William's arm, then remembered that the Chinese did not like to be touched by strangers. He said, "William, I'm very grateful for your help. I'd be lost without you."

"No, no. My English is improved already. It is I who is helped."

"I'm sure it was frightening, earlier, with the soldiers. I appreciate your sticking by me."

William looked trapped, which is what Stone had intended, in case the poor guy was thinking of ducking out. Mr. Wang called impatiently.

"Shall we?" asked Stone.

William nodded, reluctantly, and they hurried after the driver. Wang led them along the wharf, past the unloading operation, to a slip where an empty coal sampan was tied. The crew, a middle-aged man and wife and three teenaged children, were sluicing coal dust from the deck with buckets of river water.

Wang jumped down into the waist of the boat and gestured Stone and William aboard. Stone surveyed the sampan. It was about sixty feet long, with a squat wheelhouse aft and a capacious, open coal hold. Perfect: he much preferred concealment to using his letters of introduction. The grimy wooden boat looked identical to thousands plying the river, while the wheelhouse would hide a bearded American who was bound to draw the attention of the PLA navy boats patrolling the river.

The captain nodded brusquely to Wang, but he and his wife and his coal-smudged sons and daughter carefully avoided looking Stone and William in the face. There was barely headroom in the wheelhouse. A half stair led down to the idling engine, which Stone recognized as a General Motors 4-71 that had to be forty or fifty years old. Behind the stair hung a curtain, and when the daughter, a startlingly beautiful child a couple of years older than Ronnie, slipped through it, he glimpsed mattresses and a cookpot on a gimballed coal stove.

"So many children," whispered William, clearly astonished that the sampan captain had twice circumvented the one-child-one-family laws.

The daughter passed through the wheelhouse again, sneaking a shy glance at Stone. She returned within a minute. Her father spoke sharply, and she ran out on deck to help her brothers cast off the lines, while he moved the long shift lever into reverse. The thumping diesel started, rattling the windows, and the boat backed into the stream.

Stone took out his chart, which he folded to display this upper section of the river, and showed the captain two dry docks he wanted to see—the coal yard's immediate neighbor and the second a mile upstream.

Neither dry dock, nor the deepwater piers between them, held the *Dallas Belle*.

"Okay," he said. "Downriver. There!"

The empty sampan swung through a broad turn. Stone indicated the long curve of the river from the coal yard past the Bund, and had the captain hug the right bank where numerous large ships were docked. Once past the Bund and his hotel, and the Suzhou Creek, he had the captain cross the river and continue down the left bank, which was lined with piers, including the Waihongqiau passenger terminal where the *Tin Hau* was still docked, looking, as Stone had predicted, like a Maserati in a junk yard.

The weather was cooperating. The rain had stopped and the lower clouds had lifted. With the glasses Stone could see three or four miles. But the winter sky loomed heavy, and there remained, at most, two hours of daylight. They motored along another mile of piers: Gaoyanglu, Gonpinglu, Huishan, Huangpu. Suddenly his heart raced. Just past the Huangpu Pier was the dry dock of the Shanghai Shipyard West, and in it, a tan ship, sand-colored, square and boxy.

The dry dock gates were closed. The ship stood high and dry, covered in scaffolding. He focused the binoculars with shaking hands. It seemed the size he remembered the *Dallas Belle*. Then Stone groaned.

"Are you well, sir?"

Stone shook his head. It was not the gas carrier, only a container ship with the square lines typical of modern freighters.

Past the dry dock lay shallow water, the channel shifting east. "Other side."

The sampan crossed to the right back, where the Shanghai Shipyard East sprawled along the shore. The captain hugged that bank for several miles, stopping the sampan suddenly for another false alarm. By now the night was coming down hard and lights were burning on the piers and in the yards and factories that lined the shore.

The hitherto-silent captain spoke.

"Dark," William translated.

"Keep going."

The boat made about eight knots and they covered four more miles in the next half hour. He got a good look at the refinery, which he had missed in the rain. But no gas ship. "Other side!"

Again they crossed the channel, dodging ships and tugs. They were nearing Wusong when Stone saw the cruise ship under the shed that he had seen from the yacht early in the morning. He motioned the captain in closer. The berth beside the cruise liner was still empty. Arc welders and cutting torches lit the cavernous shed like black light in a discothéque. The sampan continued downstream past the yard, by which time it was pitch-dark.

"Okay, let's turn around and work our way up this side." They retraced their wake, passed the liner again. It was a breaker's yard, he realized, where retired ships were cut up for scrap. Behind it were busy train tracks with switch engines shuttling boxcars and gondolas. Stone wanted to get closer, but the captain shook his head, and his wife, who had popped out from the curtain, looked grim and uttered a shrill, "Aaaiiyaa."

"What's the matter?" asked Stone.

William seemed reluctant to answer.

"What is it?"

"Shanghai Supreme People's Court Project Eighty-six."

"What's that?"

"The execution ground. Where prisoners are shot for being . . . convicted."

Stone peered where he pointed. A dark space in the middle of nowhere, out beyond the railroad tracks. Appropriate neighbor for a breaker's yard.

Stone stepped out on deck and stared at the night-shrouded riverbanks. He told himself that he had covered some pretty good territory. And seen a number of places he had missed in the rain earlier, he added, fighting disappointment and exhaustion. Get some sleep. Early start tomorrow. He prayed there'd be no morning fog.

The Bund—the building façades floodlit—came into view after an hour. Stone, chilled to the bone and dizzy with hunger—for he had ignored Mr. Yu's dim sum and had not eaten since breakfast—told William to ask the captain to drop him at the park across from the hotel. The sampan nosed against slimy stone steps. Stone left instructions to pick him up at dawn and, assuring the protesting William Sit he could negotiate his own way to the hotel, shambled through the brightly lighted park.

Katherine was waiting in the lobby. Her face was drawn with tension. She had one hand deep in her bag. "Come to my room."

"What's wrong?"

"Security sucks."

She had had the hotel change her room to a suite with two exits. Before she would let him eat or sleep, she painstakingly walked him through an escape plan, demanding he memorize routes to the nearby fire stairs. She had embedded slivers of mirror in the wall opposite the door so she could scan the corridor through the peephole. When room service delivered, she answered the door with a gun behind her back.

When he awoke at midnight, she was sitting on the edge of her bed in a loose shirt staring at him.

"You okay?" he asked.

"Yeah. Great."

"You want to talk?"

"No, I don't want to talk. I'm thirty-three years old, I never had a guy more than six months, all I know how to do is fuck and be a cop and they won't let me be a cop. I can't see what's going to happen next."

"Well . . ."

"You gonna tell me it's gonna work out?" she asked.

"No. But I got some antidepressants in my bag."

She gave him one of her quiet, empty laughs. "Thanks. I'll pass. I'm an uppers woman, myself."

Stone closed his eyes. "Well, if you change your mind . . ."

"How can you sleep, worrying about Sarah?"

"Old habit from the boat. I sleep when I can. Doesn't mean I'm not worried sick. Every day I don't find them the ship could be steaming away or scuttled with them drowning inside."

20

THE *DALLAS BELLE* WAS MOVING AGAIN, TOWED BY SMOKE-belching tugs. The murky, squall-spattered sky had swallowed the land moments after they had departed the generating station, and when night had descended on the water, Sarah felt totally disoriented. It would be many hours before Mr. Jack slept and she could risk checking their position and course with Ronnie's GPS.

He was ensconced in his easy chair in the luxurious main lounge, drinking Canadian Club. His visitors had delivered a glossy brochure, which he pretended to read while he watched Sarah pace.

She poured herself another Pellegrino water at the bar, sipped distractedly, and made the round of the windows again. Reflected in the black glass, she and her captor looked as dead as statues.

He tossed the brochure on the coffee table. Sarah picked it up. The jacket showed a sleek black-and-white liner, the *Asian Princess*, registered in the Bahamas. It looked similar to the *QE-2*, which she had seen most recently in Singapore. The brochure was done up with four-color travel photos of Japan. The text was seductive, aimed at well-off passengers who preferred comfort to reality.

> *Ordinary liners stop in Yokohama, a fifteen-mile traffic jam from downtown Tokyo. Your* Asian Princess *docks at Takeshiba Pier in the heart of Tokyo, where she remains as your luxury hotel a short walk from Ground Zero of the dynamically modern metropolis that twelve million Tokyoites call home.*
>
> *Within steps lies the famed Ginza, with its wealth of department stores; the Marunouchi District, whose banks contain much of the world's wealth; the gardens of the Imperial Palace, home to Japan's revered royalty; and Tokyo Tower, Japan's tallest structure, which surpasses the Eiffel Tower of Paris, France.*
>
> *Tired feet? Simply activate your personal pager to summon the* Asian Princess's *fleet of private limousines waiting to whisk passengers to the destinations of their choice.*
>
> *No overpriced, expensive hotels. No outrageous taxicab fares. No mob scenes at the airport. No crush to board public transportation. See Tokyo as it's never been seen before from your luxury stateroom aboard your floating hotel, the five-star first-class* Asian Princess.

"Are you booking a cruise, Mr. Jack?"

"I bought the line. Whadaya think of my new ship?"

"You do seem to guarantee your clients absolutely no contact with the real Tokyo."

"That's what the cruise business is all about. Ever go on one?"

"I'm afraid that luxury cruises are a bit beyond our means."

"Tell you what, when this is all over, let me comp you and your husband. Honeymoon cruise, on the house."

"Perhaps we could embark this evening?"

"Sorry, Doc." He drained his glass and motioned for a refill. "Say, tell the kid I got a surprise for youse, tomorrow."

The small, dark, high-ceiled suite that Stone shared with Katherine had an ancient telephone that chirped like a cricket. Katherine answered and passed it to Stone. It was Ronald.

"Hey, sailorman. Our Hong Kong friend say call friend in hospital."

"I'll be damned."

"Got it?"

"Thanks."

The Matilda Hospital operator switched the call through to Kerry's room, where the patient answered with, "Where the hell are you, mate?"

"China," Stone answered cautiously, sitting on the bed. "How's your shoulder?"

"I'll survive."

The salvage captain sounded friendly. But he spoke in his clear, loud master mariner's voice, and Stone could almost feel his probing eyes. "I've had second thoughts lying here. About your story."

Stone stood up, pressing the phone harder to his ear. "Did you speak to your—"

"Never mind how. I checked out the SOSUS, and they don't have much in the way of fixed sonar arrays in the western Pacific. It was intended for tracking Soviet subs entering the open oceans."

"I was afraid of that."

"But subs and helicopters are still listening. And some of what they pick up goes into ADAC—the ship-noise library."

"Good."

"It's more than good, mate. A lot more. You got lucky. Twice. As near as I can reckon, this is what happened: one of our subs on a training cruise was near the Southwest

Islands when some new recruit learning sonar picked up a ship. 'What's that?' 'I don't know, sir.' 'Well, let's find out.'

"They checked their recording against the sub's library," Kerry continued. "No match. So it wasn't a warship. But the instructor probably said, 'That's a mighty heavy ship for out here. He's two hundred miles from the shipping lanes.' Tells the captain, 'Hey, skipper, listen to this.' Skipper says, 'Check with HQ in Brisbane.' The Brisbane Library interfaced with your Pentagon and back came a match. Liberian-registered fifty-thousand-ton LNG vessel, *Amy Bodman*."

"Bodman?"

"Bodman Line. Old petroleum fleet, bought up years ago, conglomerated fourteen times since then. But by the time the data came back, the ship was long gone and the sub had more important business. And that would be the end of that . . ."

"Except?" Stone prompted.

"Except that in the East China Sea the Japanese and the Australian Navy were holding a joint exercise—Aussie subs, Japanese Defense Force surface craft. Helicopters dipped sonar arrays and what did they pick up but *Amy Bodman*."

"Where?"

"About four hundred miles from Shanghai."

"What course?"

"Northwest."

His heart leaped. She was here! "Straight for Shanghai. Like Sarah said."

"There's more."

"What?" Stone demanded. "Come on. Spill it."

"Rushing this will not uncomplicate it. They heard a gas vessel right about where they'd expected to hear gas vessels, so it was no big deal. But with all the communications exercises, it got transmitted to Brisbane and automatically to the Pentagon. *Amy* is in the library."

"So she's in Shanghai," said Stone, relief washing over him.

"Not necessarily."

"What do you mean?"

"The ship stopped."

"What do you mean, 'stopped?' "

"Dead in the water. Midway between Okinawa and Shanghai. One minute engines. Next minute no engines, no propeller. I asked a mate to check out some satellite pictures for me. No go. Heavy cloud, fog, rain three days. No pictures."

"Infrared?"

"Nothing."

A chill clenched Stone's heart. Scuttled. "They sunk her."

"Maybe," said Kerry. "Maybe not. Four days after they recorded her, one of the helicopters was dipping arrays again and they recorded a strange noise. Not a screw, not an engine, not a whale. A heavy thump-thump-thump."

"I don't get it."

"Think."

"Stop fucking around!" Stone shouted. *"Tell me."*

"I don't want to put words in your mouth, Michael. I'm only guessing. The Navy didn't bother to analyze it. It was a commercial ship, they're busy with warships. I think I know what they heard. See if you think the same."

Stone closed his eyes and sank to the bed, trying to order the thoughts whirling through his brain. Katherine knelt behind him and started massaging his shoulders.

"Clue," said Kerry. "Remember she's a gas ship."

"A compressor!"

"Yes!"

"The cooling gear, to keep the gas cold."

"I looked her up. *Amy Bodman*'s new enough to have cooling equipment. The old ones were just a thermos bottle, but she's new. So what they heard was a compressor going thump, thump, thump, while she sat in the rain for four days."

"Why'd she stop?"

"Repairs, probably."

"Did she start up again?"

"Don't know. Joint exercises ended, everyone sailed home to their respective beer and saki."

"Well, has the *Amy Bodman* been reported missing?"

"Not reported missing. Not reported overdue."

"Who owns her?"

"Hard to tell. She's been leased, unleased, and released. I've had my Admiralty lawyer on it for two days. There's a cat's cradle of interlocking companies and lease schemes. I do know she picked up her cargo in Surabaya."

"We expected that."

"You know the name Jack Powell?"

"No."

"Big petroleum shipper. American. Started up back in the days of Ludwig and Aristotle Onassis. Powell was the Ludwig type, secretive. My people think it could be his."

"But why wouldn't he report it missing?"

"Maybe he owns so many he doesn't notice. Maybe he's leased her out to somebody else."

"Shouldn't be hard to ask."

"He's not returning messages. Got offices in New York, but there's no reason why he'd respond to a lowly salvor's call."

"He's certainly not going to answer mine. Have you talked to Lydia Chin?"

"Lydia tried, too. Cold shoulder. She even got one of her mega-ship friends to try. They blew him off with assistants."

"Maybe Jack Powell's on the ship."

"Doubt that."

"Of course not— Jesus, that close she could have come into Shanghai."

"I wish you luck, my friend. It could all be nothing, all coincidence. But if they were trying to hide the ship from satellites, then they got stupid, forgetting the compressor, and you got lucky. I'll keep trying to find out who owns her and I'll also keep trying Mr. Powell."

"God, I wish he were aboard."

"Why?"

"My biggest fear is they'll sell the cargo and scuttle her with Sarah and Ronnie inside."

"What would a guy like that want with your wife and daughter?"

Stone hung up the phone and thought it through, isolating the good news, ignoring the unanswered questions, the doubts, and even the mystery of what the hijackers were up to. The ship had stopped near Shanghai, hidden under cloud. He was sure they had started up again. They wouldn't scuttle her with her cargo. And he knew she was laden because they were still running the gas coolers.

Katherine kept massaging his shoulders. She had the strongest hands of any woman he'd ever known. "I can't wait for daylight," he said. "They've got to be here."

There was a knock at the door. Katherine picked up her gun. She stood to the side of the door, checked the peephole with her makeup mirror. Then she called, "Step to your left," checked the mirrors across the hall, and opened up.

Ronald sprang in, his eyes like pinpricks. "What's new?"

Willing to bet money that the Triad had bribed the switchboard operator, Stone told him what he had learned. Ronald bounced around the room and Stone wondered what he was on.

"Sound good. Hey, sailorman?"

"I think so. Are you all right?"

"Yeah, fine."

Katherine said, "You got blood on your pants cuff."

"My guys got chopped. No big deal."

"No big deal?" Stone asked. "You were thin on the ground already."

Katherine asked, "Is Michael safe here?"

"No problem."

She said, "I don't like this."

Ronald whirled on her. "You no like? Fuck you-no-like."

Katherine was still holding her gun. "He's my ticket outta here. I'm asking you, Is he safe?"

Ronald moved to slap her. She raised the gun, not quite leveled at his groin, but no longer pointing at the floor. And this time, to Stone's surprise, the Triad backed off. Reaching for the door, he said to Stone, "You no worry, sailorman. I take good care."

When he was gone, Stone asked, "What do you think?"

"He's scared. I'll bet you Chang cut him loose."

"We better move."

"If they know we're here, they'll know where we move."

"Do you advise we stay?"

"I advise you find that ship tomorrow."

21

"HEY, DOC! DOC! BRING THE KID. SURPRISE TIME."

Ronnie looked up from her book. "Surprise?" She hopped off the bed. "Come on, Mummy."

Several paces behind, Sarah heard her daughter gasp. "Ohmigod! Oh, it's beautiful, Mr. Jack."

Sarah paused in the doorway and stared in disbelief. In the corner opposite Mr. Jack's chair, a Christmas tree stood tall as the ceiling with blinking lights and sparkling glass ornaments. Its fresh evergreen scent permeated the cabin. Ronnie crept to it, her face bright with wonder.

"What's the matter, kid? Never seen a Christmas tree?" He was still drinking, against Sarah's orders. His face was flushed.

"Only in pictures. Mummy and Daddy make a baby one, but this is so *green*. Mummy, smell!"

"We decorate a little palm tree," Sarah explained, touched by the old man's gift despite the whiskey smile that made him look like a hellish Santa Claus. "How did you find this?"

"Told you, Doc, Shanghai's my town."

The captain came in, red-eyed and weary from three days of maneuvering the ship in coastal waters.

"What's up, Cap?"

"Wusong Kou, Mr. Jack. Almost in the river. We'll anchor up till high water, scoot in on the flood."

The Huangpu, thought Sarah. Or did he mean the Yangtze?

"How long?"

"Dockside, three hours."

Shanghai. A giant city, where they could run and hide.

"Hey, what do you think of the tree, kid?"

"It's beautiful."

"What do you want for Christmas?" Mr. Jack asked, then cut off her answer with a shout. "We're going to have a bang-up Christmas. Just you wait."

Sarah was appalled. "*Christmas* is ten days off, Mr. Jack? Surely you won't hold us ten more days."

"Surely I will, Doc. But it'll be a Christmas to remember. I promise."

"Is daddy still in Hong Kong?" asked Ronnie.

"Far as I know," the old man answered.

The photograph had virtually erased the child's fears. She acted now as if she and her mother were on holiday. Although Sarah wondered how much it *was* an act, designed to make *her* feel better. Ronnie had always been closely attuned to her and Michael's emotions, the result of a life lived in confined quarters, and she was a generous child, quick to give. Too generous by half, Sarah feared. A bitter smile tugged her lips: ordinary motherly concerns seemed bizarre when her and Ronnie's—even Michael's—lives were hostage to a harsh old man who was as lunatic as he was powerful.

Ah Lee arrived with dinner, a huge bowl of steamed Shanghai crabs. Sarah helped Mr. Jack out of his chair. He was stronger, but the pain in his chest and shoulder made movement difficult. When she had settled him at the table, where Ah Lee was cracking shells and showing Ronnie how to pick out the meat, he demanded his drink.

Moss came in when they were turning to dessert, Ronnie's favorite coffee ice cream. As he glowered at the scene, Sarah thought how they must look like some comic television family: mother, daughter, and grandfather, eating while Daddy worked late. Or master and slaves.

"What is it, Moss?"

"Company. Patrol boat brought 'em aboard."

"Ladies? How about you pull a vanishing act? We picked up some Disney laser discs. Catch a movie."

It was an order, and they retreated to the sleeping cabin, Sarah wondering whether Mr. Jack had banished them so they wouldn't be seen, or whether they were not to see his guests.

Ah Lee crept in with tea, cookies, and the movies and scurried off. Ronnie loaded *Snow White and the Seven Dwarfs* into the disc player, with the volume low. Sarah put on her stethoscope and pressed the diaphragm to the door.

Ronnie whispered, "What are they saying?"

"They're speaking Chinese."

"Even Mr. Jack?"

"Shhh!"

"Let me listen, Mummy."

Sarah surrendered the stethoscope.

"They keep saying, 'Old friend,'" Ronnie whispered. Then, suddenly, "Wait, he's speaking English— Here, you listen." She pulled off the earpieces, handing the stethoscope to Sarah, and settled down on the bed with *Snow White.*

Sarah pressed the diaphragm to the door again and heard Mr. Jack joking, "Hell, even communists can make a killing when they know ahead of time the Nikkei Exchange—" He finished in Chinese. Whatever it meant was greeted with laughter.

Sarah listened in vain for more English. She could hear glasses clinking and low-toned conversation, friendly laughter, and then the arrival of Ah Lee with food and more drink. Cigarette smoke wafted under the door. Were it not for the absence of female voices, she might have been eaves-dropping outside a pub.

The movie ended. Ronnie fell asleep. Sarah covered her with another blanket and was thinking of getting ready for bed, herself, when she felt the ship stop.

She moved the porthole curtain and looked out. Power-ful floodlights illuminated a pier and the framework of a massive crane. Beyond the glare she sensed more than saw a wall. She had the eerie feeling that the ship was indoors, inside an enormous shed.

When she went back to the door, the talk had ceased. She knocked softly, so as not to wake Ronnie.

"Come in, Doc."

Mr. Jack was alone, slumped wearily in his chair. His eyes were glazed with exhaustion, his tongue twisted with drink. "Bedtime, Doc?"

"You've been up much too long. You've overdone it." She fanned the air with her hand. "May I assume you haven't smoked?"

"Not me, Doc. Just my old pals. Smoke like chimneys. Always did. Crazy bastards would ambush a Jap tank col-umn just to steal their cigarettes." He looked at her blearily, but suddenly he was alert. "Wha'd you hear, Doc?"

She fingered her stethoscope before she realized she had forgotten to take it off. She moved quickly to him, opened his robe, and placed the cold disk on his chest. His heart sounded strong, and his lungs, much less congested.

"Cut the comedy. I asked wha'd you hear?"

"Do you blame me?"

"Doc, you're playin' with fire."

"I said, 'Do you blame me?' You're holding my child and me prisoner. My poor husband is God knows where."

"You just earned yourself a session with Moss."

He pressed one of the many buttons that signaled Moss's beeper, and returned her startled gaze with a cold stare. "I warned you, Doc. No mercy."

It seemed important not to show him fear. But she could feel her mouth twitching. "May I ask you something?"

"I'm through being your patsy. You pushed once too often."

"How does a man like you acquire someone like Moss?"

Mr. Jack chuckled. "You're a pistol, Doc. God, if I'd met a woman with your balls forty years ago . . . You know what's a second-story man?"

"No."

"Cat burglar. Climbs in the second story-window. Except in a city like New York, where Moss grew up, it's the twentieth story. Some 'uncle' or mother's boyfriend or whatever put the kid to work scaling the sides of buildings. He was great at it. Coulda been a tightrope walker in the circus if he'd gotten the right breaks. He got caught and sent to a juvenile home."

"How old was he?"

"Ten, eleven. Skinny little bastard, apparently."

Sarah's thoughts fled to Ronnie sliding down the forestay.

"When they let him out he was sixteen. He'd grown up fast, lifting weights, surviving. Found gainful employment pimping—like I told you. Graduated from disciplining whores to chief enforcer for a drug cartel. The big time, till he got caught again. Murder, etc. Twenty years in Attica—prison, upstate New York. Hard time. I found him there. I was underwriting a rehabilitation program. You know—big business gives the criminal a second chance."

"That sounds like a wonderful contribution, Mr. Jack."

"Great way to recruit staff . . . Saw right away Moss was a cut above—a sociopath with the self-discipline to excel. Sprung him. Hired tutors, taught him reading, math, electronics. Shipped him out to California to learn computers, over here for weapons training. Brilliant kid, if a little bent."

"He seems grateful."

Mr. Jack shrugged. "He'd be a damned fool if he

wasn't— There you are, Moss. Come on in. Miz Doc here's steppin' pretty far outta line."

"Oh, yeah?"

"Hurt her. No marks."

She could not believe it was happening until he was leaning over her and her mind was darting to where he would hit her first.

"Hold it, Moss. . . . Hey, Doc?"

"What, Mr. Jack?"

She could barely control her voice.

"Try and keep it quiet. You don't want the kid waking up and watching it, you know?"

She stared back in disbelief. He said, "Do you understand?"

"Yes."

"All ready?"

Even then she could not fully believe that he would sit by while Moss deliberately hurt her. But now the black man's hands were moving, teasing the air near her face. An ugly smile twisted his lips.

His hands moved faster than she could see. A stinging blow to her ear set it ringing. Her own hands flew to the pain, exposing her belly and her breasts. A flurry of blows doubled her over and drove her to the floor, gasping and retching for air.

Now pain swept like fire, and she fought with all her might to swallow a shriek that tried to climb from her throat like a frenzied animal. A moan she couldn't smother brought a warning from Mr. Jack.

"Let's not wake Ronnie, shall we? You're not going to be in any shape to sing lullabies."

A stab like a white-hot knife seemed to pierce her left kidney and she thought, with sudden raw fear, that Moss would accidentally kill her. The pain leaped from her kidney to her chest and into her brain and she felt herself spiral into blackness.

Moss emptied the melted ice water from the bucket on her face.

Sarah woke up spitting, holding her body, and moaning. "Quiet."

She bit her lips.

"Okay?"

She nodded. He hadn't killed her. It only felt that way.

"More," said Mr. Jack.

She prayed for unconsciousness, again. But Moss was more careful, and diabolically subtler, and there came a time when Mr. Jack had him pause to gag her—"In the interest," as he put it, "of Ronnie's beauty sleep." He used a bar towel and secured it with his belt.

She became aware she was on the bathroom floor, a dark red haze of pain before her eyes, head spinning, body shaking uncontrollably. Nauseated, she dragged herself to the toilet and threw up, then sank to cold tile, biting her lips so Ronnie wouldn't hear her.

Every breath hurt.

She concentrated for a long time to gather strength to stand. Straightening up, at last, she caught sight of her face in the mirror. She looked feral. And terrified. Amazingly there was not a mark on her. Though her face was slightly swollen. She would tell Ronnie she had puffed up from too much Chinese food.

Ronnie! She dragged herself to the door, opened it a crack, and peered out. Ronnie was curled up on the bed, under a quilt, fast asleep. How had they carried her in without waking her?

Sarah locked the door and sank again to the cold tile. The child was a sound sleeper, but why had Mr. Jack shielded her from the vicious attack? Was it to leave *her* a shred of hope? Hope that if she devoted herself to Mr. Jack's health, Ronnie would be spared?

She lay aching, pondering that, and concluded that there was no hope. The beating was proof that Mr. Jack would kill them both when he was done doing whatever he was doing with the Chinese generals and could go home to a western hospital. More than ever, they had to escape.

They were so close to land. The pier was sixty feet below, less than twenty feet from the side of the ship. Moss was the chief obstacle. She knew in the deepest part of her soul that even after the beating she couldn't pervert medicine to kill him. But could she disable him?

Hands trembling with fright, she opened her medical bag. Ketamine was used in anesthesia to obtain muscle paralysis. Its onset of action was slow, but it might do the trick. But to attempt to inject a powerful attacker with an ordinary hypo would depend too much on luck. She had to be able to hit him fast and hard, just once.

She had one-shot epinephrine auto-injectors for emergency treatment of severe allergic reactions. The bee sting victim merely punched the needle into the thigh and the dose was injected automatically. She studied the plastic barrel under the light, reckoning whether she could remove the epinephrine and replace it with the ketamine. She broke several insulin needles trying to bore into it, before she realized that she wasn't thinking clearly: the dose it injected would be too small; it would take five or six ccs to stop a man the size of Moss.

She couldn't stand any longer. The bed seemed miles away. She curled up in a ball on the cold floor again. Her teeth were chattering. Her chest burned with pain and rage. Worse was the fear she'd lose her nerve.

Frozen to the bone by another long, fruitless day on the river, Stone took a hot shower and staggered into bed. Katherine had hidden all day above a false ceiling, watching the hotel lobby. She hadn't seen any "hitters." But Ronald had not made contact, and she was anxious to leave Shanghai.

"One more day," he promised her. "Just one more."

She offered to share her wine. "Help you sleep," she

said, extending a bathroom glass half full. Stone sipped it, propped up against a pillow, and started to drift off.

"You ever cheat on your wife?"

"Nope."

"Never?"

"No need to."

"Okay, but what if somebody turned you on even more than her. A lot more than her."

"Such a turn-on would be banned under the terms of the nuclear nonproliferation pact."

Katherine returned his grin. "You'd let a *treaty* stand between you and the greatest sex of your life?"

"It's my sacrifice for humanity."

Suddenly sober, she said, "God, you're lucky."

"I know. That's why I want her back."

Katherine folded her hands and smiled over them at Stone. "No, you'd want her back anyway—you're one of those guys who takes care of people."

"And my daughter."

"I'm never going to have children."

"Don't say that. You're young and—"

"Back off!"

She glared away, angrily, then screamed, "Look out!" and threw herself desperately at her bag.

The Brit was standing in the living room door. His pistol was silenced. Stone could hear the bullets thud like punches into Katherine's chest.

22

KATHERINE TUMBLED OVER THE BED. THE BRIT STEPPED INTO THE room, pistol raised. "Merry chase," he said. "You're a hyperactive bloke."

Stone roared back, "Where is my wife?"

"Haven't the foggiest, mate." He leveled his weapon and Stone felt his world spiral into the black orb of its barrel. "Just finishing my job."

Suddenly twin thunderclaps boomed in Stone's ear. Katherine was firing from beside him. He saw blood pouring from her mouth, and she clearly couldn't control the recoil. Her first shot smashed the Brit's arm, spinning him back through the living room door. Her second missed and she collapsed on the blood-soaked bedspread.

"Run!" she whispered, pushing her gun toward Stone. "Take it!"

"What about you?"

"You can't help me. Run! For your wife and kid." Her blood was pouring freely. She gagged on it, coughed. "Make sure I got that jerk. Pop him or he'll come after you for the rest of your life. Fucking psycho."

Stone picked up the gun.

"Safety's off. Just pull the trigger."

He bounded into the living room.

The Brit was on the carpet, crawling painfully toward his gun, which had landed near the hall door.

"Don't move," said Stone.

The Brit turned, saw Stone standing in the door with Katherine's gun. "You haven't got the balls, mate."

Stone looked back at Katherine. She had fallen lifeless, eyes wide and staring. The Brit was crawling faster. Three times the man had tried to kill him, "just finishing" his job. To shoot him now in the back would be nothing short of an execution, but Katherine was right: the professional killer had made it a twisted point of honor and would keep coming after him as long as he lived.

He stepped close, pressed the gun to the back of the man's head. "Either I'll kill you or cripple you for a year. Your call."

The Brit turned his head. When he saw Stone's face his own expression changed from contempt to respect. Or fear. Stone didn't know which and didn't care. "Your call," he repeated.

"Look, mate, why not just take my weapon? I'll be in the hospital with this arm."

"Not long enough," said Stone. From far below in the street he heard sirens. He moved the gun muzzle to the back of the man's left thigh and immediately pulled the trigger, shattering the femur. The Brit's body bucked, arced; he screamed. Then he fainted, flattening on the floor as if he had melted. Stone pulled the trigger again, breaking his other leg.

He grabbed his backpack, his clothes and his coat, checked the hall. A middle-aged Japanese peered from his doorway. Stone ran to the stairwell, where he put on his pants, shoes, socks, and wool sweater. He heard sirens. He ran down the stairs.

Uniformed militia were pouring into the lobby, shouting at the desk clerks, who were shouting back. Stone backed into the fire stairs again and ran down to a basement, and, following the scent of garbage, exited by a loading bay.

Sirens filled the neon-lit night. He boldly crossed the street and pushed through the door of the first business he came to, a jazz club, lit by candles and a disco ball. Elderly American tourists were listening to an even older combo. A waitress zeroed in on Stone. He ordered Scotch and tossed it back. His hands were shaking so hard the woman stared.

He gestured for another.

The set ended. He let them bring more drinks, and food that he couldn't eat. He sat through the final set and at one o'clock they began to shut it down. If he stayed any longer he'd draw attention to himself.

He ventured into the street, taking cover behind a party trooping toward their hotel shuttle. Cops everywhere. He veered off in the direction of the old city, trying to stay on streets that were fairly busy.

A glare of light ahead announced a night market. There he mingled, among the temporary stalls, shaking his head "no" at postcards, Peking Opera dolls, toy pandas, lace handkerchiefs, and jade jewelry. Then, thinking to change his luck, and blend in like an ordinary tourist, or jet-lagged businessman who couldn't sleep, he bought a miniature stuffed panda for Ronnie and a lace handkerchief for Sarah. A crowd gathered to watch him make his purchases and hawkers descended.

One old man was particularly persistent, an old, old man in a quilted jacket selling Baoding Iron Balls—a pair of shiny balls with bells inside, which he demonstrated, crying, "Good healthy, good healthy," rolling them in one hand like a benign Captain Queeg. Stone retreated. The old man followed. "U.S.? U.S.?"

225

Here, too, it was getting to be closing time and the peddlers began to shut down their stalls.

"Yank?" the old man cried. "Yank. Air Force."

"What?"

A joyful grin showed a half-dozen yellow teeth. "Tenth Air Force. 1945. Mechanic. Airplane mechanic. Tenth Air Force. Bomb shit outta Japs."

Stone stopped, which was all the encouragement the old man needed. "You try!" He pressed the iron balls in Stone's hand. "Airplane mechanic. Bomb shit outta Japs."

Stone looked at the shiny balls and as he did, an orange street lamp flared like a tiny Betelgeuse in each of the balls. He reached for his money. It had to be an omen. He pressed the money in the man's hand and put the balls in his pocket.

"No, no. You take." The old man shoved the money back at him. "Tenth Air Force. 1945. Airplane mechanic. Platt and Whitney. Bomb shit outta Japs."

"Thank you, sir. Thank you very much. Here, from me." He took a pack of Marlboros from his bag and gave it to him.

The grin got huge. "Very good. Lucky Strike."

Stone scanned the emptying streets. "Where was your base?"

The old man pointed east. "Top secret. Very secret." And bending to fold up his table and chair, he repeated, "Tenth Air Force. Yank friend," pounding his chest for emphasis.

"I could use one now," said Stone. "Here, let me give you a hand with that."

Sarah's body ached in every muscle when she awakened to the distant bang and clatter of heavy machinery. Her kidneys burned, and she thought she tasted blood in her mouth. Bracing herself, muffling a groan so as not to wake Ronnie, she staggered through the sleeping cabin and out to the deserted lounge. She looked to see what lay on the port side of the ship. To her surprise, she saw another ship, immediately alongside, a passenger liner which appeared to be about as long as the *Dallas Belle*.

Its superstructure was covered with bamboo scaffolding. Through portholes and windows, she could see the jagged light of cutting torches flickering upon gangs of workers in hard hats and overalls.

As she had surmised last night, the slip was roofed over by a gigantic shed. Cranes and gantries hung over the liner from the far pier, and traveling hoists rode massive beams in the roof. Astern, the river was shrouded in thick fog.

She longed to climb the stairs that led to the bridge deck, but the beating filled her mind and she had to muster her spirit. Now more than ever, her life and Ronnie's depended on her courage. She *had* to act.

When she was finally able to climb, she found the corridor empty, as were the chart and computer rooms. She stole forward and opened the curtain to the bridge. She saw no officer on watch, only a seaman, who was sleeping in the big leather captain's chair at the windscreen. Moving silently, she went to the windscreen. Ahead, there was little more to see than what she had seen already: the crews at work on the neighboring ship, the vast shed roof over the double slip, the bow of the *Dallas Belle*, disappearing in shadow.

But as she watched and the day grew lighter, she could see that the back end of the shed was open to a rail yard, with freight trains shuttling by. If they could get to a train, they could ride into the city proper, lose themselves in the streets. Perhaps she could make it to the British consulate, talk her way in on her accent. A daunting thought: a tall black woman and a little black girl would stand out in the Chinese city like an invading army.

She saw movement down on the main deck. The bosun was leading a work party out of the house. They went to the Swan and began releasing the straps that held her to the cradle. Sarah ran below and woke Mr. Jack.

"What are you doing to my boat?"

"Take it easy— Ah Lee. Ah Lee. Where the hell are you? *Coffee!*— Doc, I'd have thought after dancing with Moss last night you'd have slept late."

"They're moving my boat."

"Relax. We'll drop her in the water and sail her around the other side out of the way."

"Let me do it."

"Doc, you're starting to annoy me again."

"Please. Call the captain." She handed him the phone. "Tell him I'll move my boat. Please, it's our home. They'll make a mess of it."

The old man shrugged and dialed. "Keep your shirt on, Doc. . . . Captain? Let the doctor move her boat. She's worried you'll bang a hole in it. Right. She's on her way." He hung up. "Okay, run down to the main deck. And, Doc? No monkey business. Put the boat where they tell you and come back. Ronnie stays here."

She took the elevator to the main deck, opened a heavy steel hatch, and stepped over a high sill into the cold. The air was damp, and the noise from the workmen on the passenger ship was deafening. The ship's crane was already hooked onto the sling. A seaman held a ladder for her, and Sarah climbed up to *Veronica*.

Her decks were gritty with salt and coal ash. But, as she had seen from the bridge a week ago, they had stowed things properly. She started the engine to make sure it would run, then shut it down, as the cooling system required the hull to be in the water. She hung the fenders, which the ship's crew had dumped in the cabin.

Moss came out on deck. Her heart leaped with fear as he headed for the ladder. Sarah shoved it away and the seaman dodged it as it fell.

"Moss," she called, "tell the crane driver to be careful of my mast." She pointed at the roof and was satisfied to see Moss confused as she had first been by the optical illusion. There was, in fact, plenty of room for the mast, which barely reached the bridge windows, while the roof soared higher than the ship's smokestack and radio mast.

The slings tightened. *Veronica* lurched under her feet. She grabbed the handrail on the compass pedestal and steadied herself as the boat was hoisted from the cradle.

"Watch the keel," she shouted to Moss. "Make sure it clears the bulwark."

She looked over the side and saw Moss step under the hull as the crane operator swung *Veronica* slowly over the ship's bulwark. Now, clear of the hull, it descended, swaying between the two ships. Halfway down, it began swinging like a pendulum. Sarah tried to fend off with a boathook, but the momentum was too great and twice the hull scraped the steel ship with a heart-wrenching screech.

She looked up. Ronnie was waving from the bridge wing, accompanied by the captain, who was issuing orders into his walkie-talkie. Then the hull smacked the water. The slings slackened and Sarah, familiar with the operation from boatyard repairs and bottom painting, started the engine and released the shackles. The crane hoisted the slings and *Veronica* was free.

There was not enough room to turn around in the canyon between the ships, so she had to back out—never an easy operation for a sailboat. The trick, Michael had taught her, was to start a strong flow of water over the rudder by gunning the engine, which was precisely what every instinct said not to do in close quarters. It worked. The boat started backing toward the river and, after one awful moment when the bow threatened to veer against the cruise ship, Sarah got control, throttled down, and eased slowly from between the sterns of the two ships.

The tide was ebbing, the river current strong. The Huangpu spread tantalizingly before her, nearly half a mile wide and dense with junks, lighters, sampans, coastal freighters, and oceangoing ships.

Moss plummeted down one of the mooring cables, swooping onto the pier like a huge bat. He landed grace-

fully, removed his work gloves with the dignity of an aristo-
crat home from the opera, and pointed to where she should
moor the boat.

"Mummy!" Ronnie waved gaily from the bridge wing.

The current was sweeping *Veronica* toward the pier.
Sarah left the engine in reverse and nudged the helm, angling her stern to the current, backing slowly into the river.

"Right here!" Moss yelled through cupped hands.
"Move it!"

She eyed the river, longingly. Upstream was the city.
Downstream, the sea and freedom. Foolishness. She couldn't
leave Ronnie. Unless she could find help, immediately. As
she hesitated, weighing the impossible, a small Navy patrol
craft veered from the line of outbound traffic and came skipping toward her, red lights flashing.

Her heart jumped and she felt an immense joy shoot
like adrenaline through her veins. A siren whooped. She
saw an elderly Army officer steadying himself on the windshield. His coat appeared to glitter like fish scales, and as
the boat drew nearer, she saw it was covered with medals
and decorations. His hat was speckled with a general's stars.
He waved. And from above, on the balcony behind the owner's cabin, came a shout. Sarah looked up.

There was Mr. Jack in his bathrobe, grinning ear to ear
and waving his good arm. "Hey, pal. Where you been?"

The old general waved a bottle.

"Doc," yelled Moss, "get your ass over here."

Crushed, Sarah put the engine in forward and steered
toward the pier. The patrol boat burbled to a stop at the
pierhead, leaving room for *Veronica* farther in. The crew
helped the general up the ladder with solemn deference, and
a pair of polished young officers trailed him up the gangway
of the *Dallas Belle*.

Moss was gloating. "Throw me a rope, Doc."

She could not tell whether he had goaded her into defi-
ance, or whether she was in the grip of a survivor's instinct,
but without thinking, she turned the boat around. Her hands

moved surely about the helm and throttle. Using the current to advantage, she backed *Veronica* into the space between the ship and the pier, so that when she finally threw Moss a line, the boat was facing out, bow to the river.

"Way to dock, Mummy!" Ronnie called down. "Daddy should have seen that."

Sarah looped the stern line over the pier bollard and secured it on the boat. Then she climbed onto the pier, undid the bow line which Moss had tangled around a bollard, and led it back to *Veronica*. Moss watched suspiciously as she went below for more line, which she ran as stern and bow spring lines. She doubled them through a mooring ring in the side of the pier, and secured them on the boat.

She shifted all the fenders to pierside. Finally, she brought up two anchors, which she looped over the bow and stern lines as tensioning weights. "For the tide," she explained to Moss, who was watching suspiciously.

"Are you done?"

Sarah closed the hatch and stole one more glance at the river. She had tied every line so that she could release it from the boat. Right under his nose.

"I'll need to check her at low tide."

"Let's go. I'm freezing."

It *was* cold. She had been so busy she hadn't noticed it, and had even forgotten the pain. Until now, when both penetrated to her bones. She was still shivering as they rode the elevator to the owner's suite deck. She stared ahead. The aluminum reflected Moss's grin.

"Good time last night?"

"I'm in pain, if that is what you're asking. You did your job."

He seemed startled that she had answered him and said, only, "Mr. Jack wants you to meet his friend."

The Chinese officers were guarding the door. Moss reached between them and knocked. Mr. Jack called to come in. He and the general were sitting with a mai-tai bottle between them. The room was thick with smoke, and the general was lighting a fresh cigarette as she entered.

"There you are, the docking doctor. Saw you tied her pointed out—ready for a getaway?"

"I thought she'd ride the ship wakes better."

"Sure, sure." He turned to his guest. "General, here's the reason I don't need a hospital. Got my own doctor. What do you think?"

The general was a wizened old man with bright eyes and a quick smile, his skin leathery from a lifetime outdoors. He looked Sarah up and down and muttered something in Chinese. Mr. Jack laughed. "Yeah, she's a looker. My man Moss's tongue is hanging down to his fly."

The general asked Sarah, "Does my friend's health improve?"

"He should be in hospital," Sarah said bluntly.

"Very stubborn man, Mr. Jack," said the general, dismissing her with a smile.

"I've made out pretty good in my life," Mr. Jack said that night, after Ronnie had fallen asleep. "But I'm a piker compared to my pals. Think about it: a handful of old guerrilla fighters have ruled a *billion* people for fifty years."

Sarah had no way of knowing whether Mr. Jack was exaggerating his friend's power, though the fact that PLA patrol boats and soldiers kept passing the ship on water and land indicated that the general was well connected in Shanghai, if not part of whatever it was that Mr. Jack was planning to do. "How did you meet?" she asked.

"Remember, I told you I crashed in Chekiang Province?"

"Of course." She was drinking tea. He was on a whiskey, watered at her insistence. In the pocket of her white steward's coat, wrapped in handkerchiefs, were two hypodermic needles, which she had practiced palming like a weapon—one for the old man, one for Moss. The question was when to use them. Part of the answer depended on

232

when the fog that blanketed the river most mornings would next roll in.

"Crash-landed in a rice paddy. Bombardier drowned. Hell of a guy. The rest of us got out okay—pilot, copilot, armorer-gunner, and me. We climbed out of the water and there were a hundred Chinese peasants, standing there grinning at us. The whole village turned out. Huge party.

"A couple of them spoke English—the missionaries had been through there—and they told us there were a lot of Japs between us and Chungking. Then the general appeared. Just a kid, then, like me. But a set of eyes that looked right through you. And *stature.* The man stood proud—a real fighter—like Moss. Only—" he lowered his voice "—only with more to fight for.

"You see, Doc, the peasants here had been beaten down and stomped on for two thousand years. The general was a communist. A rebel. He had a guerrilla unit that had been fighting Chiang Kai-shek and now they were fighting the Japs. 'Party's over,' said the general.

"Japs were hunting us. People hid us in their houses and helped us head for Chungking. Soldiers and farmers carried us in sedan chairs, on riverboats, pony carts. Once we were on a bus that burned charcoal. The Japs were on our tail all the way.

"They went crazy, Doc. They raided Chekiang Province with fifty battalions of infantry. Slaughtered civilians, destroyed entire villages, killing the farmers who helped us, killing every Chinese they could get their hands on. Probably killed a quarter of a million peasants and villagers in two months. *Quarter million* people." He swigged his drink and motioned for her to get him more. She poured a weak one. When she brought it to him, he was staring at his hands.

"It sounds as if the Chinese paid a terrible price for your bombing Tokyo."

"Awful," Mr. Jack agreed. "But we got what we wanted, and then some. A real boost to American morale. Bonus was, we shook up Yamamoto—hurt his pride—spooked him into rushing things at Midway—and tied up half their Air Force protecting the emperor's palace, making sure we didn't pull that stunt again.

"We took them off the offensive. And when he blew it at Midway, it was the beginning of the end. The Rising Sun stopped rising after that." He laughed, bitterly. "At least until the war was over."

"I would think you must feel some guilt, Mr. Jack."

"Me? Naw. I paid. I was punished. Bastards caught me, remember?" He held up his nailless fingers. "And this was just for starters. You seen the scars on my back."

"Did you tell them what they wanted to know?"

"Didn't matter."

"How so?"

"I told you. They killed everybody, whether they'd helped us or not. Killed everybody in the villages."

"Why didn't they kill you?"

Mr. Jack looked away. Then he said, "My old friend the general rescued me. Attacked the goddammed police station the Japs had commandeered."

"Ah. Now I understand."

He jerked his head toward her. "What?"

"The Chinese say, if you save a man's life you're responsible for his life."

"Oh, that. Yeah, but I evened things up. Fought with his unit for two years. Never did get to Chungking. Then we got our mitts on some planes and I started flying for him— We been pals ever since."

Sarah could tell he had been about to say more. She had the curious feeling that he had stayed on after the Japanese were defeated, and kept fighting Chiang Kai-shek until Liberation. That would explain his extraordinary connections to the People's Republic.

"Mummy?"

Ronnie was standing in the doorway, half asleep. "Sweetheart." Sarah embraced her. "Can't sleep?"

"Bad dream."

"Curl up with your mom, kid. I was just telling her about flying in China. Do you know how we loaded the airplanes?"

"No."

"Elephants."

"No way, Mr. Jack."

"Think I'm kidding? We were flying gasoline. They picked up fifty-gallon drums with their tusks. Seen it with my own eyes. Elephants."

"Mr. Jack? When are you going to let us go home to Daddy?"

"Hey. Everybody behaves themself, we'll all be home for Christmas."

After breakfast, while fog still blanketed the river, Mr. Jack had another visitor. "Vanishing act, ladies. Run up to the bridge. I'll call you when I'm done. And, Doc, keep your mitts off the phones."

When Moss reported that they were up there, well beyond stethoscope earshot, and that he had secured the phones and radios, Mr. Jack said, "Hold it, Moss."

"Yeah, Mr. Jack?"

"Before you bring in our guest. I hear your British bulldog screwed up again."

Moss's jaw dropped. How in hell had he found that out? "I'm real sorry, Mr. Jack. It won't happen again."

"Goddamn right it won't happen again."

Moss didn't know what to make of that. Mr. Jack told him to bring in their "guest" and to stand behind his chair.

Unlike the generals who visited by boat, Mr. Yu had boarded from the pier. He was a tough-looking heavyset guy, like a Chinese mafioso. And he had some attitude, until Mr. Jack broke him down with a mad-dog stare and a string of Chinese that sounded like a firefight in the Lincoln Tunnel.

Chinese were supposed to be a hard read, but this guy's

face said a lot. He went from attitude to angry to scared shitless in about thirty seconds.

At that point, Mr. Jack looked up at Moss, ignoring the mafioso in the blue suit. "I've just explained to Mr. Yu—who's got a nice little racket on the docks—that I've been told he's poaching on our territory. Mr. Yu started to mouth off until I informed him who our friends are. Now he's having second thoughts."

Moss took the hint to add his own mad-dog stare to the Chink boy's worries.

"I'm about to explain to him how disappointed our friends will be if he doesn't do something real soon to undo the mess he's made."

When Mr. Jack was done, Mr. Yu ran backward from the room, bowing like a man ducking bullets. Moss said, "Can I ask something?"

"You learn with questions, Moss. What is it?"

"What'd the guy do?"

"The son of a bitch gave a goddammed sampan to the doctor's husband so he could look for us."

"How in hell did the husband get here?"

"Hooked up with some two-bit Hong Kong Triad."

"So you told Mr. Yu to take care of him?" He had an awful feeling Mr. Jack was going to pull an end run, and do it himself.

"No, no. Just told him to stay out of the way. Old friends'll handle it."

That was worse, thought Moss. With all these old friends, what did Mr. Jack need him for? "Why not let him find us? Bang him when he walks in the door."

"*Moss.*" Mr. Jack's patience was wearing thin. "Look out the window, Moss. Wha'dya see?"

Moss looked.

Mr. Jack said, "Last thing I need is that son of a bitch drawing attention to my ship."

23

STONE SLIPPED OUT OF THE OLD PEDDLER'S TENEMENT BEFORE dawn, into the vanguard of the men and women streaming down the Nanjing Road to practice tai chi by the river. The loudspeakers in the park weren't blaring music yet, but early risers were already warming up. They were joined by numerous western tourists in jogging suits, but, as he had noted the previous mornings, only the Chinese stepped off the paths to talk to the trees. Stone chose his for its view of the embankment steps, pressed his forehead to the soot-caked bark, and watched for an ambush.

If he couldn't find the ship today he would have to admit that he had figured wrong, that Kerry was wrong, and that the *Dallas Belle/Amy Bodman* was elsewhere in the world. One last try. Provided whoever had tipped the Brit last night hadn't laid a trap where he boarded the coal sampan.

He was half surprised to see it chugging out of the dark, and relieved when the captain's sons jumped up on the coal carrier's bow and scanned the embankment, expectantly. He'd been watching for fifteen minutes. It looked safe. His spine prickling, he hurried through the swelling crowd and down the steps.

The elder son grinned a welcome and handed Stone aboard. The younger helped him down into the waist of the boat. In the wheelhouse, their sister was waiting shyly with a covered mug of tea; her mother parted the curtain to smile a toothless greeting; even the captain offered a friendly nod as he backed the sampan into the stream. Stone pointed downriver, and the diesel yammered a rapid note.

Mr. Wang watched from the shadows, aloof as a crow in his black suit and chauffeur hat. But William Sit greeted Stone effusively. "Here we have good weather for searching for the yachtmen's marina." As usual, he was dying to practice his English. "Are you pleased with this weather, sir?"

The weather had finally given him a break. Yesterday and the day before, thick fog had blotted out the harbor until ten o'clock. This morning the wind had backed to the northeast. Visibility was the clearest Stone had seen in the city, and he felt a renewed hope that banished the despair of the terrible night.

Mr. Wang was studying him thoughtfully. When he returned the driver's gaze, Wang glanced away.

They passed the piers below the passenger terminals, the Shanghai Shipyard's dry dock—which held the container ship he had mistaken for the LNG carrier—and crossed the river to the Shanghai Shipyard East.

"Ask the captain to slow down to four knots."

The Chinese exchanged questioning looks: surely the American understood that such a busy shipyard had no extra land to lease to yachtsmen, unless, of course, his friends were extraordinarily well connected.

There were ships on ways, ships alongside piers, and ships in slips cut into the riverbank. He scrutinized each with the binoculars, regardless of color. By now they would have had time to camouflage her tan hull with a coat of black paint. But none was the *Dallas Belle*.

The chemical factory downstream, host to a number of tanker types, received the same careful study. When the sampan had passed it, Stone was confident none of them was the gas carrier. He scrutinized the neighboring factories, though most of their piers were occupied by freight and container vessels instead of tankers.

The refinery lay downriver from the factories—an enormous sprawl of pipelines, fume-belching crackers, and holding tanks. Every vessel alongside was a petroleum ship—crude carriers arriving with raw material and various specialized tankers loading up with finished product. The refinery offered ample space and natural camouflage to hide a gas carrier. He had, however, already searched it twice.

And yet it drew him again because it was so logical a site. The power plant on Hang-chou Bay had exerted the same pull and he had gone back again—to no avail—in a very reluctant Mr. Wang's taxi.

He studied each ship with the binoculars. As the Huangpu was shallow, the crude carriers came in partially laden, riding high, flashing their bottom paint, and scything the river with propeller blades partly out of the water.

The smaller gasoline, diesel, and kerosene vessels that carried off the refinery's output were bound, the sampan driver said, up the Yangtze River to supply the hinterland. Stone focused on each, however, as he didn't completely trust his sense of scale against the immensity of space and structure. Seen from a Pacific atoll so low it was nearly awash, the *Dallas Belle* had loomed mightily. But in Shanghai, he kept reminding himself, little would distinguish it from a thousand other drab steel edifices in the port.

Reaching a marshy bank, he ordered the boat to the other side. The expression on the captain's face seemed to shout: any fool—even a clumsy landsman like the translator of English—could see that this shallow, unused stretch of river would be an ideal site for barbarian yachtsmen; even

239

the gangster-taxi driver in the fancy hat could see that yachts moored here would be happy—close to the mouth of the river and therefore less likely to get in the way of coal sampans whose families had trouble enough trying to earn a living.

Stone wanted another look at the big breaker's shed. But halfway across the river, the captain growled a throaty version of his wife's *"aiyyeee,"* and changed course. Stone thought he was afraid of the execution ground hidden somewhere out past the railroad tracks.

"William, tell him to take me closer."

But the captain pointed, and now Stone saw what he had missed while he was studying the breaker's yard in his glasses. Patrol boats were cruising a sort of picket line in front of the breaker's yard. Running slowly on opposite courses, they paralleled the frontage of the ship shed, turned around and passed each other again, clearly standing guard.

"Tell him to stick to the middle." He raised the powerful binoculars and studied the shore. The cruise ship had company, a vessel in the slip beside it. The new candidate to become scrap metal was acquiring a bamboo framework around its hull. All he could see was its stern and the back of its house. Oddly, the men on the scaffolding appeared to be painting the hull black.

Stone tightened his grip on the binoculars.

"Yacht!" said the sampan captain.

"The captain says he sees a yacht," said William Sit.

Veronica lay in shadow, between the ship they were painting and the pier. He tried to fine-focus the glasses and only gradually realized he first had to dry his eyes.

Her sails were furled and covered and she was tied expertly with spring lines and tide-tensioned bow and stern lines. Studying the boat for signs of Sarah and Ronnie, he saw that the bow and spring lines were tied off aboard, which, if his eyes weren't playing tricks, meant that whoever had tied her had prepared to get under way instantly. Sarah. Had to be Sarah.

Suddenly frantic, he swept the dark pier for her and Ronnie, then the ship—the sand-colored ship they were painting black. He couldn't see her main deck behind the bulwarks, but he could see bridge wings and a sort of balcony on the back of the house one deck below the bridge.

"Tell the captain to hold her right there."

The captain replied, via William, that he was drawing the attention of the patrol boats by standing still in the channel.

"Remind him that I've got papers," Stone said as he commenced a porthole-by-porthole investigation of the gas carrier's house.

"The captain says, 'Not for those boats, you don't.' I believe you should believe the captain, sir. And Mr. Wang says he too believes so. With great respect, sir, we both believe the captain should steer away."

"Slowly," snapped Stone, peering through the binoculars. The ship was less than a quarter mile away. He could swim to it.

The captain rammed his throttle forward and the coal sampan hurried downstream. Stone stared astern. So close. In seconds the shed wall had blocked his view of the *Dallas Belle*. Moments more and the shed itself grew small, blending with the riverbank until it was indistinguishable from the ferry head, the gray flats, and the heavy sky.

"We come back in one hour," William Sit translated.

The captain caught Stone's eye and nodded reassuringly. Obviously, there would be no yachtsman marina in the breaker's yard, but just as obviously, the American cared deeply about something there.

Stone unfolded the chart and studied the area again. Breaker's yard, bordered inland by the railroad. Further inland, the execution ground, which of course was not shown on the chart. He asked Wang if there was a road through the mud flats and marsh beyond. The taxi driver said there was. "But restricted," said William Sit. "Not allowed."

The sampan proceeded downriver for several miles. To Stone each mile felt like a thousand. The captain's wife passed tea around. Stone's grew cold in his hand. Finally, the captain agreed to chance a run back up the river. But now the tide was going out. A strong current slowed the sampan, and she crept against it until Stone thought he would go insane from the waiting.

The captain tucked his sampan under the stern of a rusty Hanoi freighter and directly ahead of a Huangpu River excursion boat with a stridently amplified tour guide. At last the breaker's shed came into sight. The tour guide fell silent as they neared the execution ground. The double patrol was still prowling the river.

Stone raised his binoculars, his hands shaking in anticipation as his sight line cleared the wall of the shed. A corner of the *Dallas Belle*'s house entered his field of vision, slowly widening until he could see the entire width of it. He focused on the upper decks. The bridge wings were still empty, as was the balcony below the bridge.

He stole a quick look at the Swan—forlorn in the shadows, definitely unoccupied—then resumed his inspection of the deckhouse, scanning the round portholes and the several big windows on the uppermost decks. Lights were burning in some of the cabins. Not a sign of her.

He glanced pleading at the captain. Would he stop? The captain eyed the patrol boats and shook his head. Too soon, as the sampan continued upstream, the cruise ship began to block his view of the gas carrier. She swarmed with workmen in hard hats. But the fiery cascades and the brilliantly flashing welders' outfits that Stone had seen earlier in the week had ceased—sensible in light of the new arrival's volatile cargo—and the yard workers were occupied stringing cable and shifting cranes that rolled on rails along the pier.

He noticed that the liner was riding high—several feet below her waterline exposed—emptied of fuel, water, stores, and furnishings before her final voyage to oblivion. The *Dallas Belle,* he realized a moment after he had lost sight of her, had looked a little light, too, as if they had unloaded some of her liquefied natural gas in order to cross the bar.

"William? Ask the captain if he knows why that gas ship is in the breaker's yard."

The captain's shrug needed no translation.

"Please ask him if he has ever seen gas carriers in that slip before."

William asked. The reply was simultaneously baroque and blunt. "The captain says he is a family man, with many mouths to feed, who carries coal and minds his own business."

"Tell him to drop me on the shore."

"Here?"

"By that ferry head—no, before it. On that old pontoon."

William conveyed the order and the sampan swung out of the stream toward a pontoon apparently abandoned when a new ferry landing had been constructed two hundred yards upriver. The captain's sons ran forward and scrambled onto the bow, where they stood peering intently into the murky water. A frantic arm signal caused him to jink the boat around an obstruction. He spoke to William Sit.

"He says to get ready to jump. And to be careful because the pontoon is very old and rusted."

"Tell him to pick me up in an hour. And if I'm not here, keep coming back every hour until I am."

"Am I to come in your company, sir?"

Stone hesitated. Downriver, the patrols off the breaker's yard were converging. But this time as they met, they peeled out into the stream and headed in company upriver. He and the captain watched them intently, but they showed no interest in the sampan and continued past them, past the ferry, and on toward the center of the city.

"Yes. And tell Mr. Wang we'll need him, too."

"May I ask whether you believe you have discovered an important yachtsmen marina location?"

Stone was already out the door, shrugging into his back-pack. He ignored the question and said, "Grab Wang. Let's go!"

When all three of them were perched on the bow, the captain's sons guided him in. The bow kissed the rusty steel and when, to Stone's relief, it didn't collapse, he stepped onto it and reached to help William. Mr. Wang boarded under his own steam. One by one they crossed the rickety bridge that connected the float to the riverbank, where a footpath pointed the way toward the breaker's yard through a field of leafless brush.

It was nearing noon, the winter sun about as high as it would rise, the cold wind insistent. Far ahead loomed the gigantic ship shed. Inland at some distance across the flat ground rumbled the switch engines shuttling freight cars.

William Sit cast an anxious gaze at the bleakness and ventured a rare opinion: "It is not necessarily likely that the authorities will hurrah this place for a yachtsmen marina, because it is perhaps too close to Shanghai Supreme People's Court Project."

"I'll leave that to the powers that be," Stone replied dis-tractedly as he scanned the path. Wang, too, appeared less than thrilled with their landing, and even less inclined to follow him. "Okay, gentlemen, let's just check out this open ground between here and the breaker's yard. . . . William, please tell Mr. Wang we're going to have a look around." He plunged through the brush without looking back and was relieved a moment later to hear them crunching after him on the dead leaves and broken twigs.

He walked for a half mile. The path was on top of the bank, which was higher than the field, having been built up by repeated dredging of the river. Occasional higher humps offered views of the railroad tracks. From one such elevation he saw, with the binoculars, a wall of mud-colored brick which appeared to be topped with barbed wire. The wall was a full mile inland, and half a mile beyond the railroad.

A rail spur curved into the breaker's shed. A train of

gondola cars stood on a siding at the foot of a huge mound of scrap metal. A crane was loading the gondolas, swinging a magnetic hoist that bristled with scrap.

Stone eyed the track. If they couldn't sail out of there on *Veronica*, the train offered the option of fleeing into Shanghai itself. Last ditch, but better than no ditch.

The wind carried the bang and clatter of heavy machinery and pneumatic drills and hammers, and the thud of hoist engines straining. A steady stream of scrap issuing from the shed was added to the pile.

"William, I want to have a look inside that shed. See what the neighbors are like."

"Neighbors?"

"We'll want our letters of introduction ready."

Mr. Wang spoke, and William, already anxious, suddenly looked terrified.

"Mr. Wang reminds me that it was in front of this shipyard that the patrol boats were . . . patrolling. He respectfully wonders whether a proper introduction to the managers of the shipyard would be a wiser way to visit."

Stone saw that this particular party was over. Neither William nor the Triad driver offered the slightest indication that they could be persuaded, bullied, or even forced at gunpoint to enter the breaker's yard.

"Okay . . . William, here's what I want you to do. Go back to the boat. It's just past noon. Tell the captain to come back to the pontoon every hour on the hour until you see me. Don't stop unless you see me. Okay?"

"I am worried for you, sir."

"I'm fine. See you in an hour. Or two hours. Or three hours. Every hour on the hour, right?"

"Right."

"Tell Mr. Wang."

Stone turned away, ignoring Wang's protest, and hurried toward the shed, which loomed against the smoke-gray sky like an oversized jumbo jet hanger. There were numerous doors in its sheet metal side.

He felt suddenly, acutely, aware of the years that had passed since his first wife had been killed. If he could recall any of the characteristics of the man he had been then, it was his compulsion to act—ponder little, keep moving. He chose a door at random. Midday, it wasn't locked.

He opened the top buttons of his raincoat to expose his white shirt and necktie, carried his backpack by the hand strap, and kept his eyes peeled for a hard hat. In that respect, he chose his door luckily, finding himself next to a wall hung with hard hats and fire extinguishers. He grabbed the cleanest red one he could find, polished it with his sleeve, and adjusted the headband so it fit him properly. Then he strode onto the pier that rimmed the slip, telling himself that with Western engineers crowding into Shanghai to partake in joint projects to build airliners, telephones, and farm tractors, a bearded American in a hard hat would not be that unusual a sight.

He had entered near the middle of the building and found himself standing midships of the cruise liner's rust-streaked hull. Every hundred feet, free-standing construction elevators in bamboo-framed shafts rose to the main deck. He headed inland, toward the bow, figuring to walk around it to the gas carrier. The few people he encountered on the pier were laborers who took no notice. Judging by the noise level cascading down from overhead, the mass of workers were employed up on the superstructure. He walked briskly—a boss on a mission.

All that stood between him and Sarah and Ronnie was the cruise ship. He saw no more obstacles, only opportunity. He would round the bow, continue past the gas carrier's bow, and find a gangway to board her. For a joyful moment it seemed that simple. But as he neared the bow, he saw a big work gang clustered around the feet of one of the cranes. The foreman noticed him, shouted into his walkie-talkie, and stepped forward to greet him.

Stone turned abruptly to mount the nearest construction elevator. He jerked his thumb up. The operator engaged a hoist, and the platform clanked up to the main deck, which had been stripped to bare steel and was jammed with workmen wrestling cable.

He stepped off, his eye already on a stairway up the side of the superstructure, toward which he moved quickly, brushing past the workers. He climbed it two steps at a time, spotted a doorway, and, checking to make sure he wasn't followed, shoved through it. He caught a glimpse of a cavernous, ill-lit space. Then he was tumbling forward, falling headfirst into the dark.

24

A SHOUT ECHOED HOLLOWLY IN HIS MIND, THE CRY ITSELF SMOTH-
ered by the rumble, clank, and roar of men and machines
tearing up the ship. Below was blackness. Above, a constel-
lation of work lamps, dim as stars in a cloud-shrouded sky,
revolved majestically as they passed his eyes in heartbeats
of slow motion.

He seemed to have all the time in the world to realize
he was falling. But the single thought, *thank God for the hard
hat,* ended abruptly with a rip of pain in his side and another
in his armpit. The limb felt torn from his chest.

He started falling again, sliding off a cable stretched horizontally between unseen bulkheads. Stone seized it with his
other hand, rasping his palm on the rough strands, and tried
to see where he was. The work lights hung forty or fifty feet
overhead. Space stretched to darkness. He'd been goddamned lucky. Below, his backpack lay on a deck. He didn't
remember dropping it.

He slid his aching arm over the cable, gripped the wire

with both hands, and dropped to the deck, where he sat a moment, looking around while his heart slowed and his brain stopped pinwheeling.

They had gutted the entire interior of the ship's super-structure. He could see several hundred feet aft and forty or fifty feet to the ceiling formed by the top deck. The shell— all that remained of cabins, decks, and public rooms—was riddled by long rows of portholes and windows. It looked like a planetarium projection of an unnaturally orderly sky.

He crossed the space and looked out a glassless port at the *Dallas Belle*. Its main deck was higher than the cruise ship's. He climbed a ladder until he was looking down on several acres of pipework, gas manifolds, and fire stations. Aft loomed its house, from which he could almost feel ema-nations of Sarah.

The yard workers had rigged catwalks between the ships, fore, midships, and aft, and were trooping across with tools and material. Forward, they were unrolling canvas, draping the cloth over the pipework, creating a tent across the deck. Then he saw that the gas carrier's fire stations were fully manned. Firefighters wearing hooded coats stood by the elevated high-pressure water guns and foam nozzles. He concluded that the canvas was fire-retardant to ward off sparks from the cutting torches which had started up again on the derelict cruise ship.

Lunatics. Literally playing with fire. Even though the pressurized cargo, compressed into heavily constructed tanks, was less vulnerable to accidental explosion than the oil in an ordinary tanker. In theory, you could toast marsh-mallows on her main deck. In theory. The sooner he got his family off the floating bomb, the better.

Aft, work crews were assembling on the deck behind the gas carrier's house. The midships catwalk seemed the least active and Stone chose that one to cross, until he con-sidered that he would have to walk some three hundred feet back to the house, all the way in clear view of the bridge and the big windows on the deck below it.

Better to cover that distance inside the shell of the cruise ship. He picked his way aft, skirting heaps of rubble and the stumps of cutaway stanchions, crunching the cinder remains of burnt steel underfoot, ducking low girders and high-stepping the taut cables that spider-webbed the structure. Every fifty or sixty feet he stopped at a window or porthole to get his bearings and gaze up at the house of the *Dallas Belle*. The ports there glared back, like eyes as impassive and uncaring as Ronald's Mr. Yu.

The ceiling grew lower as the decks of the wedding-cake superstructure stepped down. Stone reached the end and looked back at the remarkable space. He could see some four hundred feet forward, and out the front of the ship through the successive rows of front windows, from the main deck to the top and right up to the windscreen where the bridge had been.

Opposite the *Dallas Belle*'s house, less than a hundred feet from the catwalk to her stern deck, he moved into an open doorway. Foremen, he observed, wore the same quilted jackets as the laborers; bosses wore coats like his. Both carried walkie-talkies.

Stone took his VHF hand-held from his backpack. He told himself again that a bearded Westerner in a red hard hat belonged in a Shanghai breaker's yard so long as he believed he did, and marched on deck flourishing the radio.

He hurried through a maelstrom of shouting workmen and thundering machinery to the catwalk where they were leading orange compressed-air hoses across to the *Dallas Belle*. Suddenly he turned away. He might fool the Chinese but not the beefy American who was directing a work gang at the head of the catwalk.

"You, you, and you," said Stone, gesturing emphatically at three Shanghainese. They looked up with universal who-me?-I-didn't-do-nothing expressions that transcended language. Stone returned a Yes, you glower and barked, "This way!"

He herded them aft with more gestures and a stream of

meaningless orders delivered authoritatively. "Grab that!" He pointed with the radio and two of them seized a keg of rivets. "And that!" The third hoisted a pneumatic drill to his shoulder. "Gangway!" He scattered a group of idlers squatting on the deck and led his men to the back of the derelict liner.

"Hold it right there!"

His Shanghaied crew squatted down on their heels.

Stone put his radio to his lips for camouflage and looked up at the *Dallas Belle*'s house, which stood almost as tall as the cruise ship's superstructure. Window by window, port by port, he surveyed the house, praying he would get lucky and paying particular attention to the upper levels—officer country—where Sarah's patient, the injured "Old Man," would most likely be.

Suddenly he saw her.

She walked past a big window, fifty feet above the main deck. Stone blinked, wondering whether he had imagined it. The window was on the starboard side of the back of the house, one level below the bridge deck. He watched and waited.

He saw her again. She was looking down from the next window. He saw her first in silhouette, her strong, beautiful profile. When she turned toward him, full face, he felt his soul fly toward her and beat like a moth on the glass between them.

Her gaze swept the bustling decks. Without thinking, Stone waved. She stood, pressed to the glass, as if every fiber in her body was yearning to be free. Her eyes drifted hungrily and he saw with awful clarity the lines of tension that scored her mouth and cheeks. An artificial smile tugged at her lips and she turned her head as if speaking to someone in the room. She stepped back, out of sight. A groan shook Stone's chest. The Chinese exchanged puzzled looks.

Suddenly aware of exposure, Stone looked to see whether his wave had drawn attention. But there were a hundred men working on the two ships' stern decks, and no one—not even the American guarding the catwalk— had noticed.

Sarah reappeared. Her smile had vanished, her expression was wooden. Stone felt fresh anger rising: he had never seen her look so beaten down and hopeless. Had he the means at this instant he would kill whoever had done this. But even as he watched and prayed she would see him, he saw her begin to recover. Her gaze turned purposeful, her eyes busily soaking up details, seeking advantage. And then, quite suddenly and without warning, their eyes met.

If when he had first seen her he had felt simple joy, now his joy was doubled by love. All their years, all their days and all their nights, all the oceans they had sailed, had come suddenly together in one precious moment of infinity.

Sarah's eyes widened and her teeth gleamed in an astonished smile, which she covered a second later with a warning finger to her lips. Stone raised his radio in his right hand and held up the five fingers of his left. Channel 5. She nodded, her finger still to her lips, then whirled abruptly from the window.

Stone ducked down beside his baffled crew. "Gentlemen, I'm outta here. I recommend you find your regular foreman before he finds you." He glanced up under the brim of his hard hat. A broad-shouldered black man was staring down from Sarah's window. Stone ducked his head again and spoke more nonsense to the Chinese. Then, motioning them to their feet when the black man had finally quit the window, he herded them toward the nearest door, through which he disappeared into the shell of the superstructure.

He emerged cautiously, midships, port side, and commandeered another construction elevator down to the pier. He heard shouting behind him. Backpack in hand, radio pressed to his ear, he crossed the pier and exited the shed by the first door he came to. Out of the shadows and into weak winter sunlight, he ran.

It was twenty yards to the leafless brush. He heard a second shout. He ran another hundred yards down the path before he looked back. The shed itself was barely visible through the twigs and branches. He listened, heard nothing beyond the pounding and clatter inside, turned and ran again.

He continued across the brush field until he reached the clearing by the abandoned ferry pontoon. He checked his watch—one-thirty—backed into the brush, tuned his radio to channel 5, and clicked it on and off three times. No response.

At five to two, he edged out onto the pontoon and scanned the river traffic for his coal sampan. He checked his watch at two, at five after, and again at ten after. By two-thirty he began to admit to himself that they weren't coming back for him. At three, he started toward the new ferry dock, hoping to catch a bus there to the Bund.

But he found he couldn't leave the area. Sarah was simply too close. He went back into the brush and tried his radio again. She had nodded when he signaled. That meant she had managed to keep her radio, as she had Ronnie's GPS. He tried again, again no response. He would wait. Darkness would fall in less than two hours. He would sneak back into the breaker's yard.

Of the whistles and horns in constant song on the river, one sounded nearer and more insistent. He looked out from the brush. The coal sampan was back, the captain's sons holding her against the abandoned ferry pontoon, William and the daughter searching the crowds at the ferry. The captain was standing in the wheelhouse doorway, his face grim.

William said, "We are all very sorry we are late, sir. There has been very much trouble."

"Where's Wang?"

"Gone."

"What happened?"

"Your associate from Hong Kong has been arrested by People's Armed Police."

"Ronald? What for?"

"Trade in cultural relics."

"Smuggling?"

"It is what you call a capital offense."

No Ronald. No Wang. Who the hell could he turn to?

"Are you implicated?"

"I don't know," William said, shaking his head miserably.

"Ask the captain if he is."

William translated the captain's reply. "Triads never talk."

The sampan reeked of fear. Her captain *hoped* that Triads never talked.

"Can you get to Ronald's friends?"

"All gone."

The smoky winter sky cast a gray-green light on the busy river, the vast brush-covered field, the distant ship breaker's shed. Inland, a coal-fired steam engine billowed more smoke into the air as it made up a train of freight cars, while twinned diesel locomotives hauled a completed train toward Shanghai.

Swift movement upriver caught his eye. He checked it with his binoculars. "Navy patrol. Tell the captain to get out of here. You run to the ferry."

"What about you, sir?"

"Get away. Lose yourself on the ferry." The captain was already backing into the stream. Stone ran across the rickety bridge that connected the pontoon to the riverbank and into the brush. When he looked back, William Sit was hurrying, head down, toward the ferry head and the sampan was chugging toward the channel, her decks deserted, her wheelhouse shuttered.

He ran to the first rise, raised his head cautiously, and looked back again. Of William there was no sight in the jostling crowds. The patrol boat, an old wooden mine sweeper, was closing in on the sampan. But as Stone watched, it swept past, rocking the sampan in its furious wake, and made straight for the pontoon.

He ducked and ran. The minesweeper slammed alongside the pontoon. A squad of soldiers stormed ashore.

25

"Doc, you look positively radiant. If I didn't know better I'd say you found a fella while I was sleeping."

"I've come to take you and Moss down to your gymnasium."

"I still hurt like hell."

"I want you active," she said firmly, and waited with her arms crossed until he telephoned Moss.

"May I come?" asked Ronnie.

"With Mr. Jack's permission."

"Come along, kid. Watch the old man bust a gut— Moss, Doc wants me on the machines." The black American had glided silently into the sleeping cabin. Snakes of muscle rippled under his skintight T-shirt as he crossed his arms.

"It's too soon, Mr. Jack. Way too soon."

"Moss," said Sarah, "if you feel qualified to doctor Mr. Jack, perhaps you'll call a taxi to take me and my daughter to the airport."

"Let's go, Moss. Something's got her fired up today."

The old man lowered his bony feet cautiously to the carpeted deck, extended his good arm to Moss, and pulled himself erect. He stepped into his slippers and straightened his robe. "Coming, Doc?"

"I'll come by after Moss has you started."

She felt his sharp old eyes probing, seeking the lie. "Moss," she said, "remember, the rule is: if he can move it, move it more. We want you to stretch, Mr. Jack. And use those lungs. All right, off you go. Hold tight to Moss's arm, Mr. Jack. Ronnie, open the door."

Ronnie, bundled like a bear cub in a wool sweater that hung to her knees, stood solemnly holding the door, then ran ahead to get the next. Sarah listened to the shuffling of Mr. Jack's slippers and Moss's vocal encouragement until, when the elevator door closed, the cabin was enveloped in a silence no less deep for the clatter of machinery outside the windows and the rush of blood within her head.

She took Ronnie's Snoopy backpack into the bathroom, turned on the shower taps, and locked the door. She had hidden the VHF radio in Ronnie's bag as Pulo Helena had faded astern, reasoning that their captors were less likely to search a child's belongings. In fact, as far as she knew, Moss had never searched her bag, either—the advantage, perhaps, of appearing to be a helpless mother and child. Which, she thought bleakly, wasn't that far off the mark.

She lowered the volume knob before she turned on the radio and tuned to channel 5. The Battery Low indicator light glowed red. Hardly surprising, as it hadn't been charged in more than a week. She clicked the Transmit switch several times and pressed the radio to her ear.

No reply.

She clicked the switch again and listened some more. When she heard nothing, she tested the strength of the batteries by turning to Receive and scanning the other channels. It picked up faint signals of Chinese river traffic. She went back to clicking channel 5.

"Doctor! Doctor!"

She jumped. The door shook as someone pounded it. "Doctor!"

She hid the radio, turned off the shower. "Who's there?"

"Ah Lee, Doctor. Mr. Jack say tea."

"Let me get dressed." She splashed water on her hair and opened the door while toweling it off.

The Shanghainese steward was waiting there with a tea tray, sent, obviously, by Moss to watch her while he was busy with Mr. Jack. His bruises were fading, the cheek she had stitched almost healed, and she wondered if his fear was fading, too. Would he help them?

"Can you take me to Mr. Jack?"

Ah Lee responded with Ronnie's latest version of the affirmative, which she had picked up from the captain, "You got it, Mum."

In the elevator she tried to picture where Michael was at this moment. It was absolutely surreal to think of him within a hundred yards, and terrifying to imagine the risk. He had no conception of the power that Mr. Jack wielded in Shanghai.

There were VHF radios on the bridge deck, their batteries topped up by chargers. She glanced at Ah Lee, who was gazing impassively at the floor. How brave could he be after a savage beating? How brave was she after hers?

She touched Ah Lee lightly on the shoulder. He started as if she had jabbed him with a cattle prod. His eyes widened as she touched her fingers to her lips and pointed up toward the bridge. The car stopped and the door slid open. Sarah lowered her hands, but gave him a questioning smile.

Ah Lee shook his head, and instead of waiting for her to exit the elevator first, as he usually did, he darted out ahead of her and practically ran to the gymnasium door.

She found Moss pressing weights with his legs, streaming perspiration and grunting with effort. Mr. Jack and Ronnie were huddled over cans of Coke, deep in conversation like a pair of yachties in the club bar. "Whoa, Doc. Caught me."

"He just stopped, Mum. He was real good. You should have seen him."

He had acquired some color. She took his wrist and felt his pulse. Brisk and smooth. "You know, Mr. Jack, you're really all but recovered."

"You going to stop harping on hospitals?"

"It's time to let us go."

Moss stopped grunting. Mr. Jack smiled coldly. "Christmas, Doc. I promised you a bang-up Christmas."

Ronnie looked up at Sarah, gauging her reaction. "Mummy," she said quietly, "Mr. Jack wants to tell me about the Japs—"

"Japanese!"

"But he said you have to give permission."

"What do you mean?"

"Kid wants to know what happened to my hands."

"No. No, I'm sorry, Mr. Jack, that is not on."

"Mummmm!"

"You're too young, Ronnie."

"No I'm not. Mr. Jack says I'm really grown-up."

"Forget it, kid. Mum's made her mind up—Hey, stop moping. You're worse than Moss in a bad mood. Tell you what. I'll give your Mum the story—straight dope. She'll fill you in when she thinks you're ready. How's that?"

"Lousy."

"Take it, kid. Best deal you're gonna get— Hey." His face hardened abruptly. "Get out of here. I want to talk to your mother. Take her upstairs, Ah Lee. Get her some ice cream. Go on. Scram. All of you. You too, Moss. *Get out.*"

He had gone red in the face. Ah Lee fled with Ronnie. Moss trailed, his expression grave. The old man shuffled to one of the machines.

"I think you've had enough," said Sarah, puzzled by what was, even for him, an unusually abrupt shift of mood.

"Shut up, 'Mummy'!" He sat on the machine, seized the handgrips, and pulled them repeatedly. "Do you need a manicure?"

"I beg your pardon?"

"You heard me."

"But I don't understand."

"Something's up. I don't know what. But I don't want any monkey business outta you."

"Nothing is 'up.' "

"I can feel it in the air. See it on your face."

"I don't know—"

He cut her off. "Doc, I don't know if you got balls of steel, or maybe you dig pain. All I know is you're not afraid of Moss. I'm thinking of having him rape you."

"There's nothing—"

"But I don't think even rape'll help. Balls of steel. Fortunately, I got an ace in the hole."

"What do you mean?"

"Did you know that the Shanghainese do a lot of business with the Arabs?"

"I was not aware," she answered slowly. Where was this going?

"They started out smuggling rhino horn aphrodisiacs. Big market, except they discovered there's bigger bucks in human beings. . . . You see, with their one-child law, the Chinese peasants sell their daughters, hoping for a son next time. They're all doing it, my friends tell me, so of course, little Chinese girls are a glut on the market. But a little *black* girl?"

"*What?*" She felt the blood drain from her face.

"Ronnie would fetch a hell of a price."

"No! You can't mean that."

"Excellent bloodlines—gonna be a knockout with such a Mum—young enough to be trained . . ."

"Please, Mr. Jack."

"Pull any funny stuff and I'll sell Ronnie to a slaver."

Her blood rushed back in furious heat. Her hand plunged without thought into her pocket, to stab him with the hypo. She could barely hear the voice that said that it would be insane to run before she made contact with Michael.

Her voice trembled. "Is your friendship with my child a sham?"

"I wouldn't call it a sham, Doc. I love the little kid like she was my own. But I got priorities. No monkey business."

Stone smeared mud on his face and prayed for night. Inland, he heard the trains, much closer. Toward the river, the PLA patrol was cracking branches and crunching dead leaves as they searched the field.

His coat was his one defense, nearly matching the gray-brown color of the brushy field and the dimming smoke-stained sky. Buttoned its full length, it had protected him as he scrambled his way off the paths into the dense growth.

They were approaching faster than the night. Shielding his bright orange backpack with his body, he retreated far-ther into the field, ducking low and trying with little success to move quietly. The dark seemed to come up from the ground, so that while he could see the branches at eye level, and now and then a glimpse of the Chinese soldiers' silhou-ettes against the western sky, he could not see his own feet. Tripping repeatedly over roots and low branches, he made only a little less commotion than the soldiers. If they ever all stopped moving at once, they'd zero in on him like a pack of wolves.

The sunset was marked by a portion of sky slightly less gloomy than the rest, ribbed with sea clouds spawned on Hang-chou Bay. A soldier raised a weapon a hundred yards away, and Stone saw the stubby automatic rifle in silhouette. A peaked cap cut another shape. Then flashlight beams began to dart.

He listened intently. It sounded as if they had brought another squad in. Hugging the dark ground, he worked his way nearer the rail yard, careful not to silhouette himself against its lights.

A thudding sound in the distance, which he thought at

first was one of the switch engines, grew suddenly louder. He looked up and saw a bright star grow swiftly brighter and bigger until it was a helicopter sweeping the field with a searchlight. The engine and thumping rotor blades were deafening.

He ran.

The light reached for him like an accusing finger. He crashed through the brush, diving to the ground as it swept closer. For a second he saw his own arm brightly lit beside him. Then the search beam swept on and away and he ran, while behind him the soldiers shouted and someone blew a whistle again and again, the shrill note chasing him like a demented bird.

The helicopter wheeled swiftly away and just as suddenly back, parting the air like a scythe. The searchlight drilled into the brush. A heavy gun started firing. There were screams, then angry shouting as the helicopter rose suddenly and hovered at a distance. Shouts and wails pierced the night—for it was night, quite abruptly pitch-black but for the glow of the rail yard and the lights of the helicopter, which backed away.

Stone ran. They had shot their own men, but when they recovered they'd be coming after him with a vengeance. A railroad track embankment loomed above him, blocking the way. He heard the soldiers crashing after him through the brush. The helicopter had landed near where it had been shooting.

He crawled up the embankment. The helicopter took off, churning heavily into the sky, searchlight blazing. Stone scrambled toward the dubious cover of a runoff gully. But instead of resuming the search, the aircraft swung away and headed up the river.

A whistle blew. Soldiers shouted. Face to the ground, Stone clawed his way up the embankment, terrified he would cast a silhouette against the glow of the rail yard. At the summit, when he raised his head warily and looked back at the field, he saw a dozen flashlight beams stabbing the dark.

The slope was littered with gravel that had tumbled down from the track bed. He shifted uneasily on it, hesitating. The PLA soldiers were working their way toward the embankment, spread out across the half-mile breadth of the field. If he didn't move, they would nail him here on the embankment. But if he went over the top to cross the track, the soldiers in the field were sure to see him silhouetted against the light.

To turn to his right, down the line toward the ship breaker's yard, would bring him closer to Sarah but into the brighter lights glaring down from the ship shed. If he headed left, up the line toward the city, he would eventually reach the road to the ferry. But unlike William Sit he could hardly lose himself in a Chinese crowd, particularly a crowd that had seen the helicopter and heard it shooting.

He considered turning back, boldly breaching the search line itself and pushing right on to the river. It would be risky, the only advantage being surprise. But then what? Even if he passed undetected through the line, and remained undetected through the long night, daybreak would reveal him still trapped between the river and the rail yard, the breaker's yard and the ferry road.

A cold, wet wind sloughing through the brush carried the crackle of breaking branches. Stone shivered. Several searchers had forged ahead of the rest, their lights flickering within a hundred yards of where he lay. He looked out over them at the river, dotted with red and green running lights, and then down at the breaker's yard where Sarah and Ronnie waited, so close.

Light swept the dark aside.

Stone pressed his face to the slope. The ground began to tremble, cold gravel vibrating against his cheek. A heavy engine thundered. The light glared and suddenly he saw the source: a diesel locomotive approaching slowly from the right, its headlamp gleaming silver on the rails and splashing the embankment.

From the field came shouts. They'd seen him.

He saw another shallow gully that rainwater had scoured from the embankment and rolled into it. Whistles shrilled, gathering the hunters. And then, as the locomotive trundled past with a string of freight cars, he scrambled up the gully to the top of the embankment and threw himself under the train.

He tumbled a foot behind the lead wheels of a freight car, landing on the ties between the rails. His backpack, which he held by the handgrip, snagged a shoulder strap on a spike, the bag itself splayed across the rail as the freight car's rear wheels rolled toward it. Stone tugged frantically. In the bag was the radio—his only link to Sarah. But as he pulled, he saw, too late, that the other strap had wedged itself under a deep splinter.

He braced to pull harder and in doing so lifted his head. Something of enormous mass—some part of the train rumbling over him—brushed through his hair, knocking him flat to the ties. As the rear wheels bore down on him, he shoved the bag over the rail, waited for the rear wheels and then the front wheels of the next car to pass, grabbed it again and wrenched it free, falling backward and rolling over the far rail and down the opposite side of the embankment.

The pack had ripped. The gun and the radio had fallen out. The train still blocked the soldiers, but the end was coming up fast. He pawed frantically, found the radio but not the gun. He rolled to his feet, crouched and running, the train at his back, the sprawling rail yard ahead, lit here and there by lanterns and the red glow of signals.

He leaped a second track and a third, running hard, sticking to the dark. Ahead was another set of tracks and coming from the right another train, moving faster than the first. He hesitated. Should he expose himself to the headlamp or wait while the soldiers advanced behind him? It was moving too fast to tumble under it.

He waited too long. The locomotive was suddenly past and he was blocked. It was hauling a long string of boxcars and it looked endless, an endless tail disappearing into the night. He heard the whistles again. He ran forward, close to the moving train, trying to judge its speed to see if he could make it between the wheels. He saw an open boxcar, ran alongside, threw his bag into the dark opening, and then, planting both hands on the splintery floor, tried to vault aboard.

It was moving faster than he could run. His feet flew out from under him. As he gripped the floor of the car, his shoes dragged on the gravel and the ties. He gathered his strength for one effort and heaved. He never knew where his legs went or his dragging feet or his suddenly pain-racked knees, but the next instant he was lying on his back in the boxcar, breathing like a bellows, his head storming, with the train trundling under him, wheels slamming hard on the seams in the rails.

It was heading toward Shanghai, gathering speed, away from the soldiers. He looked out the other side: pitch-black darkness. He had fled across the entire width of the rail yard before the freight had rescued him. Now he was safe, the soldiers, the breaker's yard, and Sarah falling behind.

If he let himself think about the signal boxes, signposts, and rusty junk that littered the yard, he would stand in the door of the boxcar halfway across China. The train was accelerating. He felt the wind of its passage begin to cut. Beyond the door it was pitch-dark.

He buried his face in the soft side of the backpack and jumped. Now he had time to regret as he flew forever through the air. Something tugged hard at his coat. A frozen second of terror. His feet skidded on gravel. He pitched forward, out of control, frantically trying to tuck his arms and legs and roll.

The impact knocked the wind out of him and splayed him like a crucifix. Sliding on his back, he saw two red lights on the back of the train, and came to a rest in a ditch below the embankment. There, he cataloged the hurts in his body and tried to assess his situation.

He could move his arms and legs. He was at the farthest reaches of the rail yard. It was blessedly dark. But before the rumble of steel on steel had faded, he heard the soldiers' whistles.

He limped silently away. Keeping the glow of the rail yard and the ship breaker's behind him, he moved across the broken ground, stumbling, falling repeatedly. He thought he had lost the soldiers, but when he stopped to listen to the wind, he heard them calling. And then a flashlight beam swirled in the dark.

He fell again, stood up, moved ahead, and ran into something hard that banged his knee and scraped his brow. He felt in the dark. It was a wall of brick or stone. Brick— the mortar lines were straight and close. He looked up and felt with his hands. It was about six feet high, and gradually he made out strands of wire across the top.

The wall of the execution ground, he realized—Shanghai Peoples' Court Project. Behind him, he heard a familiar clatter—the trigger-happy helicopter was back, searchlight blazing like an angry eye.

Stone swung his backpack high, up over the wire, tugged hard on the shoulder strap until it caught on the barbs, and hoisted himself up.

26

SARAH HELD RONNIE SLEEPING IN THE CROOK OF HER ARM AND the radio pressed to her ear. She had the volume turned down so that all she heard was faint static and the occasional muted squawk of ship-to-ship traffic on the Huangpu. It sounded like the river was breathing in the bed beside her.

The ship's clock in the lounge chimed eight bells. Midnight. Laughter through the door. Mr. Jack's cronies had come aboard at ten, and if the previous nights were any guide, they'd be hard at it until three in the morning.

There was a steady din of machinery outside the ship and occasional shrieks of tortured steel. Suddenly the bed shook and the entire ship trembled. It had happened twice earlier in the evening, a sudden jolt and the resounding boom of something enormously heavy dropped on the deck.

She wished she knew where Moss was.

The captain—who seemed somewhat overwhelmed by the turmoil of shipfitting, the nature of which work Sarah could not see from the stern-facing owner's suite—was sound asleep in his cabin. He had come to her for, as he put it, "A Valium or something," so he could catch up on his sleep. Earlier in the week she had answered the request with sample Valiums or black market Halcions. Tonight she had prescribed the secobarbital she ordinarily used to sedate a patient facing surgery. Five hundred milligrams. The captain would sleep until noon.

Unfortunately, Moss took no drugs and no alcohol, his addictions confined to worshipping Mr. Jack, working out on the Nautilus machines, and net surfing in the computer room. She feared he was there, now, and she could only pray that he was not eavesdropping on radio signals.

Armed only with a basic knowledge of radio systems— she left the electronics to her husband—Sarah reckoned that the ship's computer had been alerted to her satellite telephone call, revealing their position to Marcus in Palau, by a constantly listening radio scanner. (If it had automatically recorded her conversation, then the only reason Moss hadn't searched for her GPS was a mistaken assumption that she had taken her position from the instruments on the temporarily deserted bridge.) Such a signal monitor would work fine at sea, but on the Huangpu River, in the heart of the busiest port in the world, the hundreds and thousands of transmissions would overwhelm the system. That, she hoped, meant Moss had shut it down.

Ah Lee, too, was awake five decks below, carousing with his cousins in the crew's lounge. They were waiting for the bosun to go off watch so they could raid his storeroom for a fifty-yard coil of nylon line. After desperate internal debate—and tormented by Mr. Jack's hideous slave threat— Sarah had approached him directly. Though Ronnie had befriended him, and expanded his English, Sarah did not trust her daughter to be able to conceal the news that her father was near.

Mr. Jack, she realized bitterly, had outfoxed her, seducing Ronnie far more effectively than the child had seduced him. God knew how confused she was and how skewed would be her loyalties. She blamed herself: attempting to insulate Ronnie from fear and use her as a wedge into Mr. Jack's heart, she had abandoned her daughter to a deeper maelstrom of emotion than a ten year old could be expected to understand.

Click-click. Click-click.

She lay still, not daring to believe.

Click-click.

She pressed a trembling finger on the Transmit switch, breathed a prayer. On-off. On-off.

"Darling!"

She pressed Transmit and shifted the radio to her lips, vividly aware that the thin, unlocked door was all that stood between her and Mr. Jack, and that Moss's microphones were embedded in the ceiling. "I'm here," she whispered. "Don't board the ship. We'll lower a rope to *Veronica*. Choose a time."

He waited a full minute before he answered. *"Half an hour after the morning fog. Thirty minutes. Do you copy?"*

"Thirty minutes after the fog."

"Out."

He would have traded a year of life to talk to her a minute longer. A year to hear her whisper that she loved him, that Ronnie was well, that soon they would have their life again. It was her whisper that threw him—a throaty, intimate sound, yet fraught with the danger staring them both in the face.

He shivered, partly from emotion, partly from the damp cold emanating from the ground and the icy brick wall. The square it enclosed was enormous, with room for a baseball diamond and spectators. If the dark corner into which he wedged his back was center field, then home plate diagonally opposite was a good five hundred feet away.

A light in that corner silhouetted what he had thought, when he first scaled the wall, was a squad of soldiers standing at attention. But as he watched in silence, crouched where he had landed, he gradually realized that they were too still. Now they looked like sawed-off trees, six or eight feet of trunk shorn of their branches. The rest of the enclosure was as black as the dark corner where he hid.

Suddenly there was activity at the entrance. He thought he saw a person pass before the light. Then a gate swung open on a moving clump of light. The search party. He heard conversation—brusque exchanges that sounded military or hierarchical in tone. The soldiers were demanding entrance. He rose on aching legs to vault back over the wall. There was a shouting match, and then the guard sent the patrol away and shut the gate. But a minute later, possibly reconsidering his position, the guard commenced a sweep of the grounds himself, walking the wall with a flashlight.

Starting from home plate, he walked toward first base and on into right field. Stone followed his progress by his light and when it veered toward his corner in center field, he loped quietly in the dark toward second base and doubled behind the searcher, settling back into his corner as the man explored the edges of left field.

He dozed and woke shivering. Dozed some more, starting awake with anxious looks at his watch. The hours crept by— two, three, four. He thought of the chances he must take and grew crazy with doubt. He slept from five to five-thirty and woke feeling little refreshed, his stomach alive with hunger, his mouth dry, craving coffee.

He was gazing across the enclosure, studying the wooden posts that studded the distant ground, before he realized that dawn had already broken, casting enough light through the overcast for him to see the far walls. The posts— for that was what they definitely were, wooden posts sunk in the ground—stood like the sentinels he had imagined in the dark. Warily, he stirred, studying the walls to the left and right. The light revealed a scruffy field of uncut grass and very little cover. If anyone at the home plate end were to study the far walls carefully, they'd spot him.

The light grew stronger.

He cursed himself for waiting too long. He should have awakened earlier. On the other hand, what fog there was lay thinly on the ground. Was it the same beyond the walls, or did the walls block the fog on its route from the river? Sarah would make her move half an hour after the fog was thick. Only by climbing the wall could he see, and if he tried they would surely spot him. Yet better to try now before more people came.

He focused his binoculars on the far corner. A wooden shed sat beside a wide gate in the brick wall. It had a door and a window, and a stovepipe which emitted a curl of white smoke. The guard had disappeared. He scanned the area one last time. Empty. Not even a face at the window. It was the best chance he would get and he started to his feet.

Pain shot through his knees and lanced up and down the stiff muscles of his legs. He forced himself to stand and felt a bone-deep ache in his feet the instant they took his weight. Then his knees collapsed and he sank half falling back to the ground, virtually paralyzed from yesterday's long run through the fields, the leap from the train, and the night in the cold damp. In his bag he found three ibuprofen, which he swallowed dry, and started massaging his leg muscles and working his knees and ankles, loosening up to try again.

Suddenly the shed door banged open. The guard rushed out and put his shoulder to the gate, sliding it open for a white truck. Behind it came a line of canvas-covered-stake trucks. The white truck stopped by the wooden posts. The other trucks parked haphazardly. Soldiers jumped down, shouting, brandishing rifles.

Stone counted twenty prisoners descending awkwardly from beneath the canvas covers. Chained wrist and ankle, they were shivering in light cotton shirts and trousers. Their cuffs had been tied with cord.

The soldiers herded them toward the wooden posts.

Stone clenched his binoculars in shock and amazement,

his eye riveted by a familiar cocky stance. The prisoner's fine clothes were ripped and stained, his face puffed with bruises. But he was still Ronald, his gaze turned hopefully skyward, sure that some old friend would send a helicopter.

They forced him to his knees and removed his handcuffs to chain his arms behind him around the post. Ronald shouted something with a grin. They looped wire around his neck and the post and twisted it tightly so he could no longer speak.

The squad leader blew a whistle.

The soldiers stepped forward, one to each post, and raised their rifles. The whistle blew again and they fired a ragged volley. The prisoners' heads jerked. The boom of the heavy weapons echoed around the walls. Ronald slumped against the wire, his body convulsing like a netted fish.

Stone felt his own body tense, bracing for the coup de grâce. But no death shot was delivered. Instead, a photographer flashed a camera over each body and an official wearing white gloves removed the chains and wire. At the same time, a gang—the only word that the sickened Stone could apply—of white-coated hospital staff jumped from the white truck, which was, Stone realized at last, a large and gruesome ambulance. They listened with stethoscopes and, working quickly, carried some of the bodies, including Ronald's, to the ambulance.

Even the executioners seemed disgusted as the butcher's crew sorted out the temporary survivors whose vital organs were available for transplant. They stood to one side, smoking and staring at the ground.

When the ambulance was full, it lurched away, blaring a siren at the gate, which, when it opened, revealed a second ambulance truck waiting to come in, and fog thick as snow.

Stone jumped for the wall, dug his toes into the slots between the bricks, grabbed the wire between the rusty barbs, and hauled himself up and out of the execution ground.

The fog embraced him as he ran, but sporadically, like

an unstable lover, dissolving without warning, thinning to a windblown mist. The ship breaker's shed loomed like a distant mountain or an unconvincing mirage. Suddenly lost when the fog billowed thick as cotton, he tried to puzzle out his position by the wail of a steam whistle; wind swirled and he was just as suddenly alone in the middle of a broad circle. A train rumbled into the circle. Stone veered away, running in the direction he thought he had seen the breaker's yard.

27

At ten to seven, when the light had grown strong enough for Sarah to see the river traffic, the fog had rolled up the Huangpu and tumbled over its banks. It gathered like petticoat pleats around the vessels in the stream, doubling, lapping over, crumpling. When it had enfolded the ships entirely, she had begun timing Michael's half hour.

If the weather held to its usual morning pattern, they might have three, even four, hours before the fog lifted. But the wind, light and from the northwest, had started backing. If it backed all the way to the northeast, as it had yesterday morning, it would blow hard and disperse the fog.

At a quarter past seven, she clicked Transmit on her handheld. No response. At twenty past, she clicked again. And when Michael did not reply, she decided she had no choice but to stick to their plan. Ronnie was in bed. As Sarah paced from window to window, Ronnie followed her with her eyes.

The old man still hadn't come to bed.

Sarah leaned over Ronnie and whispered in her ear. "Daddy found us."

Ronnie's face lit like the sun. "Daddy's h—"

"Shhh!"

"He's here? Oh, Mummy, what will Mr. Jack—"

Sarah whispered, "We're going to escape with Daddy on *Veronica*. I'm going to go get Mr. Jack now. Get dressed. Your warmest things."

She felt for the hypodermic and opened the door to the lounge, which had grown quiet around five-thirty. Two leather-skinned People's Liberation Army generals were sprawled on the couches, collars open, shoes off. One was snoring. The other was so still he looked dead.

Mr. Jack was sleeping in his chair, his skull-like head slumped to one side, his thin lips shut, his breathing regular. As Sarah approached, his eyes glittered.

"Whadya want, Doc?"

"I'm putting you to bed."

"Good idea." His gaze swept the empty bottles and overflowing ashtrays. "Jesus." He rose unsteadily. Sarah took his good arm and steered him toward the bedroom. "You wanna check my pals for signs of life?"

"It's your signs I'm worried about, Mr. Jack. Are you trying to kill yourself?"

"Don't worry. I'm not jumping the gun."

She had already opened his bed. Kicking the door gently shut behind her, she guided him toward it, got him seated on the edge, and knelt to remove his slippers.

"You're good at this, Doc. Hubby a drinking man?"

She lifted his skinny legs and slipped them under the sheets. "My father drank, after my mother died."

"Thought you went to school in England."

She pressed him gently down, arranged a pillow under his head, and covered him, except for his right arm, which she held gently on top of the blanket. "After the civil war I went home on holiday. He was very lonely."

Her hands were shaking.

"Close your eyes, Mr. Jack."

"Thought you said he had a mistress."

"Not at first." She sat on the edge of the bed and patted his hand. "I want you to sleep. And I want you to promise you'll stop all this drinking."

"Life's short, Doc."

"You're making it shorter." She arranged the sheet over the blanket and under his chin. He was watching her closely, even as sleep fogged his eyes. While tucking the blankets, she slid his loose pajama sleeve toward his elbow.

"I'll wake you around noon," she said, "try and get you on a better sleep schedule. I'll send your friends packing and request that they stay away for a night or two. Would that be all right, Mr. Jack?" She could see the vein pulsing in the crook of his elbow.

"I'm on schedule," he murmured. "No sweat."

With one hand lying on his forearm, she reached with the other for the needle; snagging the rubber guard on the edge of her pocket, she drew the needle from her coat.

"Christ, I'm tired," Mr. Jack whispered. "Night, Doc." He closed his eyes. Sarah sat poised with the needle in one hand, his arm in the other. She could almost feel the wakefulness ooze from his body. "Mr. Jack?"

His chest rose with a sigh, the rough planes of his face grew smooth, and he was deep, deep in sleep. Sarah hesitated. She looked at Ronnie, watching from the bathroom door. Ronnie made a jabbing gesture. "Do it, Mum!" she mouthed.

If she jabbed him and missed, he'd be up and screaming for Moss. This was better. Also, it gave her a second shot for Moss.

Sarah hesitated a moment longer, then rose lightly from the bed, the needle at her side. She pointed at the closet where their bags were ready. Ronnie slipped soundlessly across the carpet, put on her backpack, and handed Sarah hers. Sarah took the radio, took one last look at Mr. Jack.

She opened the door a crack and looked into the lounge.

The Chinese generals were exactly where she had seen them last, both old men dead drunk and fast asleep. Mother and daughter tiptoed around them toward the door to the aft balcony deck. The fog was so thick now she could see nothing of the river. Even the pillars and roof of the ship shed were invisible. The *Dallas Belle*'s owner's suite might have crowned a mountain in a cloud.

But when she opened the outside door, there soared from the wet, smoky-smelling cloud a cacophony of machinery and ship whistles. One old general groaned and turned over. The other half rose on one knee, blinking in confusion, a hand driven by decades of instinct reaching for a sidearm. Sarah pushed Ronnie through the door, followed, closed it, and looked back through the window.

When the Chinese's hand found only rich broadcloth where weapons used to hang, he too sank back down on his couch. Sarah released her breath. "Ah Lee hid a rope in a garbage bag. Look for it."

Together they searched the narrow balcony, but there was no rope. "Maybe Moss got him," Ronnie whispered.

Sarah's heart sank. "Never mind. He probably left it on the main deck." If not, she had brought towels they could use to slide down the ship's mooring line.

"Do you think he hurt Ah Lee?"

"No. Shall I go first?"

Ronnie looked at the ladder, which disappeared down the side of the house into the fog. "I better go first."

"Now hold on tight."

"Mum!"

"Both hands. Here, give me your pack."

"It's not heavy."

With that, Ronnie swung over the railing and started down the ladder. Sarah gave her a deck's head start and, swallowing hard with fear, turned her back to the invisible abyss and climbed clumsily, haltingly, over the railing, found purchase for both feet, and started down, her arms and legs stiff with tension.

Descending past two rows of portholes, two decks, she found her knees shaking almost uncontrollably and her strength failing. It felt like fear was dissolving her muscles, and that the cold fog had penetrated every aching injury Moss had given her. Two more decks, and she could barely close her hands around the metal rungs of the ladder.

Ronnie tapped her foot. "Stop."

"What?"

"There's people on the deck," Ronnie whispered.

Sarah looked down. She couldn't see anything but fog.

"Wait. I think they're leaving."

Now she heard them talking. Chinese. The workmen who'd been swarming over the ship. Someone spoke sharply and shuffled off, dragging something that clanked. A cold, wet wind brushed her cheek. The fog parted for an instant, but before she could see more than a vague outline of the bulwark that rimmed the main deck, the fog rushed in again, thick and gray and stinking of coal smoke. Whistles echoed; the fog made them sound close, as if ships were passing directly under the stern.

Ronnie tapped her foot again. "Okay."

She climbed down, counting rungs and portholes. One more deck. One more to go. Here, in the lee of the bulwark, the fog was thinner. She saw Ronnie land lightly and step away from the ladder. Around her were dark shapes—machines, material, she couldn't tell. As she hurried down the final rungs, she searched the shadows for Ah Lee's rope.

Her foot touched the deck. She stepped down, her legs shaking so hard she had to hold the ladder to recover.

Ronnie was darting among the clutter, searching. Sarah joined her, wondering whether her arms had the strength to descend a rope, fifty feet to the Swan's deck. Ronnie started toward another shadow, then stopped abruptly as it moved.

"You looking for this?"

Moss loomed out of the fog, swinging the garbage bag with the rope coiled inside. He had blood on his white T-shirt and as he swung the bag at Sarah's face, he looked less angry than pleased that again he had license to hurt her. The blow knocked her backward, and she would have fallen if she hadn't crashed into the bulwark. Her backpack protected her from the steel. The blow of the coiled rope inside the plastic was more shocking than painful.

Sarah plunged her hand into her pocket and closed her hand around the hypo. Ronnie rushed between them. Sarah tried to push her away.

Moss raised his arm to hit her again. But before he could, his head snapped around sharply at a new sound that penetrated the machinery noise, barking sampans, and the ships' whistles. Sarah heard it too, the most beautiful sound imaginable—a familiar *burp,* and then the weary growl of an old, old Perkins diesel grumbling to life on *Veronica.*

Moss saw the joy light Ronnie's face. "Daddy's home," he smirked.

Sarah stepped inside his swing and slammed the needle into his massive bicep.

28

"BITCH! YOU CUT ME!"

Moss jerked back, mistaking the needle for a knife, and swung hard at her face. Sarah drove the last of the drug into his hand. He yelled when he saw the hypodermic needle dangling from his palm and flung it away.

"What—"

Sarah pulled another from her pocket.

Moss's eyes widened. "What was—wha'd you—?" He staggered back, raising the garbage bag like a shield. Sarah lunged. He whipped the bag around and knocked the needle from her hand.

Ronnie flew at him. Imitating a kung fu movie jump kick, she drove both feet into Moss's knee. The big man swatted her away like a mosquito. She tumbled across the deck, squealing with pain. Sarah slid her rigging knife from its side pocket in her pack and dove at Moss.

Startled by the ferocity of her attack, he backed away but quickly recovered, gauging her moves with a savage smile. The drug seemed to have no effect. "Kiss your pretty face good-bye, Doc."

He came at her, shifting the plastic bag from hand to hand.

Sarah drew the knife near her side and knew at that moment with dreadful certainty that she would kill him and spend the rest of eternity in futile penance. She remembered for the ten thousandth time her father slaughtering the men who had attacked her mother. She saw his ceremonial sword flash in the sun and knew at last that in the heat of battle her father had fought with cold precision.

She saw precisely the next few seconds: Moss would feint with the coiled rope in the garbage bag; she would dodge; he would lunge; she would be ready, turning the blade with a surgeon's hand to slide it between his ribs.

An explosion shook the deck.

Brilliant light flashed from the shed roof. Shadows leaped like black lightning. From the distant foredeck came a roar like a collapsed dam, shouts and screams, and then the ship's fire bells and, a second later, the shocking blast of its whistle.

Moss bolted to the bulwark and stared forward past the house to the front of the ship. The fog inside the shed had melted and firelight glowed on his face. His frantic gaze shot upward, up to the top of the house where Mr. Jack slept. He dropped the bag containing the rope and threw himself onto the ladder, climbing in great double-rung leaps, his huge voice thundering, "Mr. Jack, Mr. Jack!"

Stone hauled the last mooring line aboard *Veronica*, ran back to the cockpit, and engaged the diesel. The stricken *Dallas Belle* was ringing fire bells and booming a whistle almost as thunderous as the explosion. A pillar of flame rocketed from her foredeck to the roof of the breaker's shed.

The fog beckoned. The Swan moved eagerly from the pier.

In seconds, every crewman on the ship would be racing

to the fire, every PLA patrol on the Huangpu River converging on the breaker's yard while *Veronica* ran for the East China Sea.

Stone steered close behind the ship, careful not to strike her mast top against the overhanging stern. He gazed upward, searching for Sarah.

Under cover of the fire retardant canvas spread over the gas carrier's foredeck, he had aimed the hard blue cutting flame of an acetylene torch on a gas valve and lashed it in place. When the flame had cut a pinhole through the steel, it had ignited the gas that spewed forth under tremendous pressure. The pressure would blow the fire out and away from the powerfully constructed, heavily insulated tanks. But to extinguish the blaze and cap the gas, the crew was in for a busy morning.

"Michael!" Sarah's cry cut through the cacophony of bells, whistles, and shouts. She was lowering a line from the vessel's port stern mooring chock.

Ronnie slipped through the opening, wrapping a towel around the rope to protect her hands. "Daddy!" Fifty feet above the water, her grinning face shone down on him. She started sliding down the rope, one hand around it gripping the towel, waving with the other.

"Both hands, for crissakes!" Stone jinked the *Swan* against the river current as he edged the bow between the side-by-side hulls of the cruise ship and the *Dallas Belle*. Playing the throttle against the rudder, he eased the foredeck under the rope.

Ronnie dropped lightly to the teak.

But instead of running back to him, she stared up at the ship. "Mummy!"

Stone was less than forty feet from Ronnie and would have given anything to take her in his arms, but if he let go of the helm and throttle the current would sweep *Veronica* away from the rope.

"Take a wrap around the bow pulpit!" he yelled.

"Mummy!"

And now he saw what Ronnie saw. Sarah plunged through the chock, her legs scissoring frantically for the rope. He thought she was stuck in the chock hole, but a second later saw she was struggling to get loose from a black man who had her by the arm.

Trapped in the cockpit forty feet below her, Stone was helpless.

"Ronnie! Come take the wheel."

But Ronnie started climbing up the rope to help her mother. "No!" Stone cried. "Don't!" He locked the wheel and started forward.

Sarah broke free. For an instant she had both hands on the rope, but even in that instant the man who had held her started pulling the rope up through the chock.

Stone hit the throttle.

"Jump for the mast!"

Veronica surged forward. The masthead banged against the ship's hull.

Sarah, wild-eyed, let go of the rope and leaped, falling, both arms stretched wide, grasping for the mast. She missed. Plummeting, she landed on the top spreader, miraculously on her feet, and, flailing her arms, caught hold of a shroud with one hand and the mast with the other.

Stone rammed the boat into reverse. The propeller bit, and the boat backed away on boiling water. Stone looked over his shoulder, looking for room to pivot away from the towering hulls. Out of the fog came a PLA patrol boat.

"Daddy!" Ronnie screamed.

He saw a rush from the sky. The black man swept across the bow of *Veronica* as if on wings. He was swinging one armed from the rope in a broad arc like a pendulum. He brushed the forestay and scooped Ronnie off the bow pulpit like a falcon taking a sparrow.

29

MOSS TOOK RONNIE SO SUDDENLY THAT THE SWAN WAS A HUN-
dred feet into the river and Sarah still on the mast before Stone
could stop the boat. He saw Ronnie indistinctly through the fog,
kicking and clawing. The black man held her with one arm,
shook her brutally, and pumped his legs to increase his swing.

Stone gunned *Veronica* forward.

Moss swung toward the pier, let go the rope, and landed
on the edge, teetering. He caught his balance and ran for
the *Dallas Belle*'s gangway, Ronnie still in his arms.

Stone swung toward the pier.

Sarah screamed, "Look out!"

A fireboat split the fog on a course that would cut *Veronica* in half. He slewed to port. The fireboat cleaved the spot
the Swan had vacated and bellowed and frothed to a halt
in the narrow slot between the two ships.

A second boat loomed from starboard—a shaggy-nosed
tug with a fire monitor on the bridge roof, spraying river
water in a wild arc. *Veronica* tossed on the colliding wakes.

A siren whooped and another PLA patrol boat roared out of the fog. Armed lookouts on its bow and flying bridge waved the Swan angrily out of its way. Stone swerved downriver. He saw Moss running up the gangway, Ronnie slung over his shoulder like a sack of laundry. Through the roar of the boat engines and the blast of the ship's whistle and the cacophony of sirens, he heard her scream, "Daddy!"

Stone steered again for the pier.

Sarah slithered down the mast, gripping halyards, slipping and sliding, to land hard on the coach roof. She scrambled back to the cockpit. Blood streamed from her arm, shockingly red on her white coat. Her face was contorted in pain.

"No," she cried. "Get away."

"Ronnie."

He had never seen her eyes so hard. "We can't help her. He owns the army. *Turn away!*"

Stone hesitated. The pier was feet ahead. Sarah seized the wheel and fought to turn it. "We can only help her if we get away. No one can save her if we go back."

Stone refused to let the wheel slide through his hands. But as a fourth and fifth boat converged on the ship, he had to slam the diesel into reverse to keep from being rammed.

"Look out!" Sarah cried.

Something bright fell from the ship.

Stone looked up. An old man in a bathrobe was leaning out from the balcony below the *Dallas Belle*'s bridge, his arm stiff as if he had just hurled a hand grenade. It splashed beside the cockpit and instead of exploding, bobbed bright yellow to the surface.

Stone lunged under the lifelines and plucked from the water a submersible Navico Axis handheld VHF. The radio was squawking like an angry crow.

"Doc! Doc! You hear me, Doc?"

Sarah took it from Stone. The old man was screaming into the radio's twin. "We hear you, Mr. Jack. Where's Ronnie?"

284

"Get out of here."

"Give her back. Please, give her back. We won't—"

"Doc, you really piss me off. I trusted you and look what the hell you've gone and done. Doc, you hear me?"

"Mr. Jack. I want my daughter."

"Yeah, well, you can't have her. You ripped me off, Doc."

"Mr. Jack, we'll do anything."

"Get that boat out of here."

"Do it, Michael. I'll talk to him."

Stone turned the *Swan* downriver. His last glimpse before the fog closed around the bleating, howling ships and boats was of the enormous mouth of the flame-lit shed suddenly going dark. The roar of the gas fire died abruptly. But flames began leaping from the shed roof.

"Mr. Jack," Sarah repeated, "we'll do anything."

"Little late for that. You've made a real mess for me. Got my hands full. Goddammed cops all over, people I don't know."

"Mr. Jack."

"Listen to me! You want your little girl? Tokyo. Next week. You keep your trap shut, I'll hand her over. You cause me any more trouble and I'll sell her like I told you."

"Sell her?" echoed Stone.

"To the slave trade," Sarah whispered. She stepped back against him, the radio still pressed to her ear, and Stone closed an arm around her. "He means it."

Stone took the radio. "Where will you hand over?"

"Why, it's Mr. Doc! You son of a bitch, you the one started this Chinese fire drill?"

"I want my daughter."

"Don't stop till you get to Tokyo. Don't try to screw me up again. And, don't get caught."

"Where? Where in Tokyo?"

The radio hissed a long moment. Finally: *"Tokyo Tower."*

"Where will you be?"

"Right out front. Don't worry, you won't miss us. If you get there ahead of us, give you some time for your Christmas shopping."

"He's out of his mind," said Sarah.

"When next week?"

"Christmas Eve. Four P.M. Sixteen hundred."

"It's over a thousand miles!" Stone protested. "I can't make that in a week."

"I ain't hanging around. Four P.M. deadline."

Sarah took the radio. "Mr. Jack," she said soothingly. "can't we have some alternate plan in case we can't make the deadline? . . . Mr. Jack, can you hear me?"

"We've got to go back," said Stone. "I don't care what happens. At least we'll be with her."

Sarah shook her head violently. "Michael, we can't help her. The army, the police, they're all his friends."

"Not all. He's afraid we'll get arrested by officials he can't control." Stone whirled the helm. "We've got to go back."

The radio spoke. *"Doc, I don't know what you did to Moss. He's looking a little sleepy, but he can still shoot his sniper gun. If he sees you come out of that fog he's going to blow you away. Last chance, Doc. Get outta here before they catch you."*

"Let me speak to Ronnie."

"You can talk to her at twelve hundred day after tomorrow. You got a sat phone on the boat?"

"Single sideband radio."

"Channel eighteen-twenty. Noon. Day after tomorrow."

"Mr. Jack?"

"Get outta here, Doc. They're going to start asking questions soon as we get Mr. Doc's fire under control. Damned fool, you almost blew us to kingdom come."

"Please. Don't frighten her."

"I'm not a monster, Doc. Just trying to make things right."

"Don't let Moss frighten her either."

"Moss looks ready to go sleepy-bye. But if he dies from what you shot him with, then I'll cut her little heart out."

"Moss won't die."

"Better not. Over and out."

Stone felt helpless—flung back in memory to his first

wife's dying. But then, he saw with sudden clarity, there had been nothing he could do. No human act could have saved her. This was worse. Ronnie's life hung on his decision. His heart said stay and fight; his gut said run.

Sarah turned to him with tears in her eyes. "He won't hurt her. I'm sure he won't. He likes her."

"What did he mean by 'trying to make things right'?" asked Stone.

"God only knows."

He smothered his heart's desire—pushed Ronnie to a deeper corner of his mind—and turned his attention to the fogbound river.

"Let's get our reflector down so they can't track us, and switch on the radar to see where the hell we are. Is your arm okay?"

She stared at him, through him, shaking her head. "I don't know. Can we make Tokyo in time?"

"We can't make anything before we get out of the Huangpu. Go! I'll fix you up in a second. Drop the reflector. I'll get the radar."

He ran down the companionway, switched on the radar, and climbed back to the cockpit with his bag. Sarah was at the mast, fumbling with the halyards. He turned off the diesel and listened.

The receding tide and the river current had now swept them so far downstream from the breaker's yard that he could barely hear the fire bells. The ship's continuous seven short emergency whistle blasts thundered a cry for help and warnings to stand clear.

Closer to hand, he heard the bleat of small craft horns and the steady thunder of a seagoing vessel proceeding upriver. All around sounded the sharp barking noise of the unmuffled diesels that drove the coal sampans and lighters, any of which were heavy enough to roll right over the Swan and cut her in half.

Sarah came back from the mast with the reflector cradled in her arms. "Michael, I can't seem to . . ."

When he tried to take the reflector from her, she clutched it tighter.

"Michael, I—" Again she drifted off. Then, suddenly, stronger, shrill. "She's just a baby."

"They won't hurt her. You told me. The old man likes her."

"Do you promise?" she asked in a small voice.

"I promise," he answered. They stared at each other through the emptiness of the hope that made the promise, each searching for the other's belief. Their boat was drifting, their senses converging on the invisible movement around, and they quickly broke apart, spirits clinging to glimpses of each other's strength at the core of despair.

I'll believe him because I must, thought Sarah.

And Stone thought, One step at a time; get out of the river alive.

"All right," he said, still speaking softly, still holding her eyes with his. "I know the river pretty well. We're about four miles from where the Huangpu joins the mouth of the Yangtze. Harbor master's a mile downstream, this side. We've got to dodge him, the quarantine station, and any patrols that come along."

He pointed into the fog. "Do you hear that bell gong? It's a beacon tower on the far side of the channel."

Sarah cupped her ear to shield it from the fire bells and ship whistles in the breaker's yard, and isolated the mournful clang.

"Steer for that. I'll get on the radar."

He squeezed her hand, bowed his head to kiss it, and ran below. The radar screen was smeared with targets like a windshield in a sleet storm.

"Starboard!" he yelled, even as Sarah started the engine. An echo was bearing down on the *Swan*, trailing a long phosphorous tail—a small boat moving fast. Another patrol racing to the breaker's yard. He felt the prop engage, the drive shaft grind.

The Swan heeled, turning slowly. The phosphorous dot

moved closer and began to merge with the center of the screen. Stone ran halfway up the companionway, stood on the steps, and stared into the puffy whiteness. A gray, ghostly hull swept past—close enough to hit with an empty beer can. A hard wake smacked *Veronica*. She rolled once and pulled away.

The beacon tower, which the chart identified as a four-second red flasher with fog bell, returned such a strong echo that even *Veronica*'s antiquated radar distinguished it from the myriad ship and boat targets cluttering the screen. When the sailboat was well inside the inbound lane, he ran back up to the cockpit.

Sarah was steering to a compass bearing she had estimated from the sound of the bell and was listening for clues to the traffic.

"Edge a little up. We've got something big inbound." He kicked the throttle wide open with his foot, and the boat responded to a poky six knots.

A whistle boomed steadily closer.

"Watch him. Listen for sampans coming the other way."

"Shouldn't I wait and slip behind him?"

"I don't want to hang around here, and make the patrol curious. I can't trust my papers anymore. And what if that old bastard changes his mind?" At short range, looking down, radar might pick up the steel of the *Swan*'s engine or even the lead keel.

"Bear north," he called from the steps. "We'll angle across the outbound lane." He tried to distinguish the sampans from the bigger ships, but the radar was returning crazy echoes. When the immediate space around *Veronica* appeared open for a moment, he climbed back to the cockpit with a foul-weather jacket for Sarah, who was shivering at the helm.

The fog was so thick he could hardly see the bow.

The bell was clanging close ahead and to their right. Stone took the wheel while Sarah zipped up. The fog began vibrating with the bloody tinge of the flashing red blinker,

and the bell grew so loud it almost drowned out the cacophony at the breaker's yard. He steered past the beacon and
downriver on the edge of the traffic lane, then cut the engine. "Listen."

The noise had faded.

"What happened?" Sarah whispered.

"Big ship coming downstream. We'll use him to block
the harbor master's radar." He opened the throttle again. A
cold wet wind suddenly cut his face, and there was the ship
a hundred yards across the water—a fair-sized container
vessel, its hull and containers providing a six-hundred-foot
long, eighty-foot-high moving wall between *Veronica* and the
harbor master.

"They see us," said Sarah, and indeed, the sudden wind
had so thinned the fog that a ship's officer standing watch
on the container vessel's bridge wing was staring in some
astonishment at the unlikely sight of a Western yacht on the
coal-gray Huangpu River. He raised his radio, alerting the
river pilot to a small craft nearby.

Stone let *Veronica* fall behind. "Damned wind is swinging east. Killing the fog."

"Can we hide until night?"

"There's a couple creeks on the Pudong side, but we'd
be sitting ducks for the patrols."

The container ship had vanished ahead. A high, empty
sampan was catching up. Stone eyed it speculatively. According to the *Sailing Directions*, which they had left open
in the cockpit between them, a bulk carrier had been sunk
outside the river mouth as an unloading facility to lighten
ships whose draft was too deep for the river. The empty
sampan was heading out to shuttle ore or grain.

He put an arm around Sarah. "Okay, we're going to
sneak alongside this sampan. If he's like the one I was on,
he's got no radio."

"What's that?" With her unusually keen eyesight, Sarah
had seen ahead what he had missed. It stood still in the
channel, shrouded in fog, and for an awful second he

thought it was a stationary patrol lying in ambush. A wet gust whipped the fog. A red flag over a black triangle. He checked "Signals" in the *Sailing Directions*.

"A dredge."

They ran in company with the sampan, chugging toward the river mouth. The fog-thinning gusts grew more frequent, visibility frighteningly clear. Stone edged close enough to see individual bolts and pegs in its planked hull. A deckhand stepped out of the pilot house and leaned on the gunnel and eyed the sailboat. He was joined by another. Stone pulled a pack of Marlboros from his bag.

"*What* are you doing with those cigarettes?"

"Making friends."

He slewed alongside and lobbed the pack. In seconds both men were puffing smoke and waving their thanks.

"You should be ashamed of yourself," said Sarah, and they shared their first smile.

Training walls extended from the banks and swung east to form the mouth of the Huangpu River. The tide was out, just beginning to turn, as the *Veronica* emerged with her shield. Ocean vessels were waiting to enter on the flood. The Chinese waved, warning their sampan would turn toward the loading hulk.

The fog was so thin he could see the opposite training wall, half a mile away. Sarah squinted. "They're flying a red flag." She thumbed through the *Sailing Directions*. "'Large number of small craft, navigate with extreme caution.'"

As visibility increased, sampans, lighters, and fishing boats appeared everywhere on the calm water. A cool, low sun shone through the fog, its light diffused so that it was hard to distinguish the walls, the water, the sky, and the waiting ships.

Stone unfolded the chart he had bought in Hong Kong for the Yangtze estuary. The river, which drained half of China, sprawled lazily into the East China Sea, spreading silt islands in its wake and carving a dubious channel marred by sandbanks, mud flats, and sunken wrecks. He longed to swing east, slip between the islands away from the busy channel and the PLA patrols. But *Veronica* drew eight feet, and the chart and *Sailing Directions* threatened grounding for anyone who tried it without local knowledge.

It would be thirty miles before he could chance a turn east—five hours motoring before they dared raise her sails—with the thinning fog and the dense marine traffic their only allies. Fuel, at least, was no problem, having topped off the tanks in the Marshalls, and not run the engine since. He steered with one eye on the compass, the other on the depth finder. Sarah sat beside him, watching for fishing boats, river craft, and ocean ships. Low islands sprawled to port. Scattered among them were almost invisible sandbanks.

It was nerve-racking piloting. When the depth finder showed the water shoaling, Stone went forward, leaned over the bow, and watched for mud banks. They dodged fishing boats and sampans and tried to tail ships that seemed to know the way. Finally on the radar Stone spotted the navigation tower that marked the beginning of a ten-mile dredged channel. When Sarah eyeballed the marker, they altered course to 110° and hugged the edge of the narrow channel, which was packed with ocean ships.

They talked, slowly and intermittently like acquaintances at a party, reporting their separate experiences since the *Dallas Belle* had steamed away from Pulo Helena. The mud-gray water and the damp cold were in such contrast to the brilliant colors and tropic heat of the Pacific that the events seemed long ago.

"I wonder," Stone ventured, "could we sail to Taiwan and beat him to Tokyo by plane?"

"Impossible," said Sarah. "He'll have thought of that." She described Mr. Jack and his connections to his old comrades of the Chinese army. "He'll put the word out at any airport we can reach, either to arrest us or to kill us on sight. Besides, he's got Ronnie. We have to do exactly what he says."

Stone reluctantly agreed. "Who does he think we are? Did you give him the coup story?"

Sarah said, "I didn't have to. Moss guessed we were 'on the lam.' But Mr. Jack really didn't care, he was so sure you'd never find us."

Stone told her how Kerry had helped and about Ronald and the Brit assassin and Katherine and the stolen yacht.

They skirted the numbing fear they felt for Ronnie. It was necessary in order to function as they fled the shadow of China. But their unspoken agreement was at the price of intimacy and each felt like a stranger. All they had in common now was the working of the boat, and in that practiced skill they were not strangers but campaigners—old companions girding themselves for the long haul to Japan.

A red tower with a six-second flasher and a bell marked the end of the dredged channel, and here they turned east onto the Great Yangtze Bank. With thirty miles safely traversed and *Veronica* moving offshore, Stone began to hope they might have pulled it off. The fog had lifted, but the cold sky was heavy, visibility still less than a mile. The Bank was dotted with fishing boats.

The swell marching in from the East China Sea turned choppy in the shallow water, causing the boat to pitch uncomfortably. Stone felt the early queasiness of seasickness. The sails would steady the Swan, but he hated to present such a big target. They stripped the cover off the main and hanked on an inner forestay sail and a jib. Daylight began leaking from the sky. In another hour it would be dark enough to raise the sails.

"I'll get a handle on the weather."

He went below, turned on the SSB, and listened with half an ear for the English version, while he rummaged through his charts. The large-scale North Pacific Ocean, Western Part was the best he had aboard for Japan until they reached the Japanese archipelago. For Tokyo Bay and approaches, he had the charts from their visit to Hiroshi's father.

He chewed Saltines to settle his stomach, while he plotted the two legs of their route: 480 miles east across the East China Sea; through the Osumi Strait—south of Kyushu, the southernmost big island of Japan—then 540 miles across the Philippine Sea to Tokyo.

They'd be butting into the northeast monsoon wind most of the way, which meant that *Veronica's* light, full-bellied South Pacific cruising sails, designed to run before the trade winds, had to be replaced. On the first leg, the shallow East China Sea would generate a hard chop that would slow the boat. Later in the voyage, the powerful Kuroshio, the Black Current, would give them a boost. They'd need it: the wind was sure to get weird in the lee of the Japanese Islands.

The weather report switched to English. Stone spread a clear plastic sheet over the chart and plotted on it the highs and lows and ridges and troughs that the announcer was reading in a deadpan, computerlike voice. He noted the time for this baseline by which he could track the weather. A front had stalled; now it was moving again. The gale he'd feared earlier would disperse the fog would catch up with the Swan by morning. He compared his barometer to the Pilot Chart for December. Normal was 30.3; the Swan's read 29.9 and falling. Better change the mainsail, now.

He hurried forward into Ronnie's cabin, which was wedged in the forepeak like a pyramid on its side. He averted his eyes from her stuffed animals and the posters she had taped to the ceiling. He hauled out a stiff mainsail they had taken along with the carbon fiber mast off the wrecked racer. It was a mesh weave of Technora yarn, coated with Mylar laminates. Remarkably light, it would stabilize the boat by reducing weight aloft and carve a course close to the wind.

Sarah screamed, "Michael."

He dropped the sail, raced up on deck. She pointed astern and passed him the binoculars. Out of the gloom came a knife-edged hull flashing red lights and cutting an immense bow wave. A People's Liberation Army patrol.

30

STONE FELT HIS SPIRIT DISSOLVE. EVENTS OF THE PAST TWENTY hours swirled through his mind like half-remembered passages in hastily skimmed books: his first sight of Sarah, the Chinese soldiers chasing him through the brush, the trains, Ronald's execution, the black man swooping from the sky.

He raised dead eyes to the oncoming boat and stood paralyzed at the helm. A siren howled, an incongruous noise from city canyons.

Sarah went to the mast and raised the jib, which the northeast wind tried to fill.

"Trim the sheet, Michael."

His heart went to her. "We can't run, darling."

Sarah pushed past him and sheeted in the jib. The sail bellied and the boat heeled even as its motion grew steady. "A sail looks innocent. Quick. Help me raise the main."

The siren got loud.

They threw off the ties and were cranking the crackling

sail the last notch up the mast when the patrol boat burbled alongside. A bullhorn blared Chinese.

While Stone cranked in the mainsheet, causing *Veronica* to pick up speed and the patrol boat to quicken its idling engines, Sarah cupped her hands to call, "Do you speak English?"

"Stop your vessel," came the reply. They had a machine gun on the bow and another on the roof. The boat had a modern fiberglass hull, diesel powered. Stone recognized the whine of turbochargers, but what struck him forcefully was the spit and polish of the crew, poised with boarding lines, and the officer with the bullhorn.

"We're stopping," Stone called across the water. "We have to turn to port."

The machine gun tracked them as he headed to weather. The Swan spilled her wind. Sarah finished tying off fenders. The patrol boat eased alongside and sailors threw lines that Stone and Sarah secured fore and aft.

The officer boarded, preceded by two men with snub-nosed machine guns. "What," he demanded, "are you doing in PRC waters?"

"We are guests of the Shanghai government."

"Papers."

Stone handed them over. The officer's face was in the shadow of his peaked cap, his eyes invisible behind dark glasses. He read the Chinese letters and then the English translations. Surreptitiously, he fingered the embossed letterhead.

"Yacht marina?" he asked.

"A place for cruising yachts to moor and replenish and repair."

"I know what a marina is. I lived in one while I attended school in California. Marina del Ray. This would be for Western cruising tourists?"

"Exactly."

"And now you are leaving?"

"We'll be returning to Hong Kong to talk to our investors."

"I see no exit stamp on your passport."

"We waited at the harbor master, but everyone was tied up with that big fire. So we finally decided to just leave. As we were guests of the government—"

"And where is *your* passport, Madam?"

"My wife was injured," Stone said. "We were hit by the wake of a fireboat. She nearly fell overboard—lost her handbag, with the passport."

Sarah pulled up her sleeve to reveal her bandaged arm; blood had stained the gauze.

The officer frowned. "Have you weapons aboard?"

"No."

The officer gave an order and two men went below to search.

"Drugs?"

"Only medicine. My wife and I are both doctors."

"Why are doctors sent to scout marinas?"

"Many doctors own boats," Stone said with a straight face. "As I'm sure you saw in Marina del Ray."

"You were heading east. Hong Kong is southwest."

"Sea room," said Stone. "It looks to me like we've got a front heading our way. We don't want to get caught on a lee shore."

The naval officer agreed.

"And did you find marina sites?"

"Several."

"Where?"

"I'm afraid that's confidential until I've reported to the investors."

"Have you considered a military amusement site?"

Stone looked at Sarah. "I'm not sure what that is."

"It is quite the new thing," said the officer, as the boats squeaked against the fenders and the machine gun–toting sailors stood by impassively. "The tourist is invited to shoot real weapons—assault rifles, mortars, even rocket launchers.

297

Perhaps yachtsmen could try out a submarine. It is a new idea, and one to be considered. Here is my card." He unbuttoned a crisp shirt pocket and passed a card to Stone and another to Sarah. On the back, in English, it said SECTORS OF ACTIVITY: REAL ESTATE, FOREIGN TRADE, ETC."

"The People's Liberation Army has joined the march to prosperity," the officer explained in his accentless English. "Perhaps we even lead the effort to open up to the outside world."

"Excellent," said Stone.

"Perhaps if the officials of Shanghai prove difficult, you will remember my card."

"We certainly will," said Stone. He presented the business card Ronald had provided.

"Obviously the People's Naval Forces have excellent sources of waterfront property and we would supply the best in dredges and matériel. In fact, when you think about it, it is hard to imagine such an enterprise without us."

"We are most fortunate to have met you," replied Stone. "And now, my wife and I are anxious to get offshore before that gale hits."

"Of course." He snapped an order. The searchers came up empty-handed. The sailors stood by on the lines. Stone extended his hand. The officer took it in both of his. *"Bon voyage."*

The lines were cast off. A channel of water opened between the two craft. The PLA boat swung slowly away. Stone held his breath. Radio antennas swayed as the boat pitched on the chop; any second, they could get orders to track down a certain sailboat. He waved the officer's business card. The diesels roared and the boat pounded toward the invisible coast.

They gathered the fenders, trimmed the sails, and cleared the decks. The wind was freshening. The Swan grew lively. A decent sailor in light airs, she was built for the winds that sent most boats to harbor, and Stone felt her stir like a lioness waking up hungry.

He shut down the engine and feathered the propeller. His queasiness forgotten, he worked the sails, coaxing speed out of her. They began overtaking some of the diesel-powered fishing boats. Quite abruptly, the sonar showed the water depth double, then triple. They had left the rivers behind and were moving over the Great Yangtze Bank. With twenty and thirty meters of water under her keel, and nothing between them and Japan but the lights of fishing boats returning with the night, they could sail for days by the compass alone.

"What do you think he'll do if we don't make Tokyo on time?"

"He's totally unpredictable," said Sarah.

"Well, if he just drops her, Ronnie knows to call Hiroshi's father. . . . What the hell is he up to?"

A sudden gust banged into the sails, a cold, harsh wind that stung the face. *Veronica* heeled over and buried her rail.

"Let's take a reef in the main—in fact, let's take it down and put up the Technora."

"Are you up to it? You look destroyed, Michael. You should sleep."

"Yeah. Come on, while we still have the light."

Together, they humped the sail up the companionway. Then they lowered the stretched and aged Dacron main, detached it from the boom, bagged it, and dragged it below. It was getting darker. The boat was banging into the chop, and the Technora felt stiff as tin in their cold hands.

They unrolled it on the pitching deck, found the tack of the sail, and began inserting the plastic slugs on the foot into the slide that ran the length of the boom. They secured the tack to the gooseneck, attached the head to the mast, and slid in the slugs that held the front of the sail. Sarah found the battens and they installed them in the pockets, further stiffening the cloth. Then Stone put his weight to the halyard.

They turned on the work lights.

"Evil-looking thing."

The sail was black. Its aerodynamic shape molded the wind like a slab of steel.

The boat was laboring, overpowered in the rising wind. They took a reef, making the triangle of the sail narrower and lower.

The reef was quickly followed by a second reef. The wind was rising, hard and gusty out of the northeast. The *Swan* drove into it, close-hauled. She shipped some spray and the occasional sea, which sluiced the decks of the accumulated grit of Shanghai.

While Sarah steered, Stone rigged a dodger, a canvas and clear plastic screen that sheltered the cockpit. Then he heated canned soup, which he brought in covered mugs to the helm. It had been years since they had sailed in cold weather, and they were both shivering.

"You look a mess," said Sarah. "Get some sleep." She touched his face, which was lined like that of a man twenty years older.

"You okay?" he responded.

"Better than you at the moment. Go below, sleep."

He was so tired things were beginning to spin.

"Michael?"

"Yeah?" He looked back. She was trying to smile. "Give me a hug?" He bounded to her and pulled her into his arms.

"Wait." She pulled free and opened her bulky jacket. Stone opened his, and they joined again in soft warmth.

"It was a wonderful rescue."

"Half a rescue."

"We'll get her back."

"Sure we will." He looked ahead, where the horizon was turning black. "Wake me if this gets worse."

"Sleep."

He started down the companionway, paused. "Why'd he let us go?"

"All I can think is he had no clout with the fireboats—couldn't keep a lid on it."

"So what? He could straighten it out eventually, with the friends you've described."

"Maybe not in time."

"In time for what? Selling the cargo?"

"I don't know," she said. "But he's planning something, and he's afraid of our talking."

"We'll speak to Ronnie day after tomorrow. And we'll make him promise another call. The son of a bitch. He can't hurt her as long as we're loose with a radio."

He staggered down the companionway and shut the hatch. It was quiet below; the noise of the wind and water was distant. He felt guilty for deserting Sarah, who had looked nearly as tired as he felt.

The boat was heaving around on the chop. It took a long time to pull off his sea boots, and it didn't seem worth the effort to struggle out of his foul-weather gear, so he found a blanket and collapsed on the leeward berth in the main cabin. The angle of heel pressed him against the bulkhead. He closed his eyes and pulled the blanket over him. He knew he had to sleep. He'd be no use until he had rested, but seared on his eyelids was a vision of Ronnie struggling like a kitten.

He turned on a reading lamp, swung his legs to the cabin floor, worked his way the several feet back to the nav station and found the *Sailing Directions* and the Royal Navy's *Ocean Passages for the World*. He carried the books back into the berth, pored over the descriptions of the East China Sea, the Osumi Strait, and the section of the North Pacific between the Osumi Strait and Tokyo known as the Philippine Sea.

The weather in December was dominated by China's winter monsoon—the cold dry winds generated by a vast high-pressure system over the Mongolian and East Siberian hinterlands. On the first leg, from Shanghai to the south tip of Japan, they could expect northeast and northwest winds. Twenty knots on the open sea, a good stiff force 5 breeze—

which could freshen at any moment to thirty-three knots, a moderate gale which would limit *Veronica* to a triple-reefed main and a staysail.

But once they got through the Osumi Strait, the continental high would kick up violent west winds. Low pressure moving eastward would slow the monsoon ahead of the depression and leave gales behind. Storms were frequent.

He turned on the radio for a new weather report. But long before he could chart it on the plastic cover sheet, he had passed out.

When Sarah came below for a moment's respite from the cold, she removed the books and covered his huddled body with another blanket. While the kettle heated on the kerosene stove, she went forward and turned on the light in the forepeak. The waves resonated against the bow. Ronnie's little cave, her life-size dollhouse. The ceiling over her berth was plastered with pictures of cats and penguins and photographs, cut from *People* magazine, of her current heroine, Surya Bonaly, the black French Olympic skater. In a gimballed holder swung a flowerpot with a shriveled aloe plant. She brought water to the powdery soil, thinking, Scratch an African and you'll find a farmer.

She felt as if the *Dallas Belle* carried a curse from God. The innocent were not immune. She tried to picture her child asleep in Mr. Jack's cabin. Or lying awake, terrified. Fear threatened to overwhelm her. She could feel it swelling. She looked back at Michael for strength. His face looked old.

31

STONE AWAKENED IN SLOW STAGES, HIS BODY SORE, HIS MIND SUF-
fused, at first, with a sense of well-being. He was back on
the boat, the water rushing past the hull, the familiar creak
of the rudder stock filled with peaceful memories. She was
beating to windward, her heavy, shapely hull driving effortlessly on one of her finest points of sail. Felt like seven and
a half knots. The sea was choppy; occasionally the bow
smacked a wave, but she drove right on through.

Yet all wasn't right: she was carrying too much sail,
heeling too hard, and actually losing speed when gusts
angled her sharply. He looked at his watch. One o'clock. It
must be broken. But when he held it to his ear it gave a
steady ping. He sat up quickly, memory flooding back.
Sarah had been on watch eight hours. He yanked on his
boots. Tucked between the bed and the bulkhead was a thermos of coffee, with a note, DRINK ME.

Sleeping like a rock, he hadn't heard her. The memory
of Ronnie slammed into him, and he was suddenly wide

awake. He carried the thermos up to the cockpit, climbing the companionway on aching legs.

"I'm sorry," he called.

Sarah was a shadow against the night. The sky was veiled with cloud and backlit by a faint glow—a halo cast by Shanghai, sixty miles astern. Whitecaps shone in the darkness around the boat.

"I'm fine," she said. "So glad to be outside again."

She had shaken out one of the reefs, but the wind was gusting over twenty knots now and the boat leaned hard. She was usually a more cautious sailor.

"You must be beat." He poured her a cup of the coffee.

"The self-steering won't hold. The water's too choppy." As she spoke she steered out of a deep trough and through a wave that threatened to brush *Veronica* off course. Cold spray flew over the dodger and stung their faces.

"I think we're overpowered," said Stone.

"The wind dropped."

"Yeah, well, it's back. Head up a little."

Sarah steered closer to the wind.

Stone eased the mainsheet. "Want to haul down on the leech line when I give a yell?" He went forward, holding onto the lifelines, and released the boom vang. Then he tightened up the topping lift, working by feel among the familiar controls, and lowered the main halyard, feeling for a wire marker, cleated it, and pulled the slackened sail down and secured it to the gooseneck, then cranked up the halyard. "Haul the leech line!"

Sarah used a winch to pull down the back of the sail, then trimmed the mainsheet. Stone released the topping lift and pulled the boom down with the vang. Then he ran some light line through the grommets in the sail and around the boom, gathering the loose cloth between the newly secured front and back.

At Stone's request the sailmaker had added a third line of cringles and grommets for another reef, but the second was sufficient for now. The *Swan* had straightened up.

"Eight knots!" Sarah called. She welcomed him back to the cockpit with the coffee.

Stone drank it quickly and took the wheel. "Got it."

"Oh-nine-three," she said, indicating the red-lit compass. The speedometer was jumping between 7.9 and 8.1 knots. The sonar read forty-five meters. They had passed the southern fringe of the Yangtze Bank and the chop should be smoothing down some in the deeper water.

"Where's the GPS?"

"Ronnie has it."

No sweat. If the sky didn't clear, he could radio a passing ship for a position; and in the meantime there was nothing to run into between here and Japan for the next three days.

"Get some sleep," he said, anxious to work the sails.

"Have you eaten?"

"Just the coffee. I'm fine."

"I'll bring you something."

"That's okay."

"I'll bring you something." She touched his face as she had earlier, as if looking with her fingers in the dark. "Punishing your body won't get her back."

She left him a flashlight, fresh from the charger, and he shone it on the sails to see how they were drawing. Damned near perfect. The helm felt like the boat was well balanced, but if the wind rose any more, he'd fly a smaller jib and raise the inner forestay sail.

He was not a racer by nature, but—chased across three oceans in *Veronica*—he had learned how to make a Swan fly. With her taller mast and the Technora main, she was even faster today. *He* was smarter too, more experienced. But he no longer had the body he could demand so much of; his hands had been losing strength for years, and now his legs were going. And he worried about his spirit: fleeing pursuit, he had been fueled by fear. Would love be as powerful?

The answer would come with a thousand small tests:

the willingness to change a sail two minutes after he had just changed it; or, drugged by exhaustion, the energy to stand up and crank a winch half a turn when instinct said it might help make the boat go faster, but the mind groaned, Why bother?

When Sarah came up with oatmeal and honey, she panicked. The cockpit was empty. Whirling around, she saw him at the mast, working a winch, lost in the boat. For the first time since Ronnie had been taken, she felt relief. He was master of the Swan again, back in his element. For a fleeting instant she wondered what would happen to him if they went to Africa. He returned to the cockpit in a low, easy crouch, his hands brushing a jack line he had rigged along the cabin top. His face was alight. "Beautiful sail. Pulling like a rocket."

"Will you shake out that reef?"

"No. Wind's really honking. Jesus, that smells good. . . . Delicious. Here, you have some, too. Help you sleep . . ."

Ronnie stared at her breakfast, lips tight, ears shut to Ah Lee's pleas that she eat—that she hadn't eaten lunch the day before or dinner and had left uneaten the late-night pizza the ship's cook had run up especially for his favorite crew member.

She was starving, her stomach an empty pit. At first, after Moss grabbed her, she couldn't eat, but now she was hungry and it took a massive concentration on her mother and father to keep from cramming a whole blueberry muffin into her mouth.

Ah Lee started up again, switching randomly between Shanghainese and English. She pushed the plate away.

The Chinese steward bent closer and whispered in her ear, "If you don't eat, Mr. Moss will hit me."

"He's bluffing," said Ronnie. But she couldn't ignore the bruises from the last time, the stitches her mother had just removed from his cheek, and the fear in his eyes. "Truth?" she whispered back.

"Very truth."

"Very *true*, Ah Lee. Or 'truth.' But not 'very truth.' "

"You eat, please. Please.

"Okay. Okay."

He folded his arms, and watched her down both muffins and her milk. "Now eggs, missy."

"Don't call me missy."

"Yes, Miss Ronnie."

"Don't call me Miss Ronnie. I told you, a million times. Ronnie. Ronnie. Ronnie."

"Yes, Ronnie. Thank you for eating."

Mr. Jack shuffled into the lounge wearing his robe and slippers. Ronnie's face closed like stone. He took the coffee cup that Ah Lee hurried to him, drank some with a slurping sound, and peered across the table. "Cheer up, kid. Big day coming. Going to show you something that'll knock your eyes out."

Ronnie stared at her plate. She felt very confused by Mr. Jack—betrayed. And a little frightened. She could never tell when he would suddenly start yelling, and now, without her mother to intervene, what would happen if he exploded?

"What's the matter, for crissake?"

"I want to go home."

"You're *goin'* home. Told you. Christmas Eve. Bang-up holiday with the folks." He winked, his wrinkles doubling, and broke into a raspy-voiced song, "'I'll be home for Christmas, you can count on me. . . .' Oh for crissake don't start crying."

"I'm not crying," she said, though her throat was swelling and she could feel her mouth tremble in a way she couldn't stop.

"It's not my goddammed fault they ran off without you."

"You scared them."

Mr. Jack stared. His face got hard like metal. Then he

laughed. "Well goddammit, kid, if they're scaredy-cats, don't blame me. . . . Now come on, cheer up. I'm going to show you something great today. And tomorrow you talk to them on the radio. Remember?"

"Noon. Of course I remember."

"That's right. Noon tomorrow. Nice long talk on the radio. 'Cept, of course, you gotta be careful what you say— you don't want to talk about me or Shanghai or anything. Just about you and them and how you'll have a great time at Christmas." He shuffled over to the tree and flicked on the colored lights. "If we hit Tokyo a little early, maybe I'll take you Christmas shopping in the Ginza. Get something for your mom and dad. So, you want to know what's goin' to happen today?"

She didn't. But her mother, she recalled, had been very careful to tell Mr. Jack whatever he wanted to hear, so she said, "What's happening?"

"What's happening? Come on. Go get dressed while I eat some breakfast and I'll get dressed and then you'll see what's happening."

When he came back out bundled in a big down coat, he had another for her, bright red, which fit perfectly. In the pocket were mittens embroidered with dinosaurs, and a red knit watchcap with a gold tassel. "Cold out. Button up."

He bounded up the stairs to the bridge deck. "Move it. Double time."

She ran after him, up the corridor and through the curtain to the bridge. It was cool and quiet, the big windows admitting the gray light through the hole the fire had burned in the shed roof.

Daddy's fire. She hid a smile. Mr. Jack had really yelled about the fire, called Daddy a "vicious bastard" and a bunch of other names that she had learned from American cruiser kids in Samoa.

"Come here!"

She followed him onto the cold bridge wing. Far away on the bow were hundreds of workmen, staring up at the cranes arching over their heads. Mr. Jack passed her the binoculars.

"No thank you. I don't need them."

She could see clearly; binoculars always closed in the view and she sensed that something big was going to happen and she wanted to see it all at once.

Mr. Jack picked up a telephone. "Ready when you are, C.B."

A whistle blew and all the workmen drew to attention, grabbing tools and bracing themselves.

"Oh, wow!"

Four gantry cranes—two to the starboard side of the gas ship and two to the port side of the cruise liner—moved in unison. She could hear their engines thundering, the note deepening as they took the load—like *Veronica*'s motor lowering from *burp-burp-burp* to *chug-chug-chug* when they engaged the propeller. Cables tightened and the entire front of the cruise ship's superstructure—the front cabins and the bridge on top—began to rise.

Ronnie held her breath.

The section the cranes were lifting looked about half the length of *Veronica* and was as wide as the ship. The cranes raised it higher and higher. Then they began to maneuver it like a piece of Lego toward the right.

"Wow."

"Wait for it, kid." Mr. Jack chuckled.

Slowly the cranes shifted the front of the superstructure over the side of the cruise ship, across the water between the two vessels, and over the gas carrier. The workmen, she saw, were holding onto lines, like spinnaker guys. Hundreds of them, struggling to keep the piece from swinging.

She started to say, "Oh, wow," again but realized she was repeating herself. "Son of a bitch."

"Whoa!" said Mr. Jack. "Mum's away, the kid'll play. Who taught you that? Daddy?"

"Mr. Jack, what are they doing?"

"They're playing erector set."

"I don't know what that means."

"Too young. What they're doing is transferring the superstructure of that old cruise ship onto my ship."

"What for?"

"So we can go cruising."

"What?"

"It's a joke, kid."

"But why?"

"Why not?"

He stared ahead, gloating like the happiest man alive, as the gigantic six-story piece of steel moved slowly over the gas carrier's foredeck. The whistle blew. The cranes stopped, the piece swinging gently. When the men with the guy ropes had stopped the swinging, the whistle blew again and the piece began to descend. Ronnie saw that a sort of steel foundation had been laid, and as she watched, the cranes jockeyed sideways, lining it up.

"Laser guided," said Mr. Jack. "You know how that works?"

"Sure."

"Here comes the tricky part."

The piece touched with a hollow *boom,* and Ronnie felt the deck move under her feet. Again, a *boom.* Now the crane cables slackened and workmen swarmed with chattering pneumatic drills.

In minutes, the cranes were swinging back over the cruise ship, lining up the next piece. She saw now that the full length of the superstructure had been cut every twenty feet and that they were going to move it piece by piece onto Mr. Jack's ship.

"So what do you think?"

She tumbled the ship in her head to see how it would look head-on. Dazzled by the sight, she spoke without thinking, "It's like a mask."

"What do you mean?" he asked sharply.

"When it's facing you, it will look like it put on a mask."

The old man chuckled. The kid was something else. He

nodded toward the cranes, which were shifting a second six-story section of steel superstructure. "From the side, too."

"Why?"

"You figure it out, smarty-pants."

He watched her closely. She didn't get it, yet. Not yet. Smart kid, though. She would. Her eyes were everywhere. But she shrugged. "Are Mummy and Daddy really calling tomorrow?"

"We'll call them."

"I can't wait."

Moss hurried out onto the bridge wing, his breath steaming in the cold. He nodded at the kid.

Mr. Jack said, "Ronnie, run inside. I'll call you in a second."

She edged past Moss.

Moss handed him an E-mail printout. "From the bean counters," he said, using their phrase for the executives who ran Mr. Jack's enterprises in his absence.

"I told you no communication."

"Sorry, Mr. Jack. I had to set up an emergency link in case something went wrong. The bean counters thought this was an emergency. I think so, too."

Mr. Jack put on his glasses and read the one line: *Inquiries received from Hong Kong and Australia.*

"That son of a bitchin' doctor."

Jack Powell felt old, for the first time in his seventy-eight years. Why, he wondered, had he let the parents go? Roused by bells and whistles from deep sleep after raising hell all night with the generals, he had been disoriented—admit it, frightened—frightened by the fire. He had recovered pretty fast, that was for damned sure. But then the goddammed fireboats threw him again.

He knew the ropes in Shanghai—knew the ones to yank—but bureaucrats were bureaucrats, whether they were in Washington, Houston, Lagos, or China, and he had suddenly seen the whole scam fly out of control.

Reports were being filed by the hundreds: unauthorized construction; a gas ship where it had no business being on the Huangpu; the safety of the city; et cetera, et-god-dammed-cetera.

It was being handled. Bureaucrats could be made to feel terror, if you could find the right ones, and his old friends were good at finding the right ones. But in the noise of battle all he'd been able to think was how in hell was he going to explain the black-and-white doctors screaming for their kid.

Face it, if the doctors had jumped onto a fireboat in the chaos—or if a fireboat commander had seen Moss shoot the sons of bitches or drop the grenade he had ready in their goddammed sailboat, there'd have been unexplainable hell to pay. And while it was being paid and explained, some busybody bureaucrat would have slapped a restraining order on the *Dallas Belle* and they'd be stuck in Shanghai for a year.

Now, looking at Ronnie's sad brown face about to melt into tears for Mummy and Daddy, he wished he had nailed them on the spot and bulled through it. Hell, the fire was a big thing. The Chinese were as panicked as he had been in those first seconds.

Son of a bitch doctor knew what he was doing. It would take more than one burning valve to breach her heavily-insulated tanks. She was built to survive fire, grounding, even collision. To blow her up, you had to crack her open with shaped charges.

But how did the son of a bitch know? According to Doctor Mummy, Doctor Daddy was a self-taught engineer. Acoustics. Electronics. Maybe their buddy in the salvage business had taught them about gas carriers. Maybe he read *Professional Mariner*. Or *Safety At Sea*. Brass-balled son of a bitch.

"Son of a bitch!"

"What, Mr. Jack?"

"What's your name, kid?"

312

"Huh?"

"Your *name.*"

"Ronnie. You know."

"Your whole name."

Her eyes slid aside for just a second, before she answered, "Veronica Margaret Soditan Samuels."

"Yeah? Where'd you get the Margaret?"

"Both Mummy and Daddy's mothers' names were Margaret. And they both died when they were very young."

"Handy coincidence. How about the Soditan?"

"Mummy's maiden name. From her father."

"Who made up the Samuels?"

"Mummy and Daddy—I mean, that's Daddy's name."

"Sure, kid."

She looked terrified. He let her stew a moment. "Seen enough?"

"Yes, Mr. Jack."

"Run down to the cabin and ask Ah Lee for some hot cocoa."

But she stood rooted to the deck like a little bush.

Old and dumb, he thought, old and dumb.

"Moss," he yelled. "Front and center."

Then he took pity. "Hey, don't cry, little girl. I won't tell on your daddy. I'm a bad guy too."

"He's not bad."

"Well, neither am I, really."

Stupid, though. Should have made the connection right off—but it had happened after he had bailed out of Nigeria, just before it became a total nuthouse. . . . A general had been murdered. Mummy Doc's father? The cops had charged a white American. Daddy Doc? Scuttlebutt had said it was a bullshit story to cover a CIA screwup. Whatever. They never did catch the white guy. The American had escaped. Was he the loose cannon headed for Tokyo? Mr. Jack shrugged. God knew, so many crazy stories came out of Africa.

"Go on, kid. Get outta here. I gotta talk to Moss."

Moss hurried in from the computer room. "What's up, Mr. Jack?"

Ronnie circled Moss like a rabbit around a snake and made a beeline down the corridor.

Jack Powell waited until he heard her sneakers slapping on the stairs. "Beep the captain."

The captain responded a minute later.

"Mr. Jack wants you. Now."

"*Ah got my hands full up here.*"

"On the bridge. Now."

They waited in silence, Moss wanting to ask but knowing not to, Jack Powell ruminating on his shortcomings.

"Captain," he said, when the Texan clumped in looking pissed off. "I want you to plot the route that Doctor S. and her hubby are sailing to Tokyo."

"East China Sea. Osumi Strait. Philippine Sea. Hang a left at Tokyo Bay."

"That much I can figure out on my own. What matters is the wind. It's a sailboat. I want the *exact* route."

"Any objection to my chief mate crunching the numbers? I'm kind of busy. Those bozos on the cranes make one false move and they'll blow us to hell."

Jack Powell's expression turned wintery. "Captain—and I use the title loosely, since you've already had your master's ticket revoked for blowing your last command to hell—"

"That weren't my fault."

"*I* believe in you, Captain. Hell, I'm paying you a lifetime's wages for one voyage. Unless you want me to promote your chief mate . . ."

"No, sir."

"Huddle with the computers and the goddammed weather fax and tell me where the man's going to sail. And you," he shot at Moss, who was grinning at the captain's discomfort, "you work out where you're going to stop 'em. What, Moss?"

"You going to let the kid radio them tomorrow?"

"Yes."

"Maybe we can triangulate their signal."

Mr. Jack beamed. "Captain, you should have thought of that."

"Didn't have to. Been watching the weather."

The captain walked to the weather facsimile machine and tore off the latest chart.

"There's a doozy of a cold front moving off the continent onto the East China Sea. Brand-new undisturbed front, wedging under this warm air mass." He waved the chart in Moss's face. "And this here puppy's a depression." He traced the depression—a tight whorl that resembled a knot in hardwood—with a work-scarred finger. "Dropping a millibar an hour, deepening like a bastard. Keeps doing this it's going to build into what the weather boys call a 'bomb,' and bomb the shit outta the doctors. They got no weather fax and there's no way the plain language forecast is going to pin the puppy down. Any luck, it'll sink 'em by lunchtime."

32

A BROKEN SKY TEASED STONE WITH PROSPECTS OF A SUN SHOT. But while he brought his sextant up to the cockpit, he studied the sky less with an eye to navigation than to the weather. He knew approximately where they were by dead reckoning—a respectable hundred and forty miles east of the Huangpu, averaging seven and a half knots over the bottom, the eastward setting current making up for the boat-slowing chop. And with the chart showing nothing to crash into between here and Japan, they could wait for a celestial fix.

"I wish I had killed him when I had the chance," said Sarah.

Stone barely heard her. Speed was all: he had to shape a course to find the best wind—which was backing west and dropping—while avoiding getting beaten up by the storm headed their way. Not only would it slow them down, but also in the shallow East China Sea, steep waves could overwhelm even a boat as strong as the Swan. The barometer and the radio shipping reports painted a general picture. He had to know precisely what would happen within the radius of the ninety miles *Veronica* might sail in the next twelve hours.

He had thrown his weather fax overboard years ago, a victim of Pacific humidity. Lacking the upper air charts that weather stations broadcast four times a day, he had learned slowly and painstakingly to read the sky like a 3-D monitor.

Jet cirrus clouds were invading the upper atmosphere, trailing streaks of ice crystals that thickened into broad banners. It was usually hard to judge their speed without fixed references on the empty sea, but these were shooting between the horizons, indicating ferocious temperature differences between the retreating warm front and the advancing cold.

Strong jets meant severe weather.

So did their flight path from northwest to southeast.

So did the cumulus clouds, lower down in the sky, that were traveling on a different course from the west: Watts's "crossed-winds" rule said that if you stood with your back to the surface wind and the upper wind came from your left, things were going to get worse before they got better. "*Low* weather from the *left* hand."

To put "right weather" on his right hand, all he had to do was turn around and go the other way. Were time and speed less important than safety, he would do just that. But now time was everything, and the only question was did he want to run before the storm or cut across its path and try to squeeze through the canyon between the advancing and retreating systems?

Ocean Passages noted a peculiarity of the northeast monsoon: it slackened ahead of a depression. Stone felt it happening already, the wind dropping, and he wondered whether it would cut their speed too much for them to make it across the storm. The only good news was that the broken sky was growing increasingly clouded: heavy cloud suggested a smallish low. And, promised *Ocean Passages*, the monsoon would come screaming back as soon as the low passed.

He ran below to look again at the color-smeared chart he had drawn. The cold front was relatively near its breeding ground; young and active, it might shove the depression by quickly. Maybe. He looked again at the sky and imagined the clifflike face of the young front.

He decided to take a chance. Instead of cutting across the low or retreating behind it, he would run with the son of a bitch and hope for the best.

Sarah concurred, which Stone found a little unsettling. She was never a risk taker on the boat. But since they had lost Ronnie, she was driving herself and the boat way beyond the edge.

"My watch," he said. "Get some sleep."

Sarah went below. But instead of climbing under a blanket, she began methodically cleaning the galley, only vaguely aware that she had cleaned it spotless two hours earlier. She had never felt so trapped on the boat. It was like drowning in a cage. For every breath of wind that pushed them ahead, a wave shoved them back. For every two hours at the helm, an eternal two hours below unable to sleep, her mind in knots.

She kept trying to tell herself that Mr. Jack was enchanted by Ronnie. Everyone was, everyone who met the child. But the old man was completely unpredictable. And totally unrestrained.

Who would challenge him? Moss? Not bloody likely. The captain was hopeless, the ship's crew isolated from Mr. Jack's throne room. Whatever occurred in the *Dallas Belle*'s palatial owner's suite was Mr. Jack's to decide.

She was rubbing a frayed sponge on the corroded stainless steel saltwater tap—back and forth, back and forth—when she began to realize that the boat was heeling less. The noise of cutting water had quietened to a dull murmur. The wind had died. Impossible. They lived by the trade winds and the monsoon.

She darted up the companionway, slid open the hatch. "Michael!"

He had shipped the dodger and lashed it down. And to her astonishment, he was hanking the storm jib onto the inner forestay and had already taken a third reef in the mainsail.

"What are you doing!"

Without bothering to look up, he nodded astern.

Now she saw in detail what she had registered only as darkness when she ran up the companionway. The horizon had moved in close. Hard-edged and randomly crenelated, it looked like streets of old buildings in a city made of stone. Cloud formed this apparition, cloud that plummeted sheer gray from a gray sky, blackening as it fell to a thin, bone-white line that edged the rim of the sea.

The white was water churned up by a squall line that preceded the front like dragoons galloping ahead of infantry to draw first blood. Stone raised the storm jib. It hung limp in the suddenly dead air. He released the main halyard. "Get the storm trysail," he called. Sarah was already on her way, down the companionway, racing through the main cabin into the forepeak where the trysail lay in its bright yellow bag.

She dragged it up on deck as he wrapped sail ties over the furled main, and clipped on the halyard, secured the clew, and bent sheets to the sail's tack. A gust swept the water, whipping the tops off the waves.

"Ready."

Stone heaved on the halyard. A second gust smacked into the little sail. Sarah sheeted it in. The jib filled, too, and the Swan jumped ahead.

The white line caught up with a loud hiss. The wind doubled. The Swan leaned over, buried her bow, but before she could fling the sea aside, the wind doubled again, shrieking in the rigging, solid as a wall. It slammed the boat, already staggering under the weight of the water pounding her bow. She fell on her side like a heart-shot elk.

Stone and Sarah went flying, tumbling into the leeward lifelines, which were disappearing underwater. For an instant the only thought in his head was, Thank God for Ronnie's child netting or they'd be thrown through the lines. But instead of the netting, he smashed into one of the stanchions that supported the lines. He heard a loud *crunch* and both felt and saw a blaze of pain as if someone had opened his skull to shine a light inside. He teetered on the edge of consciousness. Then his mouth and nose filled with cold water and he convulsed in a half-drowned attempt to breathe.

Something was tugging at his right arm. Sarah, struggling to free herself from the grip that had kept her from tumbling over the lines into the water. The boat uprighted itself with a *whoosh* of seawater pouring from the sails, and flung them both in another tangle of arms and legs back into the cockpit. Sarah recovered first. "Can you steer?" she yelled over the shriek of the wind.

"I'm okay."

"Steer. I'll get the kit."

She dove below, timing her opening of the hatch to keep the breaking seas from washing down with her, and reappeared in a moment with Surgipads and bandage.

"Are you hurt?" yelled Stone, hands full of the helm as he tried to put the boat on a course across the wicked chop. The sea was as ragged as rows of serrated knives, and the blowing spray and something that kept stinging his eyes made it almost impossible to distinguish waves from the bow of the boat.

Sarah faced him, braced herself by locking her legs around the binnacle post, and wiped his face with a hand towel that came away red. "Oh, it's me," he said stupidly. "Bad?"

"You're still standing." She covered the wound with a Surgipad.

Stone could see better now that the blood was out of his eyes. *Veronica* looked undamaged by her knockdown. But the China Sea was a mass of wildly moving water. The sky was dark, the sails tight as drumheads, streaming spray, and banging every time the wind shifted.

"Go below," he yelled. "No sense in both of us getting beat up at the same time— What are you looking at?"

Sarah had thrown her head back and was staring at the masthead. Stone felt a stab of alarm. What had he missed?

"Is the aerial all right?"

She meant the radio antenna, tomorrow's connection to Ronnie.

"Go below," he said. "Try the radio. Then get some sleep."

Sarah tore her eyes from the masthead and stared bitterly at the raging sea.

An hour of the chaotic wind drove the shallow sea into a frenzy. At the helm he was doing less steering than dodging. For the waves were growing steeper—slab-sided monsters that charged like bulls and collapsed suddenly, dropping tons of gray-green water that staggered *Veronica*. When they fell on the foredeck, they drove her bow under, pitching her so steeply that Stone fell against the helm. When they crashed behind her, they slammed into the cockpit, filling it to his knees and pummeling his shoulders. It was like a gang mugging, a sudden one-sided confrontation with mindless violence.

A lesser boat would have broken to pieces already. But the Swan was born on the Baltic—another malevolently shallow sea—and her hull could take a strong beating. Stronger than her crew.

The anemometer was measuring wind gusts near forty knots, a force 8 fresh gale building to a force 9. Wave crests broke apart, scattering long lines of dense foam across the lumpy sea. Tall waves started tumbling heavily, booming as they crashed beside *Veronica*. Blowing spray drove the oxygen from the atmosphere, and for long moments Stone couldn't draw a breath.

Should have gone around behind it, he thought. Too late now.

Sarah opened the hatch a crack, crawled over the washboards and across the cockpit to hand Stone a pair of scuba-diving goggles. She held the helm while he put them on, then crawled below. When she next appeared, she had a squeeze bottle filled with sweetened cocoa.

Stone sensed shadow behind him as he reached for the cocoa. Sarah's eyes filled with disbelief. He looked back to see a square-faced sea reaching halfway up the backstay. It was racing after the boat, blocking the sky like a two-story building. He tried to swing the stern at right angles to the advancing face.

She wouldn't answer the helm. The rudder moved too easily as the wave sucked water out from under the stern. The hull staggered, clumsy, started to broach. A slant of wind filled the jib and pushed the bow around just as the wave crashed aboard.

Tons of water, heavy as lead, black as night, drove Stone to the cockpit sole, flattening him, his knees collapsed, his legs a-tangle. It ripped his right hand from the wheel and scrabbled at his left. Flailing with his right, he felt his fingers close on the slippery softness of Sarah's sea boot.

The stern plummeted, the bow pointed at the sky. Water filled his pants, his jacket, his boots. It rushed past his head and then suddenly the deck thrust up under them, flinging them into light and air. He grabbed a stanchion and tried to orient himself. For a long moment the cockpit resembled a bathtub. Then water drained out the scuppers and the Swan was afloat, bobbing on the surface, sails rattling like machine guns. He was still holding Sarah's foot.

She lay on her back, staring up at the mast.

"You okay?" he yelled. One of his gloves had vanished, flayed from his hand.

"The aerial?" she pointed.

He pulled the goggles from his eyes, shielded his face from the spray. Still there.

The cockpit was a snakes' nest of sodden rope. The sheets had been stripped from their winches. One of the lifeline stanchions was bent, and the torrent had shredded the child netting like strands of seaweed. But both sails were intact. He sheeted them in and set the boat back on course, stern to the thundering seas.

"Steer. I gotta douse the jib. We're going too fast."

He clipped his safety harness onto the jack line he had led over the coach roof, crawled to the mast, fumbled in the near darkness for the storm halyard. The wind seized the sail when it descended the inner forestay, the heavy Dacron banged and crackled like sheet metal. Stone fought it to the deck, attempting to smother it with his body. Fingernails were broken from his bare hand. A five-minute job stretched to twenty. Once the sail ballooned under him and threatened to throw him over the lifelines. He bagged the sail and lashed it down and crawled at last back to the cockpit.

The boat began to resonate with a low, deep moaning sound. The wind was rising again, howling through the rigging. And despite the lowered storm jib, *Veronica* was picking up speed, lunging and surfing from wave to wave, plummeting dangerously into the deepening troughs. The air was liquid, a wind-driven mix of spray, spindrift, and icy rain racing horizontally across the decks.

Stone cast a weary eye on the storm trysail. He was exhausted from dousing the jib. But the trysail, a minuscule triangle of heavy cloth, was driving the boat too fast. Sarah nodded. It had to go. She stepped behind the wheel again. Stone crawled forward.

An hour had passed before he returned to the cockpit.

Sarah tried to send him below. But that he could not do, although he could barely stand. *Veronica* was crashing ahead under a bare mast. Without a scrap of sail flying, she was making eight knots. And Stone's gut told him that if the wind blew any harder or the waves climbed any steeper, she would be fighting for her life.

The moan in the rigging sharpened to a shriek.

It was a sound he had heard only twice before: once in the Roaring Forties, a thousand miles from Capetown, and once in a typhoon that had wiped out half the Philippines.

33

HE WAS APPALLED HOW BADLY HE HAD MISJUDGED THE SIZE OF the depression. Time seemed to stop. He grew vaguely aware that he had ceased to care, that exhaustion and incipient hypothermia were separating mind and body. It didn't matter. If anything, he felt warmer. All he needed was a nice long sleep. Just close his eyes and sleep.

"Michael!"

"What? What? Ow!" His lips were burning.

"Drink this. Wake up!"

Hot, sweet tea, thick with sugar, like warm syrup. How she had managed to make it with the boat crashing side to side, he would never know. Nor where she got the strength to scream in his face until he remembered who he was. And where he was.

"Don't die!" she screamed. "Look at me!"

He drank. She came back with more. He drank half, then forced the rest on her. "Okay. I'm okay."

Then, gradually, he began to realize that he was worrying about Ronnie again. It was as if his mind had registered a minute change in the storm, a lessening of the danger. He listened. The wind shriek had dropped a decibel. The sea was still chaos. It mauled them for hours. But the wind was veering northwest, north, northeast, and at last he and Sarah allowed themselves to share a look of hope.

Dawn, two days east of Shanghai: steep waves jumping at a gloomy sky; cold rain rattling on the sails.

Veronica beat to windward, logging seven knots under reefed main and a tall, narrow slab of heavy Dacron hanked to the inner forestay. The East China Sea was gray; the horizon ragged, oppressively close; and the sky so dark that when Sarah came up at eight o'clock to relieve him, Stone was still steering by the red glow of the compass light.

"I wish," she said, "I had killed him when I had the chance."

She spoke as if the thought were new. But she said it at each watch change—the only time they saw each other—and often they were her only words. He reached to take her hand, but she wouldn't let him.

"It wouldn't have made a difference," he said. "It was the other one who grabbed her."

"Moss is a machine. He's nothing without the old man."

Stone could not agree that Moss was nothing; blazing through his mind was the recurring image of the black man swooping down like a bird of prey. "Four hours to go," he said, hoping to calm or at least distract her with happier thoughts.

Sarah looked up at the radio antenna on the masthead. "Will you check the radio?"

"Soon as I go below." He had tuned in the weather every two hours. The radio was fine.

"Where are you going?"

She had started forward. "Shake out the reef."

"No," said Stone. "She'll just heel too much and slow down."

Sarah returned reluctantly to the cockpit. He stepped away from the helm. "I'm going to get some sleep. Give me a yell if the wind starts screaming." Already the western sky was getting lighter. Sarah eyed it hungrily.

Stone woke an hour later to feel the boat laboring under too much sail. He went up on deck. The rain had stopped, but the wind and the spray pelting the dodger were colder. Sarah, shivering at the helm, tracked him with a defiant stare as he took a second reef in the main.

"Head up a little," he called. "We've got to go to the storm jib."

"No. You'll slow us down."

She was suffering, and he was trying to be gentle with her. But the interrupted sleep and the cold he felt so sharply stirred his own anger. "Don't tell me what'll slow this boat. Head up!"

Sarah gripped the helm like a weapon.

"Goddammit! I love her too!" Stone yelled. "Trust me to sail the boat, for crissake."

"You think I can't?"

"You're not doing a great job of it at the moment."

"Aye, aye, Captain."

"Head up!"

Sarah's lips set hard. Only a spasm flickering under her cheek betrayed her confusion. "My child needs me."

"Read the knot meter," Stone yelled. "What is it? Six-eight?" He couldn't see the speedometer from the mast, but everything he felt—from the noise in his ears to the wind on his face, to the minute vibrations of the deck beneath his feet—told him that the Swan was sailing at 6.8 knots and should be doing 7.1.

Sarah tore her gaze from him to the knot meter. Then, with a strange look—a look that tore his heart—she did as he demanded and steered the boat closer to the wind. Stone dropped the heavy forestay sail and raised the storm jib in its place. Sarah wouldn't meet his eye as he went below.

He sprawled on the leeward berth in the main cabin and

closed his eyes, sleep impossible. He thought he would give his arm to have his child back. But after listening to the hollow, wet noise of the bow crashing through the steepening seas, he admitted he would give his other arm to see his wife smile again. Neither seemed likely to happen.

He fine-tuned the self-steering gear so that he could join Sarah below when Ronnie radioed. While a close-hauled windward beat was among the best of the Swan's points of sail, the same was not true of the self-steering, particularly in choppy seas. The waves kept knocking her bow off course, devouring speed. He started the generator and reluctantly switched on the electric autopilot, which had a dangerous habit of shorting out with no warning.

At five minutes before noon, he took a careful look at the horizons and then went below into the relative warmth and quiet of the cabin. Sarah was at the nav station, the radio on, the mike in her hand. Stone braced himself on the companionway steps, wondering what stratagem Jack Powell would use to ensure their privacy on the open radio waves. The answer came in Ronnie's voice.

"Ronnie calling Veronica. *Ronnie calling* Veronica."

"Oh!" Sarah gasped. "Oh, Michael." She felt blindly for his hand, her gaze locked on the radio.

"Come in Veronica."

"We're here, darling. We're here."

"Mummy! Are you okay?" Used to radiophone communication, they switched from Transmit to Receive instinctively at the end of each other's sentences.

"Yes, dear. Are you?"

"Is Daddy?"

"I'm fine, sweetheart. We're both fine." How many times had he overheard one side of a radiophone conversation between sailors at sea and their families at home? *I'm fine, how are you?* The Swan lurched. He felt her turn away from the wind. The autopilot tugged her back.

"Oh, thank God. I was worried about the storm."

"No problem," said Stone. "*Veronica* did herself proud."

"*Listen, Mummy. Daddy. Do you know who I mean by Santa Claus?*"

"Yes, dear."

"*Well, Santa Claus says remember we have each other by the short hairs. Do you know what that means?*"

"Yes, dear."

"*He promised huge presents when we arrive.*"

"Do you think he'll keep his promise?" Stone asked.

There was a brief pause. Sarah's hand tightened on his. It might have been static or one of them had hit the Transmit switch later. Stone imagined the old man in the bathrobe leaning over her on one side, and the huge Moss on the other. Finally, Ronnie came back on in mid-sentence. " . . . *always keeps his promise.*"

He looked at Sarah. Her face was alight, her whole being fueled by the sound of Ronnie's voice. Stone felt it too. She didn't sound afraid. That was the big thing. Not afraid. And yet, there was so much unsaid. Sarah covered the mike.

"*There's something she's not telling us,*" she whispered.

Stone had utter faith in Sarah's psychic bond with their child. "But she does believe he'll let her go."

"It sounds that way. . . . " She hit the transmit button. "Ronnie? Are you eating properly?"

"*Oh, yeah, Mum, Mr. J— Santa Claus told the cook to make potato chips and he did. And they got more Coke. And, before we leave, we're having a huge Chinese dinner sent aboard from the best restaurant in town.*"

"What are you going to have?"

"*Peking duck.*"

"Dammit," said Stone, and Sarah looked stricken. Ronnie hated duck. She'd gotten sick on it in New Zealand. She was trying to tell them something.

He took the microphone. "Sweetie?" How to put the question? "Sweetie. When does Santa plan to sail?"

After a staticky hiss, Ronnie said, "*Santa Claus says we'll cruise away in plenty of time.*"

"Sweetheart, you really missed a great storm."

"Oh yeah?"

"Fifty-knot winds."

"You're joking."

"I wouldn't joke about fifty knots. You would have loved it."

"Hey, Mr.—Santa," he heard her call. *"Mummy and Daddy were in fifty-knot winds. What? Oh. Daddy, Santa says do you need any new sails for Christmas?"*

"Tell him all I want is my second mate."

"Oh! I gotta go. Santa says we'll talk day after tomorrow at sixteen hundred."

"Good-bye, dear," Sarah cried, but they both knew her voice was lost in the air.

Stone let loose his breath.

"We'll talk to her day after tomorrow," said Sarah. "Thank God."

"She sounds pretty good," Stone ventured.

"Yes, considering."

"What do you think she's trying to tell us?"

"I don't know."

Veronica gave another hard lurch. By the time Stone got to the cockpit, she had fallen ninety degrees off course. He put her back on, shut down the generator and the autopilot, and searched the sky for a break to shoot the sun. The cloud, which had lifted higher as the depression rushed on, was still too thick to penetrate. He hadn't had a fix since they left the Yangtze sea buoy. Dead reckoning put them a day and a half from the Osumi Strait. But the sea chop could have thrown them many miles off course, and he knew as much about his true position as he did about Ronnie's true condition.

Why sixteen hundred? he mused. Why not noon like today?

Sarah came on deck. It was her watch. She said, "I think she was trying to warn us."

"Of what?"

"I don't know. And I don't think she knows either. . . . Michael, I'm sorry about before. I was so upset. I feel so much better now that we've heard her voice. Don't you?"

"Did he offload any gas at that power plant?"

"Just enough to lighten the ship to get in the river."

"Why didn't he sell the whole cargo?"

"Gotcha."

Moss was grinning ear to ear when Mr. Jack walked onto the bridge. The OMBO monitor displayed a chart of the eastern reaches of the East China Sea. Kyushu, the southernmost big island of Japan, thrust into it like a tongue, forming the north coast of the Osumi Strait. Moss moved his fingers on a glidepad and tapped twice. Lines of position appeared on the screen. The second line crossed the first. The third line crossed them near the intersection, forming a tight triangle.

"There they are."

Mr. Jack studied the screen. "Okay. Get to the airport. But don't underestimate those two. Captain still can't believe they made it through that storm."

Moss grinned. "They never met a storm like me."

"And for crissake don't get caught by the Japs."

"Hey, I wouldn't rat you out, Mr. Jack."

Mr. Jack reached out and laid his mutilated hand on the black man's shoulder. "I know you wouldn't, Moss. But I don't want to lose you. Huh?"

The poor bastard practically wept with gratitude. And Mr. Jack thought, not for the first time, how little you had to do to hijack a lonely man's soul.

34

"WHY SELL THE GAS IN TOKYO WHEN HE'S SO WELL CONNECTED in China?"

"Maybe some crooked Japanese offered him more money."

A clear sun shot at noon the day after they spoke to Ronnie put the Swan 360 miles east of Shanghai, 130 miles southwest of Nagasaki, and less than 120 miles from the Osumi Strait. With luck, if the clear weather held, they might by nightfall see the first glimmer of the Kusakaki lighthouse.

The northeast monsoon was still postdepression boisterous—a powerful twenty-five knots—and *Veronica* was flying under double-reefed main and her high-cut inner forestay sail. But the sea, which had deepened remarkably when their course took them at last over the hundred-fathom line, was, compared to the past three days, almost orderly. Large waves moved in stately procession, crowned with white crests. A royal blue color demarked the Japanese-Pacific waters from the East China Sea.

An hour after Stone's noon shot, they saw their first ships. A bright green car carrier steamed out of the east, bound for Shanghai or Hong Kong. Another, riding high and light, overtook them at twenty knots, racing for the Osumi Strait, and dwindled quickly.

The high sky was streaked with the trails of jetliners converging on Tokyo. Though they were still some six hundred miles and four hard days' sailing from the city, something about nearing the Strait and the first of Japan's main islands felt like their goal was in reach and the worst was over.

When Stone relieved Sarah at two, she stayed up in the cockpit with him, sitting close within his arm while he steered with one hand. They talked quietly, musing over the relative merits of staying on in Tokyo to visit with Hiroshi's family or sailing due south to warm water. It helped to pretend that there was no question they'd have Ronnie back and that life would go back to normal within a few days.

The winter light faded from the sky. A few pale stars winked behind the clouds. Ducking to look under the sails, which were sheeted in hard on the starboard side, they began to sense an intermittent glow on the horizon. Illusory, at first, it materialized as a faint halo—Kusakaki Light flashing at twenty-second intervals.

The western approach began about twenty-five miles ahead. Sixty miles beyond it they would enter the Osumi Strait. There, a thirty-degree turn to the left—if the wind would allow—and northeast to Tokyo Bay.

Eight hours later, at one in the morning, Stone was below—having just signed off a VHF radio conversation with the third mate of a Yokohama-bound Korean ore carrier that had overtaken them at sixteen knots a half mile to port.

"Sixteen-second double white flasher off the port beam," Sarah called down the hatch.

He checked the chart—where he had plotted the position the Korean had given him—and the Light Lists. "It's Sata

Misaki Light on the southern tip of Kyushu. Look for a fif-
teen-second red flasher on the starboard bow. I doubt you
can see it yet—about twenty miles."

He heard her safety harness shackle rasp along the jack
line as she headed toward the bow for a look around the
sails. She galloped back, calling, "I see the glow! Fifteen-
second red."

Stone brought her a covered mug of tea. "That's Kisika
Saki. Japanese is driving me nuts. *Saki* means point. *Zaki*
means point. *Misaki* means point. *Hana* means point. *Kaku*
means point. *Pii* means point."

"We say point, cape, headland, promontory. Why
shouldn't they?"

"They're supposed to be more efficient. Why the hell, if
Mr. Jack is as rich as he's supposed to be, is he stealing
natural gas? Why go to so much trouble for ten or twenty
million bucks when he's already worth a hundred times
that?"

"Maybe he's bankrupt."

He picked up the binoculars and scanned a confusing
mass of lights between the boat and Kyushu, ten miles to
port. It was difficult to distinguish the fishing boats, coasters,
and ships from buildings on the shore.

"Goddamned carnival out there."

He jiggled the glasses. The shore lights dissolved into
strings of tiny dots as the movement of the glasses revealed
the pulsing AC current. The sea lights, which burned on
direct current, shone steadily.

"Okay, wait till we're right between Sata and Kisika and
we go to east northeast, oh-six-oh."

They stayed up all night in the cockpit, two pairs of eyes
to watch for ships. The north wind started veering to the
east. In the darkness of four in the morning, the boat appeared to be between the glow of Sata Misaki far off the
port quarter and the red-flashing Kisika Saki ahead of the
starboard bow—indicating they were in the middle of the

Osumi Strait. The wind had swung into the teeth of course 060°.

The closest they could sail was 075, which would take them increasingly offshore as the Japanese archipelago angled toward the northeast. Sarah was distraught, Stone—high on tea, chocolate bars, and the coming dawn—philosophical: he brandished the chart, saying, "Don't worry, what we lose tacking offshore we'll get back with a boot from the Kuroshio Current."

Kisika Saki dimmed behind them to a faint glow like embers cloaked in ash, while ahead, a slowly lightening sky revealed the Philippine Sea.

It was deep, an arm of the Pacific. The water was dark, the waves widespread and orderly. The monsoon was blowing a gale, steady and backing north, more to angles the Swan liked. Stone was able to nudge her closer to east northeast.

At noon, he brought Sarah macaroni and cheese and steered while she ate it.

"You know, he could sell the gas in China before he goes to Tokyo."

"Possibly." Sarah yawned. "He seems to use the *Dallas Belle* as his private yacht."

"Get some sleep. Nobody out here but us chickens. I'll wake you for Ronnie." He had caught three hours himself.

At three-thirty he went below to wake her and turn on the single-sideband radio. At five of four, he started the generator and engaged the autopilot. At four on the dot—sixteen hundred—Ronnie came in loud and clear.

"Ronnie calling Veronica. *Ronnie calling* Veronica."

"We hear you, darling. How are you?"

"How are you, Mummy?"

"Fine. How are you?"

"How's Daddy?"

Stone leaned into the mike. "Doing fine, sweetheart. How are you?"

"Fine."

They waited. But "fine" was all they got.

"Are you eating properly?"

"Great food, Mum. I ate so much duck I'm going to squawk. . . . How are you?"

"What the hell is she trying to tell us?" whispered Stone.

"We're having a wonderful sail, dear. Brilliant wind. Clear as glass all afternoon."

Stone reached for the microphone. "Are we still going to see you for Christmas?"

"Oh, yes, Daddy."

"Does Santa Claus promise? . . . I said, does Santa Claus promise?"

"Yes. He said he does!"

"I wonder if we could talk to him for a second."

Another silence. Then, *"Santa Claus said he only talks to kids."*

"Son of a bitch." Stone handed Sarah the mike and stepped up on the companionway and looked out the hatch.

"When are you leaving?" he heard Sarah ask.

"We're leaving today."

Odd, Stone thought. If they were leaving today, a twenty-two-knot ship would be in Tokyo a full twenty-four hours ahead of the Swan.

"Santa says we have to say good-bye. Good-bye, Mummy. Good-bye, Daddy."

"Wait! Ask Santa if we're still on for the same time, same place."

"Santa says yes."

"Are we going to talk again on the radio?"

"Santa says no."

Sarah sat a moment, listening to the radio hiss and mechanically rubbing the teak nav table with her fingers. "Oh, Michael." Stone laid a comforting hand on her shoulder.

"What's she trying to tell us? She ate *duck?* She'd throw up the first mouthful."

They tried to reconstruct their conversations, looking for more code words. Santa, obviously Jack Powell. He hadn't allowed her to say much. Only that the *Dallas Belle* was about to sail.

"She said, 'I ate so much duck I'm going to squawk.' "

"Ducks quack."

"Squawk. She said squawk."

"Remember when she was little?"

" 'Walkie-*squawkie*.' The radio! She has my handheld— She meant she has a radio."

"But we'd have to be within twenty, twenty-five miles to pick up VHF."

"*She* knows that— Did you notice how she kept saying 'cruising'?"

"No—yeah, last time—the first call . . . What the hell does that crazy old man want? He didn't sail the *Dallas Belle* to Shanghai just to drink with the generals. They were working some kind of refit in that yard."

Sarah shivered. She felt as if her mind had trembled.

Stone said, "We're so worried about Ronnie, we've never really concentrated on what the hell does he want?"

Sarah shivered again. She knew, suddenly, and certainly. "Mr. Jack wants what you wanted when you lost Katherine."

"I wanted monsters erased from the planet."

"You wanted revenge. So does he."

"But you told me he got the guy who tortured him."

"He blames *all* Japanese. I think he's trying to make up for betraying his friends. I'm sure he talked," Sarah said.

"What kind of revenge?" asked Stone.

"He kept talking about Christmas in Tokyo," she replied.

"Four o'clock, Christmas Eve. The Tokyo Tower—but that makes sense, an easy-to-find landmark near the waterfront."

" 'A bang-up Christmas,' he kept saying. 'It's gonna be a bang-up Christmas.' "

"The *Dallas Belle*," Stone said, "carries more thermal energy than a nuclear bomb. Maybe the crazy loon wants to blow up Tokyo— Jesus!"

"What if it *is* the gas? But he's not selling it. He's going to detonate it."

"That's not possible. The explosion would be a thousand times worse than the Kobe quake—destroy the banks, stock market, corporate headquarters, the entire Japanese economy."

Sarah's mind trembled again. "He and the Chinese are buying stock."

"If they sell short, they'll own the planet."

"And slaughter twelve million people?"

"And Ronnie."

"Gotcha!"

Moss was hunched up in the forecabin of a triple-engine ocean racer with sat phones, signal trackers, and his laptop. The computer-generated lines of position intersected on the screen.

"Oh, shit!"

He had underestimated the sailboat's speed. She was fifty miles ahead of where he had calculated he would find her. Fifty miles of open ocean. And they had stopped transmitting. He flung open the cockpit hatch. The drivers, buckled in with three-point harnesses, gazed down at him awaiting orders. "East," he yelled. "Go!"

Engines thundered. The hull began pounding, smashing from wave top to wave top like a giant skipping stone. Down in the wildly leaping forecabin, belted in like the drivers, Moss clung to a handgrip as he explained the situation to Mr. Jack on the sat phone. Mr. Jack said he'd radio the doctors, put the kid on again, and let them talk until Moss was able to locate their signal. Ten minutes later he called back on the sat phone and said, "They're not answering. Probably up on deck and don't hear it."

Moss climbed out into the cockpit again. Of course they couldn't hear their radio if they were on deck. It was wet and bitter cold. They had their hatch closed. And without a radio signal to track, no way he was going to spot that damn sailboat before it got dark.

"We've got to radio Japanese Maritime Safety."

"Who will believe us? We don't exist. Neither does the boat. Even our call sign is phony."

"How about the U.S. Navy?"

"Worse bureaucrats than the Japanese."

"CNN?" Sarah asked, then answered her own question. "If we start a panic, the Japanese defense forces will destroy the ship at sea, and Ronnie with it."

"Kerry McGlynn— No, Lydia Chin. She's better connected. And Robert works in Tokyo."

"Will she believe us?"

"She didn't believe me, but she'll believe you."

They scrambled below, and tuned the single-sideband transmitter to Lydia Chin's private shipping channel.

It was a goddamn big ocean, thought Moss. The boat was crashing from wave to wave, his stomach was queasy despite his anti-seasickness ear patch, and the light was fading. The doctors were nowhere to be seen.

"Sir!" Moss heard in his headset. The voice of his radio listener in Kagoshima, on the southern tip of Kyushu. *"I hear them, sir! They're broadcasting on nineteen-forty."*

"Lock on!"

"Already am, sir."

Moss tuned in his own tracker, then sat-phoned the *Dallas Belle* to alert Mr. Jack.

Mr. Jack was real pleased, until he heard the doctors talking.

They got a good strong signal to Lydia Chin, clear enough to convey the woman's steel-in-silk tones. *"Sarah,"* she said, *"Are you absolutely sure?"*

"Absolutely," Sarah assured her for the third time.

After a long, long silence, a silence so long that Stone thought they'd lost the signal, Lydia said, *"I will fly to Tokyo."*

"Thank you. Thank you so much."

Lydia's reply was chilling.

"But do understand that from the Japanese point of view, the lives of twelve million people will take precedence over that of one little girl—provided I can even convince them that this is not a tasteless hoax."

Stone grabbed the microphone.

"All you've got to do is convince them to watch for a fifty-thousand-ton gas carrier steaming their way! Tell them to board for a safety check while it's still at sea. Tell them the last we saw they were painting the hull black. A black fifty-thousand-ton LNG vessel shouldn't be too hard to spot."

He gave the microphone back to Sarah and stepped up the companionway to look for ships. The water looked empty, until, miles behind the boat, in the northwest where the advancing winter night had not yet darkened the water, he saw movement.

Veronica descended the sea it had just climbed and he lost sight of it. He reached into the cockpit for the binoculars which were hanging from the steering pedestal.

The Swan attained the next crest, which was capped with foam. He saw it again, closer, sheets of spray hurled skyward by a thin dark wedge.

"What in hell . . . *Sarah!*"

He needed her eyes. Feeling a sudden urgency, he dropped down the companionway and handed her the binoculars.

"Take a look astern. Five, six miles."

She bounded up the companionway and called down a moment later. "It's a small motorboat. He's heading straight for us."

"Where the hell did he come from? We're a hundred miles offshore— Hold on, Lydia."

The binoculars revealed a Cigarette class ocean racer—
a type favored by drug smugglers and the American DEA—
covering the distance at fifty knots. "Japanese customs?"

"I can't tell."

"Got to be Customs or Coast Guard. Maybe *they'll* listen
to us."

"I don't see a Japanese flag."

He looked around. Not a ship in sight.

At four miles he heard its engines, a staccato thunder,
muted but growing louder. Audible too was a *boom* each
time the racing hull went airborne and smashed down on
the next wave. It closed within a half mile and turned broadside to the Swan. Sarah moved closer to Stone and he instinctively put his arm around her.

As the black hull rose on a big sea, it was suddenly
illuminated by a flash of light. They heard a sharp *bang*.
Incredulous, they watched a dark cylinder travel across the
water, skimming the crests, hurtling toward them.

35

"CHEER UP, PAL. WE'RE ON OUR WAY."

Ronnie was still sitting in the radio operator's chair, swinging her feet and gazing teary-eyed at the radio. Mr. Jack put on a peaked cap covered with gold insignia, and held a smaller one out to her.

"Tugs are here, Mr. Jack."

"Come on, pal. Gotta give the captain a hand."

He tossed her the cap. She caught it and tried it on. Like every piece of clothing he had given her, it fit perfectly. She wondered if he'd sent storekeepers to measure her while she slept.

"And put on that parka. Going to be cold downriver. No, no. Not the red one. Uniform. Can't sail a ship outta uniform."

Sure enough, he'd brought another parka, navy blue, and it fit too. His nose, she noted, was almost as red as the parka he threw to the deck for Ah Lee to pick up later. He stank of whiskey.

"Move it! Double time."

He made a show of jogging down the corridor to the bridge, but he really just walked because his shoulder still hurt when he tried to run.

Ronnie trailed after him, her heart heavy, her mind alert. At least Moss wasn't around. She hadn't seen him since yesterday. Maybe he fell overboard. Good riddance, Mummy would say.

On the bridge, the captain was speaking into a walkie-squawkie and a Chinese pilot had come aboard, and a crewman she hadn't seen before was standing at the helm. You couldn't see out the front windows anymore. But the radar repeaters were lighted. The deck vibrated from the engine. Just like on *Veronica*, everything seemed to shimmer, all ready to sail.

Mr. Jack opened the door to the port bridge wing and motioned her to follow. She didn't want to. It was so cold. But there he was, out where the tip of the wing extended a few feet past the new superstructure, pointing and demanding she look.

The tugs were billowing smoke and steam and hooting madly. Two of them were pulling lines from the *Dallas Belle*'s stern. The third waited in the river. And boy, were they going to be surprised when they got a look at the *Dallas Belle*. Not quite the ship they had towed in. The gutted hull that remained of the old cruise ship looked like an empty soap dish.

"Mr. Jack!" The captain, calling from the door. "Scrambler."

"Be right back, pal. Stay here."

She watched him walk inside and waited, shivering. Ever since Moss left he'd been calling her "pal" instead of "kid". It was like having a friend and it made her feel a little better, which was weird because he was the one doing all the bad stuff.

*   *   *

Mr. Jack took the superencrypted satellite phone into the computer room, where he was alone. "What?"

"Radio-guided missile right in the gut."

"*Missile?* Moss, am I paying you to be stupid?"

"No, Mr. Jack."

"Why didn't you ride alongside and drop a grenade in their laps? It's a goddammed sailboat, for crissake."

"Your Japanese guy didn't have a grenade."

"But he had a missile. Terrific."

"Besides, why get close enough for a firefight if I got a missile?"

"You already searched his boat. They don't carry guns."

"What if he picked up a fullie in Shanghai? Get my ass sprayed."

"Moss, you know damned well he'd have a better chance of screwing the mayor's daughter than acquiring an automatic weapon in Shanghai."

"Okay, okay, I'm sorry, Mr. Jack. It seemed like a good idea."

"Anybody see you?"

"No. Middle of nowhere out here. Hundred miles from land."

"Did they sink?"

"They're on fire."

"Are they *sinking*?"

"They're on fire!" Moss protested angrily. "Looks like Baghdad on CNN."

"Make sure they sink."

He jammed the phone in his pocket and walked back to the bridge. Ronnie had her nose pressed to the glass. Probably oughta adopt her, take pity on an orphan.

For a long five seconds after the missile struck *Veronica*, Stone couldn't believe they were still alive. Then black smoke began gushing out of both sides of the hull, followed by astonishingly bright flame.

Their attacker had overestimated the strength of fiber-

glass; the warhead—probably armor-piercing—hadn't detonated. The missile had passed right through the hull without
exploding. But its fiery tail had ignited a fire.

He closed the cabin hatch and ran toward the bow, yelling, "Hit the extinguishers."

Sarah opened a cockpit hatch and yanked a red cord,
activating Halon fire extinguishers in the engine box and
main cabin, and a sodium bicarbonate tank in the galley.
She shut down the generator, which would consume the
Halon gas. Stone tore open a hatch in the foredeck, turned
on the fire hose, and dragged it back to the cockpit. Sarah
was ready at the cabin hatch with a portable extinguisher.

While they waited for the Halon to work—air from the
hatch would dissipate the smothering gas—they stripped off
their foul-weather jackets, which were made of synthetics
that would melt to their skin. Flame and smoke still gushed
from the sides.

Stone nodded. Sarah slid the hatch open. Black smoke
poured out. He filled his lungs with air and leaned in with
the hose.

Flames were dancing on both sides of the cabin. Neither
the Halon nor the sodium bicarbonate, which was best used
on a galley grease fire, had extinguished the fire.

Stone twisted the nozzle. The pump started clanking.
The hose bucked in his hands, and a jet of water shot into
the smoke. The missile had blasted through the nav station,
where minutes earlier Sarah had been hunched over the
radio, across the cabin, and out through the galley.

He knocked down the flames in the galley and stepped
into the smoke-filled cabin. Sarah followed him with the
portable extinguisher.

"Port side!" he shouted in the darkness, spraying fresh
flames to starboard. She directed Halon on the burning nav
station. Suddenly, it was dark. The fire was out.

They scrambled up the companionway, coughing and
gasping for clean air. Then Stone went down again with the
portable to make sure the fire didn't flare up again. The

missile had bored a four-inch hole in the port side—scattering the electronics—and, exiting starboard, had blown a jagged hole a foot wide. Water gushed in when the boat heeled.

"They're coming," Sarah called.

Across the darkening sea, Stone heard their engines getting louder.

"Get my hammer and chisel," he yelled, frantically pulling up the floorboards.

"What are you doing?" she cried.

"Chisel!"

He flung the floorboards out of his way and knelt in the bilge. When he reached back she slapped the chisel butt into his hand, and when he reached again, the hammer.

"What are you doing?"

"Get a light."

She grabbed one from a charger, found it half-melted by the fire, and grabbed another from the toolbox.

"Here! Point it here."

She aimed it into the bilge, where oily water was sloshing with the movement of the boat.

He pressed the cutting edge of the chisel to the fiberglass and banged the butt with the hammer. Sarah watched, mystified. They were directly over the keel. The sharp tool stripped away layers of white gel coat and then shards of the clear, glassy material below. Suddenly a seam opened. A foot-long rectangle of fiberglass pulled away. Michael jammed the chisel under it, twisted hard, and it popped out, revealing a deep slot into which he lowered his hand.

Veronica heeled before a gust, and seawater plumed through the hole in the galley.

"Shove a cushion into that!"

Then, to her amazement, Michael drew a narrow box about two feet long out of the slot. He popped a row of catches. Watertight seals parted with a sucking sound. Inside was a matte-black gun and three banana-shaped ammunition clips duct-taped together.

"*What* is that?"

Stone gave her a look. She had been born in a soldier's house. Like it or not, she knew a semiautomatic when she saw one. And she knew, too, the futility of carrying protection you had to surrender to island governments *before* cruising their remote and unguarded waters.

"Bushmaster," he answered. "Got it off a mercenary."

Technically a pistol—a very big pistol—it had a folding stock that extended it into a rifle. Patrick, the mercenary— he had offered no surname—had "moused" the weapon so it could be fired fully automatically by merely holding the trigger. He had taught Stone the guerrilla fighting tricks of duct-taping the spare clips to triple the thirty-two round capacity, and twisting the pistol grip sideways to let the recoil spray bullets like a scythe.

Stone banged the clip into the gun and unfolded the stock. He left the grip in the vertical position.

Sarah peered out the hole the missile had blasted through the nav station. "There are three men in the boat," she reported coolly. "Two in the drivers' seats behind the windscreen. Moss is standing in back. He's got a rifle or something over his shoulder. . . . It has a scope. Michael, you can't kill all three of them."

He didn't know whether she meant he hadn't the ability or the moral right. "Lie flat on the deck and cover your ears. This thing is *loud*."

Sarah scooped his industrial ear protectors from the toolbox and slipped them over his head. Stone shoved the wrecked electronics out of the nav station. The missile hole would do as a gunport.

The ocean racer was closer than he had imagined. Two hundred yards. They had turned broadside to *Veronica* and were matching her seven knots effortlessly, engines emitting a lazy growl, while Moss inspected the Swan through raised binoculars.

Stone tried to summon up an icy detachment. The advantage of surprise would be brief, and with one gun on the slow-moving *Veronica*, he was in no position for a pro-longed battle.

He adjusted the rear open sight to two hundred yards. His hands were shaking so hard he had to brace the Bushmaster against the shattered fiberglass.

He'd run into the mercenary in Manila and had rerigged the guy's retirement boat and repaired his radio in exchange for the Bushmaster and a crash course in how to shoot it. Stone had learned to hit floating soup cans at three hundred yards. But afterward, over a celebratory San Miguel, Patrick had grown quiet. He was a stocky little man with piercing blue eyes and the aggressive bark of a Marine colonel. "Mike? Wha'd you do in the war?" They were of an age; he meant Vietnam.

"Naval surgeon."

"Right . . . You were a real natural. You displayed a fine accuracy out there. But there's a hell of a difference between shooting a weapon and *fighting* with a weapon. Problem is, you engage pirates in a firefight, they'll kill you."

"Then what do I want a gun for?"

"Don't think of it as a gun. Think of it as a cannon. Show you what I mean . . . "

Stone clamped the Bushmaster's stock to his shoulder, found the black hull in the failing light, waited for *Veronica*'s uproll, and touched the trigger twice to get the range. Even with the earmuffs the sound was deafening, but there was little recoil. He saw a patter of spray flare just short of the racer, raised the barrel a trifle, and fired five shots into the hull.

The men in front ducked for cover. But Moss stood tall and still as a statue, hefted a long gun, and trained it on the Swan.

36

STONE SQUEEZED THE TRIGGER, AGAIN, HELD IT. THE GUN NUDGED his shoulder, smooth as a finely tuned engine. The clip emptied in seconds. Moss fired. A high-power bullet passed through the cabin, a foot from Stone's face, with a loud *crack*. He snatched the clip out, reversed it, banged it back in, and fired another close-patterned burst.

The Cigarette boat veered away, throwing Moss to the deck.

Engines thundered as the driver presented the smaller target of her stern. A mirthless grin tugged Stone's face; Patrick would have been proud of him.

He steadied the Bushmaster and fired ten careful shots into her stern. He thought he saw chips fly. It was too dark to see for sure. But the big engines stopped abruptly. The ocean racer slid to a confused halt between two waves.

When the waves raised it again, Stone could see it was listing and sagging low in the stern, where the crew were working frantically, either trying to restart the engines, which now had numerous perforations in vital parts, or, more likely, bailing the seawater gushing through the hole Stone had blown in her hull.

But *Veronica*, too, was taking on water as she heeled in the stiff monsoon.

"Start pumping."

They put *Veronica* about on a starboard tack, to make her lean away from the hole in her side.

Sarah pumped and stood watch. Stone gathered tools and material. The hole was way too big—as big around as a soccer ball—for a conical wooden patch, so he duct-taped a piece of sailcloth over it as a temporary patch, while he mixed quick-setting epoxy and laid up several thin layers of fiberglass cloth.

Sarah was reporting scores of fishing boat lights and the occasional seagoing vessel. With luck, one of them might pick up the Cigarette boat; with better luck, he thought grimly, it would run it down in the dark.

The smaller hole over the navigation station was a simpler job. But salvaging enough of the electrical board to jury-rig a charger for the surviving flashlights and the handheld VHF short-range radio took hours.

After he had cleaned up the corrosive residue of the sodium bicarbonate extinguisher from the galley, he tipped a bucket of metal and broken glass overboard and slumped beside Sarah in the cockpit.

"That was the radio. . . . It was a setup. He knew what time Ronnie would call. A listener in Japan, Moss on the Cigarette boat, the old man back in Shanghai. Triangulation. Simple as shooting the sun. But why'd he attack us? He'd set it up long before we called Lydia."

"Vengeance," said Sarah.

"For what?"

"We caused him trouble in Shanghai. That's how he thinks, Michael. An eye for an eye." They looked at each other, shaking their heads in dismay. Stone started to voice his next thought.

"Don't say it," whispered Sarah.

He didn't have to. The question loomed like the night. What would they find in Tokyo?

He dozed off, then awakened, vaguely aware Sarah was speaking in the dark. "What?"

"Where did you get the gun?"

"In Manila. When Lydia took you and Ronnie to Singapore."

"Ah." The sky was clearing and there was sufficient starlight to see her smile. "I'm glad," she said.

"It was certainly a good argument for carrying a weapon."

"No. I don't mean that."

"What do you mean?"

"I knew you were hiding something from me. When I got back from Singapore. I just knew it. . . . I thought you'd had a fling on the beach."

"Fling on the beach? You're my fling on the beach."

"Well, you know Manila. Wasn't it Race Week? I supposed . . . you know."

"Why the hell didn't you ask?"

Sarah said nothing.

"Hey, you're the one always telling *me* to talk. Why didn't you ask?"

"Michael, don't be daft."

"I'm not being daft. Why—?"

"I was afraid. . . . I didn't want to know."

"Oh, for crissake. Come here." He put his arm around her shoulders, felt her stiffness. "Sarah. You know me. I'm a one-woman man and you're the one woman."

"Well, you don't always show it."

"Am I about to be condemned for *not* having a fling on the beach?"

"I can't *believe* you hid a gun without telling me."

"I wasn't up to arguing about it."

"Or perhaps you just wanted a secret," she retorted, and

they glared at each other across a gulf of personality—their gulf of mutual attraction—broadened tonight by fear and exhaustion.

"And you've been sitting on *your* secret."

"What secret?"

"My imaginary fling on the beach."

"I told you, I was afraid."

"Or wanted something to hold against me?"

"Why would I want that? That's ridiculous."

"You tell me," said Stone. "There's been a little distance lately. I thought it was the East Timor-Africa stuff."

"Michael, you make it sound like they're not legitimate causes. Rough-and-ready doctors like you and me *ought* to go to Africa."

"Maybe they're an excuse."

"An excuse?" Sarah asked. "For what?"

"For wanting out of this life."

"I *love* our life. Except the hiding. *You* love the hiding."

They talked in circles, then sat alone in coils of silence.

Finally, Sarah took a deep breath to build her courage and reached for his hand. She said, "You know something? It's Katherine."

"What?"

"After all these years, you still love her."

Silence swelled like a following sea, and Stone looked into the night, half expecting a wall of water to crash into the cockpit. "I love you too," he said.

"What hurts me is you still miss her."

"You," he said, "are my life and my love. You and Ronnie."

Sarah said, "You named that woman Katherine."

"It was the second name I thought of."

Stone was afraid he had said too much. Or not enough. He sensed death in the silence. . . . "The single-sideband's wrecked."

"Can you fix it?"

"Nothing left to fix. Blown to pieces. So's the radar."

No long-range radio; no way for Mr. Jack to call. No way to contact Lydia. No radar; no collision alarm in the busy Japanese shipping lanes.

Sarah reached across and laid a firm hand on his shoulder. "No radar. No collision alarm. No radio. Ronnie's got the GPS. You've done it, at last, Michael."

"Done what?"

"You're finally back to basics."

There was laughter in her voice, and he felt his heart soar toward the sound.

"What do you say we tear up the deck—get a little closer to the sea?"

"Michael. You made a joke. I can't believe it."

He shook his head and grinned. "I can't believe we're still alive. You know that son of a bitch almost killed us?"

Sarah giggled. "How do we know he didn't?"

"Maybe we're in heaven."

"It's too cold for heaven."

"Besides, nobody dead could be this tired."

Exhaustion, release, fear, and postponed hysteria erupted in laughter. They reached for each other, held tight, searched clumsily for the other's mouths and crashed together in their first real kiss since they'd escaped Shanghai. Their hands grew active. Velcro hissed, snaps parted; they tore at the zippers of their foul-weather jackets, struggled with the bibs of their sea pants, frantic to press their bodies together. "Oh my God, Michael. I thought— Oh."

Loath to part even for a second, they stayed all night in the cockpit, wrapped in blankets under the storm trysail, spelling each other as they dozed and watched for ships. Sarah felt warm at last, warmed within, her body content, her mind willing to shut down for a while, stop thinking, let the boat take care of them. But as day broke, she felt Michael's body begin to tense up, and the warmth drained away.

"Where are you going?"

"Figure out where we can get close enough to the *Dallas Belle* to talk to Ronnie on the VHF."

Sarah followed him below and stood over his shoulder as he walked the calipers over the singed and sodden chart. "Assuming he left when she said—fifteen hours ago—and assuming he's making twenty-two knots, he'll be here— three hundred and thirty miles east of Shanghai and through the Osumi Straits in another eight hours—here.

"We've got to head north and cut ahead of her. At twenty-two knots, they'll come screaming up behind us in fifteen or sixteen hours. We could meet 'em here."

He tried to draw a circle over the *Dallas Belle*'s course. The pencil gouged the wet paper.

"Then what?" asked Sarah.

"Assuming all the assumptions are correct, we'll have about a fifty-mile circle we can talk in—if we raise her— which the ship will pass through in less than three hours. God, if we could get close maybe she could jump for it."

"Too dangerous."

"Down a rope or something—"

"Into the propeller."

"At least we can talk to her."

"He'll try to kill us again."

"Not if he can't see us. Fifteen hours from now it'll be dark."

"Michael, this is crazy. What are we doing?"

"Ronnie sent a message. Says she's got a radio. What else can we do but try to get close?"

"And what happens if the ship isn't there?"

"We keep on sailing."

"Let's talk about better ideas."

But as dawn struggled to pierce a gloomy sea fog that drifted down from the north, they kept coming back to the same conclusion: the best they could do was try to answer Ronnie's radio, while they raced for Tokyo.

* * *

353

For thirty hours they watched and waited and listened for Ronnie's voice to come piping over the VHF airwaves.

Stone wired their short range handheld unit to a high-gain antenna—the steel-wire backstay. The antenna for the main unit at the nav station was atop the masthead, but that long range radio had been destroyed by the missile.

They cut near the flat-topped headland at Shiono Misaki, the southernmost tip of Honshu, and passed ten miles off-shore, hugging the outer edge of the eastbound traffic separation lane. Ship traffic was heavy, but they neither heard the *Dallas Belle* nor saw any sign of the gas ship.

The northwest monsoon was blowing hard, the wind dry and bitter cold. The Kuroshio Current flowed strong, three and four knots in their favor. But still no word from Ronnie. And nothing, of course, from Lydia.

They debated what might have happened. Either the *Dallas Belle* had passed them in the dark at a time when Ronnie couldn't get alone to use the radio. Or the ship wasn't headed for Tokyo at all. Or—and this they clung to, in their frightened, sleepless state—the ship had broken down and was making repairs. In that event, the prodigious wind and the Kuroshio "Black Current" would sweep the Swan into Tokyo first.

Lydia Chin watched the neon lights of Tokyo hold the night at bay.

With her husband, Robert, his trading hong's top man in Japan, she enjoyed a lavish apartment with views few Tokyoites could afford. One end of the living room over-looked Tokyo Tower, a steel-girdered symbol of Japanese postwar recovery, and, in its likeness to the Eiffel Tower, a quaint example of old-fashioned 1950s Asian insecurity. Buildings were kept low, out of fear of earthquakes, and compared to Hong Kong, Lydia thought the much larger Tokyo resembled a massive cluster of airport hotels and sub-urban shopping centers.

An exquisitely polite gentleman who represented the

Japanese Maritime Safety Agency stood like a statue in the living room, explaining with deep respect which failed to mask his utter contempt that every fear she had raised had been investigated. There was a reserve among island peoples—her husband was English—and a dislike of foreigners. She found herself containing her Cantonese ebullience—as she would in London—closing her smile, dimming her eyes.

She could not see Tokyo Harbor, but held in memory the sight from the plane: a vast spread of black water that funneled into the heart of the city, sparkling with the running lamps of a thousand ships.

In the business districts, many of the office buildings had lit their windows in the shapes of Western Christmas trees, starry snowflakes, Nordic reindeer, and round snowmen nearly indistinguishable from burly Santa Clauses. Countless lighted windows, and behind each a human being.

"Officials representing the American Mr. Jack Powell confirm he owns a liquefied natural gas carrier called the *Amy Bodman*. They claimed it was in dry dock in Taiwan. We contacted Taiwanese authorities. They assure us the ship is there."

"What size ship?" asked Lydia.

"Fifty thousand tons."

"Has anyone actually seen Mr. Powell?"

"Mr. Powell is leading a gas exploration expedition in Antarctica. I spoke with him myself by radio. It was a poor connection, but Mr. Powell was very helpful and referred me to several mutual acquaintances in the shipping world. Happily, your claims are refuted. We are, of course, grateful that you came here all the way from China."

"I came from Hong Kong," Lydia said frostily. "And I thank you for going to so much trouble. Perhaps now you'll have a drink?"

The Japanese bowed his head. "No thank you, I promised my children I'd be home early to wrap Christmas presents."

Lydia rang for the butler to get the gentleman's coat. "May I ask, are you a Christian?"

"Of course not. But it's a jolly celebration." He softened slightly at that. "Do be assured that my agency closely inspects every gas carrier that approaches the port. And in light of your . . . information . . . we will be particularly vigilant for the next several days."

"I was led to believe there was a child aboard. I would hope the inspectors will be careful."

The Japanese turned wintery again. "With gas ships, we are always careful."

37

"LOOK, KID! NO HANDS."

Mr. Jack raised both gloves in the air as the *Dallas Belle*'s helm, a yoke smaller than a car's steering wheel, began to turn. He grinned at her, but Ronnie was sulking in a corner of the bridge, nose in a book. Earlier she'd gone AWOL, wandering the ship for hours until he caught her on the main deck, mooning at the lifeboats. She'd scared the bejesus out of him and he'd yelled at her. So now she was sulking. And he was in the doghouse. It was worse than marriage.

The good news was, he would catch the Japs with their pants down, just like last time. His cover story had held. The clincher was the Antarctica call, relayed courtesy of the sat phone and a radio operator on the Weddell Sea who had earned enough money in one night to send every child she ever spawned to private school.

"Kid! Look! No hands."

The *Amy Bodman/Dallas Belle/Asian Princess* made fifteen ponderous knots through the Philippine Sea, the Osumi

Strait two hundred miles in her wake. The tons of cloaking steel had reduced her speed by a third, and with much of the new weight forward, she was down at the head. When she pitched, she drove her bow deep into the lumpy seas and heaved gigantic wings of spray. But the captain had promised she'd hit Tokyo on schedule, and the computer agreed: twenty-three hours and counting.

"No hands."

"Big deal." She pouted. "We have an autopilot too."

"Not like this you don't."

Overcome by her natural curiosity, the child got up and crossed the slanting deck to the OMBO monitor. Etched in light was an irregular zigzagged course, with the icon representing the ship. Ronnie's eyes widened. When the icon reached the next zig, the ship began to turn without anyone touching the helm.

"No hands."

Twice more in two miles the ship changed course, heeling tenderly, but conforming precisely as if it were rounding race buoys. And all the while, Mr. Jack grinned like a snake.

"What do you think?"

Ronnie made a face. "It's an OMBO ship."

Mr. Jack looked at her sharply, the snake grin scary. "What do you know about OMBO?"

"One-man-bridge-operated," Ronnie answered. "Daddy says they're the worst thing to hit the ocean since megacarcharodon."

"Mega-what?"

"Megacarcharodon was a giant shark. A hundred feet long. He ate everything, till he became extinct."

"Served him right."

"Daddy says they're going to run down sailboats and the boats will never even know they hit them."

"Daddy tell you *why* we make OMBO ships?"

"So you don't have to pay people to stand watch."

"Yeah. Well, this is a really special OMBO. Third generation. Even your smart daddy never heard of this one."

She stared at their reflections in the windows. The new superstructure blocked the gloomy view ahead. All she could see of the sea was out the side windows.

Mr. Jack glided up behind her. "Hold on," he warned, pointing at the monitor. "Crash turn."

It was a ninety-degree turn. A siren shrilled a warning, and the gas carrier slammed to starboard. Ronnie grabbed the rail that rimmed the windshield. Mr. Jack did too, but he used his injured arm and cried out in pain. She tried to save him, but her own grip was broken from the rail and they tumbled to the deck.

Slowly, hesitantly, the ship straightened up.

"Are you okay, Mr. Jack?"

"Yeah, yeah." He was white. Ronnie sprang up and offered a hand, as the captain charged onto the bridge. "What the hell—"

"Just demonstrating the system," Mr. Jack said.

"You're going to demonstrate us into a capsize," the captain yelled. "We're carrying enough weight topside to turn turtle."

For once, Mr. Jack apologized. He was almost meek. "Sorry. Just wanted to show the kid what she could do. Don't worry, Cap. Won't happen again."

Ronnie stared at the floor while the captain grumbled. Finally, he left.

"Jeez," whispered Mr. Jack with a conspiratorial wink. "We almost got in a lot of trouble."

"*You* almost got in a lot of trouble. *I* didn't do anything."

"Captain thinks you did it and I was just covering for you." He grinned, sly but not snakelike, and Ronnie, caught up in the game, said, "No way! Mr. Jack."

Mr. Jack patted the monitor. "So what do you think?"

"Great," said Ronnie. But in her mind she vaulted a half mile ahead of the ship, saw it pawing an angry white course through the waves—the mask, turning where it wanted to. She shivered.

"You look like you seen a ghost," said Mr. Jack.

She could almost see the eyes behind the mask. Almost. "Is Moss coming back?"

"Don't look that way," Mr. Jack replied lightly. But his face had turned to stone, and she shivered again. She was scared. She had never been alone before. But she was alone now. Moss had made her feel so little when he hit her— blew her off like a mosquito. Mr. Jack wasn't as big as Moss, but he was still a lot bigger than she. And for such a bag of bones, he was mighty strong.

"Can I radio Mummy?"

"'Fraid not, kid."

"Mr. Jack?"

"What?"

"Where's Ah Lee?"

"Jumped ship in Shanghai."

"He didn't tell me he wasn't coming."

"When a sailor jumps ship, he doesn't advertise it or he'd get caught."

"Where *is* everybody?"

"What do you mean?"

"When I went for a walk—"

"Any more walks, young lady, we're going to war."

"Yeah, but I didn't see anybody."

"The crew's busy doing what I pay 'em to do. Or they're sleeping."

"I didn't see *anybody*—except that Japanese guy, and he was drunk. Who is he? I never saw him before we left Shanghai."

Mr. Jack did one of his dumb "Jap" imitations, bowing over his folded hands. "Honorable pilot-san."

"Who?"

"Captain Yakamoto is a Tokyo Harbor and Uraga Channel pilot."

"But he's drunk!"

"Got a little problem with the sauce," Mr. Jack admitted cheerfully. "Don't worry, OMBO will cover for him."

Ronnie shrugged, pretending she didn't care, and offered to take Mr. Jack down to the infirmary to change his bandage.

She knew the ship was deserted.

In her search for a place to hide when the ship got close enough to radio Mummy and Daddy, she had wandered further than the main deck. She had gone into the shell of the superstructure, which was like being inside a gigantic igloo, it was so cold. And she had ridden the elevator down to the bottom of the ship, where huge steel beams and pillars were coated with thick paint. The engine room was the loudest place she had ever heard in her life, hotter than Palau at noon. She had visited the crew lounge, which was plastered with Marlboro posters. But the only people she had seen were the drunken Japanese pilot and the captain and Mr. Jack.

The galley was empty; since Shanghai they had been eating frozen stuff cooked in the microwave. The engine room was empty. Even the engine computer room in the air-conditioned house in the middle of the roaring heat was empty. The ship was just sailing along all by itself.

Mr. Jack was so bony it was like bandaging a skeleton. He winced as she removed the old dressing.

"Does it hurt?"

"Just a little sore," he said, but she could tell he was lying.

"Mr. Jack?"

"What?"

"Can I radio Mummy?"

"I told you, no! Hey, cheer up. Tomorrow's Christmas Eve."

She turned away so he wouldn't see her press her fist to her lips to stop their trembling. Moss's fist had been big as a coconut. Hers was like a lemon. She closed her eyes and tried to form a picture of her knuckles balled tight and shooting like an X ray through Mr. Jack's shirt and bandage and skin and right through the muscle Mummy had sewn. But her stupid fingers kept dissolving like Jell-O.

Midmorning, Christmas Eve Day found Stone and Sarah deep within the Sagami Sea. Still no word from Ronnie, though they were only ten miles from Uraga-Suido, the channel to Tokyo Bay.

The chart showed land ahead and on each side, and the volcanic island O-shima far astern, but a thin December fog shrouded the vast gulf, which resounded with horns and whistles.

The VHF was alive with ship talk. They stayed tuned to channel five.

Stone had raised their radar reflector and was trying to skirt the inbound separation lanes. He had a fair idea where they were—he had eyeballed the triple thirty-second flasher on O-shima. Ahead lay water nearly a mile deep. But they both stayed in the cockpit to watch for ships, which were everywhere, rumbling and hooting in the fog.

He brought the *Sailing Directions* up and reviewed the Tokyo approaches until the print swam before his tired eyes.

Suddenly he snapped awake, his brain churning. The fog had thinned, revealing distant hills that appeared to float in front of a range of steep mountains. A couple of miles astern, he noticed a massive passenger liner knife through the haze. Black hull, white superstructure. Looked like the old *QE-2* on a winter around-the-world cruise.

"We're missing something," he told Sarah. "There's no way he can sneak a gas ship into the harbor. It's impossible. There's something in the *Sailing Directions*." He thumbed through the blue-jacketed book. "Here! 'Regulations: Tankers must enter port at dead slow speed preceded by a patrol boat, with one tug on each side of the vessel and followed by a patrol boat.'

"That's *after* picking up the Uraga-Suido Channel pilot and then the Tokyo Harbor pilot. So it isn't exactly a situation where he could just deliver a gas ship primed to explode at four o'clock Christmas Eve. . . . Now here, look at the harbor chart. Here's some gas wharves by these power plants across from Takeshiba Pier. But they wouldn't take a ship that size. They probably restrict them to ten-thousand-ton coasters—damned well should. Ship the size of the *Dallas Belle* a mile from the center of the city would be insane. . . . He *could* make a run at Yokohama. Look at this. Whip out of the fairway here and fifteen minutes later, 'Hello Yokohama'—boom!"

"No—that's not his way."

"What do you mean?"

"If Mr. Jack intends to destroy Tokyo, he will not settle for Yokohama."

"It's only fifteen miles from Tokyo and it's a very important city."

"He told me that after they had dropped their bombs, his plane spotted a fuel depot and if they had bombed that instead, the explosion would have burned the entire city."

"Well, then, he's got a problem. Tokyo's to hell and gone up the bay and there's a gauntlet of pilots and observatories and patrol boats and a naval base. Forget it, Mr. Jack. You're not even allowed in without specific permission from the port director, and to get that you've got to make all kinds of applications, and you know damned well you're going to be boarded out here" —he pointed at a quarantine area before Tokyo Light—"for a major safety inspection. Even before us and Lydia, he couldn't get the ship into the harbor. They've got thirty miles from the first pilot to stop him."

Sarah shook her head. "Michael. Put yourself in his shoes. How would *you* get that ship into Tokyo Harbor?"

"Hire an escort from the Third Fleet."

"Pretend Katherine's life hangs in the balance."

"I'll just think about Ronnie," he said with a bleak look.

"I'm sorry," she said. "That was terrible of me. I didn't mean that. I was just trying—"

"Forget it. He's making us all crazy. You're right, though. He may be crazy, but he's not a fool. So how would

363

I get the gas ship into Tokyo? . . . Make it look like something else? Cover the gas piping, make it look like a bulk carrier— Jesus, in the breaker's yard they were draping canvas over the main deck."

He recalled how he'd assumed the canvas was fire retardant for the acetylene torches dismantling the cruise ship. Then he remembered the cranes—the heavy lift cranes surrounding the slip.

"He had a brochure for a cruise liner to dock at Takeshiba Pier," Sarah said. "He said he owned it."

Stone reached for the radio. "Ronnie said they were 'cruising.' "

Before he could switch the VHF to emergency channel 16, they heard her whisper on channel 5, *"Mummy, Daddy. Mummy. Daddy!"*

"It's her. Yes! Dear, we're here. Where are you?"

She must have been holding her GPS in her other hand. *"Thirty-five degrees twenty minutes north. One hundred thirty-nine degrees forty minutes east."*

Stone traced the position along the course he had dead reckoned from the O-shima fix. "She's right behind us."

"Thank God," said Sarah.

"How fast you going, sweetheart?" Stone radioed.

"Twelve point five knots. Mummy, Mr. Jack changed the ship. We look like an ocean liner now—"

"Kid, what the hell—"

"I'm just playing, Mr. Jack. I—"

"Ronnie! Ronnie! Mr. Jack. Mr.—" Stone switched off the radio. "Jesus, I almost gave her away if he was listening." He looked back again.

The liner that looked like the *QE-2* was overtaking them rapidly, plowing a thick white bow wave. Sarah said, "Is that—?"

Stone remembered the gutted superstructure of the cruise ship in the breakers' yard. "That's what Ronnie means—he's camouflaged the gas carrier. That's the *Dallas Belle!*"

Sarah switched to channel 16 to broadcast a Mayday to the Harbor Patrol.

Stone stopped her. "He'll hear that. Let me get Ronnie first."

"What?"

"Put me aboard."

"What?"

Stone ran below, stuffed the Bushmaster into his foul-weather jacket, and came up, pulling on his gloves. "Same way you got off. I'll go up the mast to the top spreader. You tuck the boat under her bow. Windward. Port side. I'll climb onto the anchor and through the hawsehole."

"That's impossible."

He started the engine. "Wind will get crazy beside the ship. Bear away as soon as I get on the anchor."

He studied the ship's bow with the binoculars. "Not much flair. I think we'll fit."

"If you lose your footing—"

"I'll wear a life vest." He pulled it out of the cockpit locker and buckled in.

"You'll fall on the boat."

"We have no choice."

Sarah started to protest, then saw there was no other way. "Of course."

"She's doing twelve-and-a-half knots. That's nearly twice us. You'll have about ten seconds to slot me in. Can you do this?"

"I think I can."

He turned to the mast.

"Michael."

Her face looked sculpted of onyx. Only her lips were soft. "God bless."

Stone gripped the halyards on the windward side.

38

IT HAD BEEN TOO MANY YEARS SINCE HE HAD CLIMBED THE MAST while under way.

Sarah changed course to cut across the front of the ship and sheeted the sails in hard to make the boat heel. Even with the help of that angle, his arms and legs were shaking by the time he had reached the first spreader. There was no time to catch his breath; the ship was looming large. He wondered if they could see his sails yet in the haze. If they could, they might guess what he was doing and have people waiting for him at the hawsehole. The gun felt heavy and awkward in his jacket.

He gripped the halyards and kept climbing. *Veronica* straightened up suddenly, thrown by a wave. He slipped, hung, swinging wildly, then crashed into the mast as the boat heeled again. He got his hand over the second spreader and hauled himself onto it.

The ship was almost on top of them. He could hear its

bow wave, a massive ten-foot comber. It looked like it would shove the Swan away.

Sarah was watching over her shoulder, standing tall and cool, one hand on the helm, the other shielding her eyes against the glare as she tried to judge the rise of the bow.

The anchor was higher than Stone had hoped. As the ship closed the last few yards, he realized he was going to have to jump up to reach it. But he saw nothing to hold on the enormous slab of steel. A gust of wind glanced off the ship and the sails shivered, staggering the Swan.

Sarah gripped the helm with both hands, fighting the currents that the ship sent swirling around the rudder and the wind that slammed the sails. The bow wave tumbled after *Veronica* like an avalanche.

Sarah raised a hand to warn him and turned away from the ship, timing it so the wave burst under *Veronica*'s stern. The mast swung wildly in a dizzy arc to left and right, then pitched forward, threatening to launch him into the air.

The ship blotted out the sky. Sarah signaled again and eased closer to the towering hull. A gust whipped the mast away, then slammed it back. The sails rattled like pistol shots. Stone saw the black steel anchor spring at his face. The spreader tip banged into it, and he felt the composite buckle under his feet. He let go of the mast and went with the momentum, up and onto a smooth bulk of steel which he embraced with widespread arms and legs.

He could feel the ship vibrating, shaking him loose. There was nothing to hold. He began to slide off. Out of control, he looked down to see where he would fall. *Veronica* was angling away.

He glimpsed the water racing beside the ship's hull and saw a two-hundred-foot-long strip of metal which appeared to be welded along the water line. Explosives, he guessed, shaped charges to crack her hull. Near the bow was painted the symbol for a thruster to warn the tugs. A nice touch, he thought with a strange sense of detachment—it meant the "cruise ship" didn't need a tug, even at the pier. Then he was sliding faster, slipping off the anchor's rounded fluke.

Life vest or not, the ship would suck him under when he hit the water. Then his foot brushed something, caught— and he realized he had snagged a rusty ridge that rimmed the edge of the fluke. He felt with his other foot and with both feet planted precariously, straightened his knees and pushed.

When at last he was sprawled across the top of the anchor, he inched his way toward the hull. The anchor shank, a thick oblong of forged steel, lay snug against the bottom of the hawsehole, leaving a foot-high gap on top. Through this, Stone tried to climb. He had to take the life vest off to squeeze through. The wind sucked it out of his hands. Again, he got his head and shoulder through into pitch blackness, but his windbreaker hung up. He backed out and opened it. The Bushmaster fell away. Stone watched it disappear forty feet below in a silent splash. He pushed past his despair and drove through the hole and slid down a thick chain.

He landed in the windlass room, which housed the machinery to raise the anchor. Below would be the chain locker. He felt in the dark, found a dog latch, and cautiously turned it and pushed. A door swung open into an enclosed deck, lit by daylight streaming in through a grating. He found another door and peered across the foredeck at the towering superstructure, which gleamed icily in the sunlit haze.

Bizarre. Even at a distance of less than a hundred feet, Mr. Jack's camouflage job looked so real that he ducked down, afraid he'd be spotted by the bridge crew. Because it was real, or at least the skin was. They had even put glass in the bridge windows and rigged lights inside, so portholes glowed.

He crossed the foredeck in a swift, low crouch and pressed against the front of the superstructure. He needn't have bothered, he realized. There was no one around. He edged along the side, peered in a gaping slit where two sections of the cruise ship superstructure had been cut apart and fitted loosely together, and stepped into the empty cavern.

Daylight streamed in a thousand ports. The gas ship's piping and valves and fire monitors looked like ghostly artifacts in an industrial museum.

A tangle of twisted wreckage marked the valve he had set on fire in Shanghai. He hurried past it and headed for the real house, hundreds of feet aft in the gloom. Wind whistled and loose metal vibrated in songs of many pitches.

He came at last to the deckhouse of the *Dallas Belle*, found a hatch, and opened it carefully. Inside, it was warmer. The deck was filthy. In the distance the engine murmured. He shut the hatch, peered up, and found an open central stairwell.

Ronnie and Sarah had been held on the B deck, right under the bridge. He debated taking the elevator and chose the stairs. He cursed himself for losing the gun. He took a fire axe from the bulkhead and started up the steps, silent in his rubber boots, poised at every turn to strike out at a startled face. He climbed five decks and saw no one.

The door to the owner's suite was locked, as was the captain's.

Gripping the axe, he climbed silently to the bridge deck. Down a corridor was a curtain that would lead to the bridge. He checked the rooms along the corridor—computer, chart, communications—all empty.

He moved the curtain with the axe. The old man was sitting in a big leather captain's chair in front of the helm, watching a thirty-inch monitor. The phony superstructure blocked the windows; Mr. Jack looked like he was driving a space ship.

Ronnie was standing close beside him to his left. To the right, like a large telephone booth, was a glassed-in toilet.

Inside, a man was curled up on the floor. Ronnie turned, and her face exploded in a supernova smile.

"Daddy!"

The old man swiveled his chair.

He was holding a pistol in his gloved hand, aimed at Ronnie's face, and had handcuffed his left wrist to her right.

"Drop the axe, Doc."

39

"THE AXE!"

Stone let it slide from his hand.

"Sit on that stool." His voice was like a weapon.

Stone had expected the frail lunatic in a bathrobe he'd seen in Shanghai. Instead he faced a remarkably fit old man who appeared strong as rigging wire and shackles. Clean-shaven, dressed in crisp World War II khaki, Jack Powell looked like a bantam-weight boxer who had never lost a fight.

"Here's the deal, Doc. You get on the radio. You call the missus. You tell her the rules haven't changed. She keeps her trap shut. No radio, no harbor patrol, no interference."

"And you give me Ronnie."

"Four o'clock. Tokyo Tower."

"I want her now."

"Can't have her now."

"If I refuse?"

"Little girl gets shot. Dead. And then you. Look, Doc, I

like your wife a lot. I don't want to make her a widow. But I will."

He tossed Stone a hand-held set to channel 5.

"Darling?"

"You made it."

"Not quite. He's still running things. Don't radio anyone. Just follow in and I'll see what I can do."

"But what about—"

Stone switched to Transmit. "Stand by. I'll call you back when I can." He turned off the radio. "Okay, Mr. Jack?"

"Aces, Doc."

Stone looked around at Ronnie and wondered where the key to the handcuffs was.

"Mr. Jack."

"Can it, Doc."

He was concentrating on the monitor. Stone edged closer. "No, just stay there. Sit on the stool." Stone stopped.

Ronnie gave him a frightened smile. The ship leaned into a turn. Five degrees, by the compass that hung from the ceiling over the helm. Slowly, ponderously, she straightened up on the new course.

Mr. Jack looked up from the monitor. "Wha'd you do to my man Moss?"

"Blew a hole in his stern."

"You did?" said Ronnie.

"With what?" asked Mr. Jack.

"Bushmaster."

"Where the hell'd you get that?"

Stone didn't answer.

"Did you kill him?"

"Last I saw him he was alive and bailing. Any luck, he got picked up by a ship."

"He was like a son to me."

"Your 'son' came damn close to killing us."

"Yeah, well . . . "

"Mr. Jack?" said Stone.

The old man shifted in his chair and tugged Ronnie closer to the gun. "What?"

Sarah had warned him how mercurial Mr. Jack was, emotions doubling back and reversing like riptides. Stone couldn't read his mood, couldn't tell whether it was safer to confront him or humor him.

"What?" the old man repeated, color rising in his stony face.

"I get the feeling you're making a last-minute change in plans."

"What plans?" asked the old man.

Stone glanced at Ronnie. She had hunched up her shoulders and was staring at the monitor, like any child in the presence of adults in conflict. They might be arguing about money owed or where to spend Christmas.

He said, "Your plan for Tokyo."

"And what plan is that?"

"Come on, sir. Give me a little credit."

"Plan's the same. My role has changed—damn shame. I already told my bean counters to sell Jap stocks short."

"You're making *money* out of this?"

"Pretty hard not to, if you know ahead of time that the Jap economy is going to be blown off the map. . . . My Chinese pals are going to make out like bandits. . . . You and Mrs. Doc, you've really taken a lot of the fun out of it."

Stone exploded, "My wife saved your life."

"Bet she wouldn't if she had to do it over again," Mr. Jack replied mildly.

"Who shot you?" Stone asked, probing for some wedge into the man's psyche, and knowing he wasn't good at it.

"A hero," answered Mr. Jack. "One of the ship's officers figured out the plan and tried to save the world."

"What happened to him?" asked Ronnie.

Mr. Jack looked surprised she was still handcuffed to him. "I had him transferred to another ship."

"I don't believe that."

"You know something, kid? Only regret I have is you've had to do too much growing up around me."

"Will you let us go?"

"Not yet."

"When?"

Mr. Jack shook his head. Ronnie looked at Stone. He gave her a nod and a smile as he might on one of the rare occasions they went to a restaurant and she felt overwhelmed by linen and china. Ronnie winked back.

"You okay, dear?" he called softly.

"Fine, Daddy."

Mr. Jack observed the byplay. Stone thought he looked suddenly weary, and wondered if the old man had doubts.

The VHF radio broke the silence. *"Asian Princess. Asian Princess."*

"Come on, kid. Tokyo calling." Mr. Jack stepped out of the chair and walked Ronnie across the bridge to the glass-enclosed toilet. Eyes on Stone, he rapped the door with the gun. "Wake up, Pilot-san."

The form curled around the toilet raised its head and peered around groggily. Mr. Jack opened the door and handed in the radio. "Tokyo Wan Traffic Advisory Service Center. You're up, pal."

"Asian Princess. Asian Princess," the radio repeated.

The pilot answered in Japanese and spoke at length.

Mr. Jack said to Stone, "We've got our own Uraga Channel pilot."

The pilot signed off.

"What's up?" Mr. Jack asked.

"I have confirmed that I'm aboard. From Shanghai."

"Everything okay?"

"A-okay to Tokyo Light."

"I'll wake you at Tokyo Light." He closed the door.

The pilot retched in the toilet and went back to sleep.

Mr. Jack explained, "Regulations require a qualified pilot aboard. I had this bozo flown in to Shanghai."

"Maritime Safety went along?"

"Long as I was willing to pay for it. And in Captain Yakamoto's case, I think they're happy to have him away for a while. Drinking man."

"Does he know what you're doing?"

"He's got trouble knowing his own name. Forget it if you're thinking you got a pal in the guy. He's all mine. Everything's ready. The *Asian Princess* has had Takeshiba Pier reserved for six months. Harbor master's planning to welcome the passengers personally."

Tokyo Light was only seven miles from Takeshiba Pier. The ship was steaming at twelve knots, the channel speed limit. Once the ship passed Tokyo Light there would be no stopping it.

What would Sarah say to him? "It's morally wrong to kill a million people"? Mr. Jack wasn't concerned about killing a million people. He liked the idea.

"Mr. Jack?"

"Yeah."

Stone nodded at the helm, which was moving at the invisible commands of the autopilot. "What happens when something gets in front of the ship?" A good question, and he was, after all, more comfortable talking about what made things tick than about what made people tick.

"She's got more radar than Kennedy Airport. All integrated into the course computer. Something gets in our way, she slows down or turns around it."

"What if there's no place to turn?"

The old man stared, the hint of a smile on his cold mouth. "The computer blows the whistle."

"Amazing," Stone said, trying to sound impressed. "I didn't realize they had taken OMBO so far."

"This is third generation. With this outfit, you can helicopter the crew off after the ship leaves port and helicopter a docking crew on at her next port of call. Hell of a labor savings in between."

"Tough on sailboats."

"Most of 'em carry radar reflectors. Fact is, you don't

even need a crew in port if it weren't for the goddammed Coast Guard regulations."

Stone commiserated, hoping to draw him into conversation. It seemed to work. While Mr. Jack monitored the computer screen, they swapped tales of Coast Guard boardings and bureaucracy. Stone told him how he got the Bushmaster from the mercenary. Mr. Jack topped him, claiming he had seduced right-wing Japanese terrorists into supporting Moss's attempt to sink *Veronica*.

Six times, the VHF interrupted and Mr. Jack roused the pilot to reply to other ships and Tokyo Traffic. Peering blearily at the radar repeater, the pilot ordered minor course changes which Mr. Jack punched into the computer. At other shifts in the channel, the autopilot heeled the ship through ponderous turns while Stone racked his brains for ways to keep Mr. Jack talking.

Suddenly the old man tapped the radar screen and blurted, "You think I'm nuts? You see what that is?"

"That big target?"

"Bet your ass it's a big target. That's the Jap Navy's *Admiral Yamamoto*, biggest helicopter carrier in the world. Dollars to donuts they've got air-to-ground tactical nuke missiles. . . . I'm not really nuts, you know."

Stone stepped gingerly into the opening. "You've sure waited a long time for revenge."

"Not really. I've hated the Japs since the war, but it was only recently that I realized I had all the pieces in place to do something about it—the ship, the gas, my Shanghai buddies. . . . Your wife tell you I'm nuts?"

Stone didn't know what to say. Mr. Jack stared at him, then answered his own question: "Your wife doesn't think I'm nuts. She thinks I'm evil."

"The only thing she cares about right now is getting Ronnie back alive."

Ronnie had drifted into a kind of empty-eyed sleep, half leaning on the old man.

"Daddy?"

"Yes, dear."

"There's another lifeboat." She looked up at Mr. Jack as if expecting him to stop her, but he explained, "There were two boats. The captain took one last night."

"Ah Lee showed me how it works, Daddy. You just pull a lever and it drops off the ship."

"Free fall," said Mr. Jack. "Designed for oil rigs. Drops like a stone. Handy getaway for fires and explosions."

"What about it, dear?"

"You have to wear your seat belt. Because it really crashes. But it won't break. Right, Mr. Jack?"

"Belt in tight and close all the hatches."

"Daddy?"

"What?"

"Run!"

"What? What are you talking about?"

Mr. Jack laughed. "Chip off the old blockette. What a girl!"

"Run, Daddy!"

"I can't leave you," said Stone.

"Then who will be with Mummy?"

Stone's eyes filled. "Sweetheart."

"Kid's got a point, Doc. Maybe I'll let you go at Tokyo Light."

"Let her go."

"No."

"Why? She's just a child."

"Like you said before, Doc. I changed my plans. But I don't want to die alone. The way things have worked out, Ronnie's my best friend on the planet."

"Then let her go."

"Daddy. Please run. Tell Mummy I love her."

Stone took his daughter's eye, saw the bravery shining there. He said, "I couldn't face her without you."

"That's not fair," Ronnie shot back.

"Why don't we ask Mummy to decide?" said Mr. Jack, switching on the VHF.

Stone stood up.

"Where you think you're going, Doc?"

"I won't let you torture her."

"Easy, Doc." Mr. Jack waved the pistol at him, then put it to Ronnie's head.

Stone started walking toward him.

"What are you doing?"

"I'm doing what my wife would do."

Mr. Jack's eyes got wide. "What are you talking about? Back off, man. I'll kill her."

"Then what?" said Stone, drawing nearer.

"One more step and she's dead."

"Your best friend on the planet."

"Jesus, Doc, you don't know me. Get on the radio and ask your wife if I'll shoot. She knows me."

"We both know you."

Stone kept walking. He was eight feet from the chair. He felt like he was conning the Swan through coral heads in murky water.

"Last warning, Doc. Stop."

"You're going to kill her anyhow."

"You asked for it. Sorry, kid—"

Ronnie pulled away, arms, legs and torso compressing like a spring. He yanked her back with the handcuff. But her free hand had already closed in a tiny fist.

A shrill scream ended with the dry snap of the gunshot.

40

RONNIE FELL UNDER THE OLD MAN, AND THEY WENT DOWN together like a heap of twigs and branches.

Stone grabbed frantically for the pistol. But it whipped past his hand—the *O* of the barrel full in his face.

Ronnie reared back and drove her fist a second time into Mr. Jack's wounded shoulder. The old man's eyes popped wide. Another scream, shriller than his first, spewed from his mouth, then trailed off. He convulsed and dropped the gun, grabbing his shoulder and tucking his body into a fetal ball.

Stone slid the gun across the deck and grabbed Ronnie. "You okay?"

Her eyes were wild, her nostrils flaring, her lips drawn tight in a snarl. "Son of a *bitch.*"

"Where's the handcuff key?"

"He threw it overboard."

Stone ran for the axe. Mr. Jack was moaning and clutching his arm.

"Move," Stone said to Ronnie. He shielded her hand with his, pulled the chain tight from Mr. Jack's wrist, and pounded it with the axe.

The deck absorbed the blows. He swung a dozen times, aiming for one link. It was awkward swinging with one hand. He felt Mr. Jack's eyes on him.

"Too late, Doc. You can't stop it."

"Watch me."

"Did you see the shaped charge along the waterline?"

"Yeah, I saw it."

Mr. Jack was having trouble getting a breath. "Best bomb squad in the world couldn't get that off in time."

"Thanks for the warning."

"And if you turn the ship around, it's programmed to blow."

Stone continued hacking at the chain. There'd be bolt cutters in the bosun's store, but he would as soon leave Ronnie alone with a wounded jackal. "Can't be programmed to blow up if you turn her around; you've already programmed her to turn away from ships the radar spots."

"There's slack built in, smart guy. *Ah!*" He gripped his arm harder and Stone realized, belatedly, that it wasn't only the wounded shoulder that was hurting the old man, but his entire left arm.

"You're having a heart attack, aren't you, Mr. Jack?"

The old man sucked air. "Got a heart like a turbine."

"How much slack is built in, Mr. Jack?"

"Fuck you!" Mr. Jack convulsed again, his lungs rasping. *"Jesus!* Give me a shot of something."

"How much slack?"

"You gotta give me a shot. You're a doctor."

"You got the wrong guy. I'm a lousy doctor."

The link parted. Stone wrenched Ronnie's half of the chain loose and scooped her into his arms. She was breathing almost as hard as the old man, but her eyes were starting to glaze as her mind began a merciful shutdown. Holding her tight, he ran out onto the bridge wing, out past the superstructure.

The fog had lifted. The afternoon was dull, visibility clear. They had already passed Yokohama. Kawasaki was to the left, Tokyo Light dead ahead. Once past it, the ship would be locked into the channel with no maneuvering room before it hit the inner harbor. He could see the Tokyo Tower, and hundreds of office buildings. The lights of the Ginza grew bright in the lowering winter sky.

"Where's Mummy?"

Stone had already looked. "We'll see her soon."

"But Mr. Jack said we'll blow up."

"Come on, give me a hand." He carried her back into the bridge. Mr. Jack was lying quietly with his eyes closed. "Go, wake up the pilot," Stone told Ronnie. "Pour water on him."

He hit the emergency button for the whistle, which began thundering a series of seven short blasts, and ran to the helm to view the monitor. The *Dallas Belle*'s programmed course was laid out in a neat blue line between the harbor's outer break-waters into the Tokyo West Passage, past container and RoRo wharves, past the signal station, past the gas wharves and the Toden Oi power plant—which would explode in secondary ignition, destroying the harbor—past the World Trade Center, where the ship would veer left out of the main channel for a thousand-yard charge at the Takeshiba Passenger Terminal.

"Here he is," said Ronnie.

The pilot was swaying on his feet, wet and belligerent, wincing at each deck-shaking blast of the whistle. Stone shoved the VHF in his hand. "Radio Tokyo Traffic Advisory. Tell them we are commencing a one-hundred-and-eighty de-gree turn to port, across the channel and into the outbound lane. Tell them all ships stand clear. Tell them we are car-rying fifty thousand tons of liquefied natural gas which is going to explode— Listen to me!" The dissipated face had gone blank. "Explode at sixteen hundred—thirty minutes from now. Tell them we're heading for the middle of the bay."

The pilot blinked.

"Do it!"

On the monitor, the graphic ship representing the *Dallas Belle* was nearing the outer breakwater. Other ships were shown as radar targets with their speed and bearing displayed. He touched the helm, and to his relief the ship began to turn. He had been afraid the old man had locked it somehow, but the override worked and the ship was leaning in response.

He checked the impulse to run out to the wing to see. It was all there in front of him on the screen: a column of ships coming in behind him; the column opposite, outbound. As the *Dallas Belle* turned, the monitor projected a blue line ahead that kept turning as the ship turned. It looked like a scythe cutting through the radar targets. The numbers on the screen showed them changing course and speed as traffic advisory radioed warnings that caused them to scatter.

The pilot was shouting at him.

"English!" Stone yelled.

"Tokyo Traffic Advisory denies permission to stay in Tokyo Bay."

"What do they want me to do?"

"They say head for Sagami Sea."

"No way. At sixteen hundred we'd be dead center in the narrows. We'd wipe out Yokohama, Yokosuka, and Kimitsu. Tell them we're staying in the bay."

The pilot edged toward the curtain.

"Ronnie! Quick! The gun."

She darted to where it had slid and ran with it to Stone. "Go back in that bathroom, sir, and close the door. We'll take you in the boat when we're ready."

The pilot headed for the curtain. Stone squeezed the trigger. Glass shattered. The man covered his head with both hands and ran into the cubicle.

"How you doing there, sweetie?"

"I'm okay. I think. You okay?"

"Wonderful. What time is it?"

"Fifteen forty-eight."

"You know your way to the lifeboat?"

"Yes."

"How long will it take us to get there?"

"Four minutes."

"Is it all ready to go?"

"Oh yeah. You just jump in and pull the lever."

"Is the elevator here? Why don't you check?"

She ran through the curtain. Stone watched the monitor. A very large ship was cutting across the *Dallas Belle*'s bow. Stone held the whistle down and stayed on course.

"Mr. Jack? Can you hear me?"

"I hear you, you bastard."

"Can you walk?"

"No."

"We'll carry you."

"Let me die my way."

Stone looked down at the crazy old face. "I'm not leaving you anywhere near the helm."

Ronnie came back. "Elevator's here. It's fifteen fifty-one, Daddy."

He beckoned the pilot, who was watching from the glass bathroom. The man rushed out. "Help him up," Stone said. "We're outta here."

Mr. Jack rose to one knee, moaning with pain.

"Hang on," said Stone, and locked the helm hard over. A warning siren shrieked. The *Dallas Belle* crash-turned to port, heeling like a destroyer. Stone hit the automatic emergency on the whistle again and they retreated from the bridge, fighting the steep incline of the circling ship.

Mr. Jack and the pilot struggled into the elevator. Stone followed, holding the gun in one hand, scooping Ronnie into his other arm as the car descended. When the door opened on the main deck, they again struggled against the steep incline as Ronnie led them out an aft hatch onto the afterdeck.

A ladder arced over the lifeboat, which hung from davits. The heel of the ship made it difficult to climb through the hatch in the canopy, but Stone's main problem was how to board without losing control of the situation. He and Ronnie had to enter the boat first. If they didn't, the pilot and Mr. Jack could launch without them. He looked at his watch. Three minutes.

"In you go, sweetheart. Right behind you." He turned around and backed down into the boat, watching the pilot and Mr. Jack, who were mounting the ladder. "You first, Mr. Jack."

The old man's face was a gray mask of pain and frustration. Behind him, the pilot was shoving, crying, "Hurry. Hurry."

"Fucking Jap."

"Come on," yelled Stone. "We're out of time. Ronnie, get your belt on."

The pilot shoved harder. The old man whirled in one fluid motion and kicked him in the face. The pilot fell to the deck. "I'm staying," Mr. Jack told Stone. "Screw all of you!"

They were out of time. Stone slammed the hatch and buckled in beside Ronnie. Orange light seeped through the canopy. She already had her little hand on the release.

"Go!"

She yanked and screamed. Stone's stomach flew. They were falling. A second later, they hit the water with a bone-shaking impact. The boat rolled. Stone felt the backwash of the *Dallas Belle*'s propeller hurl the lifeboat away.

He unbuckled and headed for the tiller and reached for the starter. The engine fired. But before Stone could put the propeller in gear, he felt a hard thump through the water and knew that he was too late. The explosive charges welded to the port side of the ship had detonated along its waterline.

He reached for Ronnie. One or two seconds would tell him whether submerging the charges by heeling the ship had smothered the explosion before it could ignite the super-cooled gas.

41

THE LIFEBOAT STOPPED ROCKING SUDDENLY WITH A LOUD CRACK-ing noise and lay at an angle as if it had run aground in the middle of the bay.

Stone opened the hatch.

A cold wind stung his face. The ship was a quarter mile away, sprawled on its side in a field of ice.

The ice was spreading rapidly.

It engulfed the helicopter carrier *Admiral Yamamoto*, which lay between the *Dallas Belle* and the lifeboat, and raced on another thousand yards, freezing the seawater into crystalline waves as hard and bright as glass. A smoky white fog rose from the rigid surface. Sea birds fell from the sky, their feathers sheathed in snow.

The fog was thickest around the ship, where the frigid gas continued to gush from the broken hull. Stone pulled Ronnie out of the canopy.

"What happened?"

"The cold gas froze the water. Come on! It'll blow up any second."

Her eyes widened in disbelief, then locked on the *Dallas Belle*. "Look at Mr. Jack. He's frozen."

A stick figure was spread-eagled to a ladder halfway up the superstructure.

Stone lowered Ronnie off the lifeboat, and they started running across the frozen bay, climbing ice hummocks and sliding into troughs, their backs to the ship, their faces to the wind.

"Is it poisonous?"

"Only if it drives out all the air."

Around them was a strange silence broken by a tinkling sound like thousands of miniature wind chimes. Now and then the fog swirled away and they could see lights on shore, and ships fleeing the ice, which continued to spread.

"It's moving!" cried Ronnie.

They were half a mile from the ship, and the ice sheet was growing thinner, undulating on the swells. A jagged crack suddenly came at them like an attacking animal. They dodged. Seawater erupted, spraying them. Stone slipped and fell. He scrambled to his feet and took Ronnie's hand and ran. With no warning, his foot broke through a soft spot, thin and treacherously invisible. He looked back. The ship was shrouded in fog, the orange lifeboat a barely visible dot. The trapped warship was haloed in work lights, her decks a dense clutter of helicopters, her rigging stiff with frozen signal flags.

Another crack meandered their way, moving lazily with the sea swell. The surface was disintegrating into floes. They'd be swimming in another minute—miles from shore as night descended. But to go back to the lifeboat would be as deadly. Any minute, steel chilled brittle would crack in a spray of sparks and ignite the gas.

"There's Mummy!"

The Swan was heading straight for them, mainsail black, jib white as a gull. Sarah drove the boat through the slushy ice at the edge of the field and ramped it up onto a solid slab as Stone and Ronnie ran, leaping from floe to floe.

Ronnie broke through. Stone grabbed her, jumped a channel of open water, and landed hard near the boat. Both feet broke through the ice. As he fell, he swung Ronnie by her arm with all his strength.

He saw Sarah catch her hand and haul her over the safety line. Then the water dragged him under and mushy ice closed over his head. His boots filled, pulling him down. He reached up as if to tug air down to his lungs. Something banged into his palm and he closed his hand and held on for his life.

His head broke the surface and he saw Sarah braced on the deck with a boat hook, trying to pull him to the hull. He got his other hand onto the gunnel and there he hung, the cold water sapping his strength, vaguely aware that the sails were crashing like cymbals.

Sarah screamed to Ronnie. The child fumbled at the mast and led a halyard over the safety line. They worked it around him, under his arms. Then Sarah cranked the mast winch and Stone felt himself lifted slowly out of the water and over the side.

"Turn the boat around."

He crawled along the deck and into the cockpit and reached for the helm. The wind was west. The *Dallas Belle* lay east in the ice. He started the engine and used it to kick the stern around out of the ice. But instead of heading due south for the narrows and the Sagami Sea, he veered east.

"Gotta get that helicopter ship between us or the shock wave will blow us out of the water."

"There's a police patrol coming," said Sarah.

"They're not the problem." Any moment sparks from a shattering plate of the brittle, twisted steel would ignite a pocket of gas. *Veronica* caught a favorable slant of wind and picked up speed. At last, she reached the point where the helicopter carrier blocked their view of the *Dallas Belle*. He changed course and headed for the narrows, glancing back repeatedly to make sure he was in position to maintain the shield.

Suddenly a sunset seemed to break through the clouds above the gas carrier. And then the *Dallas Belle* exploded brighter than any sunset. A fireball rose roaring into the sky, painting Tokyo Bay ruby red from shore to shore.

The sea shook under the Swan like an earthquake. A shock wave slammed into the sails and knocked her on her side.

Before she stood again, the sky was bright as noon.

Ships and boats were steaming from the fire. Others, like moths, seemed drawn to it. The warship that had shielded them from the worst of the explosion suddenly blew apart, flinging fiercely burning helicopters onto the ships around it.

Ships began igniting across the crowded bay in a string of explosions, each setting off the next, like signal fires bearing a message to the harbor.

The wind turned hot. The ice vanished. Pillars of fire, twisting and spiraling like tornadoes, swooped toward the city.

On the outer breakwaters, glass buildings reflected the flames, then puffed open like red poppies scattering their petals to the wind. Cars and trucks flew burning from a suspension bridge, falling like glitter. A stand of power plant stacks toppled like fingers closing into a fiery fist.

Stone focused the binoculars on the Tokyo Tower, which stood over the heart of the city like a prisoner braced for punishment. A railroad train of tank cars on a pier exploded in a long series of sullen booms. They proved to be a coda. Overhead, the fire pillars flickered like candles in the wind. Slowly, reluctantly, they sank toward the water, and by their fading light, Stone saw that the harbor had absorbed the brunt of the destruction. Tokyo Tower stood, a sentinel now for the city that survived.

Christmas morning, thirty miles south of Nojima-zaki, Stone folded his Japan chart and turned *Veronica* southeast to the open sea. He scanned the horizons, which were empty but for Orion's Belt setting dimly in the west, and went below.

Sarah and Ronnie were sitting under a blanket on the leeward berth in the main salon, surrounded by Ronnie's stuffed penguins and alligators and the gift-wrapped boxes purchased six weeks ago at Kwajalein.

"My hero!" Ronnie had been calling him that since she woke up.

Stone kissed Ronnie on the forehead and Sarah on the mouth. "Mummy's a hero, too, sweetie. Without her we'd still be swimming."

"Or fried. Mummy, when are we going to do presents?"

"After your father's had a nap." Sarah lifted the blanket. "Come here."

Stone squeezed in with them and opened their dogeared *Ocean Passages for the World.*

"Where are we going, Daddy?"

"Well, poor *Veronica* needs her starboard spreader repaired and a permanent patch on that hole in the galley, before some shark swims in for lunch. So first stop will be a nice warm beach."

"Then where?"

"Then your mother would like very much to sail home."

Ronnie looked puzzled and a little alarmed. She gathered her presents and pulled her animals closer. "Home? We are home."